Books from *Sphere of Compassion*

THE MAIN CHARACTER!

OF THE EXPS

Table of Contents

Part 16: Sellum's Warriors

Part 17: Return to Earth

RESURRECTION OF THE EXPS

BOOK 4

DESTRUCTION, CREATION, ABSENCE

By: Alexander J McCarty

Cover Art: Gabriel McCarty

RESURRECTION OF THE EXPS BOOK 4 Destruction, Creation, Absence.

Copyright © 2018 by Alexander J. McCarty

ISBN 978 1 943733 14 9

Published by Sphere of Compassion, Inc.

https://sphereofcompassion.com
authoralexandermccarty@gmail.com
https://facebook.com/authoralexandermccarty
http://www.instagram.com/gabriel_of_the_exps
http://www.instagram.com/sphere_of_compassion
https://twitter.com/of_the_Exps
https://www.tumblr.com/blog/sphereofcompassion

Back Cover Art by Cesar Escobar/Hoshi Art

https://www.facebook.com/CesarEscobarArtworks/

https://www.facebook.com/hoshisweeteuart/

Cover design by Gabriel McCarty

http://www.instagram.com/gabriel_of_the_exps

Part 18: Propaganda & Politics

Part 19: Sellum's Ascension

Part 20: Battle for Godhood

Acknowledgments

I give reverent thanks to my brother for planning and fleshing out scenes, illustrating the book covers, and brainstorming to create new characters and hone old ones. I give thanks to my loving and supportive parents. I thank my family and friends who read any part of this book either digitally or in manuscript form.

I want to express my appreciation for the new friends and fans who have supported me during this book's production: Aleah, Uzel, Andrea, Monica, Chris, Robby, Oscar, Ariel, Cameron, Erica, Gianfranco, Pedro, Zaidy, John, Drew, and Michael. Some have helped us manage our booths at conventions and all have encouraged us with their kind words. I also want to thank the artists who've been making new fan art for the series. Be sure to check them out in the Fan Art section of sphereofcompassion.com.

Special thanks to my wonderful editor, Rosemi, who, with her vast knowledge and research, has helped make this book more accessible and more real to my readers. Rosemi has stuck by us for over three years now, and I am continually impressed by her dedication and skill.

Lastly, I thank you, the reader, for purchasing this book. I hope you enjoy the story/characters, reflect on the themes, and continue to support me in my future works. Keep an eye out for *The Main Character* coming 2019!

Thank you! =(:3)*   (That's a bunny, by the way.)

This book is dedicated to the founders of movements that bring us closer to a world where all living beings can be treated with respect. May we all give thanks to the creators of peaceful ideologies and join hands to mold this world into a haven where all individuals are treated fairly.

Introduction

Much has happened between *Resurrection of the Exps: Sellum* and this books publication. I started my first fanfiction; called *Total Drama: Action Stars Island Tour*. We've met with a comic book artist and have made plans for a *Rebellion of the Exps: Exp 8* comic. We've even been talking to game developers about working on a PC fighting game called *Clash of the Exps.* On the side we edited my friend Bec's book, *Magician's Way* and have networked with Trevor from *Ink It Comics* to increase the series' distribution.

When I first wrote this book during an extra-curicular Summer program before Ninth Grade, it was only one-hundred and fifty pages. The composition book I wrote in had less pages and by the time I realized this, I was already fairly deep in the story. *Resurrection of the Exps: Destruction, Creation,* the shortest of them all but this turned out to work in my favor. Since the book was originally short I was able to introduce entirely new story segments in this updated version. Now that it's complete, I can firmly say this is my favorite of the four! The final book of the Resurrection Arc turned out better than I ever imagined.

I hope you will follow us on Facebook, Instagram, or Tumblr, and feel free to message me. My Facebook group, Alexander J McCarty, updates often with quotes, excerpts, and character art from my book series. We also have a website *sphereofcompassion.com* where you can ask any character any question you want! Please spread the word about my series, take a moment to give the first three books a review (on Amazon or Goodreads), and enjoy the intense conclusion to the Resurrection Arc. =(:3)*

In the Last Volume:

Book 3,

Sellum: Resurrection of the Exps

The Realm of Sel broke out into a civil war once the God of Hate was defeated and humiliated. Peace was returned to the realm when the Lord of Destruction took control of a naïve boy and brought the armies of Sel under his esteemed rule. What remained of the Freedom Forcers fled, but they couldn't hide for long. Devlin, possessed by a dark influence, tracked them down, bringing back those willing to serve the Dark One and destroying Refuge in the process. The broken rebel group of Exps and mortals tried to intervene when the Dark One breached Beacon. They pitifully failed to save the God of Love from its demise and were recruited by the cowardly Great Goddess to break into the Elysium Asylum and gain new allies. Fortunately, the Dark One gained new allies, though he lost his opportunity to claim Hope. This little Exp quickly took charge of the others and openly declared war on Lum for her repeated transgressions. After escaping the Elysium Asylum, the blindly devout follower of Sellum regained his status as a god. The Dark One, confident in his impeccable plan, revealed his intent to dethrone Sellum and rightfully claim his place. The slightly stronger, though still mostly harmless, remnants of the Freedom Forcers joined with Allah's Jannah and stormed Samsara to escape from the ever-intensifying struggle between Sel and Lum. The most cowardly of the bunch reached the portal room where they would likely die while the others fled from the wrath of the Dark One as he battled the Great Goddess. The God of Creation was given an opening when Etaf sliced the Dark One in half and fled back to her palace. Back in Lotus, Demonica and Devlin failed to capture Efil. Devlin then confronted Lord Sel about the true nature of his bestowed godhood and escaped to Lum. It matters not; the Dark One's plan will proceed without delay.

Lord Sel's Game Notes

SELLUM'S FORCES

Sellum: The Current Lord of the Afterlife
Personality: Lazy, emotionally impeded, unfit to rule
Loyalties: Himself and his misguided notion of non-involvement
Powers: Immeasurable but still has weaknesses
Risks: Incredibly powerful
Benefits: Inactive and inept
Goals: Eternal stagnation and an incompetent legacy
Developments: How can something that doesn't move grow?
Current Status: Moping about his inevitable loss, no doubt

Casey: Zenero's loving and loyal wife
Personality: Desperate to bring back her husband, not much else to say
Loyalties: Zenero only
Powers: The easily underestimated ability to encase objects and beings
Risks: Could betray me but has nothing to gain and so much to lose
Benefits: Holds one of the five things needed to take down Sellum
Goals: Freeing Zenero
Developments: Met with Zenero in Absence
Current Status: Likely with Sellum in the Microcosm

Unknown: Not sure who, but I know Sellum has one more hidden ally. I'd be outright insulted if Sellum wasn't influencing the politics of Sel through underhanded means.

FREEDOM FORCERS

A faction of Exps and modified humans. Seek to return home and live freely. Are becoming increasingly involved with the skirmish between myself and Lum. Potentially useful and possibly dangerous.

DECEIVANT'S EXPS

Ada: Exp 03; Deceivant's kind, airhead of a wife
Personality: Optimistic, idealistic, and determined
Loyalties: Her husband, her children, students, practically any acquaintance
Powers: I'm going to leave this intentionally blank
Risks: She manages to avoid being crushed by the gravity of despair, but that only that increases the fun
Benefits: A great tool for manipulating Deceivant
Goals: Bringing her friends and family home safely; becoming Deceivant's one true love
Developments: Resurrected by unknown means after I captured her soul
Current Status: In Lum with her family and friends

Destructus Supplious: D.S. for simpletons; Exp 04; A fairly skilled bodyguard with a childish mind
Personality: Obsessed with justice, heroism, and other nonsense he got from watching too many cartoons
Loyalties: His family, friends, and the forces of "good"
Powers: Without his artifacts he is easily disposed of, but with them he can be fun
Risks: Might give me a mild headache if I end up killing his friends
Benefits: Provides mild entertainment
Goals: Make new friends and protect his current ones
Developments: Claimed Crisis as his ally and friend
Current Status: In Lum, likely fighting off angels with his bare hands

Hope Kagaku: Not given a number because Deceivant's a lolicon or she's his daughter; self-proclaimed Queen of the Exps
Personality: Regal, manipulative, tactical, ambitious (a kindred spirit)
Loyalties: Herself, her mother, Devlin, time will tell if she's really loyal to her people
Powers: Can turn enemies into her slaves
Risks: Could make my warriors betray me
Benefits: Could make my warriors betray me
Goals: Don't know, and that's why I'm interested
Developments: Took over the Freedom Forcers soon after joining them
Current Status: Who knows?

Demo/Fusion: Exp 08 and 09, respectively
Personalities: Nonexistent
Loyalties: Freedom Forcers, I suppose
Powers: Multiplies itself/Merges with and controls objects
Risks: Minimal
Benefits: Good control over their powers
Goals: Don't care
Developments: Was freed from Elysium
Current Status: In Lum with Freedom Forcers, floating and/or rolling

Devlin Kagaku: My once loyal pawn
Personality: Vengeful, aggressive, obsessive, clever
Loyalties: Kaity, Kaity, oh, and Kaity
Powers: I lent him an armor of Sel energy, but now all he can do is use wires to pick up distant objects
Risks: Could rally the others to oppose me and knows confidential information
Benefits: Could make things interesting if he truly means to fight against me
Goals: Protect Kaity. Ugh, where has his ambition gone?
Developments: Was freed from the Sel armor that I used to influence him
Current Status: Betrayed me and fled to Lum; Bravo!

DEVLIN'S EXPS

Nina: Exp 3; Skillful and loyal ninja warrior
Personality: Focused, intelligent, calm, and cold
Loyalties: Devlin is her obsession, but she has grown fond of Kaity it seems
Powers: Incredible skill, but without an artifact easy to overcome
Risks: Might cut me! Oh, the horror!
Benefits: Could be a good back up if Riufen leaves my forces
Goals: Fulfilling her master's mission of bring his parents home safely.
Developments: Changed back into her selfless form to avoid death
Current Status: Who knows?

Violet Gold: Exp 7; Astral warrior
Personality: Devoted, multi-religious, supportive, and helpful
Loyalties: Her friends, her self-proclaimed false god, false gods in poetry books and real gods like myself
Powers: Manipulates and wields her aura, skillful with various weapons
Risks: Can attack and harm at a spiritual level
Benefits: Could be bent to my will with the proper circumstance
Goals: Seeks balance in Sellum
Developments: Broken by Hope and turned into her vehicle
Current Status: In Lum, taking down angels without violence while her friends massacre them

Opti: Exp 11; Happy Simpleton
Personality: Blindly optimistic, full of love, a moron
Loyalties: Opti is loyal to all his friends and all the denizens of Lum; Pesi likes to kill things
Powers: Can still influence reality despite not having his artifact
Risks: A morale booster and could cause some unexpected developments
Benefits: Let's face it, this one's not going to join my side
Goals: Defend Lum; I think he's trying to get a girlfriend because of NoOne
Developments: Turned down by Tsul; transformed an Absence god into a bunny
Current Status: In Lum, probably getting distracted by a squirrel

Atlas: A brave warrior who seeks my end
Personality: Ambitious, ruthless, creative, a worthy foe
Loyalties: To the Realm of Sel and to whomever he deems his people
Powers: Can turn the souls of vanquished warriors into weapons
Risks: Can actually harm me
Benefits: Would be a tasty feast with all those souls
Goals: Seeks to cut me down so he can claim my throne
Developments: Abandoned his god powers to be free of my influence
Current Status: In Lum, plotting ways to defeat me, hopefully

ATLAS' EXPS

Crisis: An average-looking Exp with above average power
Personality: Doesn't like things to be predictable; I can relate
Loyalties: Wants to arrive to Earth safely, not sure if he cares about anyone but himself
Powers: Creates forces of nature at will
Risks: Could postpone parties, funerals, and other fun events
Benefits: Can destroy entire cities if he were given the incentive
Goals: Wants to return to his beloved planet
Developments: Protected his allies from the angels who guard Samsara
Current Status: In Lum, fending off angels with the other Freedom Forcers

Image: Atlas' wife and a psychologist of all kinds
Personality: Helpful, intelligent, a bit loopy
Loyalties: Atlas and his Exps
Powers: Manifests her own emotions in various ways
Risks: Unknown how powerful her emotional abilities can get, can also talk Exps through their problems
Benefits: Killing her would make Atlas cry
Goals: Wants to vacation on Earth with her husband
Developments: Freed from Elysium and made amends with Atlas
Current Status: Who knows?

VIPER SQUAD

Kanasta: Business-oriented Assassin Boss
Personality: Stoic, obsessed with being a good small business owner, stubborn
Loyalties: Kaity, the Viper Squad, his clients, and apparently his targets too
Powers: Physically strong, fast, has many tools of his own creation, a true testament to one who earned his merits
Risks: Will defend Kaity at any cost
Benefits: Kaity will defend him at any cost
Goals: Becoming the ultimate assassin
Developments: Successfully dethroned the Imam
Current Status: In Lotus with Kaity and BoneSaw

Kaity: Unworthy Thief
Personality: Playful, naive, vulnerable
Loyalties: Sefiwah and her Viper Squad, the Exps too, maybe the realm of Lum
Powers: Should be mine
Risks: Could steal something else belonging to me
Benefits: Will be so much to fun to destroy
Goals: Wants to be free of her responsibility; I'll happily oblige her
Developments: Learned that Lum was her darling Sefiwah and her mother
Current Status: No idea, and that worries me

BoneSaw: Killer robot assassin
Personality: Focused and protective of Kaity
Loyalties: The Viper Squad, Kaity
Powers: Skill and stealth, prefers saws as its tool for killing
Risks: Not of any concern, really
Benefits: Sadly, not important enough to be used as a hostage
Goals: Kaity's protection; success of the Viper Squad
Developments: Stood by Kaity's side while fulfilling its assigned mission
Current Status: Last seen in Lotus

NON-EXPS

Deceivant Kagaku: Leader of the Freedom Forcers, lets Kaity think she's in charge, a talented inventor who is easy to manipulate
Personality: Overconfident, clever, and a realist
Loyalties: His wife, his children, and children
Powers: Easy to kill
Risks: Could make more Exps to go against me
Benefits: Could make more Exps to work for me
Goals: Bringing his daughter and wife home safely
Developments: Was lied to and betrayed by the goddesses who promised his family safe passage
Current Status: In Lum, happy his daughter is "safe"

Captain of Carnage: A demon lord who follows Atlas
Personality: Proud, loyal, loves a good fight
Loyalties: Atlas
Powers: Very quick but lacks any true power
Risks: Papercuts can be a nuisance
Benefits: May provide some entertainment if somehow becomes a god
Goals: Aiding Atlas in the completion of his mission
Developments: He's the same blind follower he's always been
Current Status: Who knows?

Muffins: An Absence god turned into a chubby bunny
Personality: Loyal, level-headed, cuddly
Loyalties: Absence, Opti
Powers: Can go full Absence form due to her small size and can create needles out of her fur
Risks: Absence powers could kill a number of my minions
Benefits: Nothing I can think of
Goals: Balance in Sellum; the protection of Absence
Developments: Was turned into a bunny
Current Status: In Lum with the other Freedom Forcers

Napkin: A frightened kitten
Personality: Scares easily but is dangerous when it overcomes its fear
Loyalties: Kaity and the other Freedom Forcers
Powers: Can freeze gods with its overwhelming aura
Risks: Could potentially beat some of my Sorority
Benefits: None worth noting
Goals: Keeping his friends safe
Developments: Created permanent fear in Regna
Current Status: Who knows?

LUM

LUM GODS
Followers of a manipulative idealist

Lum: A festering thorn in my side
Personality: Arrogant, justice-obsessed, utilitarian, obsessed with the color white and all its meaning
Loyalties: Loyal to her realm, nothing else
Powers: Commands light to create whatever she wishes in an instant
Risks: Could potentially kill me
Benefits: If turned against Sellum, could help me bring about his end
Goals: The purging of "evil" from Sellum
Developments: Lost Evol and was nearly killed by me
Current Status: Lost faith with Kaity and her team

Efil: Goddess of Flowers
Personality: Blindly loyal, friendly, humble
Loyalties: The Great Goddess, the realm of Lum and its denizens
Powers: Makes flowers, okay, honestly, she can manipulate time
Risks: Could cut down most of my allies
Benefits: Potentially able to overcome my greatest obstacle
Goals: Ending the conflict in Lum between the angels and the visitors
Developments: Destroyed Devlin's Sel armor when she tried to kill him
Current Status: Returned to her goddess

Etaf: Goddess of Fate and Doom
Personality: Ruthless, cold, manipulative; barely a Lumian
Loyalties: Her beloved realm and her dear friend
Powers: Can bring one's destiny into the present and can create new possibilities
Risks: Almost destroyed me
Benefits: Could create very interesting prophecies
Goals: Freedom from her cursed existence
Developments: Saved Lum from my wrath
Current Status: In Lum with the other gods

Ecnedurp: A Virtue and the manager for Samsara
Personality: Dedicated to levels of obsession
Loyalties: The Realm of Lum, balance in Sellum
Powers: Incalculable strength, speed, and stubbornness
Risks: Can she overpower a realm god?
Benefits: Is too busy following her schedule to interfere with my plans
Goals: Defending Samsara; keeping on schedule
Developments: Met with those seeking to return to Earth
Current Status: In Samsara with the "who knows" group

Ytitsahc: A behemoth powerhouse and knight of the Virtues
Personality: Simple-minded, obsessed with virtuous action, immune to her enemies' pleas of mercy
Loyalties: The Realm of Lum, balance in Sellum, virtuous beings
Powers: Able to destroy an entire armada of demons without a scratch
Risks: Could shift the tide of the struggle
Benefits: Follows Ecnedurp, so is unlikely to act anytime soon
Goals: The protection of Samsara; reclaiming the Lumian scripture
Developments: Defeated Nina
Current Status: In Samsara with the "who knows" group

Fatima: Lum's newest angel
Personality: I don't bother learning about mortals
Loyalties: Lotus, and Lum as a whole
Powers: Can wield light like the other angels
Risks: Politically could be used to unify humans and angels
Benefits: Framing the angels or humans for her death could make for a fun show
Goals: Keeping Lotus and its people safe
Developments: Lost her mother and her leader at the hands of Lum
Current Status: The Observatory, changed by Lum into an angel

ABSENCE

ABSENCE GODS
Too cowardly to invade but brave enough to defend their realm

Absence: The new ruler who favors progress over stagnation
Personality: A knight's mentality with the role of king and the mindset of a pawn
Loyalties: His realm, Lord Sellum
Powers: Mastery over Absence energy and the ability to compact anything he chooses
Risks: Could cause major damage to my forces if he leaves his realm
Benefits: He has a very interesting artifact
Goals: The protection of his realm through the creation of an army
Developments: Recruited two of my demon lords as Absence gods
Current Status: Training his soldiers so they can provide my army some entertainment

Void: First Guardian; A self-aware stone
Personality: I asked but it didn't answer
Loyalties: Absence, no doubt, and universal balance
Powers: Can become weightless or infinitely heavy at the drop of dime
Risks: Can't be destroyed by me
Benefits: Would make a topnotch punching bag
Goals: Balance and safety for Absence
Developments: Survived my wrath
Current Status: In Absence doing nothing

Occupy: First Guard; A warrior monk
Personality: Fun-loving, humble, devoted
Loyalties: Void, Absence, and possibly the Freedom Forcers
Powers: Can put anything in something else as long as both things are in his proximity
Risks: Not even Riufen can overcome his power
Benefits: Serves as an obstacle for Riufen to overcome
Goals: Defend his realm, help the residents attain peace
Developments: Defeated Etah when I attacked Beacon
Current Status: Training for the coming battle

Plagiarism: Second Guardian; A chameleon skull obsessed with sensation
Personality: Needy, forgetful, deranged
Loyalties: None that I'm aware of
Powers: Can become someone and turn them into an altered version of themselves
Risks: Could buff his own allies by copying them
Benefits: What would happen if he copied me?
Goals: Find enjoyment in a bland world
Developments: None of any concern
Current Status: Probably moping about with his guard

Crystal: Second Guard; A lay-about mineral warrior
Personality: lazy
Loyalties: I doubt he cares about anyone, really
Powers: Seemingly indestructible but lost to Riufen anyway
Risks: Can create blockades to slow down the Absence party
Benefits: If broken down, would make for a wonderful throne chair
Goals: Find his beloved
Developments: Lost against Riufen who used his own power against him
Current Status: Feeling depressed, maybe training, who cares?

Loyal: Third Guardian; A massive mythical creature from times of old
Personality: Valiant and noble, a real stick in the mud
Loyalties: Limit and Absence
Powers: I mean, he's a dragon, so fire breath, talons, and a powerful tail
Risks: Can create portals to Lum and Absence
Benefits: Doesn't seem likely to leave his realm to battle my armies
Goals: Peace between the realms
Developments: Fled to escape death at my hands
Current Status: Training for the big party!

Limit: Third Guard; A heroic knight
Personality: See above
Loyalties: Loyal, Absence, maybe the Freedom Forcers as well
Powers: In addition to his great speed and power, he can create clear limiters on his enemies
Risks: Could tie down my allies
Benefits: Could tie down my foes
Goals: The protection of his new kingdom
Developments: Defeated Yvne; recruited the Baroness and Führer
Current Status: Training with his big lizard buddy

Separate: Fourth Guardian; A big amoeba
Personality: Don't know, don't care
Loyalties: Absence, I think
Powers: Can divide itself into microscopic bullets
Risks: Can bypass nearly any defense
Benefits: Doesn't seem to have a strong will
Goals: Protecting its realm
Developments: Fled when Demonica nearly killed it
Current Status: Who cares?

Spin: Fourth Guard; A bunch of tops
Personality: Do tops have personality?
Loyalties: Nobody cares, let's move on
Powers: Spins things, really, that's it
Risks: Can give you a headache if you spin around too much
Benefits: Can make hopscotch more fun by giving everyone vertigo
Goals: Don't care
Developments: Struck by the Death Scythe
Current Status: Dead

Htols: Goddess of Sloth; A traitor who left me but without the flair of a real betrayal
Personality: Lazy, inept, bad at decision-making too, apparently
Loyalties: To herself and only herself
Powers: Can stop motion of any kind
Risks: Okay, seriously, could put the whole party on pause
Benefits: If she works with me again, could be a good guard
Goals: Finding peace through inaction
Developments: Nothing
Current Status: Doing nothing as per usual

Führer of Fortune: Traitor demon lord and ex-leader of the Hero's Militia
Personality: As smart as he is fat, but as loyal to me as he is attractive
Loyalties: Himself and his idealistic vision of a unified Sel
Powers: If convincing fools to rush to their demise in an impossible war is a power, he is truly a force to be reckoned with
Risks: Could cause political turmoil if he's given a loudspeaker and a desperate crowd of fools to listen to him
Benefits: Now that he's in Absence, his rebellion is even more insignificant than it was before
Goals: The decompartmentalization of Sel
Developments: Joined Absence to escape my clutches
Current Status: Hopefully working out to lose some of that excess weight

Baroness of Blades: Ex-demon lord of Pride; a once dishonorable warrior
Personality: Battle-hungry, desperate for a cause to rally under
Loyalties: The Führer
Powers: A remarkably skilled swordsman who has utilized her inner heat to coat her blade
Risks: Nothing Riufen can't handle
Benefits: Could be bent back to my will if I have some free time
Goals: Find a meaningful battle to validate her violent thirst
Developments: Joined Absence gods in search of a purposeful fight
Current Status: Training the other gods to fight, no doubt

Tcetorp: A Lum goddess who is trapped in Absence

Personality: Does following an invisible god blindly count as a personality? I think not

Loyalties: Lum, typical goddess

Powers: Creates shields for defense and offense

Risks: Can buff already powerful opponents

Benefits: If I break her spirit, could be a fairly useful minion

Goals: Returning to Lum so she can protect Elysium

Developments: Made a deal to defend Absence in return for her release

Current Status: In Absence, thinking about Lum and its fluffy clouds

Zenero: Casey's husband and a brilliant tactician

Personality: Detached yet obsessive, pacifistic yet merciless, he's quite the unique character

Loyalties: Loyal to his ideal world, which heralds him as its ruler

Powers: Little to none

Risks: Could turn some of my allies against me with his universally acclaimed speeches

Benefits: Could be used as an excuse for me to storm Absence

Goals: Freedom from his imprisonments

Developments: Met with his wife Casey

Current Status: Trapped in the prison of Absence

SEL

SEL GODS
An entire squad of gods who follow my orders dutifully

Lord Sel: The cunning and ambitious leader of Sel's armies
Personality: Infinitely clever, powerful ambition, believes only the worthy should progress
Loyalties: They are fun to break
Powers: I can become impossible to touch and can devour souls, not much I can't do
Risks: I could destroy everything you love
Benefits: Work with me and you can have whatever you want
Goals: Taking what is rightfully mine
Developments: United all the armies of Sel; killed Evol
Current Status: Dictating notes to make sure the plan goes off without a hitch

Demonica: The Goddess of Death and my greatest ally
Personality: Violent, vengeful, playful, and fun
Loyalties: Me, the Realm of Sel, and Devlin
Powers: Blood manipulation, instant kills
Risks: Could leave me for Devlin once the plan moves along
Benefits: Has been the greatest help to me and my conquest
Goals: Making Devlin her soulmate
Developments: Had sex with her beloved many, many times
Current Status: In the Core with me and her sister

Tsul: The Goddess of Lust
Personality: Independent, level-headed, has a rivalry with Demonica
Loyalties: The Realm of Sel and its ruler
Powers: Can burden her enemies and buff her allies
Risks: Could stage a coup if given the incentive
Benefits: Keeps the other goddess of the Sorority in check
Goals: Taking Demonica's place as my greatest ally
Developments: Turned the Prince of Pleasure into her pet
Current Status: Preparing for the invasion

Edirp: The Goddess of Pride
Personality: Arrogant, insecure, talkative
Loyalties: Herself and her sisters
Powers: Can cripple her foes with insults and crush them with their own insignificance
Risks: Could wipe out my armies if she goes rogue
Benefits: Makes isolating targets easy with her abilities
Goals: For everyone to respect and worship her
Developments: Lost to Violet's aura powers
Current Status: Coming up with new insults, perhaps

Yvne: The 'Goddess' of Envy
Personality: Depressed, needy, covets others for their experiences more than their possessions
Loyalties: The Realm of Sel and her sisters
Powers: Can transform into anyone or anything
Risks: Could be a nuisance if she betrays me
Benefits: As long as they don't have Absence power, her enemies cannot harm her
Goals: Protection of her family
Developments: Defeated by Limit
Current Status: Moping about the core

Regna: The 'Goddess' of Anger
Personality: Hot-headed, driven, justice obsessed
Loyalties: The Realm of Sel and her sisters, hates angels with a passion
Powers: Can trigger any part of her body to burst, incites blind rage in her foes
Risks: Could turn my armies against one another
Benefits: Can make my enemies tear each other apart
Goals: Overtake Lum and kill the angels
Developments: Defeated by Napkin
Current Status: Complaining to me that we aren't attacking Lum

Deerg: The Goddess of Greed
Personality: Greedy, childish, assertive
Loyalties: The Realm of Sel and the Sinful Sorority
Powers: Can magnetize anything to her
Risks: Her disappearance has harmed the economy of Sel greatly
Benefits: She isn't truly dead
Goals: Killing the assassin who stole from her
Developments: Nothing since she lost to Kanasta and Crystal
Current Status: Poking me until I retrieve her head

SEL'S PAWNS
My followers who either believe in my grand vision or are just too afraid to fight against me

Gimpy: A powerful demon who follows my every whim
Personality: Needy, clingy, loyal; ugh, there's nothing redeeming here at all
Loyalties: Myself and Demonica
Powers: Can transport itself and others between realms
Risks: If he ever abandoned me, would make travel very tricky
Benefits: No need to drive to your favorite vacation spots, visit all the monuments in a single day!
Goals: My will is its will
Developments: Sent the Imam to Lum as ordered
Current Status: Writing down this list as I dictate it

Gladius: A living god sword that resembles a crocodile
Personality: Confident, deceptive, cunning; reminds me of myself
Loyalties: He had better be loyal to me, but a momentous betrayal is fine too
Powers: Can slice through absolutely anything
Risks: Could maybe possibly harm me
Benefits: Will help Riufen become even more powerful
Goals: To find the perfect host to feed on
Developments: Tried to leave to Earth despite my warning
Current Status: Ran off with the others; I don't know where he is, regrettably

Riufen: Exp 10; Samurai
Personality: Stoic, battle-hungry, easily manipulated
Loyalties: Devlin and his own code of honor
Powers: Immortal, skilled, and holds the determination to surpass his limits
Risks: Could be creating a powerful enemy if he leaves me
Benefits: May become the sword that vanquishes my every foe
Goals: Growing stronger through honorable battles
Developments: Defeated Crystal with his own weapon
Current Status: In the Core, training for the big party

Pesi: Angry Simpleton
Personality: Violently arrogant, full of rage
Loyalties: Likes to kill things
Powers: Weaker than his other half due to lack of motivation, can bring others into a state of depression
Risks: Could bring down my army's morale
Benefits: Can weaken my enemy's morale
Goals: Survival, at the moment
Developments: Survived a battle against loyal, most impressive
Current Status: In the Core with my other minions

Wringer: Apparently, an Exp made of chains
Personality: Don't know, it doesn't talk
Loyalties: Seems to want to return to Earth
Powers: Exps can't be strangled, so pretty worthless if you ask me
Risks: Could make others underestimate my forces
Benefits: Could hold up a piñata if the rope breaks
Goals: Returning to Earth
Developments: Left Samsara
Current Status: Who knows?

Absorb: A living sponge made when Deceivant was going through his down period
Personality: Hates Deceivant with a passion
Loyalties: Vengeance
Powers: Can pull in projectiles and then shoot them out
Risks: May end up killing Deceivant
Benefits: Good for skipping stones, I suppose
Goals: Killing Deceivant
Developments: Following the Freedom Forcers
Current Status: Keeping Deceivant safe as I ordered

The Vibrator: A delusional masseuse
Personality: Clinically insane, narcissistic, obnoxious
Loyalties: Wants to return to Earth
Powers: Can make any part of his body vibrate
Risks: Could accidently destroy something he shouldn't
Benefits: Is surprisingly powerful
Goals: To be acknowledged as a god by all who walk the Earth
Developments: Tried to escape to Earth
Current Status: Who knows?

Toxic: A sharp snake
Personality: Nice, desperate for attention
Loyalties: Her family
Powers: Poison
Risks: I might forget such a worthless hostage
Benefits: Fun to use her as a weapon against her family
Goals: To be loved by her family
Developments: I think she's still my captive
Current Status: I forgot, honestly

Duke of Deception: Envy demon lord and tactician
Personality: Devout, cunning, a bit loopy
Loyalties: Me!
Powers: Uses strings to trap and eviscerate its enemies
Risks: Nothing I can think of
Benefits: Could become the new God of Hate
Goals: The success of my plans
Developments: Lost to Kanasta in Beacon
Current Status: Refining its technique

Prince of Pleasure: Lust demon lord
Personality: Manipulative, seductive, cruel, and ambitious
Loyalties: Himself
Powers: Intoxication via his fluids
Risks: Could stir up some trouble on Earth
Benefits: Can spike the punch if the party gets boring
Goals: Seeks to conquer those who are powerful
Developments: Turned into Tsul's pet; Stormed Samsara to return to Earth
Current Status: Who knows?

Part 16
Sellum's Warriors

Chapter 133: Reuniting the Team

White grass, multicolored clouds, and a radiant beacon in the sky greeted Kaity when she stepped out of the portal.

"Okay." The girl in the purple skintight suit took a deep breath. Her cat ears stood up, detecting nearby sound. "Nothing. Got to find the others," she said in a soft but energetic voice. Noticing a nearby hill, she raced up it and disengaged her sniper rifle from her pack. The metal weapon folded out in her grip; she raised the gun and steadied the sights. "Come on. There!"

Not only had the young assassin located her friends but when zooming in, she noticed an angel hawk had the same discovery.

A well-placed bullet in its wing downed the scout before he or she could relay the news of their whereabouts.

Looking back at her allies, Kaity noticed there were projectiles assaulting them, but the attackers were hidden by the slope of Mainaka Mountain.

Kaity climbed up a nearby tree to get a better look but soon realized that it wasn't high enough to get a clear view. "I know better. What am I doing?" grumbled the assassin prodigy as she slid down the tree.

With a single slice from her plasma claws, the tree toppled.

The clever girl rode the tree down the hillside to save time. After leaping off, she went into a full four-legged sprint to her allies.

"Couldn't the all-powerful god of our solar system just drop me off next to them? Makes me doubt everything he said." Kaity frowned, though her foul mood didn't last. "Papa!"

Kanasta came out from behind one of the surrounding hills. His spiky checkerboard hair accentuated his blood-red eyes. The black suit assassin boss was warmed by the sight of his prodigy. In his grip was a crystal suitcase given to him by a god of Absence as payment for his services.

Kaity nearly knocked him over when she leaped out from her sprint into his arms.

"Did that creature harm you?" asked Kanasta in a deep, fear-invoking voice, after releasing her from his embrace.

"No. Unless you count lying." The moody cat-girl crossed her arms.

"Glad you are well," he said, his voice showing only the tip of his elation.

Kaity was overcome by a rush of worry. "What happened to Devlin?"

Kanasta patted her head and smiled. "My brother is alive and well. Sadly, he left back to Sel with Demonica."

"That's a relief," said Kaity with a big smile.

BoneSaw popped out from behind Kanasta and nuzzled Kaity's leg.

"Glad you're okay too, little buddy," said Kaity, crouching down and giving a high five to the small metal cube.

"Devlin's love for you is of pure intent. I fully approve of you two becoming partners," said Kanasta.

"Where did that come from?" asked Kaity with a blush.

"I give you my blessing and vouch for his integrity," said Kanasta.

"Yeah, he's not a bad guy deep down," said Kaity with a small smile.

"We should help the others. I doubt they are in danger, but best to be safe," said Kanasta.

"Bet I can beat you there," said Kaity, sticking out her tongue.

"Challenge accepted," said Kanasta, increasing speed.

Kaity rushed to catch up to him but steadied her pace to make things more interesting.

They soon arrived at their allies' location, both smiling.

"Glad you two are having fun…while we're being attacked!" yelled Deceivant, shooting an enemy out of the sky. The renowned scientist combed his black hair out of the way and adjusted his rectangular glasses before shooting down a bird angel that had its sights on Ada.

BoneSaw was the last to arrive but quickly engaged the enemy angels.

"Sorry." Kaity ran up a tree and found a good branch. Lying flat on her belly she lined up her targets and took out three with a single shot.

"Crisis, keep up the barrier," said Deceivant, his usually calm tone becoming brazened by the intensity of their situation.

"I'm trying but I'm running low on energy," said Crisis as his wind shield gradually thinned. The tall, tan man's black business suit had some tears from the battle. "Can't wait to return home," he said in a calm, hopeful voice.

"I'm so looking forward to a sleepover with my cuties!" exclaimed Deceivant, his voice becoming high-pitched.

A nearby arrow nearly blindsided the cold-hearted scientist but was regrettably sucked in by Absorb's golden pores.

"Of all the jobs I could have been given. Why must the Dark One test me?" asked the annoyed sponge in a voice that echoed, accentuating its frustration. The scarlet sea sponge slammed into a rhino angel and toppled him over. "Meanwhile, Toxic is still in Sel's clutches!"

Muffins rolled as she shot out needles, paralyzing but not killing the angel warriors. The chubby brown bunny shook her floppy ears before forming a massive needle that dispersed an incoming wave of angels.

"Go, Muffins! And keep it up, Crisis!" exclaimed Opti in a sunny and cheerful voice, firing shots of enthusiasm into the team's personal weatherman. His ghostly pale arms glowed before sending out his joyful energy. He kicked off

30

the ground with his feathery legs and took to the skies with white wings to distract the angels.

Fusion jumped up and merged with an incoming spear. The colorful sticky ball used the merged spear to keep back an approaching human angel.

"Great work, my friends!" cheered Ada in a cheerful, motherly voice. "We can win this without hurting anyone!"

The sky-blue sphere inside her was shot, and her whole body deteriorated. "Nope. Guess again," said six other Adas, attempting to draw the attacks away from her friends. The real Ada leaned on her husband's shoulder.

"I won't let them touch you." Deceivant kissed her wedding ring and combed her long green hair, making her blue cheeks turn pink.

D.S. was brawling with four swordsman tiger angels. His muscles bulged before he lifted a tiger angel off her feet. A bear leaped on him but pulled away when D.S. bit his paw. "If I had Snippy, you guys woulda lost a loooong time ago," he said with a deep but childlike voice. He socked one of the tigers and grabbed the sword.

Violet was in a separate area from the rest of the group and was subduing the incoming forces through her devotional mantras. The benevolent zealot's light blue skin was covered by rags. Her eyes were vacant, but her devotion was displayed by her wispy voice.

Atlas was at the front lines, using his muscular arms to take down the biggest threats. An elephant angel lifted him with his trunk. "You are powerful, but not powerful enough," he said with a deep and rough voice. One of the tattoos that glowed on his body lost its shine. He summoned up his cherished axe and nicked the elephant, making him topple over with pain.

A portal appeared and Etaf emerged. The white paint coloring her cheeks contrasted with the black ash accentuating her lips. The warrior's dark, creamy skin was mostly covered by her pearl-white misty armor.

"Are you kidding me?" asked Deceivant, gritting his teeth.

"**Serendipity**." All projectiles missed their intended targets. The Goddess of Fate raised her hand, signaling the angels to cease their attack. "There is no need to continue this violence." Her voice was detached and firm.

The attacks instantly stopped and the angels fled.

Etaf scanned the Freedom Forcers. She smiled and then left back into her portal.

Kaity swung off her sniping post and landed in front of her team. "Victory!" The girl's cheeky smile dropped. "Where are the others?"

Deceivant looked at the young girl. His golden eyes shined as he flashed Kaity a smile. "They made it to Earth."

"Nobody died?" asked Kaity, a bead of sweat dropping from her chin.

31

"They all made it through, safe and sound," said Deceivant, opening his arms.

Kaity gave him a hug. "I knew I could count on you."

Deceivant patted her head. "Then why do you look so concerned?"

"It's natural for her to worry," said Kanasta.

Deceivant glared at him. "You don't get to talk. You left me, your mother, your sister, and your daughter behind so you could go to work in the middle of a skirmish! What is wrong with you?"

"I had prior obligations. Would you like to know how things turned out?"

"I don't care! What if one of us had died after you abandoned us? Did you even think about that?"

"Thankfully it worked out. I had faith you all would be safe and left Kaity behind to support you in storming Samsara. I underestimated my abilities. I couldn't have completed the job of dethroning the Imam without her insight and skill."

"You helped him? I thought you went there to talk some sense into him," said Deceivant, looking at Kaity with disappointment.

"I did what I could. Everything worked out okay, so just let it go," said Kaity.

"No. I can't just—"

Kaity hopped up and kissed his cheek. "Please."

"Adorable as that was, I need his word that he won't pull another stunt like this," said Deceivant.

"I promise I will not take up any more jobs until you and Mother are safe back home," said Kanasta, offering his hand.

Deceivant shook the massive arm. "Glad that's settled. So, how do we get back to Earth now?"

"We have to work with Lum to stop Sel. I'm sure that together we can take him down," said Kaity, her doubt penetrating her cheery smile.

"Kaity, I'm willing to work with you and convince the others to do the same, but first you have to tell us what you know about Lum. Tell us why you trust her when there are so many reasons not to," said Deceivant.

Kaity took a deep breath. "That's fair. Everyone, gather around! I have something to tell you!"

The Freedom Forcers made a circle around their leader.

Kaity stood on her tippy-toes at the center of the team. "The bottom line is: we have to protect Lum at all costs. Let's do it!"

Deceivant stood tall. "We should think this through. I feel that Lum is taking advantage of your trust. It's likely that Lum is using you to manipulate all of us to do her bidding."

"That does seem to be the case," said Atlas.

"Did she seduce you?" asked Deceivant.

"Maybe a bit," said Kaity, turning away with a blush.

"Care to elaborate?" asked Deceivant.

"Forget about it. We can all go back to Earth together once we've stopped Sel," said Kaity.

"As we are now, we stand no chance," said Atlas.

"We have to try," said Kaity in tears.

Kanasta lifted Kaity up and held her in his arms. "You aren't thinking clearly. What is holding you back?" he asked, petting her gently.

"I-I can't lose her again. Lum is Sefiwah!"

Ada's eyes widened.

"I knew it! Lum is lying to you, Kaity. Anyone who toys with a child's feelings like that doesn't deserve the life they have been given," said Deceivant, clenching his fist.

"I'm not a child. And I know it's her," said Kaity.

"I'm not sure who Sefiwah is or how this is relevant," said Crisis.

"Kaity is emotionally compromised. We can't be sloppy. I'll take over for the time being," said Deceivant, stepping in front of her.

"You are the last person who should lead!" snarled Absorb.

Ada stood atop a big rock. "Fighting doesn't solve anything!" She rushed to comfort Kaity in a warm embrace. "If Kaity says it was Sefiwah, who are we to question her? Kaity knows Sefiwah better than anyone."

"I'm still confused," said Crisis, turning to Kanasta.

"Lum was a member of the Viper Squad and Kaity's lover. Apparently, she was undercover, though we don't know why," said Kanasta with a puzzled look.

"She was watching over me," said Kaity softly.

"Hold on. Let's think this through," said Deceivant. "Why you? Why would a god spend so much time monitoring an incredibly cute assassin?"

"I...I don't know. But she truly loves me. I'm absolutely certain of it," said Kaity with firm conviction.

"So, what was it like to be intimate with a self-proclaimed god? Was it any different than intimacy with a mortal?" asked Deceivant intrigued.

"Heavenly," said Kaity, with dazed eyes and an open mouth.

"Did you feel bewitched in any way? I know it's hard to tell, but manipulation can be subtle. I've charmed many little ladies without even meaning to," said Deceivant with a slight smile.

"Always a pedophile," said Kanasta, rolling his eyes.

"Oh, you don't think I see the way you look at Kaity? Your inner pedo is on the brink of being released," said Deceivant.

"Don't put your intentions in my eyes, Father," said Kanasta with a glare.

"You know what? I've decided. The less I know, the better," said Crisis, shifting his attention to the partly cloudy sky.

"I fully believe Kaity. Sefiwah hated killing and loved the color white. She even said she would meet me in Heaven before she died. If she's the God of Lum, then it all makes sense," said Ada with numbers in her eyes, cross-referencing her file.

Kaity rushed up and embraced Ada with a face full of tears. "That's right. Everything you said about Sefiwah was right."

"Now you know just how wonderful she is!" exclaimed Ada, hugging her little friend extra tight.

Opti approached Deceivant with a perplexed look. "If you're such a strict pedophile, how come you're married to Ada? She's not a little girl."

"Oho! You think you've got me there. Ada may have an overdeveloped body, but her spirit is that of a child. Her youthful innocence breaches through, allowing me to see past the fact that her body is not premature," said Deceivant, glowing with pride.

"That's just how strong your love is," said Ada with tearful eyes.

"Also, Ada's not as old as she appears. I married her when she was technically a child. Therefore, I am not breaking the pedo code. Remember, she's an Exp," said Deceivant with a grin.

"Oh, cool! You have a code of honor like Riufen?" asked Opti with wide eyes.

"Can we please focus on the matter at hand?" asked Crisis, still looking at the sky.

"In conclusion, we are going to keep Lum safe by stopping Sel," said Kaity, her hands shaking.

"I agree completely!" cheered Ada.

"If Lum is Sefiwah and Bob is Sel, who is Absence?" asked Kanasta.

"Absence has no relation to any of us, which makes sense. Why would someone who is neutral try to change our fate? Perhaps both Sel and Lum were trying to convert us to their side. They had some reason to disguise themselves, whether for our good or theirs. Kaity, just don't put all your trust in Lum. We still don't know why she chose to watch over you," said Deceivant, patting the girl's head.

Kaity's tail smacked his hand off.

"I believe in Kaity's trust," said Ada.

"Me too," said Opti.

"Wait, everyone, let's think this through. Even if Sefiwah really was Lum, how does that prove that she isn't using us? If anything, it gives more evidence of her long-term manipulation. She could have coaxed Kaity into loving her just so she could later use us," said Deceivant, being sure to make eye contact as he looked over his followers.

Kaity clenched her fists. "Sefiwah isn't like that."

"If she was always a god and never told you, who's to say she won't deceive us once more?" asked Deceivant.

"Why won't you trust her? She only did what she had to do to keep her realm safe," said Kaity with an angry look.

"Why would I trust a goddess who masquerades as an assassin?" asked Deceivant.

"She was watching over me, like always," said Kaity with a fond smile.

"Has she ever tried sleeping with Kanasta, Tempo, Ego, the clients?" asked Deceivant before he was slapped. "Ow. Kaity, this is serious. If she makes bonds with the living to use them to her advantage in the afterlife, who knows what we're getting into? This isn't just about you; it's about all of us. For all we know, she could be using the fact that you love her to convince you that she is good-natured," said Deceivant.

"She made love only to me, okay? I'm the only one for her. I know she is pure. She's a wonderful person," said Kaity.

"I can vouch for Sefiwah's fidelity," said Kanasta.

BoneSaw nodded in approval.

"What happens if we don't work for her?" asked Deceivant.

"She won't hurt me, but the rest of you would be…eradicated," said Kaity.

"Finally! You're sharing what you know. Anything else?"

"She may have sent Efil to kill Devlin and Kanasta," said Kaity under her breath.

"Well then, it's settled. We protect Lum," said Deceivant, putting his arm around Kaity's shoulders.

"Can't wait to be home where things make sense," said Crisis, drawing a tornado in the sand.

"Wait." Atlas raised his hand. "I have something to add."

"Go right ahead," said Deceivant.

"Lum isn't just Sefiwah. After you all left, I saw her. She looks unmistakably like my sister. Perhaps she was trying to deceive me as well. No. I saw her eyes. It was definitely her. I believe my sister became Lum and then incarnated as Sefiwah."

"Well, if she's your sister, can you vouch for her trustworthiness? I'm still upset with what she tried to pull by classifying my little queen as a combatant," said Deceivant with a grimace.

"Absolutely. There is no one more honest than my sister. It is her kindhearted nature that allowed her to become Lum, after all," said Atlas.

"Either way, it's our best option at this point. And now that we know the whole situation," Deceivant smiled at Kaity, "we can fight with firm resolve."

"Yeah. And once Sel has fallen, Sefiwah will personally escort us home," said Kaity with a self-assuring smile.

Chapter 134: Forced Negotiations

Previously: after arriving at the portal room, Hope negotiated for her allies to be permitted passage. Hope outstretched her royal arm and smiled, knowing she had already won.

Ecnedurp's eyes flickered. "You are indeed correct. Your logic is sound. Oh…my apologies," said the silver-skinned goddess in a proud and brisk voice.

Hope was down on her knees in an instant.

Ecnedurp sped around like air, taking down the Captain of Carnage, Napkin, Image, and Nina. "Ytitsahc, capture them."

"As you command," said the goddess in a deep reverberating voice. The towering, blood-drenched armored goddess' aura came out from her palms as yellow light.

The Freedom Forcers were suddenly coated in a thin solid material, trapping them instantly.

Hope had a look of utter shock. "What happened?"

"We lost," said Nina.

"Impossible. I don't lose. Ecnedurp, explain," said Hope.

"You are to remain here as captives until your allies succeed in eradicating Sel." Ecnedurp's lip quivered. "I will say no more. Neither will you."

Hope's face was covered, all except her eyes, which glared defiantly at the cheating goddess.

"What do we do now?" asked Ytitsahc, stripping Nina to find the stolen scripture.

"We resume as scheduled."

Previously: After being freed from the Sel armor and learning of Sel's deception, Devlin returns to Lum.

"At least someone is loyal to me," said Devlin to himself.

The young scientist with black hair and golden eyes turned around to see the Freedom Forcers. They had yet to notice him.

Deceivant put his hand on Kaity's shoulder and signaled Kanasta to approach Devlin.

"Why are you here?" asked Kanasta, gazing at his brother with caution.

Kaity ran past Kanasta and into an embrace with Devlin.

After pausing in surprise, the enamored inventor put his arms around her. "You almost died."

"Yeah. Sorry," said Devlin in a youthful voice, smiling awkwardly.

Kanasta gently pulled Kaity off. "Can we trust you, brother?"

"Sel was controlling me. The armor he gave me, it clouded my judgement. I've come here to join you and stop him," he said, clenching his DNA pendant.

Kaity smiled.

Deceivant glared at Devlin. "Oh really. Then why isn't Riufen with you? Tell us the truth."

"I barely escaped after breaking apart from him. I don't know where Riufen is," said Devlin.

"What is Sel planning?" asked Deceivant.

"That doesn't matter. This time, I'm back for good," said Devlin with a warm smile.

"Oh, that's wonderful!" exclaimed Opti as he hugged his creator.

"It's fantastic, too fantastic for any skeptic to believe. What are you planning?" asked Deceivant.

"I'm planning on spending time with Kaity," said Devlin with a genuine smile.

"This seems rather suspicious," said Atlas.

"You're one to talk. I still can't believe you all let him join after what he did!" yelled Devlin.

"You can speak with them if you wish," said Atlas, summoning up the Bashful Bow and Wailing Whip.

Devlin's wires coiled around Atlas' throat. "Not another word."

"Stand down, brother," said Kanasta, gripping the wires.

The wires were pulled back in.

"I trust Devlin...I mean we have Atlas with us even though he…. Devlin is welcome to join. And…we need all the help we can get," said Kaity.

"What has he done to prove his authenticity? He's likely a spy," said Deceivant.

"I'm not a spy."

"Have you all forgotten that he killed his own mother!?" yelled Deceivant.

"Come now, honey. That's in the past," said Ada.

"There is no excuse for what I did to you. I was tricked by Sel, but that's still no excuse. I'm sorry, Mother. I'm so sorry," said Devlin in tears.

"Cut the act!" yelled Deceivant.

Wires poured out from Devlin and slammed Deceivant to the ground.

"You ungrateful—"

"Shut it. We have company," said Devlin, drawing Bravery. The golden sword spread out and its coils levitated, ready to strike.

Demonica stepped up, her misty purple lips stretched into a smile.

"Don't interfere. Devlin's the one I'm after. Just need to bring my little pet back home. But if you do want to get in my way," the dark goddess summoned the Death Scythe, "I'll slaughter you all," she said in a breathy, bewitching voice.

"I'll take care of her," said Devlin, walking toward the woman who defiled him.

Tentacles burst out from Demonica's chest and reeled the boy in.

"How dare you betray Sel!" yelled Demonica, her sharpened fingernails stabbing into Devlin's side.

Wires came out from Bravery and sliced the tentacles bound to their wielder. The sword's wires protruded out in the shape of a flower.

"Oh, have you become a flower child now?" asked Demonica.

Devlin stabbed Bravery into the ground. In an instant, wires shot out beneath Demonica. They pierced her skin but did not penetrate it.

"**BLOOM**," said Devlin, opening his clenched fist.

The wires on Demonica's skin split apart like petals, now shooting throughout her body.

"You can't kill me," said Demonica, tearing the bloody wires out.

"I don't need to."

The wires reeled Demonica toward her beloved. Opening up for a deadly embrace, the demoness was suddenly pierced by Bravery.

"**UNITE**."

The wires wrapped around each other, forming a single wire the size of a tree trunk.

"That's rather clever," said Demonica.

The unified wire shot out, sending Demonica thirty meters away.

"**PLANT**." Four wires shot out from the hilt of the sword and burrowed into the ground.

Devlin let go of the sword, but it kept its place in the air. He jumped on the wire and skated toward the dark goddess.

"Bravery is an extension of my body." As Devlin came in contact with Demonica, he jabbed his hands through her chest. He then dragged her body to the edge of the wire and jumped off with her.

His fingers shot forth wires that sent Demonica crashing into the grass. Wires shot out from his palm and grabbed the large edge of Bravery.

In an instant, the sword returned to its original size. He slowly approached Demonica and raised the weapon.

"Yes, penetrate it through me. De-virginize me with your wires," said Demonica, biting her lip lustfully.

"Demonica, we don't need to act anymore," said Devlin, patting her head.

"You sure I'm acting?" asked Demonica, playfully licking his face with her serpentine tongue.

Devlin shivered and pulled away. "Why else would you have created a portal for me to escape?" he asked with a smile.

"I don't know what you're talking about," said Demonica with a smile and a shrug.

"Hey, do you think that was convincing enough for me to join their team?" asked Devlin.

"I definitely do. You know, maybe I could join them as well," said Demonica, rubbing up against him.

"I think it'd be believable," said Devlin with a smile.

"So, when do you kill Sel?" asked Demonica.

"Once Lum is dead, before then we stand no chance."

"And how will we be able to stop him?" asked Demonica, worry flickering in her eyes.

"He wants to make me Lum and you Absence," said Devlin.

"Is that what he told you? Despite all your flower wire techniques, I can't imagine you being Lum," said Demonica.

"Why not? All I do is for the sake of equality," said Devlin, his hand to his chest.

"That's exactly why. Lum discriminates against humans and demons alike. You're too loving and not nearly preachy enough," said Demonica with a warm smile.

"And you're far too interesting to be Absence."

"Oh, Devlin, one day we shall rule Sellum together," said Demonica, wrapping her arms around him.

Devlin looked to the ground. "I want to rule Sellum with Kaity."

"I don't know why I'm not good enough. Or do you just like them tight? I can make myself as tight or as loose as you want. How does that sound?" asked Demonica, rubbing his chest.

"You defiled me. I can never love you."

"But you love her?" asked Demonica in a wounded tone.

"I love Kaity, and yes, I want to be intimate with her, but even more so I want to be one with her. To see her smile at me. To hear her laugh at my jokes. To smell her hair. To touch her lips. I want to spend every moment of my life with her. I cannot bear to love another," said Devlin, turning away.

"I understand, but I do not accept it," said Demonica, making him face her.

Devlin smacked her hand. "Don't touch me." He pulled away and shivered.

The Freedom Forcers caught up to them.

Devlin rushed to Kaity. "Will you allow me to join you?"

"I wouldn't. It's conspicuous how inconspicuous their fight was," said Deceivant.

"We need any help we can get. Besides, he wouldn't lie to me. I trust him," said Kaity, tapping Devlin's head with her tail.

"I did swear allegiance to Sel, but I can't betray my one and only love. I'm joining too," said Demonica, grabbing Devlin's hand.

"Don't you touch him," said Nina, slicing off Demonica's arm.

"Nina, stand down," ordered Devlin.

The steamed ninja exhaled sharply and put away her blade. "Are you really going to let her stay?" she asked Kaity.

"Not sure how I feel about her joining," said Kaity with a nervous grin.

"Come on. The deal was you'd remember my act of kindness. I saved you all from Etaf, remember?" asked Demonica, regenerating her arm and putting her finger to her lip.

"Don't you dare speak of kindness," said Nina with a dark tone.

"I remember! Welcome, friend," said Opti with a big hug.

"You know what? Let Sel spy on us. It's worth the risk to have more allies," said Deceivant with a nervous smile.

"So, Devlin is our friend?" asked D.S.

"An ally, that's all," said Deceivant.

D.S. went up to Devlin. "I know it's been a long time but," he took a deep breath, "so Matteria died, and I think he'd want you to have this." The childish Exp smiled as he gave Devlin Matteria's bracelet.

Devlin smiled with tearful eyes. "Thanks for keeping it safe," he said softly.

Kaity grabbed Devlin's arm and put on the bracelet. "Now you're officially one of us. So, no more secrets," she said with a smile.

"You're so beautiful," said Devlin, touching her hand with a teary smile.

"Aww! You two are so cute together!" squealed Ada.

Devlin pulled away with embarrassment. "Sorry. So, uh, what's our plan to stop Sel?"

"We join up with Lum and discuss with her," said Kaity.

"You really trust her?"

"I do," snapped Kaity. "Do you really trust Demonica?"

"She loves me in her own twisted way. Either way, we need her help," said Devlin with a shrug.

Chapter 135: A New Love

Meanwhile at the Observatory, Lum called forth a council meeting.

Etaf materialized, Efil was already seated, and Lum was behind a wall of pure light.

"You called back our troops?" asked Lum, hidden behind a barrier of blinding light.

"Yes. Should we punish the rebels for trying to breach Samsara?" asked Etaf.

"No need. Their casualties are a sufficient example…they will not make that mistake again."

"Did we have to kill them after they surrendered?" asked Efil in a voice as gentle as a whisper. The moss-covered goddess twirled her seaweed hair with worry.

"Justice must be firm, and their transgressions were severe. But I fear it may be time to bend justice yet again," said Lum, her voice becoming solemn.

"What do you mean?" asked Etaf.

"Sel's unification of his realm allowed him to vanquish Evol. Some of the Freedom Forcers and Sel's Pawns have crossed over to Earth. The others who arrived at the portal room have been captured by Ecnedurp per my orders," said Lum, her strong voice echoing throughout the structure.

"So, we make them work for the guarantee of their allies' safety?" asked Etaf.

"I am uncertain what to do. These are trying times," said Lum.

"We need to convince the Virtues to fight against Sel with us," said Efil.

"We need to unite this realm or we will fail. Efil, I need you to go with Fatima and make amends with the rebel humans. We can no longer use fear to keep the peace," said Lum.

"What about the Freedom Forcers? It appears that Kaity has already convinced them to work with us," said Efil.

"Indeed, though she revealed my identity to them. If they know, you two should know as well." The barrier in front of Lum dropped. The goddess' long white hair touched the ground. A dress of white light masked the wounds beneath. The goddess' skin was as pale as snow and her pupils were as black as the darkness that threatened her realm.

Efil was entranced by her god's visage.

"You're Sefiwah?" asked Etaf.

"She is a mere role I played to watch over the Exps. Though perhaps she can become something more," said Lum, her voice cold and loving all at once.

"That explains the incredible energy I felt around her," said Efil with a smile.

"Exp 8's rebellion and the mass death of Exps that followed served as a catalyst for the tensions between the realms. I feel our struggle against Sel is finally coming to a close."

"I feel the same. Can we trust the Freedom Forcers after they breached Samsara?" asked Etaf.

"Kaity revealed my secret but did so to bring her team to our side. I commend her for her efforts. For now, we will work with the Exps, but keep their allies as hostages in case they decide to betray us. As of now, you are not to tell them that their allies are captured so there won't be unnecessary tension," said Lum.

"As you command," said Etaf with a bow.

"Your will is my dharma," said Efil.

"Good. Now we need to talk about Tcetorp," said Lum.

"Yeah, I've been meaning to ask about that. Why isn't she here?" asked Etaf.

"She was taken hostage by Absence. If something were to befall her, Elysium could fall and all the prisoners would run rampant, including the Exp Demo. I will need the two of you to join the Freedom Forcers and convince them to go and free her. Now that Demonica is with them, they have access to Absence. Demonica already showed that even this sanctum isn't beyond her reach."

"I have something to add," said Etaf. "Until the Freedom Forcers are on our side, my divinations cannot reveal our future. We curve destiny in our favor by siding with them posthaste."

"That shouldn't be difficult. I need you to promise them that they will be personally escorted back to Earth once Sel has been purified," said Lum.

"I shall pass on your message," said Efil with a bow.

Lum looked over at the empty chair. "Before we can have Fatima unite the humans with the angels, we must first rebuild Beacon. We must discuss who will take Evol's place."

"Perhaps Fatima. It could be used to show we are representing humans in our pantheon," said Etaf.

"You two were both humans. Thankfully, I've saved you the trouble of discussing things. I have already found a replacement for Evol. And I have decided upon a worthy apprentice."

"An immortal goddess has no need for such things. You will not die. I won't allow it," said Efil, clenching her hands tightly.

"We are still uncertain how this struggle will end. Allah's Jannah was able to reach this place. There is no longer a place in Lum that is beyond Sel's reach. I think it's best to take extra precautions. This apprentice has a heart of pure gold and thinks only of the happiness of others," said Lum with a warm smile.

"I am not worthy. Thank you, Great Goddess. I will not fail you," said Efil, bowing devotedly.

"You are indeed not worthy, which is why I have chosen Violet to be the next Evol," said Lum with a slight smile.

Efil froze. "What?"

"My word is gospel," said Lum, folding her hands.

"I've served under you, given up everything for your glory. She's never done anything for you. We don't even know if we can trust her!" exclaimed Efil in tears.

"Violet, even as a broken spirit, did not attack the angels alongside her allies. She is one who is driven by love. Her unconditional love, even for Sel, makes her a worthy candidate. She alone is fitting to be Evol. I tested you by telling you to eliminate Devlin, and you tried your best to do so. My apprentice needs to be pure of heart. You must understand," said Lum with a glowing smile.

"Is this about me losing to Devlin? Please, Great Goddess, I will dispose of him if it would please you," said Efil, her hands shaking.

"This is why you are unfit for the job. It doesn't matter that you failed when you tried to kill Devlin. You failed me in the mere act of trying to kill him. My successor must be unbiased," said Lum passively.

"So, I am being punished for my obedience?" asked Efil, crying.

"Please, my Lord, say no more," said Etaf, holding Efil close to her.

"You are simply not rewarded; there is no punishment for you. You are still my most trusted ally. Now go and send Violet to me," said Lum, creating a portal in front of Efil.

"No. Is that what you want me to say? To be disobedient to my god? Who is more fitting to be the Goddess of Love than one who will obey any whim of a loved one?" asked Efil, crying deeply.

"You are already the Goddess of Life. I couldn't make you the Goddess of Love even if I wanted to. And only the God of Love is fit to rule in my absence. I will speak to Violet when the time is right. For now, meeting adjourned," said Lum sternly.

Efil slowly walked away before falling to the floor in tears.

Etaf lifted her up, and they went through the portal together.

"Don't listen to her," said Etaf, wiping away her friend's wet sorrow.

"Oh, but that is my sin. To hear and to love. I shall always be a sinner," said Efil, burying her face in her arms.

"You are the embodiment of virtue, and you don't preach about your goodness, unlike Lum," said Etaf, leaning Efil against her shoulder.

"Where has that gotten me? Violet was chosen over me," said Efil, peeking up at Etaf with teary eyes.

"You don't need her recognition. You shine on your own," said Etaf, holding Efil's cheek.

"I do need her. She is the reason for my existence. She saved me from despair. She gave me purpose. I need to serve her," said Efil as her arms trembled.

"Do what you must, but know I'm always here for you," said Etaf, holding Efil.

"You've always been so good to me. You've always supported me. I only wish I could be as good of a friend as you," said Efil, embracing her one true friend extra tightly.

"You already are. You alone have kept me going." Etaf seized Efil and caressed her hair as her eyes watered up. "I'm so proud of you, *mataki*."

"And I won't ever leave you," said Efil, kissing Etaf's forehead.

Etaf looked away with flustered cheeks. "I can't imagine anyone better to rule Lum," she said, pulling at her pal's cheeks.

"Oh, you shouldn't say such things," said Efil with a blush.

"If you were Lum, this place would be so different, so wonderful. I don't know what kind of goddess Violet would make, but I know you would be better," said Etaf with a smile.

"That's absolutely right! Lum revealed herself to Kaity before me despite all I've done for her! That girl is unworthy. She used to murder for fun and bathe in the blood of her victims. How is that noble? Oh, why must Lum torment me? Is it because of my deep devotion to her? How can faith be sin? My devotion alone makes me worthy! My soul lights up every time I hear her voice," said Efil with tears of bliss.

"It sickens me to see the way Lum treats you. Perhaps she is jealous of your purity," said Etaf.

"Oh, no, jealousy is such a primitive fault. Lum has no faults and never will. Whatever I have done wrong, I apologize for. Lum is simply trying to perfect my soul. I must not yet be worthy. Thank you for showing me Lum's guidance," said Efil with a sunny smile.

"Don't know how I did that, but I'm glad you're feeling better," said Etaf, pulling her dear friend along.

Etaf and Efil entered a portal.

They exited in front of the Freedom Forcers. Etaf eyed the Goddess of Death.

"If you want a fight, I'll be happy to oblige," said Demonica.

Deceivant stepped in between them. "Etaf, we've come to an agreement. If you'll promise to escort us to Earth once Sel is defeated, we will join forces with Lum."

"We both promise," said Etaf, grabbing her dear friend's hand.

"So why is Demonica with you?" asked Efil.

"Devlin is free now, and he wants to work with Lum. I won't let you harm him or Kanasta," said Kaity with a glare.

"Those orders are no more. We seek cooperation now," said Etaf.

"You had better not go back on your word again," said Deceivant.

"We won't. Efil, I'll manage things from here. You complete the task given to you. *Popko no okai*," said Etaf with a smile.

"And you as well. I leave the rest to you," said Efil with a smile before leaving.

"Alright. So, how are we going to go about taking down Sel?" asked Deceivant.

"First off, we need to recover Tcetorp from Absence. Demonica, have your little pet bring us there," said Etaf.

"I don't take orders from you," said Demonica with a grimace.

"Wait! We don't need to stay and fight. Demonica, you can bring us to Earth right now, can't you?" asked Deceivant.

"Yeah, but I don't feel like it," said Demonica with a shrug.

Deceivant pulled Devlin aside. "Talk to her. Don't you care about Kaity's safety?"

"I've always done what's best for Kaity, and I know for a fact she won't be safe until Sel falls. You can't run away from this like you always do," said Devlin, grabbing his father's collar with intensity.

"Always a stubborn boy," said Deceivant before he was released.

"Demonica, bring us to Absence," said Devlin.

"Wait. Etaf, after our allies were teleported, Sel said something peculiar. It wasn't the words so much as his tone that bothered me," said Atlas.

Etaf smiled. "They are safe. And as long as you continue to cooperate, they will remain safe."

"Of course. Lum is keeping them as insurance. Kaity, are you sure she is someone we should trust?" asked Deceivant.

Kaity broke down into tears. "I...I don't know."

Deceivant gripped Etaf's shoulders. "You made her cry."

"I don't care. Either cooperate with us or they will die, one by one," said Etaf.

"Hope was captured, wasn't she?" asked Deceivant horrified.

"Yes, but don't worry. She'll be the last—"

Deceivant punched the goddess in the face.

"Think I'm bluffing? I'll be right back with one of their bodies," said Etaf, forming a portal.

"Stop!" Kaity ran to her in tears, but Etaf walked through before anyone could stop her.

"Demonica, make a portal there now! We can't afford to lose any allies," said Devlin.

"Alright…for a kiss," said Demonica, seductively sticking out her tongue.

Devlin made out with her and broke the kiss. "Do it."

"Oooh, as you command."

Gimpy appeared. The slave was entirely bound in a tight black gimp suit.

"We need a portal to the portal room. Now," said Demonica.

The Freedom Forcers fell silent. Just as Gimpy made the portal, another portal appeared.

Nina emerged, setting Hope's limp body on the ground.

Deceivant ran to her side in tears.

The little queen opened her eyes and turned away. "What do you want?" she asked in a regal, imposing, yet cutesy voice.

"You're not hurt?" asked Ada, helping her daughter to her feet.

Hope stood tall on her high heels and brushed the dust off her purple skirt with her mittens. She pushed her two spiraling hair curls aside. "I'm not happy," she said, her powdered cheeks puffing out.

Image exited, with the Captain of Carnage on her shoulder. Napkin came soon after. The meek kitten with white and frazzled fur ran into Kaity's arms.

Kaity went up to Nina. "Can we talk?"

"Sure thing," said Nina, her firm voice stilted with apprehension. The *kunoichi* had a piece of the Hero's Militia flag covering her mouth. Her purple hair was short and her breasts were wrapped.

"Oh, it's you," said Kaity, noticing the pain in her friend's eyes.

"Is that a problem?" asked Nina, avoiding eye contact.

"I certainly don't think so," said Hope with a smile.

Atlas approached his wife. "Were you captured?"

"Yes, but we were freed," said Image in a logical tone with little feeling. Her body was a mishmash of different items, each representational of a different branch of psychology. The inkblots on her face formed what was either a powdery moth or bloodied body. "I'm happy just to be alive," she said, her eyes shining through her glasses.

The armored ferret on her shoulder stood at attention. "I have failed you, my lord. I was unable to bring her home. I wasn't even able to protect her," said the Captain in the firm voice of a proud soldier.

Atlas seized his great comrade in an embrace. "You've kept her safe. I cannot express sufficient gratitude," he said, tears pouring out from his eyes. He turned to Image. "Who is that freed you? I owe them great thanks."

The portal enlarged and Sellum emerged. The Omni God's black and white energy was eliminated by the clear energy coating his golden armor.

"What are you here for?" asked Kaity, glaring at the God of Gods.

"Etaf was going to kill your allies. I intervened," said Sellum in a deep and stoic voice with tears pouring from his helmet.

"We are forever thankful," said Atlas, bowing as low as he could.

"Lum must have cheated," said Hope with puffed out cheeks. "I had convinced the portal's guardian, but she suddenly changed her mind. This gentleman was able to override her order somehow."

Deceivant approached the god and bowed. "Thank you."

The God of Gods turned to leave.

"Please, let us come with you. It isn't safe here," said Deceivant.

Sellum looked over the Freedom Forcers. "I can no longer remain neutral in this conflict. Very well. All of you, come with me," said Sellum, forming a portal by mixing Sel, Lum, and Absence energy together.

"Wait. I don't think it was Lum who betrayed us. I think we should stay here," said Kaity.

"Foolish. It's only a matter of time before Etaf returns. Whether loyal to Lum or not, she will likely attack us. But worry not, I've already made the choice for you," said Hope.

"No. I have to lead this team. The choice isn't yours," said Kaity.

"You're the leader and I own you. Therefore, I shall decide the proper course of action," said Hope.

"You don't own me! I said I'd help you out not be your slave," said Kaity with a furious look.

"Now is not the time for disobedience. Hmm, it appears they agree." Hope pointed to the Freedom Forcers who were entering the portal one by one.

"Wait up. Lum isn't our enemy," said Kaity, rushing after them.

"Not if we play our cards right," said Hope, entering right after Deceivant.

Demonica popped up in front of Kaity. "Take my word or don't, but Sellum is trouble."

"What do you mean?" asked Kaity.

"He sure showed up at the opportune time, didn't he? Right before you all swore allegiance to Lum to save your comrades."

"Yeah, but he saved them and he saved Devlin too."

"That was at an opportune time as well," said Demonica before entering the portal.

After shaking away her worries, Kaity followed.

"Well, this place certainly is a sight to behold," said Deceivant, gazing up at the cosmos adorning the ceiling.

"Incredible!" exclaimed Crisis.

"Not bad at all," said Devlin with a smirk.

"Oh, before I forget, Devlin, I would like to formally introduce you to Hope, the sister you never knew you had," said Deceivant with jazz hands.

"A pleasure to meet you," said Devlin with a bow.

"Able-bodied, handsome, and polite, you'd make a fine vassal. However, I must first break your allegiance to Sel," said Hope, sizing him up.

"I have no allegiance to him. He ruined my life and wants to kill Kaity," said Devlin through clenched teeth.

"How cute," said Hope with a little smile.

"Cute?" asked Devlin, taken aback.

Hope giggled.

"I shall return shortly," said Sellum, vanishing into a Lum portal.

"I hope he's speaking on our behalf," said Atlas.

"Ugh, the floor here is hard. Violet, carry me," said Hope.

With vacant eyes, the broken devotee lifted up her queen.

"Wait, she's still like this?" asked Devlin, grabbing Violet's cheek and examining her eyes.

"Impressed? Her state of mind is proof of my power," said Hope with a smile.

A single wire pulled Hope out from her slave's arms and brought her to the ground.

"What do you think you are doing?" asked Hope, almost fully ensnared by wires.

"You will change her back," said Devlin with cold intensity.

"Oh my, I rather like that look in your eyes," said Hope with a small smile.

The wires tightened their grip.

"Do it," said Devlin.

"I will not be ordered by Sel's puppet. If you kill me, she'll remain broken. Is that what you want?"

Devlin's wires went up to her throat and strangled her.

Kaity grabbed his arm. "Stop!"

Devlin turned to his beloved, his anger instantly subsiding.

Hope coughed and held her throat, tears welling up in her eyes. "Why didn't you help sooner?"

"The team was discussing strategy. Devlin, why are you hurting her?" asked Kaity, shaking him.

"You know what she did to Violet. I'm making sure she fixes my daughter," said Devlin.

"You can't force her. And it's not so simple," said Kaity.

Devlin released the detestable girl.

"If you want my help, you'll have to give me something I want," said Hope, holding her neck in pain.

"I won't play your games. This is serious," said Devlin, crouching down to her level.

"You'll have to carry me around in Violet's place. As my brother, you have a lot of lost time to make up for," said Hope.

"Fine. I'll carry you," said Devlin.

"Not with that attitude you won't. Kiss my foot," said Hope, raising her leg.

Devlin begrudgingly placed his hand under her foot and kissed it.

"Oh, yes. That is quite a good look for you. And one last thing. I get cold at night…you must keep me warm," said Hope, gripping his hand and bringing it to her chest.

"No worries. I can do that," said Kaity with a grin.

"Silence. I was speaking to him," said Hope, her nose raised pompously.

"Yes. I'll carry you and cuddle you, but only after you fix Violet," said Devlin.

Hope snapped her fingers.

"Violet? Are you okay now?" asked Devlin, hoisting her from the floor.

"It's not so easy," said Hope, giggling under her mittens.

Devlin turned to her with aggression, but Kaity calmed him by grabbing his hand.

"I don't care if it's easy or not. Fix her," said Devlin.

"Very well, but break your word and Kaity will face the consequences," said Hope with a proud smirk.

"You hurt her and I'll break every bone in your body and drain every last drop of your regal blood," said Devlin through gritted teeth.

Hope looked away, flustered. "When she is cured, I want a kiss…on my cheek. Is that understood?" The queen wobbled a bit.

50

"Sure. Whatever."

Hope took a deep breath and looked into Violet's eyes. "MENTAL CRUSH."

"Well, go on. Say something," said Devlin.

"I'm good at breaking minds, not fixing them. It has to be genuine or it won't have any effect," said Hope.

"Then give me your artifact," said Devlin.

"No need. You can reach her now. I've made her mind malleable, but only for a little while. Better hop to it. The longer she stays in a broken state, the more permanent damage her mind will suffer. Hmm, I wonder if your feelings will reach her," said Hope with a sly smile.

"Oh, maybe this will help." Ada took out Allah's Nur and placed it in Violet's hand.

"As if it would be so simple," said Hope with a small smile.

Devlin grabbed Violet in a loving embrace. He combed her golden hair as he spoke to her. "Everything Hope told you…it wasn't true. Your belief system is not a lie. I filled your mind with religious texts when I made you, but you chose to take them to heart. You found something from each tradition that resonated with you. It's supplementary, not contradictory. And you don't use it as a tool of convenience. You realize there are times when certain beliefs will create more problems than others, and you adjust accordingly."

"He's rather good at this," said Hope, visibly shocked.

"And you're not weak. You're one of the strongest people I've ever known. You spread so much joy, despite all the tragedy you've gone through. You even fought Etah and almost won. You never failed me, Violet. You…guided me toward forgiveness, and you stood by me when I asked you to do unspeakable things on my behalf. I know you see me as a god, but I'm just a mortal, another animal just trying to do what's right, and you supported me when I needed it and stood against me when I went astray. I did use you for my own gain, but that fault is mine to shoulder, not yours. Decide your own purpose, and I'll support you every step of the way. You have no master but that radiant spirit that resonates within you," said Devlin, embracing her with a face full of tears.

Vitality slowly returned to Violet's amethyst eyes.

"D-Devlin?" she asked in a daze.

"Yeah. It's me."

"You're free," she said with joy in her eyes.

"I am," said Devlin with a smile.

"You're back with us?" she asked in a wispy voice filled with love.

"Yes. And you're back too," said Devlin, helping her back to her feet.

"Is this book for me?" asked Violet, just noticing what was clenched in her hands.

"All yours," said Devlin, kissing her forehead.

Hope clapped with two fingers on her palm. "You continue to impress me. Now, I believe we had a—"

Devlin hoisted Hope up into his arms and placed a kiss on her cheek. "You're lucky I was able to rescue her," the dangerous boy whispered in her ear.

Hope fanned herself. "You'll do just fine," she said with flushed cheeks and a warm smile. Hope turned and stuck out her bottom lip while staring at Deceivant.

"Can I give you a kiss too?" asked Kaity.

"After speaking out against me? Absolutely not," said Hope, crossing her arms.

A portal appeared and Sellum emerged.

"Kaity, I've been meaning to ask. Who is that guy?" asked Devlin, pointing at the armored god.

"He's the one who saved you. Be careful though, he's a pathological liar," said Kaity.

"So you've spoken with him?"

"Yeah. We had a one-on-one talk here," said Kaity.

"One on one? You were dating him?"

Kaity smiled. "I guess you could say that."

Devlin looked up at Sellum with a grin. "Mask covering the whole face, cape, golden armor; damn it, he's the mysterious type," said Devlin, faking aggression.

Kaity slugged him. "Stop being so silly."

"I had to. You weren't smiling," said Devlin softly.

"Is something the matter?" asked Lord Sellum, approaching the special boy.

"I heard you called Kaity to your pad here so you could talk with her alone."

"I suppose that is one way of putting it."

"Do you love Kaity?" asked Devlin.

"You misread my intentions. I wish only the best for Kaity. I'm Sellum. I observe and intervene if necessary. I thought you would be relieved," said Lord Sellum.

"Then it's really you? You're really the Creator?" asked Violet with a dazed look.

"Come now, you can't honestly believe that he watches over Earth," said Deceivant, patting the zealot's back.

"Not just Earth, the entire Milky Way. Though Earth is the only planet under my supervision that has problems."

"Can I have a hug? I've always wanted to hug God," said Violet, coated in devotion.

"Why not?" said Sellum as he gave Violet a quick hug.

"Warm and personable. You're a loving god," said Violet with a gentle smile.

"Why did you call us here? What do you want?" asked Kaity.

"Sel will commence his assault on Absence shortly. Absence is our ally, but I fear his forces won't be enough to stop Sel. We must not let Sel free Zenero."

"Whoa, whoa slow down. Stop ordering us around. We don't work for you," said Devlin.

"I concur," said Hope, grabbing her new vassal's hand.

"You are not safe in Sel or Lum. You cannot reach Absence. I may be mistaken, but it seems only I can offer you solace," said Lord Sellum.

"You are most certainly right! We should join, right away! Oh, let God's will flow through me!" cheered Violet, spinning in place.

"What do we get in return?" asked Hope.

"What do you want?" asked Lord Sellum.

Hope looked around the room. "Earth. It's a rather pretty planet."

"I can't give you Earth."

"Then what about Venus? Surely you can part with Pluto. It isn't even a planet; isn't that right, Deceivant?" asked Hope.

"Absolutely! It's just an icy meteor."

"I can return you to Earth once balance in Sellum has been achieved."

"That's a start," said Hope.

"What is your end goal?" asked Kaity, looking up at Sellum.

"I want to preserve the balance of Sellum. To do so, I will need to replace the current Lum and Sel."

"I'll take over Sel for you, once I've killed Bob," said Devlin.

"And after that? After you've created balance here?" asked Kaity.

"I will preserve it."

"And what about Earth; what are you planning to do with our home?" asked Kaity.

"To purge it of its ailments. My dharma is to make Earth a utopia for all life!" yelled Sellum with a sudden burst of extreme passion.

"A planetary doctor. That's fine with me," said Deceivant.

"Then, you'll offer your aid?" asked Sellum.

"Absolutely," said Deceivant.

"There is a species more dangerous than Exps. It threatens the life systems on Earth," said Sellum.

"One thing at a time," said Deceivant.

"I need to speak with Lum," said Kaity. "You told me so many things, and I don't know what's true and what isn't. Bring me to her throne room. Let me talk with her, and then we will discuss joining forces with you."

"Allying with the Omni God is the clear tactical choice. You're not thinking clearly," said Hope, sitting up in Devlin's arms.

"I don't care. I won't turn against her without reason. Sellum, make the portal," said Kaity with fierce eyes.

"Do not go alone," said Sellum.

"I'll come along. I have some questions of my own I'd like answered," said Hope.

"Me too! I will protect you even without Snippy," said D.S.

Sellum materialized a giant pair of scissors identical to the one D.S. was accustomed to. "Keep her safe."

"Yes, sir," said D.S. with a salute.

"I'll accompany as well," said Kanasta.

Napkin hopped into Kaity's arms, ran up her shoulders, and licked her face.

"Of course you can come along," said Kaity with a smile, rubbing under the kitty's chin.

"I should go too. We must uncover the truth," said Violet, still in a bit of a daze.

"I should go with you," said Devlin.

"You'll come along?" asked Violet with shimmering eyes.

"I won't lose you again," said Devlin, grabbing her hand.

"We don't know if Lum will try to kill you, Devlin. You're staying here," said Kaity.

"Well, if he isn't coming, who will carry me?" Hope was hoisted up into Nina's arms. "Oh, well, that settles that."

"How can we be sure she won't hurt you, Kaity? And Violet is very fragile right now. I should be there for her," said Devlin.

"I will keep Kaity and Violet safe." Nina walked past Devlin, averting her gaze from him. "But I'm not doing it for you."

"Nina, I...," said Devlin softly.

Nina took a breath and turned to him. "I protected your family as ordered." She turned away and walked to Kaity. "From now on, I'm doing what I want."

"Come now, you should be polite to your father," said Ada.

"I don't think of Devlin as my father. And you're not my mother," said Nina, walking off.

"That poor girl," said Ada softly.

"No idea what's going on, but I'm sticking with the Creator," said Crisis, pointing to Sellum.

"Do be careful," said Sellum, creating a portal leading directly to the Observatory.

"Stay with us. I think your e-x-g-f wants some s-p-a-c-e," said Opti.

"But what if something happens to them?" asked Devlin, worry weighing down his voice.

"You shouldn't look down on her because she's a child," said Deceivant.

Devlin looked up at the master inventor. "Actually, there is a reason I should stay behind."

Kaity and her team exited the Microcosm, carrying doubts as to Lum's intentions as they crossed over.

Chapter 136: Sellum's Dillema

Sellum looked out at those who remained. "I'd like to introduce you to my allies."

A small figure in a black cloak approached Sellum and grabbed his leg.

"This is Stabby," said Sellum.

"Is that a real name?" asked Absorb.

"It's the name she chose," said Sellum.

"It is a pleasure to see you again," said Deceivant as he bent down and softly kissed her hand.

The girl pulled her hand away and hid behind Sellum's leg.

"Aww, she's shy. And she's still brimming with youth," said Deceivant.

"You know her?" asked Sellum.

"But of course. I wouldn't be a connoisseur of cuteness if I wasn't familiar with this sweet little raspberry," said Deceivant, smiling at Stabby.

"Casey, come and greet the Freedom Forcers," said Sellum.

Casey approached, keeping her distance from Atlas.

"Sister?" asked Atlas.

"No need to hide yourself. You're among comrades," said Sellum.

"How can we be certain he isn't a spy for Sel?" Casey removed her cloak. The Exp had a smooth body made up of cubes. Even her silver hair was boxy. The Exp was wearing all black, still in mourning for her missing husband.

"If he works for us, I may very well select him to rule over Sel. He has no reason to betray us," said Sellum.

"I'm only working with you for Zenero's sake. There is no us," said Casey with a mechanical womanly voice.

"And I'm the one who's going to be the next Sel," said Devlin.

"Okay, why is the creep here?" asked Casey, pointing at Deceivant.

"He's harmless, don't fret." Sellum turned to address the Exps. "And finally…" A tiny pink bunny with a black tail and eyes that shimmered like crystals, materialized in Sellum's open palms. "This is Nibbles."

"So cute!" exclaimed Opti, petting his new furry friend.

"Does Nibbles have any special powers?" asked Deceivant.

"None that should concern you," said Sellum.

"Is super cuteness a power?" asked Opti, scratching the bunny's ears.

"Opti, please protect Nibbles. He is very important to me," said Sellum.

"Can't you protect him?" asked Deceivant.

"I must leave for a short period. I will return when I can," said Sellum.

"Then why not take the bunny with you?"

"He would be in more danger alongside me," said Sellum.

"Have you ever been attacked in this place?" asked Atlas.

"Only once, but I fear Sel has found a way to reach here," said Sellum.

"Maybe with Demonica's gimp, but she's with us now," said Deceivant.

"We cannot be certain of that. Also, when Kaity returns, I will need you to convince her to work with us," said Sellum.

"I'll do what I can," said Deceivant.

"We must take extra precautions. You need to be well-equipped to fight Sel's forces when they arrive," said Sellum.

"Our guns are practically out of ammo at this point," said Deceivant with a shrug.

"Then I shall give you a gun that won't run out so quickly. I fetched this from Innov Labs, an Earth facility you are familiar with." Sellum summoned up a specialized gun. The gun was pink and yellow with a thick metal coil that rode up to its opening. The muzzle had three metal prongs coming from its sides that circled around the opening like a plasma coil.

"Amy?" asked Deceivant with wide eyes.

"Why did you say that name?" asked Casey with slanted eyes.

"The Gravity Gun is fully automated and ready for combat." Sellum pushed a button that caused a bayonet to pop out from the bottom of the gun.

"Amy was confiscated. How did you get her back?" asked Deceivant, running his hand up the gun.

Sellum stared at Deceivant and gestured to his planetarium.

Casey stepped up to him. "Did you name your gun after my daughter?"

"As a mother, I expected you to be honored," said Deceivant with a bewildered look.

"That looks really cool. How does it work?" asked Opti.

"Well, Amy was supposed to be a tool for research, but I got a grant from the U.S. military and turned her into a weapon. The major problem I had to overcome was that the gravity of her bullets affected the user as well as the target. To get around that problem, I incorporated a blade on her that releases a fixed gravity field around the user. This allows the user to manipulate the gravity of the target and the surrounding area without being caught in the gravity shifts themselves. Amy is two inventions in one," said Deceivant, glowing with pride.

"So, in other words, Amy is epic!" cheered Opti.

"Truly a remarkable creation," said Image, inspecting it with her eyes.

"Thanks. I am excited to see how she performs in a combat scenario," said Deceivant.

Casey turned to Sellum. "When do we rescue Zenero?"

"When the time is right," said Sellum.

"I heard Zenero was assassinated," said Deceivant with a confused look.

"You do realize you're in the afterlife?" asked Image.

"Oh, yes…still getting used to the absurdity of it all," said Deceivant with a mild chuckle.

"Zenero is neither alive nor dead. He is in stasis," said Lord Sellum.

"Like Schrodinger's cat," said Image.

"Don't speak of that absurd denial of science," said Deceivant, rolling his eyes.

"Sellum imprisoned him in Absence. I have no choice but to cooperate with this traitor if I want to rescue my husband," said Casey.

"Stay strong. You will reach the end of your desired path if you remain focused," said Atlas.

"You don't know what happened, so butt out," said Casey.

"The loyalty in her must be preprogrammed quite thoroughly," said Deceivant.

"Her programing is only the foundation of her feelings for him. It is the love she fostered that makes her loyal to him," said Sellum.

"How much time has passed on Earth since we arrived?" asked Deceivant.

"A day in Sellum is close to the time it takes for a year to pass on Earth. A day is roughly—"

"Two minutes on Sellum," said Deceivant, flicking his glasses for added flair.

"I must be off. Each moment I remain here is another life lost," said Sellum, exiting into a Lum portal.

"What is he doing in Lum?" asked Deceivant.

"Who knows what that fool does?" asked Casey with a shrug.

Deceivant approached Stabby. "Stay with us til he's back, okie dokie?"

Stabby stepped back and nodded.

A Sel portal appeared. Lord Sel, Riufen, Pesi, Regna, Edirp, and Yvne emerged.

Devlin turned to Demonica. "Did you do this?"

Demonica turned to Gimpy, who was on all fours and bouncing in excitement. "It doesn't just follow my orders. Foolish creature thinks I'll reward it with punishment."

"Then it was you!" yelled Devlin.

"It was Sel." Demonica stared at Gimpy with hate. "I want to hurt you so badly right now, but you don't deserve it," she said through clenched teeth.

"I protected Deceivant as you commanded. Now that you've returned, what are my orders?" asked Absorb.

"Keep the bunny from interfering. Muffins, I mean," said Lord Sel, noticing Nibbles in Opti's arms.

"As you command," said Absorb, tilting his body.

"What do you want?" asked Atlas, starring at the God of Destruction.

Sel pulled in his dark energy. "Hmmmm." The beach-ball sized eyeball's intense blue pupil looked over the pawns. He pointed at Stabby. "Her. We've come to arrest her for treason against the realm of Sel," he said in a cruel and dignified nasal tone.

"I won't let you touch her," said Deceivant, standing in front of the little girl and raising his gun.

Sel burst into laughter, rolled on the ground, and then wiped his tears away. "You can't stop me. But, I could strike a deal with you. I'll send Hope to Earth, like the Lum gods were supposed to, and you come with me." He stretched out a spectral hand.

"And you'll promise to do her no harm?" asked Deceivant.

"The thought didn't even cross my mind," said Sel, shaking Deceivant's hand.

Wires came out from below and sliced into the Dark One.

Sel turned to face Devlin. "I would have made you a god."

"I'll earn that title with my own power," said Devlin, disengaging the wires as the corruption spread.

Demonica stood by Devlin's side. "The only chance we have is if the three of us attack together."

"Who's the third?"

Gimpy stood up and instantly materialized a peculiar-looking sword. The spiked black sword was bound in chains and belts. The grip of the sword was sharp, and while the center blade pointed straight, its four branching blades bent outward in different directions.

"Your slave can't be trusted," said Devlin.

"It may follow Sel's orders, but it isn't able to defy mine. I've established utter control over its mind. Gimpy, as D.S. calls it, answers to me above all else."

Riufen stepped up, searching for an opponent. "I shall cut down the strongest warrior here," he said in a strong and stoic tone. The rock-skinned samurai set his sights on Atlas.

Deceivant shifted the gun's sights to the bone-clad samurai. "Sorry. You'll have to settle for me."

"Are you sure?" asked Atlas.

"I may need a little help, but I can keep him occupied till Sellum returns," said Deceivant.

The Captain of Carnage pointed his blades at the samurai. "Then we shall both fight him."

Regna slammed her feet in a fury. "Alright! I'm not in a good mood, and I'm ready to let loose!" she exclaimed in a voice seething with disdain and boiling with rage. The magma inside her rough red skin pulsed with extra intensity.

Pesi rushed up to Opti and punched his other half with a corrosive fist. "I'm going to permanently rid this world of your ignorant insolence!" he yelled in a furious tone. The Exp's skin was black like coal, which accentuated his red spiky hair.

A slimy green puddle with deer horns protruding from it made circles around Sellum's helpers. "I've chosen you," said Yvne in a curious voice, almost like a whisper. She approached Crisis while shifting into the form of the knight who bested her.

"I stayed behind to avoid confrontation. Oh well," said Crisis, creating a current of wind around his arms.

Yvne's lancet was shorter and her armor was thinner.

"Leave the capture of the traitor to me," said Edirp, stepping up to Stabby. The demon goddess' gruesome purple body was embellished with regal relics. "Come here, you worthless little brat," she said in a haughty and narcissistic voice.

Ada picked up the child. "No. I won't let you take this poor girl away from her family."

"I don't know who you are, but you're in the way!" yelled Regna, ejecting her arms.

The arms segmented in mid-flight and started flashing.

"Case."

Each body part was instantly covered by a silver encasing.

"You can't contain my rage!"

Regna's limbs burst inside the boxes but did not even budge them.

"That's it! I'm furious!" yelled Regna, her body flashing rapidly.

Suddenly the goddess was trapped in a silver rectangular encasing.

"I'm not particularly pleased myself," said Casey, walking off.

"I have to fight a bunny? Whatever. It's better than my last task," said Absorb, sulking up to his opponent.

Muffins' fur stood on end.

"That's odd," said Absorb.

The fur shot out as spines.

Absorb deflected the thorny projectiles with powerful puffs of air. "You do realize I'm a living weapon, right? I was made for combat," said the sponge, propelling himself toward the bunny.

Muffins hopped out of the way, letting her attacker smash against the ground.

The bunny's fur stood on end once more and fused into a single needle before firing off.

Absorb swerved out of the way of the needle and hit the bunny from the side. "You left yourself open."

The giant needle exploded, showering Absorb from behind with tiny thistles.

The weaponized sponge sped out of the way only to get pierced from below by a second giant needle.

"You're surprisingly skilled." The sponge's wound pulled in the large needle into its center.

Giant needles popped out from all its pores.

"You couldn't have chosen a worse—"

The needles exploded all around Absorb, piercing him from within.

The spongy Exp fell to the ground in a daze.

Having won her bout, Muffins rushed to Opti's side to aid him in his battle against his other half.

Pesi fired black shots of negativity at his sworn nemesis.

Opti used a white shield to keep the blasts at bay while closing in. "We don't have to fight anymore."

"Shut it! I want you dead!" Pesi formed a black sword once he was within range.

Opti countered with a white sword of his own.

The swordplay continued until Pesi fell back, paralyzed.

Muffins hopped up to the nice mortal and snuggled his leg.

"Thanks, friend," said Opti, patting the bunny affectionately.

Yvne, having taken the form of Limit, rushed at Crisis.

A powerful gust sent the weatherman up into the air. He followed this maneuver by sending a hailstorm at the knight.

Yvne braved the storm and leaped up, turning her hand into a lance.

Crisis' body became molten as the lance pierced him, melting it into ash.

Yvne's arm extended, grabbed the enemy by the foot, and slammed him hard against the ground.

Crisis stood up. "You can't overcome nature." He used a torrent of air to keep the armored enemy airborne.

Yvne layered her armor further, weighing herself down to avoid being pushed back after landing in front of her enemy.

"Not the best choice," said Crisis, adding a cold front to his torrent and freezing the goddess.

"You really think you can oppose a goddess?" asked Edirp, forming insult arrows.

Blades shot out from Stabby's sleeves and pierced into Edirp's leg as she fired.

The arrows hit the ground and bounced up.

They went right through Ada.

"So, that one was a fake. No matter. I only need the girl. **Imperial Atmosphere.**" All the Adas and Stabby were brought to their knees by the sudden weight of their insignificance.

"**ILLUSIONARY INSANITY!**" yelled Ada, creating a thick wall in front of Stabby.

"Pathetic tricks, nothing more." Edirp walked through the wall. Once she reached the other side, she saw thirty-six Stabbys. "You are a fool to defy me!"

"I will show my worth to you. Taking you down won't be easy, but with Amy, I can do it." Deceivant hoisted up his beloved gun.

Riufen and the Captain bowed to each other.

The samurai unsheathed his spine as the armored ferret glided up to him.

The Captain kicked off the samurai's blade after attaching a hook to it. He then spun around the sword, slicing Riufen's throat with each revolution.

The blood that splattered on the sword collected on the tip and hardened it like steel.

Riufen closed his eyes and slammed his sword into the Captain.

The clever ferret used the momentum to slide up the warrior's back, cutting it along the way.

Riufen fell to his knees.

"As the God of Hate's personal assassin, my blades are often poisoned. Since you are immortal, I used paralyzing toxins." The Captain sliced up the samurai's body, coating his blades with more toxins as soon as they ran dry.

"Ingenious. This is a new obstacle for me to overcome." Riufen closed his eyes.

Blood sprayed out from his body, and the toxins went along with it.

"Go on. Shoot him. I can't keep this up," said the Captain.

"Then move aside else you get caught in the crossfire," said Deceivant.

"Fine!" The Captain sliced Riufen's hand as it reached for him, creating distance between the two.

"Deceivant. You are human. This battle will only result in your death," said Riufen as he approached.

"Humans are weak animals, we can't tear through flesh with our fingernails, camouflage, or release toxins, but we can create tools to overcome our weaknesses. I'm not arrogant enough to think we're the only animal who does that, but some of us are better at it than others. No longer will I be viewed as a coward. Now, I will fight for my own cause. *GRAVITY SHOT*." Deceivant pressed down on the trigger.

The bullet zoomed by Riufen, but the power swept the warrior off his feet.

"Hit him now," said Deceivant with a confident grin.

The Captain flung poison-tipped paralysis knives in a circle around the samurai's chest.

The knives bounced off the warrior's hardened skin.

"You are not just fighting me. You are raising your sword against every opponent I've battled. Their techniques have been inscribed upon my inner scroll." Riufen caught the knives and flung them at Deceivant.

Another bullet redirected the knives and pushed the samurai back.

"You seem more cowardly than ever," said Riufen, flicking his blood out from his fingertips to destroy the special bullets.

"Don't you judge me. I have to live with the fear of dying."

The back of the bulky gun opened up, revealing pink containers.

"*GRAVITY GRENADE!*" Deceivant grabbed a grenade and tossed it at his opponent.

Riufen dodged it with a quick shift of his weight.

Deceivant pressed a button on the gun.

The grenade exploded behind the samurai.

Riufen slammed to the ground and lost his grip on his spine. "Very intriguing," said the warrior with a smile. He leaped off the floor and grabbed his sword after kicking it.

"Alright, I've only got one shot at this. Captain, be ready!"

The sides of the gun popped open, revealing two tubular missiles.

"*GRAVITY MISSILE.*" Deceivant disengaged the missiles from the Gravity Gun with the press of a button.

Riufen tore out a second spine with his left hand and cut the missiles in half. In doing so, he released the gravity field contained within. His body was crushed by the opposing gravitational fields and shot up into the air after it squeezed out.

"Splendid work!" The Captain rode the gravity field of a bullet and connected his hooks to the samurai. He sped around, slicing Riufen to stunt his recovery.

"I can choose whether or not to be affected by the gravitational distortions created by Amy." Deceivant flipped a switch just above the trigger. "Amy gives me the power to defeat you!" He faced the opposite direction and fired the gun.

The bullet's gravitational field sent him backward until he was right below Riufen. The sides of the gun turned down, revealing that they were machine guns. The guns fired downward rapidly, propelling Deceivant upward to the samurai.

"I am the first organism to conquer and control gravity!" Deceivant flew up to the powerful Exp with his blade posed.

Once his opponent was within range, Riufen turned the gun around so the blade was at Deceivant's neck.

Deceivant sharply closed his eyes in a sudden surge of fear.

Riufen put his hand on Deceivant's shoulder as he healed. "I won't kill you. You fought well. We must do battle again sometime. Grow stronger and defeat me."

"Okay. I did." The inventor stabbed the immortal with the Gravity Blade.

The samurai was trapped by the blade's zero gravity field. "This is indeed impressive! I must become the second organism to overcome the power of gravity if I plan to win when next we battle."

"No. You should really take your time to ponder your loss instead."

"Ah, wise words. I shall heed them," said Riufen with a nod.

Devlin, Demonica, and Gimpy watched the ground after Sel sunk into the floor.

"Can we really win? I can't use Sel powers anymore," said Devlin, creating a grid of wires to detect movement.

Gimpy mumbled excitedly and pointed at a black spot on the ground.

Dark tendrils came out from the corrosive area.

Devlin fired wires into the mobile muck, but they disintegrated.

Gimpy leaped back and tapped its sword against the ground.

The puddle instantly moved to that place, throwing off its trajectory.

The tendrils shot forth and pierced into Gimpy.

"Don't worry. I've got this," said Devlin.

Bravery fired out golden strands that sliced the tendrils in two.

When the dark energy dispersed, Gimpy turned to Devlin mumbling angrily at him.

"Am I being berated for saving your slave's life?" asked Devlin.

"Gimpy is complicated," said Demonica with a shrug. The Dark Goddess created a blood barrier around the Sel puddle. "Now he has to come out."

The blood barrier was quickly taken over by dark energy.

"Not good." Devlin spun the strands of Bravery in a circle to deflect the incoming projectiles.

Gimpy seemingly teleported around the area, purposefully getting hit by as many shots as possible.

"That's a very unique approach to battle," said Devlin with a raised eyebrow.

Lord Sel emerged from the barrier and fired a powerful beam directly at the treacherous boy.

Demonica liquefied the ground instantly, causing the beam to zoom just over her beloved's head as he descended.

"Devlin, are you honestly foolish enough to stand against me?" asked Sel in an ominous tone.

"I don't fear you! You will fall by my hand," said Devlin, pushing out his chest.

"I knew it! I am so proud! You are becoming just like me," said Sel all teary-eyed.

"You're proud?" asked Devlin with a confused look.

"Very proud! Try your best to kill me; you will fail," said Sel with a smile before sinking into the ground. He popped up behind Demonica. "As for you...why have you allied with the Freedom Forcers?"

"It's either you or Devlin. I've chosen him," said Demonica, riding a torrent of blood while readying her scythe.

"So, it's treason then? Glorious!" cheered Sel, firing a single beam that split apart to target her from multiple angles.

The attack connected, but it was Gimpy who took the damage.

The slave gripped its chest in euphoria and let out an ecstatic moan.

Lord Sel summoned up the Atma Blade and sped toward Demonica's new location.

"Lord Sel!" Edirp held up Stabby, who was now unconscious. "I've completed the mission!"

"Splendid!" Sel changed his trajectory and used the miniature Sel barrier to make a portal.

Lord Sellum spontaneously appeared in front of Edirp. His gaze slowly shifted to the thief. "Set her down."

Lord Sel fired a beam at the God of Gods.

"You're here as well." Sellum raised his arms, summoning up a meteor storm.

"Get out of here now!" yelled Sel, leading his allies into the portal. "Deceivant, come with me now and I'll save Hope!"

"I'm still thinking about the offer. We'll talk later," said Deceivant.

Adas appeared in front of the Freedom Forcers and told them to stay put.

Deceivant fired a gravity bullet at Edirp.

The goddess fell over. She dropped the girl who was pulled to safety by Devlin. "Wait for me!" she yelled as she ran into the portal.

Yvne carried her encased sister and fled.

Lord Sel and Absorb were the last to leave.

The meteors crashed, bursting into confetti.

"What just happened?" asked Devlin.

Sellum deteriorated and Ada popped out. "Surprise! That was me! I made an illusion to keep everyone safe."

Devlin rushed up to her and hugged his mother. "Mom, you're incredible."

"Fantastic work, darling," said Deceivant, joining the hug.

"I feel forgotten," said Riufen, suspended in the air.

"What happened to you?" asked Devlin.

"I was bested...by Deceivant," said Riufen.

"Haha! Like that could ever happen," said Devlin, holding his sides.

Deceivant hoisted the Gravity Gun. "It did. I bested your greatest warrior."

Devlin looked at the gun and the blade, recognizing the same colors and patterns. "So, Riufen, you allowed him to win. I understand. You wanted to be left behind so that you can serve me."

"I have yet to decide what path I will take in the coming war," said Riufen.

Opti looked up at the static samurai. "Hey, so then what do you see when you look at the Lum clouds?"

"I...don't know," said Riufen softly.

Sellum appeared before them. "You were attacked," he said, noticing the wreckage.

"Daddy!" Stabby ran up to him and was lifted into his arms.

"They were after Stabby," said Ada.

"Cowards," said Sellum calmly with a quaking fist.

"When do you think Kaity will return?" asked Devlin.

"I am not so certain Lum will allow her to leave," said Sellum.

Chapter 137: The Third Option

The remnants of the Viper Squad along with D.S., Hope, Napkin, Violet, Nina, Atlas, and Image arrived inside the Observatory.

Lum was seated upon her aura, facing away from them. "I have not summoned you here. Leave at once," she said, refusing to turn around.

"We need to talk," said Kaity.

"Fine. I'll talk with you and you alone," said Lum.

"No! We all deserve to know what is going on!" yelled Kaity.

"You do not demand things from me." Lum looked over the intruders. "Who brought you here? Oh, of course, it was Demonica, wasn't it?" She turned to Kaity. "I specifically asked you not to tell them that I was Sefiwah."

Kaity, rushed over to the front of the goddess. "I want the truth."

"I haven't the slightest clue as to what you are talking about. Has Sel twisted your mind with lies?" asked Lum.

"Etaf tried to kill our allies. Did you order that?" asked Kaity.

Lum stood up from her chair. "I most certainly did not. I specifically warned her against threatening your allies."

Atlas approached. "Sister, I trust you entirely. And I know that our only chance at stopping Sel is to join forces."

"I agree," said Lum.

Kanasta approached his old colleague. "Before you faked your death at the hands of the Forces of Hate, you sent your angels to me with a request. The Viper Squad has dethroned the Imam. We expect proper compensation for the completion of that job and the rebels we killed in the pursuit of this goal."

"Fixed in your ways as always. A year's worth of bliss for Ego, Tempo, myself, Kaity, BoneSaw, and you. That was the agreement?" asked Lum.

"Indeed."

"You killers are all the same. Always looking for an excuse to justify your obsession. You don't care about the bliss. You only seek justification."

"I demand payment."

"Very well." Lum sent out her energy.

Kaity stepped in the path of the dangerous light. "The bliss will only mess with your mind and make you forget who you are."

"I would drink a keg of poison if it were my payment," said Kanasta, stepping in the way. "Ah, it feels like I'm leveling up."

"Violet, come here," said Lum.

"You want me, Great Goddess?" asked Violet, reverently approaching.

"Evol was vanquished, and I've chosen you to replace her," said Lum.

"I'm not worthy," said Violet, moved instantly to tears.

"You are indeed worthy," said Lum.

"Hold on," said Kaity.

"What is the matter?" asked Lum.

"Are you really my mom?" asked Kaity, looking deep into Lum's eyes.

"I don't know what you are so flustered about," said Lum with a dismissive wave of her hand.

"Answer me," said Kaity, almost in tears.

"Oh, I think she would make a great mom!" exclaimed Ada.

"Are you just going to ignore me?" asked Kaity.

"I was your lover, Kaity. I've always been honest with you," said Lum.

"You ordered Devlin and Kanasta to be killed? Or was that Etaf?" asked Kaity.

"Please, calm yourself, my little kitten," said Lum, slowly pulling the worrisome girl into a calming embrace.

Kaity started to sob.

"Don't tell me you forgot the times we shared," said Lum with a smile, kissing her lover's ear.

Kaity's plasma claws shot out. She put the claws to her own neck.

"What are you doing?" asked Lum.

"Family shouldn't fight!" exclaimed Ada, rushing over to her.

Kanasta stopped his mother. "We should leave this matter in Kaity's hands."

"Are you my mother?" asked Kaity, staring intensely at Lum.

"How could I be your mother?" asked Lum.

Kaity said nothing but pressed the claws to her neck. They seared her skin.

"Kaity, you need to stop this foolishness. You know I love you," said Lum, sending out a healing ray of light.

"What is a destined Sellum?" asked Kaity.

"Who told you about that?" asked Lum, her eyes widening.

"I can't trust you unless you explain everything," said Kaity in tears, slowly clawing her sides.

"I ordered Kanasta and Devlin killed. Devlin was an agent of Sel, and Kanasta had become too unpredictable," said Lum.

"Then you told Etaf to kill our allies too?"

"I did not."

"What is a destined Sellum?"

"One who has been chosen to take up the role of the Omni God after that god has either stepped down or been killed."

"Are you my mother?" asked Kaity.

"That's not a simple question," said Lum, approaching the girl.

"Tell me or I'll kill myself!" yelled Kaity.

"You can't," said Lum.

Kaity pierced into her side, gasping in pain.

Lum rushed to her and healed the wound. "Stop this foolishness." The goddess kissed Kaity's lips lovingly. "I...I'm your mother, okay?" She embraced her precious one.

Kaity pressed her claws to Lum's neck. "You manipulated Father, didn't you?"

"Everything I do is to protect you," said Lum, with a gentle smile.

Kaity stabbed her plasma claws into Lum's shoulder.

The wound healed the moment it was created.

"You can't harm me, dear."

"You can't kill Sel, isn't that right?"

"It would be against the laws of Sellum."

"Is that why you made me? You wanted me to do your dirty work for you? Tell me the truth," said Kaity in tears.

Lum's embrace tightened. "Don't cry. I'll tell you, so there's no need to cry. I faked my death to protect you. I reappeared as Sefiwah, who had just enough of my traits to catch your attention but enough differences as to not arouse suspicion in you. I let you live as an assassin so that one day you would come to Lum and kill Sel. That's the truth."

"I thought you loved me," said Kaity as tears dripped softly from her cheeks.

Lum's embrace became like steel chains. "I do, I love you dearly. But I also detest you. You are a killer, a murderer! I did unforgivable things to keep up my appearance as an assassin. I've tarnished my virtues and sinned for your sake. I've defiled every inch of my body to keep you safe. I've tried to make amends for the innocents I've put to rest by granting them boons in Lum, but the sin won't leave me. I've tortured myself in repentance, drenched my body head to toe in scars and blood, but I can't cut out the sin, I can't escape the guilt. You have tainted my soul, and yet I can't let go of you. I hate you!" Lum pushed Kaity to the ground.

"That's enough." Kanasta stepped between them and helped Kaity back to her feet.

"Sel will come after you and you will kill him. I've already won," said Lum.

"And once he is no more. You'll get rid of any potential threats to your kingdom," said Kaity under her breath.

"I will simply correct my mistake. Those who would not have gained entry had I not lowered the karmic bar will be removed," said Lum.

"Do you want a civil jihad?" asked Hope.

"Evil must be purged."

Violet stepped up. "War does spread faith. It is the work of merchants and missionaries that creates true converts."

"I chose well," said Lum, smiling at Violet.

Hope stood in front of Violet. "I suppose you'll take those who surrender and have them spread the glory of your monotheism to unite the realm?"

"No. All humans who gained entry from me lowering the karmic bar will be removed from the realm. No exceptions," said Lum.

"Not just humans. She'll kill all the Exps too," said Kaity.

Hope shook her head. "A liar has no right to rule. You seek to penalize those who have aided you in your troubled times."

"I must keep this place pure of sin," said Lum.

"You are sin," said Kaity with a dark glare.

"If you were never chosen, my soul would be a perfectly clean pearl. I won't allow you to leave again," said Lum, creating a portal.

Etaf emerged.

"If any of you try anything, I'll bring your doom into the present," she said, pooling her aura into a weapon.

"But that's only if you try to harm me. We don't want any trouble," said Lum with a smile.

Etaf nodded and ceased the summoning.

"You expect me to permit you to hurt my friends?" asked Kaity.

"Violet, if you wish to become a goddess of Lum, you need only aid me in Kaity's capture. Know that all I do is for her own good," said Lum.

"Kaity, do we stay here or leave? It's your decision," said Kanasta.

"Let's go," said Kaity softly.

"You have no means of escape," said Lum.

"Of course we do. Napkin is a Lum god. Come on, little buddy. Get us out of here," said Kaity.

Napkin turned away in tears.

"Come now, you can't really be that dense." Etaf lifted up her companion and pet him. "I gave you Napkin so the Great Goddess could watch you when you leave Lum," she said, rubbing under his chin.

"Napkin. No. You're on the wrong side," said Kaity with watery eyes.

"What significance do your few lives have when compared to that of every living being in my glorious realm?" asked Lum.

"Your obsession with purity has made you dark, sister," said Atlas.

"Napkin, please, make the portal," said Kaity.

"He doesn't listen to you. Now, my little friend, if you paralyze them all, we won't have to hurt them," said Etaf, setting her furry companion on the ground.

The conflicted kitten kept his head down.

"We best not wait for his decision," said Atlas, summoning up the Bashful Bow.

Napkin looked up and let out a fearsome "*Meeew*." An ominous aura erupted from the feline and surrounded the Freedom Forcers.

Violet looked at her allies, who were all frozen like statues.

"Fear not. You were not his target. Come now, devoted one. And become a god," said Lum, pulling her chosen one in by creating a wind current.

"But, what about them?" asked Violet.

"They are in no danger. Please, I only want peace," said Lum with a smile, reclining into her throne.

Violet crouched down before the goddess.

Atlas broke free of the trance and kicked Napkin.

To his surprise, his allies were still trapped.

"They cannot overcome the power of the God of Fear so easily," said Etaf, summoning up the Destiny Sword. The blade of the sword thinned out all the way down to the gleaming star at its tip.

Atlas swiftly summoned up the Appalling Arrow and fired.

Etaf sliced the air, causing the arrow to appear behind her. "I can deny destiny itself."

"Violet! If you become a god, then—"

Etaf appeared behind Atlas and sliced his back.

The ex-god swiftly turned around while summoning up the Searing Sword.

The two blades clashed.

Kaity steadied her breath and reached for her sidearm. She rushed in, emptying an entire clip into Lum's head.

The wounds healed as they appeared.

"So utterly futile. INFINITY GENESIS."

Vines sprouted beneath Kaity and wrapped around her, growing faster than they could be cut.

"P-Please. L-Let's negotiate," said Hope, just now becoming calm enough to speak.

"This shouldn't be a sad moment. Being welcomed to the pantheon should be a joyous moment," said Violet in tears.

"The decision is yours," said Lum.

"Wait, I have something." Violet pulled out Lum's religious text.

"The second copy. I had thought it had perished along with Refuge," said Lum, standing up from her throne.

"If I hand it over, you must allow them to leave. Those are my conditions," said Violet.

"Loving as always. I fully agree to your terms," said Lum, placing her hand on the book. "What about your ascension?"

"I humbly accept." The devotee bowed to Lum and held out her hands.

The Great Goddess pulled out a radiant white cloud of energy from her body. She condensed the energy and placed it just below Violet's tilak.

Violet's body was quickly coated in a pink aura, lifting her off the ground.

"I chose well," said Lum with a smile.

"Fool. Now you're susceptible to Lum's influence," said Atlas, using a staff to deflect Etaf's barrage as she teleported around him.

"My friends, they can leave?" asked Violet.

"As promised," said Lum.

Violet pooled her energy into a Lum portal.

Lum pressed her hands together.

Gusts of wind pushed all the Freedom Forcers into the portal; all except one for the Viper Squad.

"Not the reunion I had hoped for," said Kanasta, rushing at the goddess.

Lum created a growing tree from her hand that Kanasta sliced with a thin wire.

BoneSaw snuck up behind Lum and slashed her body with his saw.

"It is not yet time," said Lum, creating two portals and sending the assassins into them.

"Where did you send my family!" yelled Kaity, slicing at the growing vines.

"Evol, in order for you to become a proper god, you must become detached. You must love all equally." Lum created a barrier with her aura, boxing in Kaity and Violet. "Strike her down. Eliminate our enemy."

"But everything you've done was to keep her safe," said Violet.

"If she dies fighting you, she is of no use to me. I kept her safe so she could eliminate Sel in my place. Sel's recent attack against me has given me grounds for retaliation, so I no longer need her. You're my new salvation," said Lum, caressing her goddess with strands of light.

Violet turned to the goddess, tears welling up in her eyes.

"Come now. We're connected. You know that my word is genuine and my mission is just," said Lum.

Lum flicked her fingers, stopping the growth of her vine trap.

Kaity squeezed out of it. She looked at Lum but did not show fear.

"Kaity, for the sake of balance, I must end you." Violet's aura came out of her hands like daggers.

Kaity ran up to her and rolled, firing a round of bullets at her corrupted friend's legs.

Violet dodged through rapid motion. She created an arching path behind Kaity and rode it, slicing her back.

Kaity's plasma claws clashed against Violet's aura blades.

"Wake up! She's using you!" With her hands occupied, the assassin's tail gripped her sidearm and shot into Violet's chest at point-blank range.

The wounds swiftly healed, pushing out the bullets.

"If we attack Lum now, we can take her down," said Kaity.

"I am a Lumian. Her will is my religion."

A pink trail sent Kaity swerving from side to side, repeatedly crashing against the barrier.

Kaity pulled out her sniper as she was slammed and fired at Violet's heart.

The Goddess of Love gasped and collapsed.

Kaity rushed to her friend's side in tears. "Violet, look past the devotion. Think about what Lum's doing."

Violet created a circular trail around Kaity, rapidly slicing her as she sped around.

"*VIOLET, LOVE, KAITY.*"

Lum smiled. "As if a mere artifact could overcome a god. You just wield love, Violet embodies it."

"I don't want to hurt you!" Kaity fired blindly but to no avail.

Violet cut deeper, slicing chunks of flesh from her foe's body.

Lum looked away from the gruesome scene. Napkin covered his eyes with his paws. Etaf watched passively.

The aura daggers came together as blades and sliced Kaity open.

A blinding light came from the wound, materializing as vines that knocked Violet out of the trail.

Lum stood up from her chair with a slight smile.

"How did I do that?" asked Kaity, noticing all her wounds had healed. "It was you, wasn't it? You were protecting me, Violet."

Lum teleported behind Violet and pooled energy into her warrior's head. "Now you know why I must do this."

Violet nodded with a face full of tears. "I shall put my faith in your love."

"I can't bear to watch this violence any longer. End it," said Lum, looking away.

Violet's eyes were now buried under Lum energy. "Understood, Great Goddess." The pink energy fully coated her body and became thin sheets of armor. Evol placed her hands together to form a single blade from her aura. She created a pink trail leading directly to Kaity.

"I'll kill her. I'll kill Lum and free you," said Kaity in tears.

"I am free." Evol sped in for the instant kill.

Kaity smacked Violet's hand aside with her tail the instant it came in range. "Kill or die. That's what I've been taught ever since I was orphaned. But it's not true. There's always a third option." The ex-assassin created a Lum portal and exited the Observatory.

Lum laughed and smiled.

"Is that what you expected?" asked Etaf, joining Napkin in giving the Great Goddess a curious look.

"No, but it's what I hoped for," said Lum with a smile.

Chapter 138: A Safe Haven

Previously: The Freedom Forcers who went to the Observatory were pulled into a portal and arrived in Lum. BoneSaw and Kanasta arrived soon after.

"Can any of you bring us back? Demonica can, where is she?" asked Kanasta, sweat dripping down his face.

BoneSaw nuzzled the Boss' foot, trying to calm its creator.

"She isn't here. We are stranded," said Atlas.

"Perhaps Violet was better off as my toy," said Hope with a worried look.

"I failed Devlin," said Nina, holding her head and overcome with tears.

"You are not to blame. And I feel that Lum won't hurt her," said Image.

"What is going on?" asked D.S. in tears.

"We need to figure out a plan. Yes. Someway of rescuing Kaity," said Kanasta, holding himself and shaking with worry.

"We need to find somewhere to hide before Etaf appears," said Image, lifting up Hope and running for the trees.

A portal appeared in front of them, leading to the Macrocosm.

"Sellum can help! He can save her!" yelled Kanasta, rushing in.

The rest of the Freedom Forcers followed.

Devlin was the first to greet the Freedom Forcers when they arrived. "Where is Kaity? Where is Violet?"

"We need to go to the Observatory now! Kaity is in danger!" yelled Kanasta.

"Demonica, you heard him!" yelled Devlin. "I should have been there!"

Sellum reappeared, holding Kaity. "She is safe for now."

Kanasta opened his arms as she leaped into his embrace.

Kaity cried in her papa's arms.

"Where is Violet?" asked Devlin, turning to Hope.

"Her mind was overtaken by Lum's influence, but that doesn't mean you can escape your obligations." Hope plopped herself into Devlin's arms. "That lying goddess is now our true enemy. Unlike Sel, she wants us all killed."

"It is as she says," said Atlas, his voice heavy with regret.

"Violet is the strongest person I know. She would never break," said Devlin, his face pale.

"That quick fix didn't allow her psyche to fully heal. She was still fragile at the time. And did you forget that I broke her?" asked Hope.

Devlin glared at the little monster.

Kaity turned to Sellum. "Lum forced bliss into Kanasta. Is there any way you can remove it?" she asked, drying her eyes.

75

"Absolutely." Sellum pulled the light energy out from Kanasta and BoneSaw.

"Can robots absorb bliss?" asked Kaity.

"BoneSaw asked me to remove it."

"Wait, you can understand BoneSaw?"

"I am Sellum. I can understand all things."

BoneSaw communicated with Sellum using various gestures.

"He wants you to know he was only with Sel so he could be informed when the Viper Squad members were in danger," said Sellum.

Kaity lifted BoneSaw into a hug. "I knew there was more to you than just killing!"

"Unless he's lying," said Kanasta.

"Is everyone here okay? Was there a battle?" asked Atlas.

"There was. Ada rescued us all. Also, Amy and I...bested Riufen!" exclaimed Deceivant, gesturing to a now-empty spot. "Where is he?"

Demonica turned to Gimpy and sliced open the slave's stomach. "Don't get confused. This was your reward for helping us fight Sel," she said, stomping on the slave's open wounds. "Your punishment for letting Riufen leave will come later."

Gimpy tilted its head curiously.

Opti rushed up to his friends. "Where is Napkin!?"

Kaity broke out into tears all over again.

"He's with Lum and his other allies. They must think they can still use us against Sel or else they would have killed us," said Hope.

"Napkin isn't like that! We're friends," said Opti, starting to cry.

Ada hugged him. "It's a misunderstanding. I just know it."

"Napkin, didn't want to hurt us. He's...he's still my friend," said Kaity, using her arm to continuously clean her tears.

"So, what is the plan now?" asked Deceivant.

Kaity slowly slid out from Kanasta's arms. She approached Sellum. "Will you bring us back to Earth after we defeat Sel and after I end Lum?"

"Wait, what? Isn't she Sefiwah, your lover?" asked Devlin.

"She's even more than that apparently," said Hope with wide eyes.

"She was once. But that was just another lie. She's lied to me so many times." Kaity pulled in her tears. "Well, will you?"

"If that is what you wish, then it is done," said Sellum.

"Is he lying?" asked D.S., poking Image.

"I can read faces, but his is concealed," said Image.

"Why should we trust someone who hides behind a mask?" asked Devlin.

"I believe him without a doubt," said Kanasta.

"I don't care if he's lying. Right now, he's our best option," said Hope.

"I still have more conditions," said Kaity.

"I'm at your command," said Sellum with a bow.

"Nobody hurts Efil or Napkin or Violet. I mean, you can defend yourselves, but don't kill them."

"What about Etaf?" asked Deceivant.

"She has to die," said Kaity, unflinching.

Kanasta smiled.

"Understood. What else?" asked Sellum.

"If I say they live, they live. Got it?"

Sellum nodded.

"Lastly, I get to kill Lum," said Kaity.

"Absolutely," said Sellum with a nod, tears leaking from his helmet.

"Good. We'll join you," said Kaity, offering her hand.

"This union must not be spoken of," said Sellum, shaking her hand and sealing the deal. "If any of you have requests, please share them with me anytime. This is an alliance, not a bargain," said the God of Gods, bouncing up and down.

"I already told you I want a planet," said Hope.

"I thought that was a joke," said Sellum.

"Well, do we have a deal?"

"Ownership is an illusion. I cannot abide."

"Ugh. Fine. Then I have some questions. What exactly are Exps?" asked Hope.

"Come now, sweetie. You can ask me. I know all there is to know," said Deceivant, approaching her before she kicked him.

"Good kick," said Devlin.

"Exps are living weapons created by those who seek change," said Sellum.

"Such a vague answer," said Hope.

"Can they reproduce?" asked Devlin.

"They can only be created," said Sellum.

"Can they provide the sperm necessary to knock up someone who isn't an Exp?" asked Demonica.

"I do not know, but it is possible. I have seen the reverse," said Sellum.

"You mean you were there when it happened?" asked Ada, turning pink.

"Ooh! I have a question," said D.S. "I hurt some people really badly in Sel. Are they okay?"

Sellum's spirits lifted. "There is no death in Sel. The soul wanders throughout the realm. The current Sel keeps the portal closed to keep his army expanding."

77

"How very interesting. Now, tell us more about Exps in general," said Hope.

"Exps do not need to eat, sleep, or breathe because of the infinite energy their capsules emit. Most importantly, Exps have a purpose. That purpose is to create a utopia," said Sellum, thrusting his arms toward the cosmos.

"A utopia which I shall reign over. Very well, that's enough questions for now. Tell us the plan," said Hope.

"Kaity, as you know, you must kill Lum," said Sellum.

"I will," said Kaity coldly.

"Atlas, it is you who should kill Sel," said Sellum.

"No. I will end him," said Devlin with a dark smile.

Hope looked up at him with flushed cheeks.

"If you are able to, the kill is yours," said Atlas.

"Very well. Then Atlas shall serve as Devlin's advisor when he becomes Sel," said Sellum.

"Agreed," said Atlas.

"Everyone, I want you to meet with your allies," said Sellum.

"Um, I think we're all here," said D.S., waving to his team.

"Sel and Lum have become enemies to the balance. That leaves Absence as our ally in this conflict," said Sellum.

"And balance is all you seek?" asked Deceivant.

"Absolutely," said Sellum.

"Absence will serve as a suitable refuge for now. I'd like to leave as soon as possible," said Hope.

"As long as Absence is on my side, I'm safe. I will need you all to protect him no matter the cost," said Sellum.

BoneSaw bumped into the god's leg to get his attention and then waved its saws around.

"Apparently, Sel plans to kill Tcetorp as well. Be sure to protect her," said Sellum.

"Great job getting intel," said Kaity, patting her robot buddy.

Kanasta turned to Devlin. "Brother, can you confirm?"

"Who can trust anything Sel says?" asked Devlin.

"I can confirm. Sel wants to create chaos in Lum. Once Tcetorp dies, the whole prison collapses," said Demonica.

"Make haste to Absence. Opti, Deceivant, I ask you to stay here with me," said Sellum, creating the portal.

"I object," said Hope.

"You do?" asked Deceivant, eyes lighting up with hope.

"We can't allow another hostage situation like what happened in Lum. Opti must come along," said Hope with a smile.

"But he could still hold Deceivant hostage," said Crisis.

"A hostage is only useful if their life is valued," said Hope, glaring daggers at the deplorable man.

Deceivant broke down in tears.

"Such a splendid look. Truly suits you," said Hope.

"Why hurt when we can help? Come on, mommy's here to talk if you want," said Ada, picking up her not-nice-at-the-moment daughter.

"Set me down. He must carry me as per our agreement," said Hope, pointing at her contract-bound brother.

"Let's just go," said Devlin, picking her up.

"Deceivant and Opti will be there by the time you arrive," said Sellum.

The Freedom Forcers entered the portal.

Deceivant, Opti, and Stabby were the last to exit.

Limit hopped out from a clear portal. "You are no longer welcome here."

"They are with me," said Stabby, pushing out her chest.

Limit stared at the girl, confused.

Absence appeared. The blue-haired man with flaming eyebrows raised his hand. "Leave, great knight. I will handle this," he said in a soft-spoken and devout voice.

Limit bowed and left into a portal.

"Who's the new guy?" asked Devlin.

"He's not new. This is my brother!" cheered Atlas, embracing Absence. "Casey, aren't you going to say hi?"

"Are you going to betray Sellum again?" asked Casey.

"I did not let Zenero escape, and I will not allow him to escape again," said Absence.

"Hmm. Good to know," said Casey.

"Hello again. I see you've killed the old leader," said Demonica.

"If you're here, does that mean your master cannot enter?" asked Absence.

"Who knows? The Absence before you was smarter. He kept the peace. Lord Sel will take your army as a challenge, not a deterrent," said Demonica with an excited look.

"We will only attack if he invades. I will lower my head to keep my people safe, but I will not leave them without protection."

"Oh, so you don't know? A few of your gods fought against Etah's armies. Sel already has reason enough to bring ruin to this realm. That's not a threat, just a warning."

"Enough. We were sent here with a mission." Kaity approached the new realm god and bowed down. "We wish to stay here."

"Absolutely not," said Absence.

"Why not?" asked Kaity, visibly surprised.

"Only those who are bound to this realm and the guardians are permitted to stay here. It is not a place for refugees," said Absence.

"Worry not. I'll negotiate with him," said Hope with a smile.

Stabby approached Absence and whispered in his ear.

His eyes widened. He gestured to Demonica and whispered something.

After a bit of back and forth, Absence stood up. "You are all welcome to stay here. Leave and come back anytime you want. My wish is your command," said the realm god with a gentlemanly bow.

"I could have handled it just as well as that creature," said Hope, crossing her arms.

Stabby turned back to face her allies. "Thirsty."

"Umm, does anyone have anything she can drink?" asked Deceivant.

"I'm sure if you collect all your tears in a flask, she'll be satiated, fufufu," said Hope, keeping her hand over her mouth as she giggled.

Nina bent down and handed the girl a container filled with water.

Stabby shook her head. "I want blood."

"Well, isn't she delightful," said Hope, resting her head on Devlin's shoulder.

"Absolutely!" Deceivant crouched down and pulled up his sleeves.

Stabby's topaz eyes intensified. She sliced into his arm with blades hidden beneath her sleeves and lapped up the blood like a kitten.

"Sooo cute," said Deceivant, beaming with adoration.

"Bwood!" she exclaimed happily, her teeth shining like blades.

"Makes me call into question for what reason this gremlin is serving Sellum," said Hope.

"Well, Sel said something about her being a traitor to his realm. I'm not sure, but I don't think we'll get an answer out of her," said Devlin.

"Shall I introduce you to the guardians?" asked Absence.

"We already met most of them," said Devlin with a shrug.

"Building relations is important," said Image.

"I concur. Let us greet them." Hope turned to Deceivant with a glare. "I will not carry you if that imp drains you dry."

"That's enough for now, okay, sweetie?" asked Deceivant, patting Stabby's head.

"Okay, mister scientist," said Stabby with a bladed smile.

"Miraculous! She's even cuter than before," exclaimed Deceivant in passionate tears.

Hope turned to Absence to hide how flustered she was. "Proceed."

"We shall start from the beginning. The first guard and guardian will now greet you," said Absence.

Occupy and Void appeared.

The monk with a shaved head and amber eyes was holding his venerated guru. The smooth rounded rock in his grip was covered with symbols and mantras.

"Aren't you the seconds?" asked Deceivant.

"I don't get it. What happened to Eil?" asked Kaity.

"I destroyed him. Turns out he was an old enemy. These two are the new firsts," said Absence.

"You've changed," said Occupy in a soothing and youthful voice, staring at the former God of Hate.

"For the better," said Atlas.

"Hmm. I'm not sure even I could break that one," said Hope with a contemplative look.

"Indeed. Occupy has a powerful spirit," said Atlas.

"Not him. The rock," said Hope.

"Void has taught me all that I know," said Occupy with deep reverence.

Absence welcomed in the next group.

The man of crystals was carrying the chameleon skull he was sworn to protect.

"Was there a Crystal before you?" asked Deceivant.

"Oh yeah. Word is he was a real troublemaker," said Crystal, his rough-around-the-edges voice sounding less depressed than usual."

"Then you aren't the one who manipulated Etaf?"

"I was a Mawali when I was in Lum. Etaf was way too high in the chain of command for me to manipulate her."

"I appreciate the information."

"Oh, hey Kanasta. How's the suitcase working for you?"

"Greetings, friend. It works splendidly," said Kanasta, opening up the large diamond suitcase to reveal his smaller silver one inside.

"Glad you're with us now. I'm sure you're a fine leader," said Crystal, shaking the assassin's hand.

"Kaity is the leader," said Kanasta.

"And I am her owner," said Hope, patting her little friend's head.

"Where is the pretty one?" asked Plagiarism in a shrill and exuberant voice.

"I'm here. But I'm not the one you know," said Nina.

"Not you. The colorful one," said Plagiarism.

Atlas summoned up the Bashful Bow. "He is with me."

"He?" asked Plagiarism with a curious look.

"Yes."

"Beautiful, valiant, and able to transcend boundaries. I was lucky to have met Matteria," said the skull with a fond smile.

"He fought and died because of me," said Devlin softly.

Hope patted his cheeks. "That is not a look I will permit you to have. You must be strong, understood?"

Devlin smiled slightly. "Okay, little sis."

"Um, it's best if you address her as queen," said Deceivant.

"Do not speak for me," said Hope with a glare.

"Let's move along," said Absence.

Loyal landed before them, and Limit hopped off his back. The massive pearl white dragon stretched his wings as his pearl white knight stood at attention.

"Any ally of Absence is my comrade. We shall fight together!" exclaimed Limit in a muffled heroic voice.

"I see new faces," said Loyal in a wise and thunderous voice.

"A dragon. My word. I didn't know such fantastical beasts were real," said Hope, holding her cheeks with shock.

"I try not to think about it too much," said Deceivant.

"I want it," said Hope, reaching her hands out.

"He is my greatest ally. Loyal is not a possession," said Limit.

"Not yet," said Hope with a sweet smile.

"Next are the fourths," said Absence.

Spin and Separate appeared. The massive amoeba and a collection of spinning of tops were frightened when they noticed Demonica.

"Didn't I kill that one?" asked Demonica, pointing to Spin.

"Apparently not," said Devlin.

"What you killed was not its entire body. Part of it remained in Absence and has now reformed," said Absence.

"Finally, the fifths," said Absence.

The Baroness of Blades and the Führer of Fortune emerged from the portal.

The Baroness was a living armory of swords and other weapons. Her scorched flesh showed her body had been split both horizontally and vertically in past battles.

The Führer was an obese demon resting on a living bed that was held up by sharp metal legs.

"It's an ambush!" yelled Deceivant, aiming his gun.

"Not so. I have left Sel," said the Führer in a regal and boisterous flamboyant voice.

"Where is the samurai?" asked the Baroness of Blades with a proud and raspy voice.

"He's on the wrong side," said Devlin.

"Wonderful," said the Baroness with a smile.

"Greetings, Führer. It is my pleasure to meet a fellow ruler," said Hope, offering her hand.

"Are you the Queen of the Exps?" asked the Führer, shaking her hand with his metal appendages.

"Most certainly. So this is my army." Hope looked out at the floating battalion of empty armor. "I suppose it will have to do for now," she said with pride.

"I am training every willing resident how to fight. We will defend this realm," said Absence.

"You're a fine leader. I gladly agree to our alliance," said Hope, shaking his hand.

"There is…one more. He has been waiting so long to be reunited with you all," said Absence with a big smile.

Chapter 139: Return

A figure emerged from the portal and approached Kaity.

He was clad in full-body armor that had dents, burn marks, and cuts on it. The rebel's talons had dried blood splotches, and his orbs glowed as bright as his resolve. The rebel's piercing black eyes seemed to stare off into a future known only to him.

Kaity looked at him blankly and then slapped him across the face.

"What the hell was that for?" asked Exp 8 in a strong and gruff tone, pulling his head back.

"I'm just making sure you're real," said Kaity amazed.

"I'm real and I'm ready to fight." Exp 8 looked out at his comrades, moved to tears. "You're all alive."

Ada and Opti knocked him over as they rushed into an embrace.

"I missed you guys too," said Exp 8, joyously hugging them back.

"Didn't I kill you?" asked Atlas.

"What the hell is he doing here?" asked Exp 8, jumping back.

"He joined us," said Kaity.

"It's true," said Atlas, showing off his companion bracelet.

"He murdered our friends!" yelled Exp 8.

"I don't like it either, but we need him to stop Lord Sel," said Kaity.

"We have the same enemy then," said Exp 8.

"Yes. And that enemy is Bob," said D.S.

"What?" asked Exp 8.

"Bob is the ruler of the Realm of Sel," said Kaity.

"I thought he worked for Etah," said Exp 8 with a curious look.

"I am no longer Etah. I am Atlas."

"So, Bob is Sel. Is Lum someone we know too? What about Absence?"

"Sefiwah was made by Lum to control me," said Kaity angrily.

"I'm sorry, but didn't she die?" asked Exp 8.

"No, but she will," said Kaity coldly.

"I thought you and Sefiwah were lovers," said Exp 8.

"She used me!" yelled Kaity.

"I missed a lot, didn't I?" asked Exp 8.

"You sure did. Why don't you fill us in how you are even alive?" asked Devlin.

"I was rescued. Sellum teleported me to safety after Etah's attack covered me."

"And what were you doing instead of helping us?" asked Deceivant.

"I assumed he had killed all of you," said Exp 8.

84

"Did Sellum tell you that?" asked Hope

"He gave me a mission. I was in Sel working with the Princess of Insight. We're building up a new rebellion," said Exp 8.

"What do you know about Sellum? Why would you follow his orders?" asked Hope.

"You're new. It's nice to meet you. I'm Exp 8," he said, offering his hand.

"Answer the question," said Hope.

"Sellum is the watcher of worlds. I followed his orders because I wanted to stop Etah. The armies were unified under a dark knight. I believe it was Etah's second in command," said Exp 8.

"That was me, actually," said Devlin.

"Oh, I'd love to see you in shining armor," said Hope.

"The armor was a prison. I won't be trapped again," said Devlin.

"So, how did you arrive here?" asked Hope, gazing into Exp 8.

"My mission kind of ended before it began. There was a prison break in Lum. I don't know all the details, but afterward a new Absence was crowned. Sellum brought me here to fight with and protect him. I've been training with Absence ever since," said Exp 8.

"Care to vouch for his claim?" asked Hope.

Absence bowed. "All he says is true."

"Hope, you don't know him, but Exp 8 was once the leader of the Freedom Forcers. I absolutely trust what he says," said Deceivant.

"Leader? Well then, I suppose it's best we get acquainted," said Hope, offering her hand.

"Actually, we usually do group hugs," said Exp 8 with a smile.

"I already went through that shameful initiation ritual. I shan't do it again," said Hope, crossing her arms.

"Oh, sorry." Exp 8 shook her hand. "Glad to have you on board. Devlin, I'm proud that you moved on from Kaity. You've grown a lot."

"What? Hope and I are siblings. That's all," said Devlin.

"Siblings." Exp 8 paused.

"Do you wish to speak to them?" asked Atlas, summoning up a weapon in each hand.

Exp 8 summoned an orb and slammed it into Atlas, knocking him off his feet. "Don't talk to me!"

"I'm not even going to ask what's going on," said Crisis.

Exp 8 approached the weatherman. "Thanks for joining my comrades."

"Oh, uh. You're welcome. I have my own reasons, honestly," said Crisis.

"Then your fighting spirit shall shine even brighter," said Exp 8.

"Welcome back, fearless leader," said Kanasta with a smile.

Hope hopped out from Devlin's arms and approached the old commander. "I am the leader of the Freedom Forcers now. Don't think your return changes anything."

"Fine by me. Being a leader is rough," said Exp 8.

"Glad you understand."

"So, what are you all doing back here anyway?" asked Exp 8.

"We are working with Sellum. We're here to protect Absence, like you are," said Kaity.

While Exp 8 was greeted by his old allies, Casey approached Demonica. "Send me to the Core."

"And what do I get in return?" asked Demonica.

Meanwhile at Lum's throne, Evol is being trained by Etaf.

"Spacing is absolute in combat. If your opponent cannot hit you, they cannot win."

Etaf dodged Evol's aura blade and pressed her weapon to the new goddess' neck. "We're done for today."

Evol suddenly embraced Etaf.

"What is with the display of affection?" asked Etaf.

"The world is wonderful. I prayed to the gods every day, and now I am finally a god. I feel ecstatic! I'm overcome with feelings of love for everything!" exclaimed Evol before kissing her teacher.

Etaf pulled away. "Get ready, Evol. Our mission is to go to Absence to free Tcetorp. We will likely be met with resistance."

"How will we get there?" asked Evol.

"Sellum already made arrangements for us," said Sefiwah, gesturing to the Absence portal on the ceiling.

Previously: Riufen vanished from the Microcosm. He arrived at the Core, greeted by a familiar face.

The green and blue crocodilian sword's blood red eyes were softened by the swordsman's joy.

"Gladius?" asked Riufen, moved to tears.

"What's with him?" asked the living sword.

"We are one. Do not leave my side again," said Riufen, patting his trusty blade.

"I'm only back here because Lord Sel needs me. I've already become quite the celebrity on Earth," said the living sword in a vicious and sly voice.

"I'll be with you in a moment. Seems we have a visitor," said Lord Sel.

The woman in the veil approached the God of Destruction and bowed. "Greetings, Lord Sel."

"We can skip the pleasantries, Casey. What do you want? Spit it out," said Sel, not even looking at her.

"How did you figure it out?" she asked amazed.

"Well, you put forth effort, that's good. But in order to truly deceive someone, you must deceive yourself. How do you expect me to not know who you are when you do?" asked Sel, removing the veil.

"What?" asked Casey.

"It's an acting fact. The audience will only believe you if you believe yourself. Whatever, it doesn't matter. You have a message for me, I presume."

"Exp 8 has returned," said Casey.

"I thought Etah disposed of him."

"Sellum saved him."

"I want to know as soon as they leave."

"I will inform you."

"Good. Now, what are you really here for?"

"We need Zenero's help."

"Zenero, eh? Hmm, are you sure?"

"Yes. He's the only one to have ever defeated Sellum."

"There were likely others in the past, but who knows who they are? You make a good point, but bringing him back would be quite risky."

"What risk can he pose to you?"

"I would say you're obviously kissing up, but you're absolutely correct. I can handle him if he gets rowdy. One slight problem: I don't know where he is. I thought he may have been in the Elysium Asylum, but I didn't sense his presence there."

"He is locked up in Absence."

"Is he now? Well then, it's too much of a hassle to get him out. Not worth the effort, sorry."

"If I capture Efil, will you free him?"

Sel turned around and floated up to Casey. "Your offer is rather enticing. But how will you capture the Goddess of Life? My dear Demonica was overwhelmed by her power. I would have helped if I wasn't busy fighting the Great Goddess herself."

"My powers are not affected by time. I will capture her."

"Such conviction! Splendid! We have a deal!" exclaimed Lord Sel, gripping her hand and shaking it with his spectral energy.

"Thank you."

"But once he is free, you will make it very clear that it is his duty to help me take down Sellum."

"I doubt he'll need much convincing."

"Good point. Pleasure doing business with you. Send her off," said Lord Sel, turning to Gimpy.

Casey vanished along with Gimpy.

"Now then, moving along. Riufen, Gladius, get over here!"

Riufen approached Lord Sel. "Is Devlin-sama truly our enemy now?"

"Who cares? I've chosen you," said Sel.

"Chosen me for what?"

"I'll let you think about it. You know, you caught my interest the first time we fought back in Devlin's lab. Ever since, I was shaping you into my warrior. There were times where it may have seemed that I was disappointed in you—and, well, I was. But I never gave up on you. You're so very special."

"You honor me with your words," said Riufen, his voice quivering with reverence.

"That's why I've decided to make you immortal."

"Immortality is the bane of my existence. I will never have an honorable death. Even so, you cannot give me what I already have."

"You aren't immortal. I could destroy you, so could Demonica. There are quite a few who could. I already killed you once, remember?"

"I cannot forget."

"What makes a swordsman immortal? I've been asking myself this for quite some time." Lord Sel manifested the Atma Blade. "The answer: it is their bond with their blade that gives them life eternal. At least, that's the poetic poppycock explanation."

"That makes perfect sense. A warrior aligned with his blade cannot be struck down."

"Oh, but you can. That's why I've decided to fuse your souls."

"You can fuse souls?"

"But of course! The Atma Blade is made up of my essence after all," said Sel, caressing his weapon.

"I would be honored if you could join Gladius' soul with my own," said Riufen.

"Now, it won't be quite so easy. You must share a strong bond and both be willing to join together. Plus, it will take time—my time, that is." Lord Sel shoved the Atma Blade through the samurai.

Riufen fell to the floor, unconscious.

Lord Sel pierced the spectral blade through Gladius, absorbing his soul as well. "If all goes according to plan, the spirit of the warrior and his blade will be forever entwined," said the God of Destruction as the two souls mixed.

"Riufen is already powerful. This is unnecessary," said Gladius.

"In order to kill Sellum, I will need a Lum and an Absence realm god capable of breaching his defenses. I've chosen Riufen to be my Absence. Without true immortality, he stands no chance of taking down the current ruler."

"Then who will be your Lum?" asked Riufen.

Sel's pupil contorted into a mischievous smile. "I've already chosen, but it's a secret. Victory is all but certain now. With Efil and the realm gods at my command, Sellum will fall and I shall rise anew."

Gimpy reappeared and rushed to Lord Sel. He mumbled something illegible.

"Lum has made her move. Casey, return with Efil alive and we have a deal," said Lord Sel, signaling his minion to make a portal.

"I cannot do it alone," said Casey.

"I am occupied with Riufen, but I'll send in sufficient reinforcements," said Lord Sel with a wide smile.

Chapter 140: Capture

The Freedom Forcers transitioned into a battle formation as soon as a Lum portal appeared in Absence.

Efil, Evol, and Etaf emerged from the portal.

"Violet, do you recognize me?" asked Devlin, approaching.

"Of course I do," said Evol with a smile.

"Ooh, ooh. What about your best friend? Remember me?" asked D.S.

The Goddess of Love embraced him. "I remember all of you."

Demonica nodded to Gimpy, and her minion vanished from Absence.

Absence appeared in front of Etaf. "Why have you entered my realm?"

"We mean no harm. We only wish to bring Tcetorp home," said Efil.

"My apologies, but the Goddess is staying with me. She's the only insurance I have against a Lum invasion," said Absence.

Etaf summoned up the Destiny Blade. "Where is she?"

"You're hopelessly outnumbered," said Absence.

Sel portals appeared in a perfect circle around the Freedom Forcers, the Lord of Absence and the Lum goddesses.

Demons screamed as they charged out of the portals, numbering in the thousands in mere moments.

"You're working with Sel?" asked Absence, calling all the guards and guardians to his side.

"This ambush has nothing to do with us, but they are likely after the same thing," said Etaf.

"He cannot hide the goddess from us," said Evol, approaching Absence.

"*TCETORP, LOVE, ETAF.*"

A silver ball came out from under Absence's tongue and landed in Efil's hands.

Absence smiled. "Without my help, she'll be stuck like that. I can keep her hidden from the enemy. Help me fend off this invasion. Then we can negotiate."

Two dragons joined together to create a barrier of flame and ice.

"Splendid. Now, Crystal, use the ice formation to whittle down their numbers," said the Führer.

"Not a bad plan," said Crystal, using the frozen barricade to gun down droves of demons.

Limit and the Baroness joined the Freedom Forcers in taking down any demon that managed to get over the icy wall.

"Nina, do you have any explosives?" asked Occupy.

"You want one?" asked Nina, whipping out an explosive tag.

"Just seeing it is enough." Occupy closed his eyes.

The ground around the demons was instantly littered with explosive tags.

They all triggered at once, debilitating the current forces of Sel in an instant.

"Remarkable," said Hope, seated on Devlin's shoulders as his wires eviscerated a gold-plated demon.

"We need to close the portals," said Etaf, slicing one of the gateways in two.

As the demons exited the portal, their bodies split in half.

"Stand at attention. There are Sel gods mixed in with their forces," said the Führer.

Regna climbed out of a pile of her people's corpses, her body boiling with rage.

The Baroness leaped over the ice wall and engaged the goddess.

"A demon lord cannot hope to stand against me!" yelled Regna, throwing the bodies after turning them into bombs.

"I'm no longer a demon lord," said the Baroness, unsheathing her sword and slicing the bodies.

The corpses were defused by the cuts but uninjured.

"You're in my way!" yelled Regna, firing off her arms.

The Baroness sliced the arms in two and kicked them into a group of approaching demons before they could detonate. "Becoming a goddess has given me clarity on many things."

Yvne emerged from a pile of burned bodies by the south end. Her body enlarged and contorted until she resembled her sister, the Goddess of Gluttony. Though the size was exact, her version of Ynottulg had fewer mouths.

Efil sliced through a crowd of demons until she arrived at the behemoth.

Crisis created a tornado beneath him and flew to the gruesome monster. "I'm here to provide back up."

Efil released a pod of seeds and dispersed them with the wind.

"TIME LAPSE."

The seeds grew into powerful vines that created a cage around the demon goddess.

Casey boxed in her enemies and then kicked them into incoming demons. After creating a spherical encasing around a group of seven, she rode it all the way to Efil, squashing demons along the way.

"I'm the Hero of Sel! Stop fighting!" yelled Exp 8, taking on three sword-wielding demons with his bare hands.

"Actually, I defeated Etah and unified the armies, so that would make me the Hero of Sel," said Devlin, wrapping up twenty demons before using them as a living wrecking ball.

"Something doesn't feel right. Most of these demons are amateurs. I think they are just trying to keep us busy," said Demonica.

"Indeed. They seek to kill Tcetorp, but they don't know where she is," said Limit, protecting Ada and Deceivant by piercing any enemy who approached.

"Oh, I think I know what's going on," said Demonica before collapsing into a puddle.

The Goddess of Death slid through the mess of demons and up to Efil.

Chains came out from the puddle and bound the goddess.

Yvne slammed her massive fist into the Lum goddess, spraying her with bile in the process.

The bile ate at Efil's skin like hydrochloric acid.

"She's all yours," said Demonica, tapping Casey's shoulder.

"No, for cases."

Efil was imprisoned in an ever-expanding series of cases.

Tsul popped out from behind Yvne. The slender self-reliant goddess wore her own tentacles as a suit with feather legs and dark pink skin.

"I still don't trust you," she said in a composed and commanding voice with buried rage. "I never will." Pink smoke escaped from her mouth as she glared at the goddess of death.

"You shouldn't," said Demonica with a smirk.

Tsul created a portal and entered it along with the imprisoned goddess.

White flags suddenly littered the battleground.

Sel's forces began a full-scale retreat back into the portals from which they came.

Etaf appeared in front of Absence. "What happened? Did they claim Tcetorp?"

"They did not," said Absence, holding out the compact.

"Perhaps they realized they couldn't win," said Occupy.

"Either way, she is yours as promised. I hope the Great Goddess will see that this gift comes in good faith. **Revert**."

The silver ball unfolded into the Goddess of Protection.

The hefty goddess wore shields like armor and had vacant white eyes. Tcetorp smiled upon seeing a fellow goddess. "Thank you for coming to my rescue," said Tcetorp in a firm and stoic voice.

Etaf froze up. "Where is Efil?"

Crisis flew up to Absence. "Um, I saw Efil get trapped and carried into a Sel portal. I know we aren't exactly allies with them, but just thought you should know."

"Why didn't you stop it?" asked Etaf, pointing her sword at him.

"I was fighting my own battle. By the time I realized what was going on, it was too late," said Crisis.

Tcetorp pooled her energy into making a Lum portal.

Etaf joined her until it was formed.

"We have to return to the Great Goddess and tell her what happened," said Tcetorp.

"I know that. I know," said Etaf, her hands shaking.

The three goddesses left Absence.

"What could they want with Efil?" asked Hope.

"I can only imagine," said Demonica with a shrug.

"I think I know," said Exp 8.

"Really?" asked Deceivant.

"They want to use her ability to rapidly accelerate time, most likely. Though for what, I can't say," said Exp 8.

"Casey was a spy, which means she probably knows about you trying to recruit the Exps on Earth," said Crisis.

"If that is indeed true, you must hurry. I was to send you there after Sel's forces retreated anyway." Absence tossed a compact to the ground.

It unfolded into a portal.

"Where does that lead?" asked D.S.

Hope smiled. "It's obvious isn't it? It leads to home."

"You mean...we can finally go back?" asked Deceivant.

Absence nodded.

"What about Toxic? We can't leave her," said Ada.

"I promise I will free her. But I won't miss this opportunity," said Deceivant.

"Freedom Forcers, let's finally go home!" cheered Kaity with a huge smile.

Part 17
Return to Earth

Chapter 141: Earth Chronicles

Iron doesn't feel anything. Not warmth or cold, not fear or mercy. I wait by the bus stop in Washington, D.C., the central mainframe of the corporate infection. It's dark out and my trench coat keeps my features hidden from the pedestrians. I skim today's newspaper and see that I've gained notoriety, though my motives are fiendishly misconstrued. Wringer, from Vigilante to Serial Killer.

When the system fails the people, they have to stand up and act. An innocent man was sent to death because of this corrupt system. I can't shake off all responsibility though, considering was my actions led to his death. You see, the superhero movies got it all backward. A true hero doesn't clean up the streets while letting greed fester in the skyscrapers. A true hero uses fear to weed out corruption. I'm just one man. I work alone, always will. I look over the sob story of the vamp in the obituaries. Of course, I know they aren't vampires—they are all too human—but for whatever reason, viewing them as biological monsters makes tightening those sturdy chains around those soft throats so easy. See, we all need air, whether you're living in the ghettos or profiting off of dividends in your comfy chair as the richest stockbroker in D.C.; we all need to breathe.

Suffocation is a really great way to die. It's not too quick but not too slow either. It allows time for struggle, agony, and most importantly, regret. I didn't believe in heaven or hell before I was killed, but let me tell you…all the remorse and regret for their actions, all the apologies and guilt won't bring them even a step closer to the pearly gates.

There was a time I had doubts about my actions. Was wrestling the life out of corporate crimes a viable strategy to take down the behemoth of capitalism, or was it simply a violent cry for help from a desperate man? When I died, I gained new clarity. I went to Heaven and I didn't see a single one of my victims there. My mother used to take me to church before she was murdered by someone who had been so twisted by the system they actually snapped. There I learned all about morality and ideals. Problem is, there's no room for either in the corporate world. It's a narrow street paved with the misfortunes of others. Each purpose comes at someone's expense, whether the overworked middle-class single mother or the droves of children working for nickels to stave off starvation. I'm sick of this world and want to wring the corruption out of it. If that causes it to suffocate, collapse, and die…so be it.

He was late, Patrick Jones, advisor to our current governor and friend to the banks he regulated. From Goldman Sachs to politics and then back to lobbying; the revolving door of capitalism truly is a magical thing.

Patrick pulled up to the bus stop. He had a new watch, likely a gift from the generous donations from the oil companies he was in bed with. I waited for him to get out of the car.

My body was shaking. Excitement overwhelmed me.

I could hear his throat singing the National Anthem. His body begged me to destroy it for the sake of justice.

Patrick dropped his suitcase. Four seconds of confusion in his eyes before he realized he was going to die.

Then came the look. Utter desperation, like a child mining for diamonds in Africa, or the look of an innocent man before being sent to Guantanamo Bay for practicing a controversial religion. I always wondered if the victimizers understood the irony of it—that they made others feel this hopeless their entire lives—but I doubt it. All I could see in those pitiful blue eyes was a pathetic "why me?"

Nothing changes. The victimizers abuse until they get caught, then they act like victims. There is no empathy in them, only greed. Capitalism fosters this greed; it feeds on it and seduces good men and women to it like a siren. "You can too." The hope that we can one day be rich like those we despise is what keeps us bound to the system that sees us as mere products to be bought and sold. The global imposition of sameness is based upon the accumulation of wealth and power by the few over the rest. Capitalism offsets the speed of productivity and has channeled thought and work into a soulless monster. I am the hero who must slay this monster. Yet all I'm able to do is remove those already intoxicated by its siren song.

It had only been a few months since I got back from Heaven. Things were too complicated there. Here it's simple. Find the vamps and wring their throats till their eyes bulge. Then repeat the process and keep myself from falling into a thoughtless pattern and becoming a machine.

My spirits dropped when I heard the snap. I was lost in my own thought; missed the show. I don't do it for the spectacle, but a man who doesn't enjoy his job won't perform quite as well. Just ask Karl Marx, a man ignored by Capitalists and Communists alike.

I remember Judy, my old girlfriend back when I was in college. She would ask me what I wanted our country to be. I was more Keynesian at the time, thinking that Liberalism and Capitalism could somehow lie down and make a child without deformities, but now I just don't know. I leave that vision to the future generations; I'm just here to make the transition to that new world smoother.

As I dragged the body into the bushes, I felt eyes upon me. They weren't those of an innocent witness either. They were eyes like mine, those of a hunter.

The car door opened and a young man in a mask, head to toe in a skin suit, came out.

It was over. Reality was gone. I had become the misunderstood villain of a comic book, and this kid was going to stop me with nothing but peaceful ideals and his fists.

"I'm here to help," he said tossing one of the chains onto the lamppost above us.

A fan boy. Oh no. Disciples never once followed in the footsteps of their predecessors. If Freud and Jung ended up at odds, what's to say this relationship would end better?

I haven't been paying attention to the best sellers. Did some desperate fool looking for a quick buck make a book to sell my ideology to the masses? How long before my simple job gets misconstrued into an ideology of perversion and revenge?

The boy, likely in his twenties, was aware of my work. He started going on a fanatic rant about each one of my victims. He had a lot of anger, something that had no place in my line of work.

He picked up the man's wallet, pocketed the cash except for the symbolic fifteen dollars. I figured Charon, the ferryman to the underworld, wouldn't ask for more than minimum wage; and I wanted to be sure that each one of these corporate pharaohs was delivered to their eternal tomb without delay.

"Alright. Here's the truth. I'm not here for an autograph. I've got a job for you." He handed me a folder with photos and bios on all the biggest scum in the United States. "Well, several jobs."

I turned away. I wasn't an assassin. I don't seek to profit off of death like those wannabe vultures.

"Oh, my apologies. I wasn't asking." The young man pressed a device to my back.

I felt energy escape me like how breath escapes my prey. I grabbed his ankle with my chains and slammed him against the farthest car I could reach. My chains pulled in four other cars, creating a wall to mask my location. I ran down several alleyways, hoping he had lost sight of me.

My chains tried to pull out the device but it wouldn't budge. Before I could smash it, my consciousness abandoned me. The world looked as black as it truly was.

"What I had lost in years, I gained back in a few months. My death shook the globe. After all, what could kill a god? Some spoke of me as a false messiah, slandering me with accusations of sorcery and unprescribed medicine. The acupuncturist society, or ACS, demonized me for going against their ancient teachings, but what are mere words to a deity? Those I healed sang songs of deep devotion that dispelled any darkness around my namesake. Now my empire stands at the top of the massage community. Lepers and common folk alike come to me for salvation.

My journey to the Heavens has been shared with only my most faithful disciples: Mary, the saintly woman who packs my groceries every Saturday; Isis, the parakeet who speaks only the truth; and Hermes himself, disguised as a mere postal worker. Even they do not believe my story, but such is the way things are for a prophet.

The naysayers and my competitors have banded together in a group called Humans First. It's as bigoted and volatile as any hate group and uses its rage funds to undermine the property status of Exps. I, of course, am not a mere Exp. My birth records alone are proof of that. What I truly am cannot be detected through the limited tools of man."

"So, you tell this to everyone you give a massage to?" asked the masseur's patient.

"What?"

"All I did was ask, how are you? And you started ranting on and on about the Heavens and Exps."

The masseur's hands were gloved, but this didn't hide their bizarre shape and his spa robe wasn't able to conceal the large pistons poking out from his elbows. "What do you think of Exps?" asked The Vibrator.

"They need to be controlled. That's what the media says, right?"

"You can't think beyond what the sorcerers speak?" he asked in a boisterous aristocratic tone.

"I don't like politics. I just want a simple life…you wouldn't understand," said the girl.

"How does it feel to be so mediocre? How do you mortals find joy in your fleeting lives?"

"Well, that's easy. We lie to ourselves. Tell ourselves we're part of a bigger picture. Another cog turning the world toward a peaceful tomorrow. But we're not. We're insignificant. We spend our whole lives searching for a meaning that isn't there," said the girl softly.

The massage ceased for a mere moment.

"Are you crying?"

"Your words are just so pitiful. As an avatar, I'm not beyond empathy, though my true form is."

"Pierre Dubois. Such a fancy name."

"A mere alias," said The Vibrator, now blessing her lower back.

"You were born without the ability to feel pain."

"No god can. We merely act as though we do."

"You tried to kill yourself when you were eleven years old. Must have been hard. Your suicide note said you were cursed by demons. It was a fun read."

"Oh, uh that. Well, if you've read the Ramayana with a keen eye, you'll realize that Ram was not fully aware of his divinity. At that point, I had yet to realize my gift."

"To rationalize your sickness into a delusion of divinity…that's rather admirable."

"Alright, who are you? You one of Judas' friends here to pull me down to the Earthly plane?"

"Just don't get too involved in politics, okay? What has risen can fall. Oh, and thanks for the massage." She placed a tip in his lap and ran to pick up her clothes.

"Are you threatening me?"

"It's just a warning. From the top," said the girl, pointing up with a grin.

"Ahhh. You're from Heaven. That explains your perfect skin."

"I already gave you your tip," she said with flushed cheeks.

"The gods cannot threaten me. Once I've siphoned the faith from their followers, I will return and claim the kingdom of Heaven as my own."

The 5'1" girl was in her early twenties. Her black hair shaded her light blue eyes, which complemented her glossy pink lips. The girl's slender body was easily able to slip into her slim black dress. "I can't believe they expected valuable intel from you," said the girl in a cute spunky voice, pressing her hand against her chest. A black suit spread out from beneath her dress, stopping at her neck. "See ya." She walked out of the room and down the red carpet.

"This is more of a palace than a massage parlor," said the black suit commander, sliding out from behind a marble pillar. His helmet looked like a human skull and he was wearing a tuxedo.

"What are you doing here?" she asked under her breath.

"Checking on you, of course," he said in a carefree but chilling tone, ruffling her hair.

"I'm more than capable of handling myself."

"Yeah, actually, you did alright this time. Other than running off and doing a job nobody asked you to."

"You…you were spying on me," she said in a hushed voice.

"Yeah. I'm your brother; it's my job to look out for you."

She gripped his arm. "Was killing Daniel your job too?"

"Hey look, I vouched for you when the Boss said you weren't ready for real work. Don't prove him right."

"Well, I don't need you chaperoning me," she said.

"Sis, you busy tonight?"

She turned around, eyes lighting up. "Movie or dinner?"

"Um, a performance actually."

"Ooh, I love theatre!" she exclaimed with a little bounce.

"Wait." The black suit puts his finger to his ear. "Change of plan. Wait back at home."

"I'm not a child."

"This one could be dangerous."

"I live for danger. Teetering on the edge of death is true—"

"Cut it out. I'm serious," he said, grabbing her and bringing her down the pearly steps.

"Well, I'm seriously starving for some excitement. You know, Daniel had a brother who I could swear had a thing for me."

"Stop it. Killing people you like isn't a hobby of mine, you know. I try to avoid it when I can."

She slugged his arm. "You attacked him in the shower! We were about to make love!"

"Keep your voice down." He opened the door. "Ladies first."

"When you do it, it just seems like misogyny," she said, kicking him on her way out.

"Look, sis, I'd love to go out with you tonight, but this mission is dangerous. Possibly even for me."

"What is it, a gay strip club or something?"

"Ugh! No. Don't even joke about that."

"Few people are so homophobic that they actually get an allergic response from it. You're a credit to bigots everywhere."

"Can we not do this?" He noticed a black limo with tinted windows. "Finally, it's here."

The man in the black suit opened the driver side door. He shot the driver and shoved the body to the passenger seat.

"Why couldn't you just let him drive?"

"Orders from the Boss. And don't worry, he's not one of our men," said the man, starting up the car.

The sister begrudgingly sat in the middle seat in the back. "You should apologize to me. You know I like to ride shotgun."

"I can move him if you really want me to."

"And sit where a dead guy was? Uh-uh, no thank you."

"Then why even bring it up?" he said under his breath, speeding past a red light.

"Are you trying to get the police on our back?"

"Hey, you were the one who wanted some excitement. Better buckle up."

"Wait. You're taking me?"

Her brother tossed her a folder. "Read it and decide for yourself. Actually, read it out loud because I haven't read it yet."

"Person claims to be Satan? Demons confirmed real. Seltanic Churches. What is with these articles?"

"The guy drops into existence six months ago. He's got to be an Exp, right? That's what I thought, but all known Exp creators are dead. Xholk, Zenero, Atlas, Deceivant, and Devlin are all deader than the American dream."

"Maybe he was in hiding."

"Yeah, but why come out then? There's really no reason."

"Oh my god!"

"What's wrong?"

"He's totally my type."

"Now's not the time for jokes. The guy's a whacko."

"I'm serious. Look at him! You can't say he's not hot!" She shoved the photo in his face.

"Hey, I'm driving and put on your seatbelt."

"He's sooooo hot."

"Stay focused."

"I am focused, on those charming eyes. Mmm."

"Okay, so the mission is to infiltrate the Seltanic church and find out what this guy is."

"You know, I was once part of a suicide group. Maybe I'll see some of my old friends here."

"Can you not talk about that? Look. I don't think it's safe. And if it turns out this guy is a real freak, I'm going to have to clean house."

"Why is killing the only way you solve things?"

"It's protocol. Give me a break."

"Well, then, give me a gun. I'll cover you."

"No way. Not dirtying your hands over something like this."

"My hands, my choice."

"Please don't make this an issue."

"You expect me to go in there unarmed?"

"Sis, I'm not taking you there."

She grabbed his face and gave him a loving peck on the lips. "Please."

He smiled and blushed. "I'm really not negotiating."

"But you said it was my choice!"

"Well, I changed my mind."

"You're going to take me or else—"

"Wait up, I'm taking a detour."

He drove off the street and into the woods. "Three cops behind me. Take care of them. Thanks, Sigma."

The girl turned and saw the three cop cars crash into each other. "You are taking me." She stretched her arms out and hugged him.

"No, I'm not."

"Fine." She opened the door. "Then I'll just have to kill myself!"

"Stop it! Now isn't the time for your games. Plus, falling out at this speed wouldn't kill you. It would just injure you, and we both know what a wuss you are. Now buckle up." His smile dropped when he saw her in the mirror.

His little sister had a revolver pressed against her head.

"Your life isn't a game. Put the gun down."

"Make me," she said, sticking out her tongue.

"Fine! You win! I'll take you there. Follow my orders exactly. Things get dicey, we leave. Got it?"

"Yes, sir," she said, saluting with the gun in hand.

Chapter 142: Super Spy

"So, brother dearest, should we get into special disguises?"

"What, you expect everyone there to be in black robes or something? It's a formal event. They are welcoming new members."

"Oooh, can I join?"

"Sis, you don't want to be in a shady group of scripture junkies, do you?"

"Well, what better way to keep tabs on this hunk?" she asked.

He removed his helmet, showing slicked back black hair and a charming yet unsettling smile. His dark demeanor even shined through his sky-blue eyes.

"Your skin looks darker."

"Yeah, I'm undercover. Just don't stick out too much, okay?"

He parked the car and opened the door for her.

She leaped into a hug, almost causing him to topple over. "Thank you! We're really going on a mission together! You know, it's almost like," she leaned in and kissed his cheek, "a date!"

"We aren't going in together. I'll go in first, then you come in with the next group, got it?"

"Sir, yes, sir!" she cheered with a salute.

"Thatta girl."

Her brother went to the front door, slipping into the crowd. "Just in time."

"I am Demian," said a jovial man in a jolly and reverent tone. "Welcome to Satan's sanctuary." He stood at the door's entrance and personally greeted each person who entered.

The man was in his later years, but his positive attitude gave his skeletal face vibrance. He was wearing an all-black robe with an emblem of a green eyeball with a red heart-shaped pupil. The hood of his robe was pulled back, but the girl spy noticed it had plastic goat horns attached to it.

The male spy shook the man's wrinkled hand. "I'll be honest. I'm a little worried about being here."

"Worry is natural."

"Well, I don't exactly believe in the Devil or God for that matter."

"Ah, but you have doubts. This is the home for those who hold doubts." The jovial man opened the door.

"Hi! I'm Kioshi," said the sister spy, shaking the man's hand.

Her brother turned to her with a frustrated look.

"I am Demian," said the jovial man.

"It's very nice to meet you, Demian," she said with a salute. "Whoops." She bowed.

"You have quite an exuberant spirit. What brings you here tonight?"

"Well, I love the occult and all that stuff. And rumor has it you're having a special guest tonight," she said with a smile.

"Yes. I hope that once tonight ends, we will no longer have to pray in the shadows. Our love for Lucifer shall be a beacon for those without refuge!"

"That's a great attitude. Smile for the camera!" she exclaimed, taking a selfie with her phone.

"Your youthful spirit is refreshing. But I ask that you refrain from taking pictures of the temple at any time during the ceremony."

"Oooh. So, what happens if I break that rule?"

"You'll be politely asked to leave."

"Oh. That's it?"

He smiled.

"So, where do I sign up?"

"Once you get inside, there will be a table on your right. On behalf of Satan, I thank you for coming here," he said, holding her hand.

"Well, thanks for having me." She skipped inside and up to the table but was stopped when someone grabbed her wrist.

"Does the word covert not mean anything to you?"

"Is that a trick question?"

"You told him your name."

"And I got him to tell me his annnnd I got his picture."

"We don't need his picture."

"Hey, you said we shouldn't stick together. So I'm just doing my own thing. Can't break your orders, after all."

Her brother placed what looked like a credit card in her hand. "In case we get separated."

"Thanks. So, do you think they have events on Sundays or—"

"You're not signing up to this creepy cult, understood?"

"Ooh." Kioshi slipped out of her overprotective brother's grip and went up to the handsome young man behind the desk. "How old are you, cutie?"

"Fourteen. Um, would you like to sign up?"

She hopped over the table and crouched down. "Say peace!"

"Uh, peace?"

"Great photo," she said, noticing she got the list of members in the shot.

"So, umm, want to sign up?"

"Hmmm." She takes out a card and writes her number. She slips it into his shirt and then walks off.

"Hey, bro. Why is everyone dressed so normal?"

"Because, to them, this place is normal. Try to be a bit more culturally sensitive, would you?" His attention shifted to a woman in a red dress who walked by. "Well, I'm not going to go hungry tonight," he said with a smirk.

"Koshi, you're on the prowl in the middle of a mission? I can't believe you would…oh, if you'll excuse me." Kioshi sped through the crowd and took a seat at the very front between a hot thirty-five-year-old man and his stud of a son.

Koshi rolled his eyes and followed the tasty woman to the back pews.

Kioshi smiled at the father and the son. "Hey there! What brings you both to this place?"

The man smiled. "It gives me a certain peace of mind."

"And you?" she asked, leaning into the hot-blooded eighteen-year-old to her left.

"I was raised here. It's like a second home to me. So, why are you here?"

"Well, it may seem a little silly, but back in middle school, I had a thing for guys who were Goth. So, in order to get their attention, I studied up the occult and stuff like that. I guess you could say my love for hot guys is what brought me here," said Kioshi with a wink.

"My girlfriend is Goth," said the young man.

"That's nice," said Kioshi, putting her hand on his lap.

The man who greeted everyone at the door stepped up to the temple area. He was now wearing a black flowing robe with an intense blue eye design at the center. "They say we are children of God, but if God shaped us from the earth and the earth is Pan, is it not more apt to think of ourselves as children of Pan?" He smiled a big smile. "Welcome, sinners, wayward spirits, homeless, outcasts, and those with the slightest bit of curiosity. Welcome to Satan's Sanctuary. This is the place where those not welcome to God's church are welcomed in with open arms. The Creator God, much like kings, pharaohs, and other figure heads, seeks to create a divide between those who reach a certain moral criterion and those who do not. He deems those created in his image worthier than those who are not. Well, I can't speak for Sel, but I can say that from what I've seen, our Lord doesn't care if you like men or women, it doesn't care if you have been incarcerated, it loves you whether your karma is as white as an angel's or as black as a demon's, whether you have feathers, fins, or fur, whether or not you belong to a faith that does not deem Sel as the true god. From what I've seen, what I have experienced, Sel welcomes all who seek a home. And on behalf of Sel, I welcome all of you here tonight."

Kioshi started clapping excitedly then stopped when she noticed nobody else was.

Demian smiled. "I'd like to open tonight with a prayer and then welcome our very special guest."

Kioshi leaned on the young man's shoulder, found the page for the hymn and spoke the words while caressing his leg.

"When light claims truth,
We turn to you.
When the Heavens rule Earth,
We seek your warmth.
Sel, our Lord, we humbly thank thee,
For giving all a home.
Through rain or shine,
Death or life,
You take away all our strife.
Through sin we are kin.
Through hate we find love.
The love we feel within
We know comes not from above
For a seed does grow from the earth
A seed you sowed to give life worth
God may claim the land, air and sea,
But you have won over me.
Sel, our Lord, we praise thee.
One who does not glorify mercy.
The truth is not for one to claim.
But one truth will always stay.
Satan, Lucifer, Beelzebub,
Pan, Destruction, God of Love,
Nature, Gaia, Earth and Hell,
Hades, the Devil, our Lord Sel,
We love you as a mother loves her child
And you love us like a creature loves the wild.
Sel, our Lord, we humbly thank thee
For giving all a home.
When I die, I gladly give
My soul to you and not to him.

Kioshi wiped her eyes.

"Are you alright?" asked the father to her right.

"Yeah, I guess. It really spoke to me," she said with a little smile.

Demian folded his hands and welcomed the special guest as the altar boys and girls passed out drinks to the people in the pews.

The Prince of Pleasure stood tall at the podium. He now wore a real tuxedo with a red rose and had centered his once contorted grin. The demon lord's glowing purple lips and pink eyes remained unaltered.

Kioshi's eyes lit up.

The crowd was filled with gasps and whispers.

"I am a man who needs no introduction. You all know of me," he said in a suave, sultry voice that almost masked his dark tone. The Prince slowly lifted his shirt, showing his toxic purple skin.

Some of the people in the back row fled. Koshi, making out with the woman in red, turned his attention back to the stage.

"Drink, sir?" asked a young man with a tray of cups.

"No, thanks," said Koshi.

"I am the Prince of Darkness himself. In these times where faith has been replaced with science and science has been replaced with politics, a savior is needed. I incarnated from Earth into the form you see before you now."

Demian was overzealously shaking with religious passion. "It is my great honor to have you here. The Matriarch herself has come tonight to greet you."

A ghostly pale little girl with long white hair and wise green eyes stepped up to the Prince barefooted. She was dressed in a black see-through cloak with the same eyeball emblem as the priest and congregates. The girl was wearing a frilly black leotard under the transparent cloak.

"Thank you, my dear, for helping my gospel spread in these troubled times," he said with a smile and a wise and gentle voice that belied his age.

The girl peeked up at him through her deer-horned hood and said nothing. She turned to face the crowd. "He is indeed a demon. A high-class demon at that. But he is not Sel. He is not the one I spoke to."

"Heathen. You dare accuse the Lord of Destruction, the Dark Prince himself, of lying."

She smiled ever so slightly. "Lord Sel relishes lies. You are not him."

"You're not a true seer. You've all been duped by this girl and her father." He gestured to the priest. "But I am not without mercy. I shall allow them to keep their placement as long as they admit their transgressions against me."

"Mercy is a word Lum uses, not Sel."

"Do not test me, girl," said the Prince.

Demian stood in his path. "If she says you are not Satan, then I trust her. There is no need to lie. You're a demon, aren't you? That alone is miraculous. Tell us why Lord Sel sent you here. Surely he is not testing our faith like the Creator God would."

"Lord Sel can control men without even touching them. I'll prove my word is gospel," said the Prince, snapping his fingers.

107

The people in the pews stood up at once, all except the spy siblings, who quickly stood up to follow suit.

"Kill the girl and her father. May they repent as they are torn apart," said the Prince with a toxic grin.

Kioshi ran up to the podium and pulled out the credit card-shaped object.

The object unfolded into a thin pistol that was now aimed at the Prince.

"You dare aim a gun at your benefactor?"

A bullet shot into the Prince's leg.

"Release them from your spell, Exp," said Kioshi, aiming at his head.

Koshi pushed through the crowd and lifted up the Matriarch. "Don't just stand there, run! I'll keep your daughter safe!" he yelled to the priest.

"I do not fear him," said Demian, pushing aside the mob as they clawed at him.

"Sis, take the girl and get out of here. Wait by the rendezvous spot. That's an order," said Koshi, firing into the crowd to keep them at bay.

Kioshi saluted and took the girl into her arms. "Your daddy is going to be just fine. My brother is like a ninja warrior," she said, calming the girl as she fled the place of worship.

Each member of the crowd fell silent after the spy shot their necks.

"It was the fruit juice, wasn't it? You put something in it. I've seen a lot of poisons, but this one is special," said Koshi, turning to face the so-called demon.

"The blood of a deity makes mortals into slaves. You will be no different." The Prince fired toxins from his fingertips at the enemy.

Koshi dodged the attack and swiped the legs of the target.

The Prince looked up to see a gun pointed at his face. "If I so chose, I could have them tear each other to pieces here and now. You wouldn't want that, would you?"

"If you can't have fame, you'll settle for infamy. But you misunderstand. I'm not here for anyone but you."

"Go after his sister! She's waiting by the limo past the garden!" hollered the Prince.

The followers ceased their assault on Demian and rushed to the exit.

"Ugh. I'm going to get a lecture about this later. Sorry, Boss, but the tranqs have a small clip." Koshi reached into his coat and pulled out an automatic gun.

He sprayed bullets into the crowd, turning his back on the Prince of Pleasure to ensure his sister's safety.

The Prince seized the opportunity, exuded mist from his body, and fled the area.

108

Koshi rushed to the front door as he shoved a third magazine into the gun. He noticed the woman in red. "Shame. I really wish I could have gotten to know you better. Oh well, see you in the papers," he said with a smile before blasting her head open.

He aimed his gun at the crowd and noticed there were a number of kids. "Shit. Oh, I know." He shot their legs, reducing them to crawling machines.

"Exp poses as demon and massacres a church. Hmm, yeah. I think the Boss will dig it," said Koshi, gunning down anyone who looked over the age of eighteen.

Once he was out of bullets, he ran out the door and sped to the car.

"Start it up! Now! Umm, where the hell is she!" he exclaimed, noticing the car was empty.

The Prince made his way through the trees in the dark.

"Hey there, hot stuff," said Kioshi.

"Who are you people?" asked the Prince, pointing his finger at her like a gun.

"Me? I'm just a girl looking for a good time. And, I'm your best bet at getting out of here without getting caught by the cops."

The Prince smiled. "Very well. I'll allow you to help me."

"Good!" Kioshi ran up to one of the eight police cars that parked near the premises. She whipped out her badge. "C.I.A., I need your vehicle."

The cop nodded and got out.

"Come on, let's go," she said, opening the back door for the Prince.

Kioshi took out her phone while starting up the car. "Gamma, I need a safe house. Any nearby?"

"Yeah, I'll upload it to your car's GPS. Is there a problem?"

"Nope. I'm just carrying precious cargo," she said, winking at the Prince.

Koshi was in the limousine driving backward through traffic. His phone rang and he picked it up. "Boss, did you find her?"

"No, but I'll send someone out looking in your stead," said a deep voice on the other line. "There have been Exp sightings in different parts of the world. I'm sending my best agents to investigate and that includes you. I've already scheduled your flight to Moscow. It leaves in an hour, so you better hurry."

"I don't care about that! My sister is missing. Get Gamma to do a full scan of the area. She could be in danger."

"Think clearly. You are the leader of the Hunters. You must serve as a proper example or else your disobedient nature will create a ripple effect through my warriors."

"I don't give a damn about you or your mission! My sister could be tortured! She could be dead!" yelled Koshi, breathing heavily.

"You need to learn discipline. This is not the time for this! I am your leader. Now, get on that plane!"

Koshi dropped the call. His phone rang.

"What do you want, Gamma?"

"Your sister called me."

"Is she okay?"

"She's fine. Said she was taking precious cargo to a safe zone," said Gamma on the other line.

"When did she call you?"

"Just now. I'll put her destination on your GPS."

"Thanks, kid."

"You're welcome. Were you two together?"

"Yeah, some freaky Exp tried to attack her!" Koshi slammed his hand against the roof of the car. "This is all my fault!"

"It's not far from where you are. You can make it in just a few minutes."

"I just hope I'm not too late," he said, his face riddled with worry.

Kioshi was on route to the safe house.

"You're a most peculiar girl."

"Ooh, caught your interest, have I?"

"Most certainly."

Kioshi drove to an abandoned building and beckoned the Prince in.

They walked into the bedroom.

"Looks like a recent foreclosure. That means we're," she stripped out of her clothes and down to her underwear, "all alone."

"You're really foolish enough to lower your guard when you know what I'm capable of?" he asked with a grin.

Kioshi leaned into him. "But I don't know what you're capable of. Why don't you show me?"

"If you actually knew who you were dealing with, you would be trembling at my feet."

Kioshi dropped to her knees and looked up at him. "Like this?"

"I'm a demon lord of lust, one of only a handful."

"Lust, oh my, that explains a lot," she said, pawing at his crotch through his clothes.

"My fluids, all my fluids, are toxic. Some paralyze, others kill, there's even one so addictive it turns those who drink it into my slaves."

"Is that what happened at the church?"

110

"Yes. It's even more effective on humans than demons."

"Demons?"

"Yes. Demons. I'm not from Earth. Can't you tell?"

"Then how did you get here?"

"A portal from the Heavens to Earth."

"Is that where The Vibrator came from too? Oh no, don't tell me you two are friends. That would explain the delusions."

"He crossed over as well; we are not friends. I speak the truth." The Prince removed his shirt, showing off his toxic body.

"Wow, you're really hot," said Kioshi, rubbing his arms.

"And clearly not a human."

"So, you're the Devil's lackey or something?"

"Hardly. In fact, I nearly took over Sel."

"So hot and yet so odd," said Kioshi, putting her hands on his bare chest.

"You're not a bad catch yourself. What say you work with me? Through the Church the two of us can gain great influence in politics."

"I'm not really that into politics. What is your goal anyway?" she rested her chin on his shoulder.

"I don't have a goal. I'm simply one who finds great joy in turning others into my slaves, the stronger they are, the more satisfying it is."

"Oooh, I can totally relate. I love making sexy studs into my servants, treating me to dinner, breaking up with their girlfriends, fighting with their fathers, I love being in control. It's so invigorating."

"Ah, so that's why you rescued me. You think you're capable of making me into your servant?"

"Maybe." Her hands moved in a flash, stabbing a small metal object into the Prince's chest.

"What's this?" he asked, pulling at the device.

"It's an energy suppressor, designed to cut off the flow of energy from your capsule. See, I'm not just a spy; I'm a trained Exp Hunter! Now that you're helpless, why don't you tell me what's actually going on?"

The Prince gripped his chest and fell backward onto the bed. "Hahaha! I did tell you." He tore out the device, creating a bloody wound in the process. "I'm a demon lord."

Kioshi stepped back.

"Too late, my dear." He slipped his fingers into his chest wound and shoved them in her mouth.

Her eyes lost their will and she began lapping up his blood.

"Good girl. Now, you're going to tell me everything you know about the man you work for." His face contorted into a wicked smile.

Kioshi spit the blood in his face and roundhouse kicked him.

"What are you?" asked the Prince, looking up at the dangerous girl.

"I'm a super spy! And you're under arrest," she said, whipping out her gun.

"You're immune to my charms?"

"Well, not entirely," she said, licking her lips.

The Prince raised his hand at the girl.

Koshi bust in through the window and slammed his foot down on the monster's hand.

"My prince!" cheered Kioshi, kissing his cheek.

"I thought you were in danger."

"Not this time," she said with a grin.

Koshi slammed four energy suppressors into the Prince.

"Apparently, he's immune to that. We'll have to improvise," said Kioshi.

"So, the Exps found a way to combat it. Did you get any information out of him?"

"Well, just a bunch of nonsense about him being a demon and stuff, buuut I did learn his motives."

"Which are?"

"Hmmm, Thursday you have a date with Debby, right?"

"That's correct."

"Cancel it and take me to a movie instead and then I might tell you."

"Heheh. Alright, you've got yourself a deal."

"I wasn't lying about what I said. We don't need to be enemies. We can work together," said the Prince.

Koshi fired a round into his chest. "You threatened my sister's life. The only place you're going is a body bag."

Kioshi smacked her brother's bottom. "He's mine. I caught him. If you kill him, the Boss won't think I'm capable of being a spy."

"You aren't. You put yourself in serious…are you crying?"

Kioshi wiped her tears. "This means a lot to me. I want to help out. I'm tired of just staying at the base. Please, brother. Don't ruin this."

Koshi hugged her. "Okay. Okay. Dry your tears. We'll take him to see the Boss. Good work," he said, ruffling her hair.

"Super spy!" she cheered.

"I'll come along peacefully," said the Prince, allowing Koshi to cuff him.

Chapter 143: Zenero's Exps

Previously: The Freedom Forcers left Absence and entered a portal to Earth. They came out of the portal and arrived in the living room of a house.

"Where are we?" asked Kaity.

"Home!" cheered D.S., rushing off to another room.

"I'm confused," said Kaity.

"Don't be. We've arrived at a safe zone. This is my kingdom," said Hope, having her handsome knight lower her onto the sofa.

"Everyone, welcome to my home. I'll get you all something to drink," said Deceivant, leaving with his wifey to the kitchen.

"It's been a long time since we've been here," said Atlas, sitting on the couch with his lovely wife.

"See? I got you back here just like I promised," said Exp 8 to Nina.

"We've never met. You're Devlin's creation, right?" asked Nina.

"His greatest creation. What do you mean we've never met?"

"I'm the original Nina. The narcissist you're familiar with is a different person entirely. The others speak highly of your bravery. I'm honored to meet you," said Nina with a bow.

Exp 8 hugged her. "This is how Freedom Forcers introduce each other. We're family now."

"Th-thanks," said Nina with a blush.

"Hey, who want to come to my room and play some board games?" asked D.S., smiling at Kanasta with an excited look.

"We came here on a mission. Let's not get sidetracked," said Kanasta before turning on his portable console. "Vitality. I feel alive again."

"Put the game down. We have important business," said Devlin.

"I put this game on hold to finish the job you asked of me. Now that we have returned, I ask that you forward the proper amount of pay to the Viper Squad. BoneSaw."

The robot popped out from beneath a desk.

"Calculate the number of hours we were working for our client," said Kanasta.

BoneSaw saluted.

"I'll pay you what I owe. Then can we get to work?" asked Devlin.

"Certainly," said Kanasta, his eyes glued to the screen.

"So, Exp 8, do you have any intel for us?" asked Devlin.

"I'm curious? When we died, our souls created an image of us in Lum. Are we truly alive again or is this body fake?" asked Kanasta.

"I'll explain," said Atlas. "Now that you all crossed through the portal to Earth, your body is real but your dead body still exists."

D.S. jumped up on the couch. "Way cool! Hey wait, what about our artifacts?"

Opti reached into his chest and pulled out a burgundy garnet gemstone. "Wow. Does this mean there are two of each of our artifacts now?"

"Your current artifacts are forged by your memories. They aren't as strong as the real deal, and chances are the Senator's men already took all the originals." Exp 8 stood in front of the widescreen TV. "Let's focus on our mission. Sellum told me about the Exps on Earth. There are currently nine Exps on Earth. I'm not sure which you're all familiar with, so I'll go over them one by one. There's The Vibrator."

"We know him. And we know Wringer too. They made it to Earth before we did along with the Prince of Pleasure," said Hope.

"Damn it, he's here. I don't like that guy. He's manipulative and cruel," said Exp 8.

"Are any of these Exps powerful enough to take on Sel?" asked Hope.

"Well, no, but they can help us beat his followers, and together I know we can destroy Sel," said Exp 8.

"Who are the others?" asked Crisis, peering into the digital fish tank on the desk to the right of the TV.

Deceivant and Ada came into the room, offering juice and grapes to those who would take it.

"Where is my tea?" asked Hope, popping a grape in her mouth.

"Still brewing," said Deceivant.

"It had better be to my liking."

"So, how many have you convinced to join us?" asked Image.

"Well, that's the thing. I haven't spoken to any of them yet," said Exp 8.

"So, it's up to us to convince them?" asked Devlin.

"Well, we can try and convince five of them. There's one who must be avoided at all costs," said Exp 8.

"And why is that?" asked Hope.

"He's been compromised. He works for those who seek our subjugation," said Exp 8.

"Oh, you must be talking about Codename Famine," said Hope.

"You know him?"

"I know what he's done. Either way, I wouldn't want someone so unstable as my vassal. I'm assuming the others you speak of are Chipko, August, Flash Girl, February, May, and Durga," said Hope.

"That's…correct," said Exp 8, visibly surprised. "How do you know about them?"

"I make it my business to know what my kind is up to. Since I've been away for so long, I don't know where they are. But you do, right?" asked Hope.

"Flash Girl is in New York City, which is also the closest locale of them all. Chipko is in Moscow. February is in the Amazon. May's location is currently unknown…she may have been killed. Durga is at Guantanamo Bay, and August is in Israel."

"Great work. How did you get all this information?" asked Kaity.

"I may have gotten some tips from a government spy," said Exp 8.

"They never give something for nothing. What was the exchange?" asked Kanasta.

"Well, it took some convincing, but I think they honestly want all the Exps in one place. I don't trust them, but I'm not afraid of them either," said Exp 8.

"Alright. So, we need to split up to cover more ground. Who's going after who?" asked Kaity.

"My wife and I will go after August. He's the strongest of the bunch, and I know him well," said Atlas.

"I'll come with you. It's best I get to know you so I can put our past behind us," said Exp 8.

Stabby walked up to Exp 8 and looked up at him.

"Alright. You can join us. Just be careful okay?"

"I'll go after Flash Girl. Always wanted to meet a superhero," said Crisis.

"Did you say superhero? Oh, I'm going with you for sure," said D.S.

"Oh, I've got something for you, son. Much better than that relic you've got with you."

"Really? Thanks!" cheered D.S.

"Why you waste your time making toys is beyond me. Now who wants to go after February?" asked Hope.

"Being in the Amazon means he will likely be difficult to track. I'll find him," said Kanasta.

"And I'll go with you. If that's okay," said Nina, turning to Devlin but not looking him in the eyes.

"You, uh, you can go wherever you want," said Devlin.

"We're going to Russia," said Hope, raising her knight's arm for him.

"I have some things to talk about with Devlin, so I'll join you," said Kaity.

"You…you do?" asked Devlin a bit flustered.

BoneSaw sped to Kaity's side and saluted.

"Guess my little buddy is coming too," said Kaity.

Opti took a sip of carrot juice and then froze up. "Wait, that means…Muffins and I have to go to the prison alone!"

"Well, if it makes you feel better, Fusion can come along," said Deceivant.

Ada grabbed her husband's hand. "We should go with him."

"Absolutely not! You have to stay here where it's safe!"

The Captain cleared his throat. "I have an idea. I'll stay with Ada, keep her safe, and you accompany Opti to Guantanamo Bay."

"On second thought, I will stay here as well. Now that I'm alive again, I have a lot of things to sort out," said Hope.

"Mediator, you stay behind and keep her safe too, okay?" asked Exp 8.

Stabby shook her head and grabbed onto his leg.

"Alright, you can come along. Deceivant, let's arrange the flights," said Exp 8.

"Since Exps are property, we actually save money on tickets," said Deceivant with a smile.

"My people are not property," said Exp 8 with a glare.

Hope pointed at Exp 8. "Forward-thinking is necessary when planning for the future. But it's best not to get trapped in a bog of optimism. Exps, at the moment at least, are property. If we seek to change that, we must first accept the reality of our situation. I'll take this moment to remind you all that your actions are no longer your own. They represent us as a species. Be mindful of your actions and wary of your surroundings. I won't have years of work undone by reckless behavior."

Devlin looked at Hope and smiled, causing her to blush and look away.

Hope handed out phones to everyone. "Call me if things get out of hand. Now, we ought to get moving. Chances are Sel's forces are aware of the other Exps and will try to capture them. After all, killing them would almost guarantee they would be sent to Lum and thus escape Sel's figurative clutches. If it appears that Sel is going to get away with an Exp, killing them is our best option. Is that clear?"

"But we'll do our best to make sure it doesn't come to that," said Exp 8.

"I'll take care of the flight arrangements," said Hope.

"Or we could just ask Demonica's little friend for some help," said Devlin, turning to the demoness.

"He's with Sel at the moment. Best to prepare the tickets and modify things if and when he returns," said Demonica.

"If all goes well, we'll have five new allies fighting for the balance of Sellum," said Exp 8.

116

A masked person in black and yellow spandex sat atop a high-rise building and scanned the alleyways of New York City. The yellow mask had black eyeholes that looked like action bubbles and a permanent smile on it. Her black braided hair extensions came out from the back of the mask and rested on her shoulders. The suit had a computer-generated image on the back that mimicked a neon blue cape. At the hip of her suit were two zipped side pouches. Her pink sneakers were snug and had a pad at the bottom with reinforced steel. On the front of the suit was a hot pink star emblem. The hero raised a pair of binoculars and noticed a group of three men approaching an old lady.

"Six in the morning and the grime has already clocked in. With grace and intent, our heroine races down the building, arriving at the perpetrators within a mere instant," said the hero, performing the actions alongside narration.

The men were swept off their feet by an unseen force.

"Flash Girl, using the powers given to her by her benefactor, handcuffs the villains and picks them up. After dropping them off at the nearby police station, along with photographic evidence of their suspicious activity, she returns to her post on the top of the building. This may seem like an adrenaline rush to most, but for Flash Girl, it's just another morning in her beloved city," her voice was exuberant, high-pitched, and heroic. She raised the binoculars and smiled with relief as the old woman walked out from the alleyway. She placed the binoculars back into her right side pouch and felt around inside the bag. "Being a hero is a thankless job, and a thankless job it must remain." Flash Girl lifted her mask just enough so she could pop a piece of cinnamon gum into her mouth. She blew a big bubble as she checked her phone for the news, reading about another incident in Moscow. "The line between hero and villain is dangerously thin." She punched the air, having the letters on her fingers join to read "KAPOW!"

In Moscow, a freckled woman with green hair stood at a podium surrounded by people carrying signs. She wore a shirt that said 'End Speciesism: Live Vegan'

Police men tried to keep the protesters at bay and drew their guns.

One of the cops exploded into blood, showering his people and the protesters equally.

Fear took over and the air became filled with the sounds of gunshots and screams.

More policemen exploded. Protesters fled.

In minutes, more cops arrived at the scene, coming face to face with the only protestor willing to stand her ground against the gunfire.

"You will not take this land from the Earth's creatures. Leave now or die," she said in a pained but passionate voice.

The cops opened fire at the woman.

After a few bullets pierced her, she slammed her fist to the ground.

The resulting shockwave burst the nearby cops into pieces and flipped the police cars.

"The Furies have returned, and their revenge is certain," she said under her breath.

In Israel, thousands of people are walking along the Judean Desert.

A young man approached a man with a beard and shook his hand.

The walk continued.

The bearded man collapsed, but not from heat stroke.

"There he is," said a man under his breath, his face concealed by a hood. He asked the young man for directions and waited for the others to walk off.

A gun pointed at the hooded man.

"Go home. I was faster than you. The bounty is mine to collect, my friend," said the young man, cocking the gun.

"You don't know who I am, do ya, boy?"

"Just another bounty hunter trying to make a living. We are like brothers, and I don't want to shoot my brother."

The man in the cloak took a step toward the target.

A bullet bounced off his chest.

He reached into his coat and slammed a wanted poster into the young man's face, decking him.

The young man pulled the poster off and reached for the gun he dropped only to have his fingers crushed under the hooded man's wooden sandal.

"I don't hunt bounties. I hunt bounty hunters. No pay. Just the thrill. I'm the Crimson August," his voice was gruff and weathered. The hooded man sucked on his e-cigar. He lifted up his hood and put on a cowboy hat with a falcon's feather on it.

The young man looked up at his attacker's face.

The scruffy bounty hunter had a gruff-looking face and wore shades over a red eye patch. His braided black hair reached his shoulders.

"Recognize me now?" he asked, tossing the cloak aside and pointing to his own wanted poster tattooed onto his bare chest.

The young man froze with terror.

August twirled his e-cigar in his hand. "This was too easy. Hard to find real thrills when you're this skilled," he said, helping the young man to his feet. "I'll give you thirty seconds to run. You can call in back up too. Just don't bore me, okay?"

The young man fled the area as fast as he could.

"What's the point of living without excitement? After all, the hunt is only as good as the prey," said August, taking another puff of his e-cigar.

In the Amazon rainforest, a bizarre humanoid resembling a pastel-colored Mayan portrait sat on a log, breathing heavily.

Something zoomed by and burst the bark of the tree behind the creature.

Four men came out from the bushes, their faces concealed under wraps and their arms weighed down with rifles.

The humanoid made a mad dash as bullets screamed behind him.

Sweat dripped from its pores, giving its body a yellow sheen.

A stray bullet shot into the creature's leg, causing it to lose balance and tumble down.

A truck pulled out from the foliage and the six men riding trapped their prey in a laser net.

"I just want to be left alone," said the creature in tears.

"The demon speaks," said one of the men.

"Then the price must be raised," said another man, likely the leader.

The men cheered and raised their guns. The demon of the jungle was now their prisoner.

In the unseen corridors of Guantanamo Bay, an Exp sits in a locked room with two guards and an inmate.

"I don't deserve to be here!" yelled the man, his fists shaking with fury.

"Fear is what brought you here, isn't it?" asked the woman with a soft flowing voice.

The woman was dressed in white yoga pants and an orange long-sleeve shirt with black stripes. Her pink hair was combed over to conceal her left eye. Her right eye was pink and calming.

"Not my fear! They fear my people."

"You were prosecuted for being an accomplice to known terrorists," she said.

"The Furies are not terrorists."

"One of their most prominent members killed twenty-eight policemen this morning."

"That woman. The eco-killer is not a Fury. She is a monster…like you."

The Exp grabbed his hand. "You're still frightened. Does it hurt?"

"I don't want to go back in there. I…I've had a fear of drowning since I was a child. But I'm not going to tell you anything either. So just give up on me." The grown man sobbed like a child.

"I'm not here to interrogate you. My job is to take away the pain…and transform it." A light pink aura came out from her fingertips like needles.

The man suddenly started laughing. His tears of pain became tears of joy. His smile stretched from ear to ear.

"Much better. Now that you're relaxed, these men would like to ask you a few questions, okay?"

The man laughed and smiled. "Okay," he said, squirming in his seat like a child.

The Exp brushed aside her hair, revealing her right eye was red, veiny, and terrifying. "Just in time for yoga," she said, putting a pink contact lens over her red eye. The Exp left the room and closed the door.

Chapter 144: Airport Anxiety

The Freedom Forcers arrived at the Douglas Adams Airport, except for Deceivant and a few others who were waiting their arrival at the base.

"It must be hard for you coming back here," said Exp 8, gripping Devlin's shaking hand.

Devlin escaped the affectionate grip. "This place helped set me on my path. I don't regret what happened here. I'm only shaking because there's no way we'll get past security and bringing any attention to ourselves is dangerous."

"It's not my fault. Everyone keeps staring at me," said D.S., hiding his face.

"Kagaku!" hollered a young man in a suit, running up to them.

Devlin and Kanasta turned around.

"I'm here on behalf of Deceivant Kagaku. My booth is right there, and I'll be happy to help you," he said, leading them to the area.

"Not all of us have IDs," said Exp 8.

"Well, some of you are property and would be put with the luggage, but not to worry, I've got you covered," said the man, handing boarding passes to all of them.

"We are people, not property," said Exp 8.

"Do you have any luggage?" asked the young man.

"It's all carry on," said Kanasta, gripping his steel suitcase as he distributed the boarding passes.

"We appreciate the help, but who are you?" asked Devlin, eyeing the suspiciously helpful man.

"You're Devlin, right? Well, your father helped me find a foster family when I was a kid. Helping out his creations is the least I can do," said the man.

"They weren't all made by him," said Devlin with a glare.

"I can't imagine why a bunch of Exps are going out to different countries," said the young man with a curious look.

"We should get moving," said Kanasta, pulling his brother along.

"What's wrong?" asked Devlin.

"I didn't say anything was wrong," said Kanasta.

"He's a spy, right?" asked Devlin.

"I don't know for sure, but Father didn't inform us about getting additional help," said Kanasta.

"Are we in danger?" asked D.S., looking at the growing crowd of travelers with worry.

"The quicker we move the better. Let's get past the security check," said Kanasta, moving along.

They pushed through the crowds only to get in line.

"Place all laptops, cell phones, and other electronic devices in the bins!" hollered a woman. She had brown eyes, soft features but carried herself like a soldier. Upon noticing the bizarre travelers, she motioned for another employee to take her spot. She approached them, her hand on her gun.

"Have we been randomly selected for a routine search?" asked Crisis, pronouncing the word 'randomly' in a way that conveyed his sarcasm.

"Come with me," she said, beckoning them along.

Everyone but Devlin followed.

"Are you coming?" asked Kaity, grabbing his hand.

"Yeah," said Devlin, a hitch in his voice.

"Don't worry. You're not alone like last time. We're all here for you," said Kaity, smiling at him.

Devlin couldn't help but smile back. "You're right. Things are different. Kaity, stay calm, but I know that woman."

"I'll keep an eye on her then," said Kaity.

"She's the one who tortured me. She's incredibly dangerous," said Devlin.

"So are we," said Kaity with a wink.

The Freedom Forcers followed her into a door marked 'Only Authorized Personnel Are Permitted Entry'.

The room was a rather stuffy office. Curtains covered the walls of the room and the metal desk was spotless.

The woman motioned for them to sit in the four available seats, but she remained standing.

"What appears to be the problem, officer?" asked D.S., looking at the lady with a smile.

"The problem is, you have no way of getting past security. So, help me out, and I'll help you out," said the woman.

"How may we help?" asked Kanasta.

"Just answer a few questions for me, and I'll personally escort you past security and onto some private jets where you won't be bothered by anyone," she said, sitting on the room's metal desk.

"Wow! You're really nice," said D.S. with a big smile.

"I can be," she said, crossing her legs.

"Your generosity is greatly appreciated," said Kanasta.

"My reports indicate that many of you were killed a few years ago. Yet here you are. Explain." She folded her hands in her lap.

"Your reports were wrong, it appears," said Kanasta.

"So the camera footage was false too?" she asked, rolling her eyes.

122

"Your people have no right going into my security feed," said Devlin.

"I would think that after all you went through, you wouldn't be so naïve. Privacy is an illusion and rights can be bent. How are you alive?" asked the woman.

"We faked our deaths," said Exp 8.

"You faked self-destructing?" She raised one eyebrow and stood up from the desk. "You're traveling to unite your people. Each second you waste is a second that my people come closer to catching your people. And you know what will happen once they are captured, right?" asked the woman, smiling at Devlin.

The artificial scientist turned away.

Opti put his arm on her shoulder. "We did die. And we struggled even after death. We fought to survive in the afterlife, and we made our way back here."

"I don't think she'll believe that," said Kaity.

"It's absolutely absurd. But then again, so is the existence of Exps. He's not lying. That much I can tell. Right this way." She parted the curtains and opened up another door.

The door led to the runway.

Crisis, noticing the wind had nearly knocked over Stabby, created a gust to cancel out the current.

The woman pointed at five jets. "New York, Russia, Israel, Guantanamo Bay, New Zealand. You know who's going where, so say goodbye and get inside."

"Is it a good idea to go along with this?" asked Kaity.

"We'll keep each other safe," said Devlin.

"That's right. But stay extra wary. Our top priority is staying alive," said Exp 8.

"Yeah." Devlin approached Nina. "Stay safe, okay?"

Nina turned away from him. "Is that an order?"

"Nina, I care about you," said Devlin.

"Just go," said Nina.

Devlin turned away and joined his team at the Russia-bound jet.

Nina ran up to him and hugged him.

He patted her head and smiled.

"I'll keep your brother safe. And when I return, I'll keep your little sister safe too," said Nina, looking away. "Bye." She broke the hug and rushed off to join Kanasta in the New Zealand jet.

They sat down in the compact plane.

"Ah, the sound of victory," said Kanasta with a small smile as the credits played on his handheld game.

"You do everything with such dedication," said Nina.

"Yet, I have a job still left undone. Even with a diamond from an Absence god, I doubt I could end Reflector."

"Who is Reflector?"

"A client and a target. Let's see if there are any new jobs posted." Kanasta whipped out his phone and cycled through his mail. He started crying.

"Um, are you alright?" she asked.

"The Viper Squad is done for," he said softly.

"What makes you say that?" asked Nina.

"Two years of unanswered messages. One hundred and eighteen job offers, and what's worse, sixteen jobs I left incomplete. The business my father passed down to me. The ultimate group of assassins is done for," said Kanasta, sobbing into his palms.

Nina scratched her knuckles and stuttered as she tried to find the right words to say. "Wait. Those sixteen unfinished jobs could still be completed. It's not too late."

Kanasta's phone rang and he picked up. "Hello?" asked Kanasta, instantly regaining his composure.

"You owe me," said the voice on the other line.

"Who is this?" asked Kanasta as the plane gained speed.

"The guy who kept you in business. I had to fly across the globe to take care of those jobs for you. And if you check your account, you'll see that the payment for those jobs has been forwarded to you."

"Once an assassin, always an assassin," said Kanasta with a tearful smile.

"You're welcome. When you get back from your trip, I expect you to return the favor. Till then, enjoy the flight."

"How did he know you were on a plane?" asked Nina.

"He's part of the same organization that was kind enough to fly us to our destinations." Kanasta's shoulders drooped. "Even if the jobs were completed, the number of unanswered requests is enough to tarnish the name of the Viper Squad forever."

"You're not thinking straight. This is just another tricky situation, and you've escaped those many times, right?" asked Nina.

"The severity of this cannot be understated," said Kanasta.

Nina grabbed his hand. "Close your eyes. Take a deep breath."

Kanasta did as commanded.

"Clear your thoughts and you'll find the solution."

After a few deep breaths, he opened his eyes and smiled at her. "If I explain that I was detained and complete all the jobs within the next month, I can help bring the Viper Squad out of this pit. I cannot thank you enough."

"You're Devlin's brother. It's my duty to help you out," said Nina with a smile.

"He should be very proud of his dutiful daughter," said Kanasta with a nod.

"I don't think of him like a father. Let's stop talking about Devlin," said Nina, shuffling in her seat.

"Understood. Time to get back on track, one job at a time," said Kanasta, copying and pasting his response and sending it to multiple recipients.

"You may now unfasten your seatbelt," said the flight attendant over the speaker.

"No way am I doing that. Safety comes first." D.S. turned to his seat partner. "You should only move about a plane if you have to."

Crisis was shifting in his seat, his eyes darting back and forth.

"Do you need to go potty?" asked D.S.

"I just really don't like getting into planes," he said, shivering.

"Because they are unnatural?" asked D.S.

"Bad memories," said Crisis, covering his mouth with his hands.

D.S. put his arm over his pal's shoulder. "Let's play a game then! It will help get your mind off of things. I'll say an animal and then you have to say another animal that starts with the last letter of the animal I said. Okay?"

"Yeah, sure. Sounds fun," said Crisis.

"Octopus!"

"Swallow."

"Whale!"

"Egret."

"You don't have to sit next me, you know," said Devlin, blushing as he looked at Kaity.

"Maybe I want to," said Kaity with a smile.

"You're so cute," said Devlin, stopping himself from seizing her in a hug.

"You're cute too," said Kaity, poking his cheek.

"I am?" asked Devlin.

"Yep. You're almost like a kitty," said Kaity.

"That form…doesn't frighten you?" asked Devlin.

Kaity held her chin inquisitively. "Nah," she said with a grin.

"Thanks."

"For what?" asked Kaity, tilting her head.

"For being a part of my life," said Devlin.

"You know, there's a reason I didn't object to you riding alone with me."

"Oh, planning on convincing me to abandon my conquest of the Heavens?" asked Devlin.

"No, silly. It's because I trust you," she said with a smile.

Devlin looked away and wiped his tears.

"Are you okay?"

"Kaity, I'll never stop loving you," said Devlin, crying more.

"I know, but just tone it down a bit. I have a lot going on right now," said Kaity softly.

"And I'm here to support you through it all."

Kaity smiled and then shuffled in her seat. "So, uh, how do you feel about Nina?"

"I care for her dearly."

"Do you love her romantically?"

"I...I don't know. But it doesn't matter anymore."

"Yes it does! It matters to Nina a lot! And as her friend, it matters to me a lot."

"Kaity, I—"

"You take her for granted. She fought against you to save you. And when you hurt her...she wanted to die. Did you know that? She wanted to die because she felt like you'd never love her. Be there for her Devlin, please. Even if you're only doing it to make me happy," said Kaity, turning away in tears.

"I'll talk to her when we return...I promise," said Devlin softly.

Opti pet Muffins in his lap. "It's okay. I know it must be scary, but trust me, I fly all the time. It's perfectly safe."

Muffins licked his finger affectionately.

"It's just a few hours long. And I'll be right here the whole time, okay?" Opti fiddled with her ears.

Muffins let out an affectionate squeak.

Image and Atlas were seated hand in hand.

Stabby was in the adjacent seat, clinging onto Exp 8's arm.

"She's sure taken a liking to you," said Image.

"Yeah, makes me think about my little sister," said Exp 8 with a solemn tone.

"Would you like to speak with her?" asked Atlas, summoning up the Wailing Whip.

Exp 8 reached out and touched the whip. "Sister, you can rest easy. I'm still alive, still fighting for the freedom of our people. And I promise you, I won't stop until we attain it."

"Your words are inspiring," said Atlas.

"Please don't talk to me," said Exp 8, tears coming out from his helmet.

Image leaned over a bit. "Sorry to complain, but you really put us in a bad spot by getting the Exps' whereabouts from a government spy."

"If we're going to make Earth a home for our people, we'll need to cooperate with others. If the spies wanted to take them out, they would have done so in our absence," said Exp 8.

"You did what you thought was best. We are fortunate to have you back," said Atlas.

"Is there any way to bring them back?" asked Exp 8.

"Not that I am aware of." Atlas looked away.

"Then they're really gone," said Exp 8 softly.

"Do not think of them as dead. They will be fighting alongside us, just in a different form. All of them are within me. And it is with their power that I will take down Sel."

"That means a lot to me," said Exp 8, smiling at his former foe.

"It is my honor to work alongside you, but a word of advice." Atlas sat up straight in his chair. "Be aware of your limitations. Don't get yourself killed by being reckless again."

"Says the guy who almost killed me. Don't worry. I'm not the same arrogant rebel who fought you back then. I'll be careful," said Exp 8, smiling beneath his helmet.

Chapter 145: The Search Begins

Ada was in the kitchen making up a falafel salad. Hope was reclined on the sofa, having her feet massaged by Deceivant.

"They are in the air and en route to their destinations," said Deceivant.

"Did you make some sort of deal to keep them safe?" Hope giggled and then kicked him. "Do not tickle me. I'm only allowing you to massage me because Mother is incompetent. Don't test me."

"It was a mistake, my darling little queen. And no, I absolutely did not make a deal with those spies. Thankfully, the security systems are up and running again, so my home is as secure as when I left it," said Deceivant, applying strawberry-scented lotion to his hands before continuing the massage.

"Exps have become more feared in my absence. It appears that Exp 8's self-destruction killed a whole building's worth of scientists," said Hope.

"That's impossible. The only scientist around when Exp 8 exploded was Devlin," said Deceivant.

"Then those thirty-six scientists who disappeared are either held captive by the government or dead. No remains were discovered," said Hope, taking a sip of tea.

"That means the only way to disprove it would be to infiltrate the government facility where they are being held."

"Not worth the trouble. Rather than disprove it, we need to create our own positive propaganda. Thankfully, though, the Humans First movement has grown and so has the Deus Ex Machina group. I'd rather not associate with religious fanatics, but we must make do with what we have," said Hope.

"You're absolutely right. I actually have a colleague who works there. I'll see if we can schedule a meeting with one of the heads. As far as I know, they are pacifists," said Deceivant.

"Indeed. Thankfully, there is also a sub-branch of Progressives vying for Exp rights. And there's one other group that may be of use," said Hope.

"Are they pro-Exp?" asked Deceivant.

"Not quite. But they are anti-human. The Furies are eco-terrorists or planetary freedom fighters, depending who you ask. Their numbers have been growing steadily and so has their success. Currently, they are trying to gain sovereignty on a self-made Earth ship, which would make them the newest federally recognized nation since Israel. If the Exps offer them aid in this endeavor, then surely we can get them and the radical progressives on our side," said Hope.

"It's nice that we're finally talking again," said Deceivant with a lax smile before his daughter's footsies slammed into his face.

"Do not ignore me. I realize that if I'm going to live with you, I cannot simply avoid you. This in no way changes my utter contempt for you," said Hope, puffing out her cheeks.

"A thousand pardons, my queen," said Deceivant with a bow. "I'm not sure it's a good idea to work with the Furies. I personally agree with their methods, but wouldn't such an allegiance create a bigger divide between Exps and humans?"

"One must first show their strength before they can gain respect. Globalized or not, we live in a divided society. We must stick with the side that favors my kind." Hope closed her eyes and fell asleep.

Deceivant looked at her neck to see a small dart. Unable to discern where the dart originated from, he seized a cushion from the couch.

A figure popped out from the curtains. Black spandex covered its entire body. The identity of the intruder remained a mystery as it was hidden behind a metal helmet shaped like a skull with a one-way visor.

"Come with me and I'll hand over the antidote," she said, patting her utility belt.

Deceivant vaulted over the couch, removing the cushion and pulling out a large metal object hidden beneath it in the process. He turned on his ear piece as he held up the shotgun at the girl. "Intruder in the living room."

"Not fast enough," said the girl, shooting the shotgun out of his hand. She then ran into him, knocking him to the ground.

Deceivant turned his head to peek into the kitchen, seeing his lovely wife collapsed on the ground. "She had better not be hurt."

The girl looked at the fire in his eyes and pulled away. "I didn't hurt her. And Hope is okay too. The energy dart is harmless."

"What do you want?" asked Deceivant, whipping out a pistol and pressing it to her chest.

"I've come to retrieve you. My client is in need of your skills," said the girl.

"How did you bypass the alarm?"

"Controlled EMP. Knocks out specified electrical functions for a more covert approach. You may not be aware, but I'm actually a super spy," she said before swiping the gun out of his hands.

The Captain of Carnage sped by and sliced her back.

The girl's suit hardened on impact, leaving her without wounds.

"Is this a new Exp of yours?" asked the spy.

"You were foolish to come alone," said Deceivant, seizing her in his arms.

The Captain sped in but had to change course when the girl flipped Deceivant over her back.

She whipped out another pistol and fired at the Captain as he raced across the ceiling.

"Keep her busy! I'll get Amy!" yelled Deceivant, making a break for the hallway.

The spy lifted up the shotgun and whacked the armored ferret before blasting the new Exp into the kitchen. "Wow! I'm really doing this! Who says virtual training doesn't count? Wait till brother hears about this."

"You're Koshi's twin sister, aren't you?" asked Deceivant, reaching inside a large pot and hoisting up the Gravity Gun.

"No. My name is uh, Margaret. Margaret Dunsberry," said the spy.

"Well, Kioshi, I think it's time you surrender," he said, pointing the gun at her.

She looked down, realizing the shotgun was out of ammo.

D.S. and Crisis were on the streets of New York City.

"Look, a pigeon!" cheered D.S., waving at the cute bird.

"Yes. There are hundreds of pigeons here, and you don't need to greet them all."

"Each pigeon is a different person, so I'm saying hi to all of them."

"We need to find Flash Girl, so let's split up and ask around," said Crisis, checking the local newspaper for any stories leading to her most recent whereabouts.

"Yeah, uh. The thing is…I'm not really good at talking to strangers, and the people here are looking at me funny," said D.S.

"Says the guy waving to every pigeon we come across." Crisis turned to D.S. and smiled. "Of course. I know how we can get some information." He ran ahead and D.S. increased his pace to keep up.

"We just passed by a lot of people," said D.S.

"Yeah, but why ask someone who's never met her?" Crisis turned into an alleyway.

"Um, my mother said to avoid these kinds of places," said D.S., holding his nose as he walked down the messy alleyway.

"And your mother is absolutely right. Under normal circumstances, going here would be a bad idea, but if we're looking for a hero, why not ask some criminals?" Crisis found a group of unsavory-looking fellows. "Hey, we're looking for someone. Think you can help?"

"Actually, maybe you can help us. See, we need money for the bus and—"

D.S. caught up.

"Whoa. Uh, yeah, sure. What do you need?" asked one of the men, looking at D.S.' muscles with wide eyes.

"We're after Flash Girl. Have you seen her?" asked Crisis.

"Every criminal in the city is after her, but not one of us has ever seen her. The only reason we even know she's a girl is because one kid drew a picture after he was rescued. You're not a cop, are you?" asked the man.

"Do we look like cops?" asked Crisis.

The thug looked to his friends and shrugged. "Look, we've got a plan to catch her. We're planning a big crime a little after lunch time. You want in?"

"Um, I don't know about this. I promised Mom I wouldn't get involved with bad people again," said D.S.

"We're not the bad guys. We are victims of a system that benefits the rich and throws away the poor. Sure some of us are addicts, but we're just doing what we can to survive," said the thug.

"Addicts, like drug addicts?" asked D.S.

"Yeah, what's it to ya?" asked another thug.

"Drug addicts are really nice people. We'll help you," said D.S. with a toothy grin.

"So, what is the crime?" asked Crisis.

"A bank robbery. Well, three at once, actually. The money gets divided up based on how much you contribute," said the head thug.

"That sounds like a lot of fun!" cheered D.S., bouncing up and down.

"Will you excuse us for a moment?" Crisis pulled D.S. aside. "Do not use your powers under any circumstances. We can't let anyone know Exps were involved in criminal activity. If you do use your powers, I'll tell your mom that you robbed a bank. You'll likely get grounded."

"I won't, I promise," said D.S. with a salute. He turned to the addicts and waved. "Hey guys, we're not going to kill anyone, are we?"

The head thug tossed him a shotgun. "Not part of the plan, but we have to be able to defend ourselves. The only one we're killing is Flash Girl, but she's an Exp, not a person."

Opti and Muffins stood at the door of Guantanamo Bay.

"Hi, can I come in?" he asked with a smile.

The frowning guard looked up. "ID."

"Oh, yes, of course," said Opti, pulling out his face-card.

"Mr. Goodsmile, you may enter, but you can't bring the rabbit inside. No pets."

"Oh, Muffins is my friend, not a pet."

"It's against the rules regardless."

"Can Muffins stay in the waiting room? I don't want to leave her outside."

"That's fine. You may enter."

Opti entered the prison and was delighted to see the waiting room was sparkly clean. He set Muffins down on a plastic chair and approached the bald woman at the front desk. "I'd like to talk to Durga. Is she available?"

"She is busy at the moment. You'll have to wait. Is it urgent?"

"She's my cousin. It's time sensitive, but not urgent."

"I'll tell her you're here."

"Thanks so much. I really appreciate you helping me!"

"You're welcome. You know, I'm not used to getting such genuine gratitude. Tell you what, I'll have a guard escort you there, and you can speak to her as soon as she's done. Sound good?"

"That sounds wonderful. Oh, and can you keep an eye on Muffins?" Opti pointed to his rodent friend.

"Sure thing. Have a nice day."

"I will have a nice day," said Opti, following the officer.

The hallway was compact but surprisingly clean. Still, Opti felt that a bit of color would do the granite walls wonders.

"She's currently talking to a visitor," said the guard, once they arrived at the door.

"Can you tell her I'm here?" asked Opti.

"Proceed." The guard opened the door.

Opti peeked in. Seated in the chair beside Durga was Pesi.

"So, you're finally here. Come on in," said Pesi with a grin.

Kanasta finished chatting to the park ranger before meeting up with Nina.

"Any news on February?" asked Nina.

"Oh. I forgot to ask."

"Then what were you talking about?"

"Seems there's a problem with poachers. Three K for alive, two for dead. Why less for dead, I wonder," said Kanasta with a curious look.

"Does it matter?"

"Absolutely. The value of a life should be a fixed number."

"Didn't Kaity convince you that taking up a few bounties would increase your group's credibility?"

"She spoke to me about the subject, but I'm not convinced."

"Devlin entrusted me with this mission. We can't afford to get sidetracked."

"How were things on your end?" asked Kanasta.

"The barkeep told me a story about a strange creature in the jungle. Usually stays by a lake," said Nina.

"Think it's just a legend?" asked Kanasta.

"Legends don't have bounties on them." Nina raised a wanted poster.

"Is there any way to narrow the search?" asked Kanasta, texting a client.

"Actually, there is." Nina led Kanasta into the jungle and pulled a man out from the bushes. "I caught him after he left the bar. He's a poacher, so he can tell us where the Running Beast is."

"Have you asked him yet?" asked Kanasta.

"I was thinking you might be better at getting information," said Nina, pressing her katana to the man's throat before tearing the tape off his mouth, ripping clumps of his facial hair along with it.

"We need to know where the Running Beast is. Tell us," said Kanasta.

"If we knew where it was, the thing would be dead already."

"Then lead us to where you last saw it," said Kanasta, bending the bounty's fingers back.

The phone in the man's shirt pocket rang. Nina put the phone on speaker and held it to the man's ear.

"George! You there?"

"Yeah, I'm here," said George, his eyes widening when the katana's tip pressed against his throat.

"We caught the Running Beast. We've got traders from all over the world bidding for it. Heheh! Maybe next we can catch Bigfoot. Meet us at Traitor's Keep. We're throwing a celebration!"

"I'll be there within the hour," said the poacher.

"Here's what we'll do. Every ten minutes, you lose a toe." Nina tossed the filth into the jeep. "Drive us to the rendezvous point."

The poacher gulped. "I'll get there as fast as possible. No need to hurt me."

"You seem to have no trouble with negotiations," said Kanasta, patting Nina's shoulder.

"I suppose you're right. I won't fail Devlin. I'll show him how dependable I am. He needs me, just like I need him."

Kanasta put his hands over hers. "You're trembling."

"I'll be fine."

"Your skills would be put to good use with me," said Kanasta.

"I'm not becoming an assassin," said Nina.

"Did you just say assassin?" asked the terrified poacher.

Kanasta turned to Nina. "You just cost me a thousand dollars. Thank you."

"What does that mean? I'm freaking out here! I can't drive right if I'm freaking out!" yelled the man.

"Oh, the first ten minutes are up," said Nina with a smile.

Atlas, Image, Exp 8, and Stabby were at a bazaar in Israel, questioning the locals about information on August.

"I think we've attracted enough attention. If the guy is a bounty hunter, he'll likely come after us. I don't want this densely populated area to become a battleground," said Exp 8, turning to Atlas.

Image stepped in between them. "Actually, it's exactly what we want. Most of the time, he chases his targets to an open area. And every target without witnesses ends up dead. Being around witnesses is our best bet at keeping his powers contained and thus keeping us alive."

"I'm thirsty," said Stabby, tugging on Exp 8's arm.

"I'm getting a bad feeling. You two can stay here, but I'm going to draw him out elsewhere," said Exp 8, picking up Stabby.

"He is incredibly skilled. It is best if we stay together," said Atlas, grabbing Exp 8's arm.

"We can't stay here," said Exp 8, looking out at the crowds.

Sharpened teeth like blades popped out from Stabby's mouth. Her eyes glazed over. She leaped out from Exp 8's arms and dug her fangs into the back of an elderly man in front of them.

"This wasn't part of the plan," said Image with a curious look.

Exp 8 fired his turrets at the nearby stalls and created a massive orb. "If you want to live, you had better run!"

Atlas raised his binoculars and spotted a single man moving against the crowd. "He's here."

Stabby ran off after the crowd.

Exp 8 zoomed into her and picked her off the ground. "What has gotten into you?" he asked as she gnawed on his armor.

"Hey, Atlas, here on vacation with your wife?" asked August.

"In a manner of speaking. Brother, we have come to see you. We need your help," said Atlas.

"You've heard the stories about Chipko, haven't you? We've changed. If you want my help, then beat me."

"Very well then," said a woman, appearing behind August. "**Case Creo**"

Kaity, Devlin, and BoneSaw walked the chilled streets of Moscow.

"You sure you don't want something warmer?" asked Devlin, pointing to a nearby clothing store.

"This suit regulates temperature. I'm as cozy as a kitten," said Kaity with a stretch.

Devlin's wire receded, bringing a scarf into his hand. With great care he put it over Kaity's neck. "Cozy?"

"And pretty. Purple makes me think of Nina," said Kaity with a twirl.

"Thanks for supporting her in my absence. Hey Kaity, you know we could get more intel if we split up," said Devlin.

"That's true, but I'm surprised you'd want to end our date early," said Kaity with a grin.

Devlin blushed and looked away. "I'll call you if I find out anything. Contact me if you run into trouble."

"Roger," said Kaity with a salute.

Devlin saluted her and ran down the snowy sidewalk. "Excuse me, sir. I couldn't help but notice that tattoo on your arm."

The man smiled and lifted up his sleeve, revealing a gruesome tattoo of a bird-humanoid tearing out the innards of the goddess Athena. "You seem like a smart boy. I like that look in your eye."

"Thanks. I'm looking for someone. She's a member of the Furies," said Devlin.

"Well, you've met the right person. I know everyone in the Moscow branch. My name is Blood Beak."

"Drake," said Devlin, shaking the man's hand.

"You'll fit right in with the others. Follow me," said the man, turning the corner.

Devlin followed along till they arrived at an old warehouse.

"We have four bases of operation and relocate accordingly. You're interested in becoming a member, aren't you?" asked the man.

"I'm definitely considering it. I've dedicated my life to fighting injustice in my own way already," said Devlin.

"There are only five requirements to become a Fury. One: you live vegan, no flexitarian or vegetarian, full on vegan, and you encourage others to live the same. Two: you don't drive anything that runs on petroleum, and you encourage others to do the same. Most of our members use bikes or eco-cycles, but electric cars are fine. Three: you take a vow of anti-natalism, and you encourage others to do the same. Four: you accept that the world is better off with the human race extinct, and you encourage others to think the same. Five: you put the greater good over your own sense of morality. Bottom line, you do what must be done for Gaia. Is that all clear?"

"Absolutely," said Devlin.

A man placed his hands on Kaity when she turned the corner.

"You're alive after all," said the black suit commander.

"What are you doing here?" asked Kaity with a shiver.

"Just checking up on an old friend," he said, placing his hand on her shoulder.

Chapter 146: Cornered

D.S. and Crisis joined a posse of five criminals at the bank.

"This is a robbery!" exclaimed D.S., shooting into the air.

"Are you trying to get us killed?" asked the head thug, shoving an ID card into his own shirt pocket.

Crisis pointed his pistols at the civilians. "We don't need to hurt anyone. Just stay on the ground and don't try anything heroic."

Police sirens shook the glass doors of the bank.

"How do they know we are here? Do we bail?" asked one of the thugs.

"Don't let them inside. Big guy, you're with me," said the head thug, beckoning D.S. to follow.

"Did you guys hear that this place is under tornado watch?" asked Crisis, moving his hand in a circular motion.

The wind outside circulated into a twister, lifting the police cars off the street.

"Do as I say not as I do. How like an adult," said D.S.

"My powers are discreet, so cool your jets, kid. I just hope we're safe inside," said Crisis.

D.S. ran to the safe where two other men were setting C-4 explosives. Four security guards opened fire. The bulky Exp rushed them, taking the bullets for his new friends.

"Great work! Keep your eyes peeled. Flash Girl will be here any moment," said the man.

In the blink of an eye, D.S. was flung off his feet by a blurry figure.

A thin wire coiled around the blur, making the figure faceplant to the ground.

"Hey there, girlie. Once you're dead, we're taking over this city," said the head thug.

Bullets sprayed into the criminals before they could fire.

"What are you doing?" asked D.S., turning to Crisis.

"Taking out the bad guys," said Crisis.

"They trusted us!" yelled D.S.

"We just needed them to get to Flash Girl," said Crisis.

"You're the bad guy! Don't worry, buddies. I'll get the money and I'll get you patched up," said D.S., using glue to seal their wounds.

"Flash Girl found herself tied up, face to face with a power-augmented person. The question burning in the back of her mind was, 'is he a hero or a villain?'" said the superhero.

"Hey, Flash Girl. A powerful enemy has appeared, and we'd like your help to take him down," said Crisis.

D.S. shot the C-4, blasting the bank vault open. "We haven't failed yet."

When the smoke cleared, the steel-plated walls of the bank were empty. There was a figure clad in tight latex with a mouth gag.

"Gimpy? Um, where's the money?" asked D.S.

"An empty bank vault and a mysterious figure. What sort of trouble has our heroine run into this time?" asked Flash Girl.

The six-toed poacher parked the jeep near a gathering of tents in the damp jungle.

"Still in business," said Kanasta before snapping the target's neck.

"If they are planning on selling February, we don't need to worry about his safety. Capture or kill?" asked Nina.

"Kill, but keep their faces intact so they can be identified," said Kanasta.

Nina leaped back. A metal beam appeared seemingly out of thin air. "Demo. I'll keep him busy. Find February. Don't get sidetracked," said Nina, countering a metal bullet spray with her katana.

Kanasta nodded and ran off inside the first tent. "The Running Beast, where is he?" he asked a bearded man with the added persuasion of a loaded shotgun.

"The green tent by the Northern end. Please don't—"

With a *blam*, the man's life was put to an end.

Kanasta ran out of the tent and fired at the poachers as they came out from their hiding spots.

Bullets zoomed by, a few nicking the assassin boss. But none of them were strong enough to breach his bodysuit.

Rather than reload, Kanasta used a tether to grab the guns of the fallen targets and then used them to open fire on more targets. "Semi-automatic. Not bad at all."

A sharp pain suddenly burst from his shoulder.

The assassin boss looked at the tree tops to see several snipers.

"This isn't covert at all. But a sloppy job is still a job."

Kanasta opened fire at the tree tops as he ran toward the green tent.

Three men came out of the green tent, all holding rocket launchers.

"Not too bad for the first job of the year." Kanasta whipped out his pistol and fired the first rocket after it was ejected.

The blast killed the three gunmen.

Something sped by Kanasta and went into the bushes.

The assassin boss followed. "February, is that you?"

The figure stood up from the damp bushes. "Nothing personal," said The Vibrator before poking a hole into the assassin boss' chest.

Kanasta slammed his fist into the attacker, knocking him over. The sound of a jeep starting caused the assassin boss to turn.

February, his primary target, was in the back of the jeep asleep in a cage.

Kanasta's sprint came to a sudden halt when he heard Nina's voice in the distance. She was calling for help.

Pesi led his lesser half into the rigid metal chair next to him.

"Is everything alright?" asked the guard.

"I'll be fine. Leave us," said Durga, not even turning to face the guard.

The guard nodded and left the room.

"I'm Opti. It's very nice to meet you," said Exp 11, extending his arm.

"I'm aware of who you are…and what you want," she said, her pupil-less eyes gazing at him.

"Great, so, shall we go?" asked Opti.

"I'm not a fighter. And I have no family. I live by myself now. And I find solace in alleviating the pain of others. I want to make it perfectly clear that this prison is where I have chosen to spend my life. Lum's conquest of Sellum is no longer my concern," said Durga, gazing beyond them.

"Umm, wait up. Lum isn't the problem, at least not the big problem. Sel is the one who wants to take over all the realms," said Opti.

Durga smiled. "Two truths. Now things are interesting."

"Ignore him. He's a pathological liar and an idealist. He fails to see Lum's scheme because of his rose-scented glasses," said Pesi.

"Rose-colored," corrected Durga.

"He's the one who is lying. Pesi is working with Sel. That guy is majorly evil. He killed the big ball of love and that deity was really nice," said Opti.

"Fragments of a more complex story…how can I decide?" asked Durga quizzically.

Opti and Pesi leaned in at once. "We need you!"

A pink mist came from Durga's mouth as she spoke. "Very well, I'll come with you."

"Wonderful," said Opti.

"As expected," said Pesi.

The two of them stood up and left the room.

Durga folded her hands and smiled.

Devlin followed Blood Beak to the top floor of a creaky staircase. "So Chipko is the head of the Moscow branch?"

"She is our icon. The belief of the Furies given power and form. We act on the behalf of the planet, but she is Earth's vengeance. And what's more, she's too strong to be brought in by the police." Having arrived at the top of the stairs, Blood Beak knocked on the metal green door.

The door swung open on its own.

The woman who had led the nearby protest was staring up at the sky from the rooftop. She was wearing a tank top and running shoes made from cheap materials. Her amber eyes shimmered, and her freckled cheeks lit up in the sunlight.

"Are you augmented? Or are you an Exp?" she asked, not even turning to face him as she pet a small white rock.

"Wait, you're an Exp?" asked Blood Beak, taking a step back.

"I am indeed," said Devlin, releasing wires from his fingers.

Blood Beak's smile nearly split his face in two. "Well, that's fantastic! Having two Exps will exponentially help our cause."

"Brother Blood Beak, please leave," said Chipko, blowing a strand of her green hair to the side.

"Gaia's love upon you, sister," said Blood Beak before leaving.

"It's just a formality. I haven't seen my real family in a long, long time," said Chipko, slowly rising to her bare feet.

"Is Atlas your brother?" asked Devlin.

"Yes, and he's also a murderer," said Chipko, clenching her red gloves into a fist.

"Myself and many other Exps are coming together to fight someone who threatens the afterlife," said Devlin, walking up to her.

"The afterlife is the concern of spirits. The planet is the concern of the incarnated. Are you a ghost?" asked Chipko.

"No, but the realms are connected," said Devlin.

"If those who walk the path of spirituality dedicated their lives to the well-being of the planet rather than chasing mysticism and lore, this world would be a far better place," said Chipko.

"Okay, let's negotiate. What is it you want?" asked Devlin.

"What I want doesn't matter. I'm discarded trash trying to carve a purposeful path despite my utter insignificance," said Chipko.

"I have somewhere to be, so just tell me what you want in return for your help," said Devlin.

Chipko placed the rock in her tank top. "All the protests, petitions, and marches do absolutely nothing to sway the whims of the elite. Sadly, to change the world you either need to end demand or make compromises. I alone cannot end demand, but I can make compromises," she turned to Devlin, a distortion around her gloved fist. "You can rest easy. Your defeat will save many lives." The environmentalist wiped a tear from her eye.

"What do you want?" asked Kaity, turning away from the dangerous man.

"A hug would be nice. It's been years," said the black suit commander.

"I haven't forgotten our last encounter, Koshi. I doubt you have either," said Kaity, ejecting her plasma claws.

"Easy now. Let's not make a scene," said Koshi, taking a step back.

"What do you want?" asked Kaity, backing him up against the wall of the alley.

"I saw you on the airplane and—"

"Yeah, I was almost certain it was you, but the eye color and nose were off, so was your chin."

"Wow, you have my every feature memorized. I'm flattered. What gave it away then?"

"The sick feeling in my gut when you smiled at me," said Kaity, her claws now singeing his suit.

"I came here to see you. I thought you were dead. Been searching for two years. Even with global surveillance I couldn't track you down. I thought I had lost you."

"Drop the act. You only care about yourself."

"Oh really? If that's the case, why did I keep the Viper Squad in business while you were gone?"

"Because you want something in return."

"You know me so well," said Koshi with a grin.

"So what is it?" Kaity brought the claws up to his throat, slicing his suit.

"Hey, if you want me to strip, you can just ask."

"Answer me!"

The agent's tone became solemn. "You've changed a lot. I just want to spend some time with you. Maybe we could even do a job together."

"I need to find Chipko. Do you know where she is?"

"Chipko is one of my best friends! You know, when she's helpless and broken, she's actually kind of cute."

"You're sick," said Kaity.

"So, are you and Devlin dating now? Cause that's what it looked like to me," said Koshi.

"You know where she is. Lead me there or else," said Kaity.

"Or else you'll slice my throat open, fill me full of holes, what?" asked Koshi with a big grin.

"Or else I'll ignore you," said Kaity, turning away.

"Hey now, don't get upset. Alright, I'll—" Koshi grabbed her and pulled her into him, getting burned by her claws in the process.

The wall bloated up like a pimple before bursting, releasing a hot flame that would have burned them had Koshi not pulled Kaity with him to the ground.

BoneSaw came rushing down the alleyway, pursued by a pale-skinned woman draped in bandages.

"Nobody told me this was going to be a reunion," said Koshi.

Kaity broke out from his arms, rushed past BoneSaw, and plunged her claws into Sefiwah's chest.

"What is going on?" asked Exp 8, noticing the eight-foot-tall, twenty-foot-long encasing that came out of thin air.

"Enemies incoming," said Atlas, pointing to Edirp as she approached.

"How does Sel know where we are?" asked Exp 8, landing next to his allies.

"It's a curious situation, isn't it?" asked Demonica, walking alongside her sister.

"Flee the area. It isn't safe here," said Atlas.

"I'm not leaving you again," said Image.

Exp 8 put Stabby in Image's arms. "Please, we're counting on you."

Image nodded before running off.

Atlas rushed at Demonica, hoisting up the Agony Axe.

Edirp brought him to his knees by concentrating her aura.

Demonica sped past Atlas and Exp 8.

"You're not getting Stabby!" yelled Exp 8, firing at her with his shoulder turrets.

Demonica collapsed into two puddles, which headed off in opposite directions.

Exp 8 activated his jets before being floored by a sudden surge of gravity.

Previously: August was captured by Casey.

August looked at the steel prison around him and back up at the woman in front. "What is this, Casey, a family reunion?"

"I've been tasked to retrieve you," she said, taking a step forward.

"Here I thought Zenero forgot about me." August tossed three grenades her way, all of which were swiftly encased in an instant.

"I'm sorry we have to meet under these circumstances," said Casey.

"Don't act like you care about me. The only one you care about is your creator. Not your fault though; he designed you that way. Doesn't that upset you?" asked August, circling around her.

"Only a fool worries over that which cannot be changed. My programming is me and I fully accept it," said Casey, sending metal boxes flying at her brother.

The boxes bounced off as if they had hit a wall of rubber.

"You're too attached to Zenero. I was worried I'd have to kill you one day." August ran up to Casey and punched her to the floor. "*SURFACE BOUNCY.*"

The metal floor morphed into an elastic material. Acting like a trampoline, it sent Casey into the air upon impact.

August hopped on the bouncy spot before shooting up into the air. "Come on, fight back a little."

Casey created a wall of boxes to shield herself.

The boxes bent like paper before his leg slammed into her, sending her into the encroaching back wall.

August's body became like metal, accelerating his drop.

His feet grew springs by the time he hit the bouncy floor.

With the combined strength of the springs and bounce pad, he was sent flying into his attacker.

"Got you," said Casey, summoning up a metal case around him before his iron punch made contact.

The case fell to the ground and Casey slowly stood up.

The front of the case collapsed into a liquid puddle.

August walked out with a stretch.

Casey was frozen in shock as he approached.

The bounty hunter pressed his hand through her chest and pulled out the Encasement Artifact.

"If Zenero wants me captured, he should have come himself," said August, twirling the chunk of Titanium on his finger.

The puddle on the ground stood up and took form. "Zenero doesn't want you. But I do," said Demonica, blowing a kiss.

The Gravity Gun was aimed at Kioshi and she was out of ammo.

The girl stomped her feet against the ground.

"Is that some sort of signal?" asked the Captain, ready to strike.

"Not fair! Not fair! This was my chance to prove myself. How did I lose?" she whined.

"Who knew there was such an adorable girl working for that horrible man? Don't worry, we won't hurt a cutie like you," said Deceivant, stepping toward her.

"You think I'm cute?" asked Kioshi, her eyes shining behind her visor.

"You did your best. Why don't you lie down, relax, and I'll make you up a cup of tea," said Deceivant, patting her shoulder.

"That sounds great!" she exclaimed, launching into him with a hop.

Smoke suddenly filled the area.

The girl ran down the hall with the famous scientist hoisted over her shoulders. "Super spy!" she cheered, rushing into the bathroom.

The girl stopped in place.

A round floating sponge was in the air above the sink.

"What a tragedy! Deceivant Kagaku found dead in his own bathroom. Killed by a government spy," said Absorb before knives grew out from all of his pores.

Chapter 147: Persuasion

Opti and Pesi walked out of the room triumphantly.

Durga reached out and grabbed a cup of water. "In a world of dreams, pleasure is easily attainable and pain does not exist." Her eyes widened. Without a moment to think, she kicked off the table.

A small metallic snake coiled itself up, gazing at the woman.

"You're here for me, aren't you? I'm sure we can negotiate," said Durga.

"If I'm successful, Mother will remain safe. If I fail, she dies. I, Toxic the corn snake, will not fail her," said the segmented metallic snake before shooting into her target.

Durga kicked the living projectile, her leg getting sliced in the process. "It is foolish to harm me." She raised her hands and then froze up.

"My poison is set to paralyze. You won't be able to escape. Do not worry. Sel wants you alive, not dead," said Toxic in a reverberating mumbling voice, coiling around the Exp's injured leg.

Durga smiled. "You lost the instant you told me your motive. *Nightmare Hex*."

A red aura came out from the wound and took the shape of needles before entering the snake's head.

Toxic thrashed around. "Mother, no!" she screamed.

"Now to remove the poison," said Durga to herself. The whimsical woman looked down, noticing her hand was stuck in some sticky yellow goop. "Is this a secret power, or is there another one hiding here?"

Durga pulled out a dagger from her coat with her left hand. "I knew trouble would find me eventually." She screamed as the knife went back and forth against her wrist.

A chubby brown bunny appeared in front of her.

"Were you the one who did this?" she asked, pointing to the goop that glued her hand to the floor.

Muffins did not respond. Her fur extended and hardened before shooting out as needles.

Durga dropped the knife and her body fell limp. "You won't be able to take me out of this place undetected." Fear crept its way into her eyes as her legs vanished from sight. It wasn't long before her whole body was invisible.

Fusion came out from beneath the woman's hand and pulled her along to the exit of the room.

"Our hero trapped, an encounter with a PAP and a mysterious figure of unknown gender inside an empty vault. Was this situation a result of the recent crime lord's imprisonment, or was something more sinister afoot?" asked Flash Girl, struggling to break free. She looked up at the others. "Okay, so seriously, what is going on?" she asked in a snarky tomboyish voice.

Gimpy pointed at her and stood up.

"D.S., we have two primary objectives and one secondary objective. Keep Flash Girl alive; make sure she doesn't get captured; those are our top priorities. Capturing her ourselves is only a secondary objective now, understood?" asked Crisis.

Double barrel shotguns materialized in Gimpy's hands.

"You're on," said D.S., reaching for his gun. "Um, where did it go?"

"Grab her and run! I'll hold it off!" yelled Crisis, firing a gust that dispersed the bullets and knocked Gimpy back into the safe.

"Okay, so, I know we're kidnapping you, but we're the good guys," said D.S., lifting Flash Girl onto his shoulders.

"Our hero, hoping to gain more intel on the situation, chooses not to escape from the strings coiling her legs like a lonely anaconda," said Flash Girl as she was lifted up.

"Um, if you can move, you really should run," said D.S.

"Hey, don't break the fourth wall, buddy," said Flash Girl, smacking his head.

"Then don't speak out loud!" hollered D.S.

Crisis was sent flying back, careening through several office stations before smashing through the glass of the bank.

Several policemen gathered around him, guns at the ready.

"The only laws of this world are natural laws. By imposing order, you only create chaos. *Elemental Armor.*" Wind circulated around Crisis, coating his whole body. Not only did the wind coating lift him off the ground but it also deflected the ensuing bullet spray.

D.S. grabbed a pistol and aimed at Gimpy. By the time he pulled the trigger, he realized he was holding a banana. "You're so funny, Gimpy!" The ex-gangster held his sides.

Gimpy covered its face beneath its hands in embarrassment.

"It was then that Flash Girl realized she could no longer keep the act up!"

"Ow! Why are you so loud?" asked D.S.

"Flash Girl slipped her feet out of the metal strings, picked up the injured criminals and…." The superhero Exp vanished.

"Wow! She's so fast!" exclaimed D.S.

Gimpy spawned a pistol into its hand and fired, launching grenades at D.S. instead of lead bullets.

"Time for you to meet," D.S. whacked the grenades aside with two extended blades, "Snippy the Second!"

The new and improved scissors were longer and sharper. It had a hook on the outside, and the scissors were detachable, allowing him to dual wield.

D.S. flung Snippy the Second at Gimpy.

Realizing the attack would only hit the bound figure's feet, Gimpy slid down and opened its arms, welcoming the weapon.

"Flash Girl suddenly swoops in and seizes the scissors in midflight. She turns to her foe with questionable hobbies and holds the scissors to his or her neck. You've lost, now tell me your plan," said the young, able-bodied heroine.

Gimpy mumbled.

When next the heroine blinked, she was on her knees and Gimpy was holding the scissors at her throat.

"Whoa! Okay, what just happened? I'm seriously confused," said Flash Girl, raising her hands in alarm.

Crisis slammed into Gimpy from the side. He fired a torrent, sending Demonica's minion outside the bank with him.

"It's really cool to meet a real hero! Now come on, let's get out of here!" exclaimed D.S., picking up Snippy Two and helping Flash Girl to her feet.

"I'm not joining your league of avengers. I work alone, so you can forget about it," said Flash Girl, speeding to the front of the bank.

The police opened fire, but she dodged while seemingly staying in place.

"You should get out of here. This is no place for a kid," she said to D.S. before speeding off.

"A wall of cars appeared before her, but the nimble heroine simply ran across the tops of them, escaping the blockade, and...oh crap!" Flash Girl sped back to the other side of the street when civilians rushed into the intersection to grab hold of cash falling from the sky. "She rushes in and speedily saves them one by one. Oh no." Flash Girl leaned over a woman on the asphalt, her body was limp. "Okay, guys, no more playing around! Someone was killed!"

"Is there anything you can't do?" asked Crisis, firing a chilled wind in hopes of freezing Gimpy.

Gimpy snapped its fingers, suddenly littering the intersection with mines.

Flash Girl sped into action, pulling people out of cars before accidentally stepping on a land mine. She fell to the ground, holding her scorched legs. The girl cried out as explosions littered the streets. "I have to get out of the city. You want me, then come get me!" she yelled, flicking off Gimpy.

Demonica's slave appeared in front of her, dodging Crisis' lava fist in the process.

"Flash Girl fled the scene, ignoring the screams of the innocent in the hopes of minimizing the loss of life that day," she said to herself, wiping away her tears. "She soon arrived in a mostly abandoned alleyway. It was here that she would take down the criminal and bring the fiend to justice." The heroine tumbled when something sliced through her feet.

Metal strings then wrapped around the injured heroine's body.

"Eheheh! Lord Sel will be most pleased to see that I've captured you," said the Duke of Deception in a sly feminine voice that sounded a bit forced. The demon lord was a mishmash of body parts and had half a woman's face sewn onto its face.

"Another enemy appeared and our heroine was trapped…sir, madam. I know you're my enemy, but I need medical attention. I'm bleeding out," said Flash Girl in tears. She removed her mask, showing she was a young black teenager with freckles, amber eyes and a Band-Aid on her nose and right cheek. "I'm just a kid. Please. I don't want to die."

Wringer came out from behind a grimy trashcan. Without a sound, it coiled chains around the Duke's neck.

"You came to rescue me," cried Flash Girl, hope blooming in her eyes.

"Wrong. He was following me," said the Duke, slicing the chain around his throat with a single string.

Gimpy materialized in front of them and created a Sel portal. It pulled Flash Girl into the black vortex. The Duke entered the vortex, and it closed just as Wringer's elongated chain entered it.

Just as Kanasta began his sprint, he heard Nina scream behind him.

The Vibrator leaped back to his feet and attacked the assassin boss in his moment of hesitation. "You best surrender. You won't be able to reach that truck with your mortal speed."

"Then I ask for your aid." Kanasta pierced his hand into The Vibrator and tore out his artifact. After slamming the red spinel stone into his chest, the assassin boss sped to the origin of the scream and flung the stone back to its owner.

"What are you doing?" asked Nina, drenched in blood. "The mission is more important."

"You need to think like a businessperson," said Kanasta, ducking under Demo's pincer attack. "If you die, you can't complete any more missions. A failed job is not as important as the employer." He hoisted her onto his shoulders.

"I won't die here. Have faith in me. Go after the Exp before it's too late," said Nina, deflecting incoming projectiles by spinning her sword.

"I've already balanced the risk–reward ratio." Kanasta turned to the silver sphere. "Demo, your target is in a jeep heading north. You've succeeded in stalling us; now leave," said Kanasta, tossing up Nina and standing firm as another pincer attack came his way.

Nina flung a handful of shurikens into the surrounding foliage where the attacks originated from. "Demo was sent here to kill me. It won't leave until it completes the mission. I'm the same way," she said, rushing north to catch February.

Kanasta opened his suitcase up as Demo came out from hiding and sped after Nina. "Luckily, I came prepared." He whipped out a liquid nitrogen gun and blasted the baseball-sized black dot, freezing it in place.

Nina arrived at the tipped-over jeep.

"That's right. Flee before my divine power!" exclaimed The Vibrator as the poachers sprinted away.

Nina unsheathed her sword. "Stand down or I will kill you."

"Have you seen yourself? You're covered in wounds. So absolutely pitiful," said The Vibrator, rushing up to her with his fingers engaged.

Nina kicked him aside.

When he got up, The Vibrator noticed an explosive tag on his chest. "What is this sorcery?"

"It's a bomb," said Nina, limping up to the cage.

"I surrender. No need to blow me up," he said, his arms in the air.

Kanasta arrived and met up with Nina, having her lean on his shoulder. The Vibrator sped off in terror.

"Mission accomplished," said Nina, slicing open the lock.

"Thank you all so much for rescuing me!" wailed February, bowing repeatedly.

"I'm the one who should be thanking you." Kanasta slammed his foot down on the Exp's head, bursting it open.

"I've never fought her before. Anything I should know?" Exp 8 hollered to Atlas as he fought against the increased gravity.

"The vertical distance between us and her is the difference in power. To take her down, we need to bring her to our level," said Atlas, flinging the Chaos Chain at the goddess.

Edirp's platform extended, reaching farther than the chains could reach.

"Thanks for the tip," said Exp 8, looking up at the sky. "ORB CONTROL." He brought his hand down.

The orb he had fired to disperse the crowd came crashing down into Edirp.

In a frantic attempt to dodge, her platform rapidly descended.

"I'll leave the rest to you," said Exp 8, forming a massive orb in his hand.

Atlas nodded and attached the Agony Axe to the end of his Chaos Chain. When Edirp was within range, he sent the axe into her, slicing her side and flooding her with agony.

Exp 8 slammed the orb against the side of the case arena housing August, but it was no use.

Inside the case, Demonica's blood tendrils were sliced by August's sharpened arm. The blood turned to bats, which were suddenly pierced by the spiky floor.

"You're a shape-shifter? This should be fun," said August.

"Fun as this is, there's really no need to fight," said Demonica, sending her arm out like a whip.

"Really? And why is that?" he asked, hardening part of his body while coating the rest of his body in blades.

"I want your help in breaking Zenero out of prison."

"When was he imprisoned?"

"Does it matter? I know you want to kill him, but the only way you'll get a chance is if you help us break him out," said Demonica, creating a trail of blood spikes as he ran up the wall.

August kicked off the ceiling and slammed his sharpened foot into Demonica, who parted her body to dodge it.

"So, do we have a deal?"

"Absolutely," he said before punching her.

"Then why are you still attacking me?" asked Demonica, dodging by splitting her body up.

"We can leave once this fight's over. I'm having a blast!" he exclaimed, catching her off guard by piercing her with spikes.

"If you insist." Demonica's arms sharpened into sickles and pressed against August's throat. "I win."

"Fair enough," said August, raising his arms.

"Good, now follow me," she said, creating a portal.

Devlin put his finger to his ear as Chipko approached. "I'll be right there!"

"Who was that?" asked Chipko.

"Kaity is in danger. If you really want to fight me, it will have to wait." He ran off before the ground beneath him burst.

Chipko leaped after him and thrust her aura-coated fist into him.

Devlin tumbled over the side of the roof.

Chipko leaped off and slammed her legs into him, bringing them both down to the street below. "I too have friends I must protect."

"Now is not the time!" Devlin's wires coiled up Chipko's legs, strangling them.

Chipko kicked him and blasted the wires off her all at once.

Devlin was sent skidding down the street. He pulled his wires in and put his head to the floor. "Please. Kaity is in danger. I love her more than anything."

"I…I was in love once," said Chipko softly.

"Then you understand that I have to save her."

"If I don't bring you in, they'll set fire to a forest. So many lives will be lost. Give up and you can save them."

"Alright. I'll surrender. I'll let you take me in, but only after I rescue Kaity. You have my word."

Chipko looked at him blankly. "You're serious?"

Devlin raised his head. "Absolutely."

"Then we'll go together," said Chipko.

Previously: Kaity plunged her claws into Sefiwah's chest.

"Okay. Hold the phone! Did you two break up or something?" asked Koshi.

Sefiwah kicked off of Kaity. Her flesh stretched out and covered the searing wound.

Regna climbed out of the hole from the wall she made. "I'm not in a good mood today."

"You look like you're never in a good mood," said Koshi, jumping back to dodge her glowing claws.

"I don't know who you are, but you better not get in my way!" yelled Regna, shooting off her arms. The enraged demoness watched in amazement as her arms traveled backward and shot into Sefiwah.

"My Love Artifact is working at full power. Now die!" yelled Kaity, firing at the glowing arms and triggering them to burst.

"Not sure who made you, hottie, but I know who beat you." Koshi slammed his palms into Regna, attaching two energy suppressors to her.

"Don't touch me!" yelled Regna, growing new arms and slicing the man.

"Oooh, feisty," said Koshi with a grin.

Kaity emerged from the smoke and rushed at Kaity.

"Now I'm even more confused," said Koshi.

"She's not Sefiwah. Her skin color is a bit off. She's a shape-shifter," said Kaity, as Yvne's arms extended and pierced her side. "Devlin, can you hear me? I've been ambushed! Come as soon as you can. There may be more of them."

"Hey! Hands off her!" yelled Koshi, shooting a full round into the mimic's face as Regna slashed his back. He flipped around and slammed his gun into Regna's face. "How are you still walking? Wait? Do you know the Prince of Pleasure? Are you two a new type of Exp?"

"The Prince is a mere demon lord. I'm a goddess!" exclaimed Regna, lunging at him.

Koshi leaned back to dodge the lunge but was hit head on by the aura blast that followed.

BoneSaw saw a chance and leaped into action, sawing the Kaity clone in two.

The two halves became BoneSaws that quickly cornered the little robot.

Koshi suddenly rushed at Kaity with a knife.

"What are you doing?" asked Kaity, dodging the first two swipes before slamming her arm into his and seizing the knife.

Blue energy burst out from Koshi's body, pushing out the red energy and knocking Kaity off her feet.

Koshi caught her in his arms. "Sorry about that. It appears she has multiple artifacts. But it's nothing I can't handle."

"Put Kaity down!" yelled Devlin, sending wires into the government spy.

Kaity sliced the incoming wires. "Wait. He's helping out...for now."

"He's their top agent. He can't be trusted," said Devlin.

"Not the top. And I went rogue recently. I'm just here to keep your girlfriend safe," said Koshi.

Chipko dropped in from above.

Koshi leaped back, dodging both Chipko's fist and Regna's next aura wave.

"Everything he's saying is a lie. He's Agent Alpha. And if he's smart, he'll tell his boss to call off his attack on the forest. Otherwise, your best will die here!" Her eyes flared up, and the red aura coated her body.

"Wonderful! She's welcoming the rage into her body," said Regna.

"New plan! Get Kaity out of here! I'm going to...run!" yelled Koshi, speeding off.

Chipko raced after him.

"At least he was useful for something. Are you hurt?" asked Devlin.

"Don't ignore me!" yelled Regna, firing off her arms.

Wires seized the arms and then slammed into Regna, triggering them to burst. "She'll regenerate quickly. Go after Chipko but keep your distance," said Devlin.

Kaity nodded and rushed off.

Kioshi was surprised when she found a floating sponge in Deceivant's bathroom. The surprise morphed into fear once the sponge grew blades from the large holes in its body.

Deceivant pulled her back and fired a gravity bullet.

The field from the bullet tore the sink out from the wall and sent Absorb smashing into the bathtub in the back.

"Get out of here! He's after me!" yelled Deceivant, detaching the Gravity Blade from Amy.

"But so am I. I can't leave without you," said Kioshi.

"Enemy!" yelled the Captain of Carnage, racing down the hall as the ground bloated beneath him.

Tsul rushed after him.

"Where is Ada?" asked Deceivant, crossing swords with Absorb.

"She's helping out in her own way," said the Captain before zip-lining toward Tsul.

Automated turrets popped out from the ceiling and opened fire on the goddess.

"Finally! Hey, you want me? Come get me!" yelled Deceivant, running around the bullet fire to the exit of the building.

Tsul rushed after him.

Just as Absorb left the bathroom, he was struck from behind.

"Do not test me little girl," said Absorb.

"I'm an Exp Hunter, not a little girl. My people are trained in advanced VR simulations to take your kind down. I've prepared for this moment my whole life!" she exclaimed before fleeing in terror as the giant sponge chased her.

She tossed anything she could find at the killer sponge and then dropped a smoke bomb to the floor.

"That won't work on me," said Absorb, pulling in the smoke. "What's this feeling?" The living sponge wobbled in the air, suddenly overcome with fatigue.

"Leeches are not only adorable, they are also the inspiration for many of our spy tech. There was a young Exp girl named Kawai who was able to leech energy off her opponents, allowing her to take down Exps stronger than her. Exp Hunters have made that power accessible to all our members. Have another!" she exclaimed, slamming her palms into Absorb and attaching a second energy suppressor.

"Deceivant must pay for what he's...." Absorb dropped to the floor and collapsed.

Deceivant leaped over cars as Tsul approached. "I can't use the grenades as long as there are civilians nearby. I wasn't thinking this through!"

A young, elegantly dressed girl stepped in Tsul's path. "You there, stop at once. I won't allow you to tarnish the credibility I've worked so hard to attain."

"Hope!" exclaimed Deceivant, rushing after her by maneuvering through the traffic. He yelled out as he came in proximity. "Tell me what you want? Please, just don't hurt her." The scientist fell to his knees in tears.

"Did you say something?" asked Hope with a smile.

Tsul had a vacant look in her eyes and was holding herself.

Deceivant grabbed Hope in his arms and ran down the street.

"I wasn't done with her. Having a sin in my forces would be most beneficial," said Hope.

"Come now, sweetie. How about we go see a play together?" Deceivant beamed at her.

"A play?" asked Hope with wide eyes. "Well, I'm not sure you're dressed for it."

"Then we'll stop by the tailors on the way."

"It has been awhile. Very well, I permit you to spoil me," said Hope, patting his head with a smile.

Chapter 148: Government Intervention

D.S. meets up with Crisis while searching the alleys.

"She's really good at hiding," said D.S.

"Gimpy is gone. I think he took her away already." Crisis slammed his fist into the wall. "She's just a kid…damn it!"

"Hey there!" hollered a black suit agent, dangling their feet over a rusted balcony.

"Did you see what happened to her?" asked Crisis.

"Nope, but you better hurry back to the jet. We leave in twenty minutes with or without you," said the youthful agent, hopping down and landing in front of them.

"You're the nice guy from the airport! I'm Destructus Supplious. What's your name?"

"Don't have one. My friends call me The Pilot," he said.

He was still in his teens based on his voice and height. His pilot helmet covered his face, and he was wearing military clothes over his black suit.

"How young were you when they took you from your parents?" asked Crisis.

"James, relax. You're so paranoid. You know humans are just another part of nature," said The Pilot, putting his arms beyond his back.

"Biologically, I agree. But we've lost our connection. Our instincts are dull and our respect is gone."

"I'm not here to argue with you. Now hurry up. I've got orders to bring you back," he said, leading the way down the alley.

"Um, so, are you the good guys or the bad guys?" asked D.S., his finger on his bottom lip.

"We're agents of change, that's all. We keep the peace while paving the way toward the future," said The Pilot.

D.S. tugged on Crisis' shirt. "So, are they good or bad?"

"I certainly don't trust a government funded by Big Agriculture, Big Oil, and Big Pharma," said Crisis.

"You sound like someone I know," said The Pilot with a grin.

"Really, who's that?" asked Crisis, tilting his head slightly.

"No more talking. Just follow me."

Toxic awakes in a daze, noticing her target has left. When she speeds to the door, a spongy ball blocks her path. "Why do you serve someone who sees us only as tools?" The snake lashed her tail at her opponent.

Rather than dodge, Fusion merged with the tail on impact. The sticky ball spun around, skidding Toxic across the ground. Toxic lunged and sank her fangs into the adversary.

Fusion combined with her head.

"It's already over," said Toxic muffled.

Fusion slammed the attacker against the metal tiles, trying to knock her off.

Toxic finally released her fangs and was sent flying across the room.

Fusion raced up to the attacker.

"My toxin will only paralyze you. I'm saving my fatal venom for emergencies."

The poison took effect, and Fusion froze in place. Toxic slithered out of the room and rushed down the halls.

Muffins met up with Opti in the waiting room, dragging her invisible prisoner behind them.

"Well, we got what we came for. Let's go," said Opti. "Wait, where is Fusion?"

Toxic entered the waiting room.

The woman at the front desk looked up at the metal snake as it approached.

Muffins fired out needles each time Toxic lunged, knocking the snake back but unable to pierce her metal plates.

The lady at the front desk held her finger to her ear. She had red hair and wore slim glasses with a red trim. "This is Agent Iota. There are five of them here. Do I engage?" she asked in a shaky voice with false bravado.

"Don't fight!" yelled Opti, stepping in the way. "Can we please talk this out?"

"With pleasure. If I don't bring Durga back with me, Sel will kill Ada. She's my mother and I will protect her," said Toxic.

"You're worried about nothing. Sel is a liar. He wouldn't kill Ada. He wants her alive so he can control Deceivant."

"He tried to devour her soul in Elysium! There is nothing he won't do!" yelled Toxic.

"Elysium. Possible gathering spot for them. I repeat, do I engage?" asked Agent Iota.

"Okay, but do you really want to work with someone who would harm your mother?" asked Opti.

"No. I don't." Toxic dropped her head.

"Then why don't we go back together and figure out what to do then, okay?"

"Okay," said Toxic with a frown.

"Don't frown, Auntie. Your smile is so pretty," said Opti.

Toxic beamed at him.

"Yeah! I'm going to go in and fetch Fusion. I'll be right back," said Opti, slipping on the special handling gloves.

"Alright. I'm sending the data now," said the lady behind the desk.

Nina held her katana to Kanasta's throat. "Why did you kill him?"

"For two hundred fifty K and, more importantly, for the credibility of the Viper Squad."

"I failed Devlin because of you!" she yelled.

Kanasta ducked under the sword and lifted the jeep up. "You did nothing wrong. I apologize for ruining your mission. But you must realize that Devlin's feelings for you won't change because of one success or failure."

"I have a duty!"

"As do I! I will not allow the Viper Squad to lose their importance. This world needs honorable assassins."

"Devlin needs honorable warriors, and you just killed one."

"Don't kid yourself. You saw his eyes. He was a coward. He's worth more to us dead than alive."

"Perhaps you're the same way," said Nina, sliding her blade down his shoulder.

"You won't kill me. Leave. I must round up the bodies and deliver them to the client."

"Absolutely not. You're coming back with me now, and you're going to explain to Devlin why the mission was a failure."

"I'm not returning until I've turned in the bounty. And there are a few stops I'd like to make for some other clients. It may be a few days before I can return."

Nina dropped her gaze to the floor. "If I kiss you, will you come? I know you like me."

Kanasta looked over his shoulder. "I'd like you to join the Viper Squad. My feelings toward you are purely business related."

"I know why you're so obsessed with your killer's code. You're afraid of realizing you're just a murderer in a suit."

"Either help me round up the bodies or leave," said Kanasta through clenched teeth.

"We're better off without you anyway," said Nina, walking away from the selfish man.

Once she was gone from sight, a large black suit agent appeared hoisting four bodies over his shoulders. He was wearing a helmet with a bat-like design.

"Much appreciated. What is your name?" asked Kanasta.

"The less you know the better," said the agent in a surprisingly youthful voice considering his size. He tossed the bodies into the back of the jeep.

"I like you already," said Kanasta, walking alongside the man to fetch the rest of the bodies.

"You've been a great help to us. I'm happy to return the favor."

"I'm looking for new members. Would you like to apply?"

"I already have a family, but the offer is appreciated. Well, if I'm going to ask for your help, I suppose I should introduce myself after all. I'm Agent Kappa." He offered his hand, which was firmly grasped by Kanasta. "I have a job offer for you from my boss. And as you know, government jobs are reliable and secure."

"I'm listening," said Kanasta.

"Richard Dawkins, head of the Humans First movement. We want him dead by the end of the week. Make it showy and bloody too."

"I'll consider it."

"We'll go over the documentation on the ride back, and we can make a few stops as needed if you'll comply."

"There is a woman traveling with me. She won't approve."

"Not to worry. Someone will be escorting her back to the jet you came from. A little ways in the jungle is my jet. We can go where you'd like once you agree to the terms."

"I thought Richard Dawkins supported your boss. Why is he the target?"

"That is confidential. That won't be a problem, will it?"

"Absolutely not. I'll look over the contract and confirm he is indeed the target by speaking directly with your boss."

"Absolutely. I'm just the messenger. Um, can you identify these guys? Their faces are charred," said the agent, lifting up the poachers who were killed by a rocket bursting.

"Just the teeth will be enough to identify them."

"I'll just take the top off then," said the agent, cutting off the head with his extended knife. "It's true what you said. The world needs assassins. Some revolutions need to be snuffed out and others need their fire stoked. The death of a figurehead can do either depending on how the news delivers the message."

"You're a journalist. Be careful, bending the story to the whims of the highest bidder can ruin your credibility," said Kanasta.

"I'm true to the facts, as true as needed. Either way, my competition keeps dying off. It's such a wonderful coincidence," he said, sawing off the head of another poacher.

"Cutting corners is efficient, but it's a slippery slope to mediocrity," said Kanasta.

"I've buried a few stories about a credible group of assassins. There was this one story where a prominent journalist was shot dead in his own bathroom. Didn't seem like front page material."

Kanasta smiled. "Help me with some jobs. You can intern."

"Well, I can't very well refuse that offer. I'll have a lot of new stories to write by the time I return."

"We shall write them together." Kanasta placed his hand on the agent's back.

After taking three turns through the forest, Nina leaned against a tree and cried. "I don't even know the way back."

"Dry your tears, heathen," said a deep evangelical voice brimming with compassion.

Nina turned around to see a broad-shouldered white suit agent, as muscular as a rhino and as tall as a gorilla. His Hunter suit was designed like a priest's robe. The agent's helmet had a cross design and only showed his intense brown eyes. "Were you the one who brought us here? He isn't coming, so just take me home."

"Your people threaten everything we've established." He grabbed Nina's hand.

The warrior pulled back. "What is this thing?" she asked, tugging at the device she had snatched.

"It is like holy water to you demons," said the agent with a benevolent tone.

Nina held her sides and screamed out in agony. She leaped at the enemy only to be slammed down by his massive fists. The injured ninja drew her katana as his fist came down, her body shaking from the pain.

The agent punched the blade, having it poke out his elbow. He pulled Nina into him by pulling back his arm. "The Messiah takes away my pain, insignificant as it is." His head smashed against hers. "I ask the Lord to lend me his power." The agent lowered his head.

The ninja warrior took this opportunity to toss a spear into the man.

The suit expanded on its own, covering his head for an instant to deflect the spear.

"My flesh follows the lord's will," said the agent, smashing the heathen's weapon and tossing it aside.

Nina tore out her sword, slicing the man's trunk of an arm open.

The agent did not flinch. "What is a demon doing with a religious blade? Do you know what the transcription says?"

"Not a clue and I'm not a demon." Nina pressed her sword to his neck. "The only reason I haven't cut open your throat is because I realize that my every action determines the future Devlin has sacrificed so much for."

Tears dripped from the agent's face to the floor.

"What are you sad about?"

Nina froze for an instant when the man's eyes met hers. They were like a violent flame behind a waterfall.

His fist, coated in a blue aura, smashed through her sword, breaking it before smashing into her.

Nina gagged before being launched into a tree. The tree broke upon impact, and Nina was pierced by the jagged wood. "That sword was a memento. You'll pay."

He approached her as she pulled herself out of the wood. "You demons dare to feign devotion? I should send you back to the pits you came from!"

Nina tossed shurikens before breaking free and falling to the ground.

The shurikens bounced off the agent's suit.

"Your devotion to your dark lord is hollow and weak," he said, smashing her hand beneath his foot.

Nina stabbed his leg with her free hand, but her dagger wasn't sharp enough to pierce. "If it were weak, it wouldn't hurt me. If it were hollow, I would have lost the will to fight long ago." She wrapped her legs around his arm and tightened them.

"You will see how little your dark lord cares for you. I'm bringing you in as insurance. Your dark kin will learn to obey the Lord's will or they will die." The agent walked to the tree and slammed her against it repeatedly, piercing her with the wooden spikes. "Suffering is the only way to cleanse you of sin. As beings of sin, your only chance at salvation is a constant bath of agony."

Nina's grip weakened and she released his leg.

The agent tore her from the tree and tossed her down onto the dirt road. "If you keep struggling, you will die." He opened up his robe and placed a white blanket onto her back. He poured a green salve on the blanket that entered her wounds and expanded like foam, sealing them up. "You've spat on the Lord's merciful wishes yet his mercy does not waver." The agent took a rounded dart from his belt and pressed it into the back of her neck. He placed his hand to his ear. "The demon has been captured."

"Good work, Sigma. Bring her to base."

"It shall be done." Sigma turned his attention back to his captive. "Rest now, heathen. You will see soon enough that Hell is more than myth. I cannot bring you home at this time, but I assure you your stay with us will remind you of the inferno you covet." He picked her up by her hair and walked off.

Hope watched the performance from the back row, seated on Deceivant's lap to get a better view. She leaned back with tears in her eyes.

"After all those years, she's finally reunited with her father. It's beautiful," said Deceivant, his tears dripping down onto Hope's face.

Hope grasped his hands. "I'm not crying because of the play, you buffoon. I…I missed this." She leaned against his shoulder. "You brought me back home as promised. As a reward, I order you to be my servant again. You will follow my every—" She squeaked in surprise when he suddenly embraced her.

"I gladly accept."

"D-Don't think this means I've forgiven you for what you've done. There are many reasons I made this decision. Scowling at you will leave me with horrid wrinkles, after all. And a good queen must put politics before personal feelings. After all, we've got a long road ahead of us before my people gain equal rights and are treated equally. You're still my servant and you will obey my orders, understood?"

"Absolutely, my queen," said Deceivant, planting a kiss on her forehead.

"No talking. It's incredibly rude to speak during a performance, even if we are in the back row because you weren't punctual," said Hope, raising her nose and crossing her arms.

Deceivant zipped his lips and smiled at her.

Hope smiled a little, sat up straight, and diverted her gaze back to the play.

Kioshi, having stuffed Absorb in a very large suitcase, was now stuffing the case in the back of her purple car. "Come on!" she exclaimed, slamming the trunk a third time before it sealed shut.

"You're back," said the Prince in the back seat. "I was starting to worry."

"Aww, why would you worry about me?" asked Kioshi with flushed cheeks, starting up the engine.

"The most beautiful flowers are the most delicate," said the Prince, caressing her shoulder.

"Well, this pretty flower has been through a few storms and made it out just fine," she said, slowing down when her car signaled she was over the speed limit.

"The plan remains, I assume. Your boss will speak to me directly?"

"Yep, and since I brought you in, I get to be there when you two have your discussion," said Kioshi.

"That's no good. I'll be distracted the entire time," said the Prince.

Kioshi blushed, signaling a car to pull in front of her. "After the discussion, maybe you could come to my room. I doubt my brother will be back by then. He's on an important mission," she said, rolling her eyes.

"Weren't you assigned to capture Deceivant?"

"Oh, I lied about that. I just wanted to prove my worth, and he's eluded the Boss so far. I did put a tracker on him, and I did capture something."

"There's nothing I find more alluring than a confident woman," said the Prince, rubbing her shoulders from the back seat.

"Hey, uh. Stop light." She leaned back and kissed his lips. "So, um, do you have a girlfriend back home?"

"I parted ways with her. She was a princess."

"Oh, hope I don't feel like a downgrade," said Kioshi softly.

"Not at all. I'll take a confident young lady over a broken princess any day. You're a very special girl, you know," he said.

"Okay. We're here. Annnnd there's the jet," she said, pulling behind a warehouse.

Kaity rushed after Chipko as the environmentalist pursued Agent Alpha, knocking aside anything in her path with powerful shockwaves.

"You came to rescue me? I'm touched, but I can handle her," said Koshi, keeping his hands behind his back as he ran backward through the alleyways.

"I'm making sure you don't take her. She's coming with me," said Kaity.

"I totally understand. She's my type too," said Koshi, running backward and waving at her.

Chipko slammed her fist to the ground, making the spy lose his balance.

"Flying Shockwave!" exclaimed Chipko as she rapidly punched up, sending the government agent to the skies.

Koshi whipped out a machine gun and fired as Chipko leaped after him.

The bullets were pushed away by a pulse of her aura.

The agent tensed his body as her fist slammed into him. After being blasted into the side of a building, he rolled and ran up it.

Kaity went on all fours to catch up to Chipko and then pounced on her. "He's leading you into a trap."

Chipko slammed Kaity into the ground and collected energy in her fist. "Call off the attack on the forest or I'll kill her!"

Koshi hopped off the building and approached Chipko. "I'm not the one who ordered that attack. Right now I'm supposed to be on a mission in Israel. I came to Russia to see Kaity. So threatening me is pointless."

Chipko fell to her knees in tears. "Please. I beg you."

"Nothing more beautiful than a powerful woman crying at my feet." Alpha put his hand to his ear. "Epsilon, I'm pretty sure you're still in charge here. Oh, by here I mean Russia. Yes, I know I'm supposed to be...look, don't tell the Boss, okay? Yes, I'll make it up to you, babe. But the reason I called is I was hoping you'd call off the forest burning." He looks up at Chipko. "What forest was it again?"

"I'm not sure."

Koshi held his head. "You really are way too easy. Surprisingly virtuous for a mass murderer." He turned his attention back to the agent on the other line. "Oh, thanks, babe. You're as kind as you are beautiful."

Chipko looked up at him.

Koshi bent down and patted her head. "Dry those pretty eyes; random forest twelve is safe."

Chipko embraced him and cried on his shoulder.

"Like I said, she's adorable," said Koshi, winking at the cute assassin.

"Chipko, I'd like to talk to you alone. I need your help," said Kaity.

"What, don't trust me?" asked Koshi.

"I don't."

"Then you'll have to kill me because I'm at least bringing back some intel from this vacay," said Koshi.

"Fine. Chipko, there is a great enemy we need help fighting. Many Exps are coming together."

"Where is the enemy?" asked Chipko.

"I can't say," said Kaity, eyeing the grinning agent.

"Then I can't help," said Chipko.

"Just threaten to burn Stacy over there," said Koshi, pointing to a potted plant on a balcony.

"Chipko, the afterlife is in danger," said Kaity.

"Mother Earth is my concern. I'm doing what I can to help in my own way," said Chipko, lifting up one of the trashcans she had knocked over.

"You know, you could ask for my help," said Koshi, grabbing Kaity's hips.

"Chipko, you were made by Zenero, right? Well, we need your help to keep his power from falling into the wrong hands," said Kaity.

"Zenero has been dead for decades," said Koshi.

Chipko turned to Kaity. "You'll take me to see him?"

"Absolutely."

"Then I'll help in any way I can," said Chipko, her fist to her chest.

"Alright then. If you two lovely ladies would just follow me, we can head back to my jet and—"

"Devlin and BoneSaw are still fighting. We have to help them," said Kaity.

"Kaity, there was an agent assigned to monitor each group. The agent watching your team was tasked with capturing Devlin. I'm only telling you this so we don't waste our time backtracking. Devlin is probably already captured and being delivered to my boss."

Kaity ran off on all fours.

"You're wasting your time!" hollered Koshi.

Devlin and BoneSaw teamed up to fight against Yvne and Regna.

The little robot created smoke clouds and slid out while the two copies battled.

Devlin's wires shot out to deflect any projectiles Regna sent his way.

"Once we're done with you, your gal pal is next. You must be punished for betraying Lord Sel," said Regna, shooting her aura into him.

Devlin closed his eyes and released the aura out from the tips of his wires. "Funny. Your boss was rather thrilled about the betrayal. Oh, and by the way, Kaity is too skilled to be taken down by you." His wires poured dark energy into the ground beneath Regna.

The ground collapsed beneath her. The buildings fell into the pit as the puddle of darkness spread.

"Sister!" Yvne turned into a puddle and rushed into the pit to save Regna.

Devlin pulled the dark energy back into his wires. "I guess I've been in that armor so long, my body internalized the energy. Fancy that." He picked up BoneSaw, leaped over the pit, and ran off in the direction Kaity was in.

Something stabbed into his leg and he toppled over.

He scanned the nearby windows but saw no one.

Three glowing blue needles were poking out of his leg.

Another volley of blue needles came flying from behind.

Devlin's wires sped past the needles and seized the one throwing them.

The white suit agent was camouflaged with the building behind her. She was wearing a belt with various torture devices on it. Her helmet had a spider design and stared at Devlin with its many eyes. When she removed her helmet, her short purple hair fell. The woman had full purple lips, rosy cheeks, and a slender build. Devlin's wires shivered when he saw her merciless green eyes. "Hi there," she said with a wave.

"W-What do you want?" asked Devlin, freezing in place.

"I'm taking you back to base. There are so many experiments I never got a chance to test on you," said the woman, shifting between a seductive and playful voice as she hopped up to him.

"You're not taking me anywhere!" Devlin tried to will his wires to attack but they wouldn't listen.

BoneSaw rushed in only to be lifted up by her foot and sent into the air.

The agent detached a glowing blue marble from her belt and flung it into the robot.

BoneSaw lost power and fell to her feet.

"Fear is such a powerful weapon. Your wires act on your subconscious. After all these years, your body still remembers me." She walked up to Devlin with an excited grin and dragged her hands down his chest.

Energy suppressors pierced into his skin and ate away at his vitality.

She placed neon green cuffs on his hands and feet, then put a collar around his neck. "I wonder how long before I break my new toy."

The case collapsed and Demonica walked out.

"I thought you were going after Stabby," said Exp 8.

"Kidnapping her would give Sel bargaining power over Sellum. I'm on Devlin's side," said Demonica.

"Where is August?" asked Atlas.

"He's with Sel now," said Demonica, digging the sand out from under her nails.

"Why would you turn him over to our enemy? August is one of the greatest fighters I've ever known," said Atlas.

"It's a bit of a gamble, but I think it will end up helping Devlin in the long run. Time will tell," said Demonica before lifting up Edirp and strutting into a portal.

A large black suit agent approached the team. "The longer I keep the police away from this area, the more suspicious things become. Let us leave shortly. Your other two partners are already on board," he said, gesturing to the jet in the distance.

The plane exploded, sending a jet of fire into the air.

Smoke covered the team.

Atlas ran out of the cloud to the plane, but Exp 8 adjusted his vision and searched for the attacker.

The man placed his palm on Exp 8's chest. His Hunter suit was red, which matched the red patterns and demonic teeth of the oni samurai helmet concealing his face. "The others are fine, I assure you," he said in a kind and dreary voice that contrasted his intense demeanor.

Exp 8's eyes widened as a sudden burst of energy exploded into him. He skidded down the bazaar, crashing into several stands.

The agent chased after his target. "Every cause needs a martyr," he said under his breath.

Exp 8 sped up to the agent with his jets at full throttle.

Two energy orbs exploded into the agent.

Ripples of energy traveled from the point of impact on the agent's suit and gathered onto his fist, giving it a red hue.

"Your own power will destroy you." The agent gripped Exp 8's shoulders. "**IMPACT RELEASE**."

Metal shred and twisted.

Exp 8 fell to the sand, his body in tatters.

"I may have gone overboard." He picked up the fallen rebel and hoisted him onto his shoulders. "I'm returning to base with the target. The reports are wrong. He is not the Ultimate Exp."

Chapter 149: The Long Journey Home

Hope and Deceivant, having finished the theatrical performance, were taking a stroll down the street.

"Eyes ahead. Don't want you tripping because you were ogling some little girl," said Hope, slamming her foot into his belly.

"I'm just appreciating nature's art."

A woman with long braided hair and blue eyes made larger through her spectacles stood up from the table she was seated behind. "Lovely lady, would you like your fortune told?"

"No, thanks. We don't believe in hocus pocus," said Deceivant.

"Don't be rude. We would absolutely love a fortune," said Hope, stuffing Deceivant's hand into his pocket.

"Yes. Apologies about before," said Deceivant, giving the woman her payment.

"Come in and sit," said the woman, beckoning them past the strings of beads into her tent.

Deceivant set his darling daughter down.

"Wait outside. I shan't have your skepticism get in the way of my reading," said Hope.

"Okay. Daddy will be just past those beads," he said with a smile.

"Ugh. Go!" commanded Hope.

Deceivant bowed and then left.

"So, shall we begin?" asked the fortune teller.

Hope stared into her eyes. "You're a hard one to read."

The fortune teller grabbed Hope's hand. "Close your eyes."

"Are you reading my mind or my fortune?" asked Hope, her eyes shut.

The fortune teller held her phone beneath the desk, skimming information about the Exp. "You're afraid of your father," she said, reading an article about Hope's murder.

The little queen's hand trembled. "Mind your tongue."

"You fear getting close to him."

"I fear him getting close to me."

"You should be cautious of your every move. I sense a great struggle on the horizon."

"Are you threatening me, Debbie?" Hope opened her eyes.

"I never said my name."

"An agent who can't even keep her name secret. How pitiful. Why are you Agent Beta, the penultimate Exp Hunter, if you can't even manage to fool your prey?"

The fortune teller smiled. "You're a clever little girl."

"Indeed. I came into this tent because I would like a meeting with your boss at his place. Do forward my message." Hope turned around. "Escort, we're done here!"

Deceivant came inside. "Is everything alright?"

"Fine. Except my dress. It's old. I want a new one," said Hope as they left the tent.

D.S. and Crisis followed The Pilot out of the alleyway.

The ex-gangster looks at the chaos on the street, crashed cars, police lights, and screaming humans. "We should help them."

"If we help them, we'll only bring attention to ourselves. We've caused enough trouble already," said Crisis.

"And I have orders to get you out of here as soon as I can," said the agent.

"This doesn't feel right. They're hurt because of us," said D.S.

"Things we do or don't do end up causing others pain. Sometimes we just have to look the other way and move on," said Crisis.

"I thought you were a nice guy. I guess I was wrong," said D.S.

"If we go in there to help, we'll end up getting shot at. And that will mean more will end up getting hurt. We're heading back and that's final," said Crisis.

"You aren't my mom!" yelled D.S.

"But your parents expect me to watch over you. I won't fail them," said Crisis.

"Fine. Let's just get on the stupid plane so I can talk to mommy," said D.S.

"We're being followed," said The Pilot, turning around and aiming his pistol.

Wringer emerged from the shadows.

D.S. approached the chain guy. "So, we're going to stop a big bad guy. Want to help?"

Wringer nodded.

"Good. At least we won't be coming back empty-handed. Come along," said Crisis, sending a wind gust that lifted a car off of a screaming person.

D.S. looked up at Crisis and grinned.

Kaity found BoneSaw and noticed the marks left by Devlin's wires. She approached Koshi with her head lowered.

"See? Told you. Waste of time."

"Rest easy. As far as I know, they've never killed an Exp," said Chipko.

"What do I have to do?"

"Are you asking me or yourself?" asked Koshi, crouching and looking up at her.

"What do I have to do to get you to save him?" asked Kaity, her hands shivering.

"Hmmm." Koshi slid his hand up her thigh and to her face. He then brought his hands down to her shoulders and grasped her hands. "You don't have to do anything. I'll get him back to you." He smiled.

"Really?" asked Kaity, still shivering.

"I owe you so much already. Consider this just part of my past dues. Oh, and add a couple assassinations, which I credited to the Viper Squad, as part of my payment."

Kaity nearly knocked him down as she launched herself into him like a joyous missile. "Thank you! Thank you! Thank you!"

"Come on, we're practically family. Oh, crap." Koshi put his hand to his ear. "Hey, boss. Did you hear that Venus will be out tonight? Better get out that telescope. Who knows? You might even spot a UFO."

"Why aren't you at Guantanamo Bay?"

"Because we always pin the murders on someone in our way. Thank you so much for keeping me safe despite the truckloads of bodies I've—"

"The mission! Why aren't you there completing it!?"

"Well, funny story about that. See, I was going to go there, but something urgent came up," said Koshi, getting up from the ground and walking off.

"You do realize who keeps your sister safe, don't you?"

Koshi's face went pale. "What are your orders?"

"The agents at the prison aren't fit for the task, but the Exps are already leaving. Return to base immediately. Is that clear?"

"Absolutely. As soon as I drop off Kaity and Chipko."

"Chipko is with you?"

Alpha spoke in a hushed voice. "Yes, sir. She was attacked by some unknown Exp."

"Then it's a good thing you were there to defend her."

"See? Not a total waste of time, after all. Sometimes you gotta just go with your gut feeling."

"Your insubordination ended up working in our favor this time. Don't let that encourage future acts of disloyalty."

Alpha bowed. "Your mercy will never be forgotten. I'll be back at base by midnight."

"Don't fail me."

"Ask him about Devlin," said Kaity.

Koshi hung up. "I know who has Devlin, and I'll talk to her as soon as I get back to base."

"Promise?" asked Kaity, looking at him with worry.

"I promise," said Koshi, patting her head with a shaken smile.

Kanasta pulled out his phone as he waited to speak with the park ranger.

"Kaity, are you there?"

"Yeah. Is everything okay?"

"I'm going to complete a few jobs before returning to base. It may take a few days. Would you like to do the same?"

"I know the Viper Squad is counting on us. And I'm sure we have a lot to catch up on since we went away, but there are more important things at stake. There are so many who need our help right now. I'm heading back to base and hope you'll do the same."

"There's a target in the city you're in. Could you at least take him out?"

"Alright. I'll do it. Send me the info. Just be careful, okay?"

"I will and thank you."

"You're welcome. Oh, can I talk to Nina really quick?"

"We're not going together. She'll be heading back shortly. I just sent you the information."

"Who's that?" asked Koshi, peeking over her shoulder.

Kaity pulled her phone away. "None of your business."

"Don't be like that. Come on, if we work together, you can get home sooner."

"He's my target. He's recently been spotted in this city. Shouldn't be too hard to track down," said Kaity.

"Is he an enemy of Mother Earth?" asked Chipko.

"I don't know and it doesn't matter," said Kaity, walking off.

"He looked like a kid. How old is he?" asked Koshi.

"About fourteen. Says he's the son of a politician."

"Having a death in the family would certainly harm someone's campaign, or maybe it could give an unknown candidate the spotlight," said Chipko.

"You're overthinking things. We get our target and we shoot them. It's that simple," said Kaity, checking her ammo.

Koshi snatched the phone from her hand. "He's thirteen. Count me out."

"What? Not properly dressed for the occasion?" asked Kaity with a glare.

"I don't kill kids. Period," said Koshi.

"Well, you learn something new every day," said Kaity, putting her arms behind her back after taking back her phone.

"Hey, don't act like that. What's wrong with having some moral standards?" asked Koshi.

"You're talking about moral standards after what you almost did to me?" asked Kaity, her hands shaking.

"That was years ago," said Koshi softly.

"It shouldn't matter if someone has been alive for thirty years or ten. Karma doesn't care about your age, neither do the Furies. What does matter is whether or not you are guilty. I don't hurt innocents," said Chipko.

"And how can you determine who is innocent?" asked Koshi.

"Ever heard of an ecological footprint? There's a certain threshold that is permissible. Anything beyond that isn't," said Chipko, adjusting her gloves.

"You just dropped a bomb! The Furies are trying to impose the Eco-Footprint Network, not in the hopes of fostering environmental accountability but as a means of tracking down the biggest threats. You terrorists sure are organized. Why did you spill that little secret to me?"

Chipko looked away with flushed cheeks. "I trust you."

"Here's what we're going to do. I'm going with Chipko for a bite to eat and to get her some new clothes while Kaity goes after her target. We meet back in an hour at that bench. Everyone okay with that?"

Chipko grabbed his hand. "I'm okay with it, but I don't eat anything."

"That's fine. The meal is just for me," he said with a smile.

"Be careful around him," said Kaity before signaling BoneSaw to follow her.

"Chipko, did you know that all three of the biggest sponsors of the Furies are UN representatives?"

"I didn't know that. Seems strange considering the likely size of their footprint," said Chipko.

"The old man I work for is one of their absolute biggest sponsors. Zenero may have helped make the environmental issue a bipartisan one, but it was my boss who removed his political obstacles."

"I thought the Furies did that," said Chipko.

"Terrorism can be used to weaken a government or to strengthen it. My boss uses conflict to get ahead. Some say he's the most Republican of the Democrats, others say he's so far Left he makes the other Democrats look like Republicans. Did you know he got voted into the Senate with thirty-two percent Republican support and only twenty-six percent Democrat support, despite running as a Democrat? Some say he's even an Independent. But you know what I see? Someone who is trying to change his party for the better. I may not agree with his politics, but I admire his charisma."

"Why are you telling me all this?" asked Chipko, still holding the agent's hand.

"I want you to know that the Furies have his support and they have my support too. You've been a great help to us, and we're likely going to need your help in the future."

"I don't do what I do to win your boss' approval. I am just trying to do what everyone knows must be done but refuses to do."

"You take matters into your own hands. It's so admirable. But most of your attacks are reactive. I was thinking it's time to catch the enemy by surprise and deal a powerful blow."

"The enemy is a lack of responsibility, a political system that fosters greed and a short-sighted ideology that proclaims humans as the only beings with worth."

"Right you are. But every movement has its icons, and when the icon is tarnished, the movement suffers."

Chipko leaned on his shoulder. "Thanks for supporting me."

"Come on, you get plenty of support from the Furies and those who support them, don't you?"

"Well, yes, but they see me as some sort of god or celebrity. You treat me...like a person, not an object." Chipko looked up at him with a torrent of tears dripping from her cheeks. "I love you." She embraced him.

Koshi wrapped his arms around her. "I love you too," he said with a grin.

BoneSaw, hiding in plain sight, scratched its top with its saw.

Hope returns home in her father's arms wearing a cute but expensive frilly purple and gold skirt. She now had blue ribbons in her blonde hair drills.

"Welcome back," said the Captain of Carnage, lowering his blades.

"Proper etiquette should be rewarded. As should your dedication to keeping this place safe. Servant, I want you to begin working on some new weapons for our new tenant, but only after you brew some tea."

"As you command, my queen." Deceivant set her on the couch and joined Ada in the kitchen.

"My word, look at the time," said Hope, noticing the digital clock above the widescreen television. "Best check up on the others." She grabbed the remote and set up a group call on the television.

"Hi!" exclaimed D.S., waving too close to the camera.

"Most of you should have completed your tasks by now. But don't all talk at once. D.S., how did your mission go?"

"Let me answer," said Crisis, taking the phone.

"Hey, she asked me."

"Just let me handle this, okay?"

"D.S., let him speak," said Hope.

"Fine," said D.S., crossing his arms and sticking out his tongue when Crisis turned to face the phone screen.

"We can't confirm, but it looks like Flash Girl was captured by the enemy. As you can see, D.S. and I are safe. We're on our way back and Wringer has decided to come along."

"You fought admirably, I assume. Opti, what about you?" asked Hope.

"I'm doing great! Thanks!" exclaimed Opti.

"Hi, Opti," said D.S., waving at the screen.

"Oh, hi!" responded Opti.

"Skip the pleasantries. Tell me whether or not your trip was successful," said Hope.

"Oh, well. Fusion, Muffins, and I are safe. I thought I convinced Durga to join, but Muffins said I was hallucinating. The good news is she is with us and so is Toxic. Say hi to everyone, Toxic," said Opti, grabbing her tail and waving it at the camera.

"Hi!" exclaimed D.S.

"Great work recovering my invention," said Deceivant.

"Yes, you've performed quite well indeed. I'm most pleased. Kanasta, what about you?" asked Hope.

"Nina is on her way back on a separate plane. I'm going to see what I can learn about the black suit agents. I may be a few days late," said Kanasta.

"Were you able to retrieve February?" asked Hope.

"He's dead," said Kanasta before hanging up.

"Um, did Nina pick up?" asked Kaity, part of her sniper rifle visible from the phone camera.

"She didn't. What are you doing?" asked Hope.

"Waiting for the target," said Kaity, returning her gaze to the sniper scope.

"Were you able to recruit Chipko?"

"Yeah. But something happened and Devlin was captured. I have someone on the inside who is going to free him," said Kaity, checking the wind with her finger.

"One of the agents captured Devlin?" asked Hope.

"Yeah. I'll be careful on the way back," said Kaity.

"Why would they capture him?" asked Atlas.

"Devlin is one of the Exps they want. Wait, where is Exp 8?" asked Hope.

"He's on another plane," said Atlas.

"Are you certain?" asked Hope.

Image took the phone. "We were told he was being brought to their base to speak directly to the agent's leader. That could be a lie, though it seems likely to be true from what my husband told me."

"We must assume the worst. How did the mission go?" asked Hope.

"August was captured, and Demonica destroyed the jet we arrived in," said Atlas.

Image leaned in. "Once again, that's only what we were told. All we know is that the jet we arrived in exploded. But considering they had another jet nearby, it seems more likely the agents blew up their own plane."

Hope clenched her dress. "I was hoping we could work with the agents and their boss, but they've spat on my offer of peace. I won't do anything brash until I've spoken directly to their leader on the matter. But if they think they can use hostages to control my people, they are severely mistaken. If they decide to make an enemy of me, I will crush their organization."

Part 18
Propaganda & Politics

Chapter 150: Awaiting Orders

Gimpy arrived at the Core and unraveled the strings binding Flash Girl with a snap of the fingers.

"What are you planning on doing with me?" asked Flash Girl, searching the area for some form of exit.

"Calm down, sister." August helped Flash Girl to her feet. "Whoever is in charge wants to break out Zenero."

"I thought you hated Zenero."

"That was a long time ago. He's needed now more than ever."

"Flash Girl encounters her brother again after so many years, and he tells her that she's been recruited to rescue the man who created her. Are his intentions pure, or is there something sinister going on behind the scenes? Find out what perils await our young heroine next issue."

"You don't trust me. I can't say I entirely blame you."

"I can't miss out on an opportunity to create suspense. It's not personal. So, where are we anyway?" She pulled out a camera from her utility belt and took photos of the dome of darkness, illuminated by a sphere of lava flowing around it.

"Honestly, I haven't the faintest idea. I'm guessing it's somewhere in Sel, but I'm not sure where."

"It's been so long I had nearly forgotten about the afterlife. Do you think I'll alienate my readers by bringing Heaven and Hell into the comics? They are more used to an urban setting. There've only been a few issues where I go outside New York, and they haven't gotten the best reviews."

"I actually happen to like 'Flash Girl in India'; one of the best in the series if you ask me."

"Wait, you read my stories?"

"It's the best way to keep track of you. I know you can handle yourself, but it makes me feel better to know what you're up to."

"What have you been up to? Chipko's becoming more ruthless as time goes on. I think one day I'll have to stop her myself, and I fear that day is coming closer and closer. Oooh, that will work great for an end quote."

"I've been traveling the world in search of strong opponents. Something tells me I'm going to run into a lot of them soon enough."

"What's the deal with Bondage Boy there? Or maybe it's Gimp Girl?"

"No clue. I was brought here by a demoness. She easily outclassed me. Oh, by the way, Casey is going to help too."

"Figured as much. I'm questioning this mission more and more."

"Don't worry. If Zenero tries to attack us, I'll take him down," said August, seizing her hand.

"What sort of powerful being took down the previous Sellum, and is he friend or foe? Hey, maybe we could make this a crossover comic."

"Do what you want. But I don't have my own comic line, so it wouldn't be a true crossover."

"Well then, maybe all you need is a debut. With superhero movies and comics as popular as they are now, you'd be a fool to miss out."

"I'm staying focused on the mission for the time being."

"So, when is the breakout?"

"Don't know. Right now we are awaiting orders."

Hope was reading the news on the New York terror attack when the doorbell rang.

"I'll get it." Ada stopped Hope's shoulder rub and danced to the door.

"Mommy!" exclaimed D.S., seizing her in a hug.

"It's wonderful to see you too," said Ada, kissing his forehead.

"Living room...now!" exclaimed Hope.

Crisis and D.S. entered the living room, noticing the scowl on Hope's face when she looked at them.

"You robbed a bank," she said, her whole body shaking to stay composed.

D.S. stepped back so Crisis was in front. "It was his idea."

"It was our only chance at catching Flash Girl," said Crisis.

"And yet you didn't catch her."

"Look, we tried our—"

"Silence! Every action one of us makes will be used to define us as a species. We've already been framed for a number of atrocities thanks to the Exps employed by the government. I'm the one who has to put out each and every one of these fires. You used your powers after robbing a bank."

"Yeah! And he told me not to use my powers and then he goes all woosh!" yelled D.S.

"Let me handle this," said Crisis, turning to D.S. with a frightening gaze.

"You attacked the police and caused sixteen deaths."

"Gimpy caused those deaths."

"As far as the public is concerned, Gimpy is an Exp! And do you know who arrived at the scene to save the victims from your attack? Humans First! Urgh. Years of work tarnished overnight. News outlets all over are talking about the danger of Exps to public safety," said Hope, squirming in her chair.

"I had to try and save her! If we didn't help with the heist, they would have killed her, and I thought Gimpy was going to kill her too!" yelled Crisis.

"You failed to save your teenage daughter. I'm well aware. Do not let your personal failures cause you to act rashly. I'd rather lose an Exp than have our movement sullied by a criminal rescue mission."

"The only people I attacked were the criminals willing to kill a little girl. I don't regret it."

"Oh really? 'Tornado created by the Exp during the robbery killed four police officers and seven civilians.' Would you like to know their names?"

"I...I didn't mean to hurt anyone."

"What you meant to do isn't what gets put in the news. Thankfully, I've found a way to turn the incident in our favor. *The Divine Machine*, that's the magazine published by the Deus Ex Machina organization, is printing an article about you specifically. 'God Controls the Weather' is the title. I'm going to deify you in the hopes of getting some followers out of this mess. But Deus Ex Machina is a pacifist organization, so turning this in our favor is going to be quite tricky."

The doorbell rings.

"I'll get it!" hollered Ada from the kitchen where she was making fruit smoothies for the guest.

Opti and company were welcomed in. The cheerful Exp set his captive on the couch.

"Was kidnapping her absolutely necessary?" asked Hope.

"I don't think she'll care as long as we wake her up with a big hug!" exclaimed Opti, shaking Durga in his embrace.

"Where am I?" asked Durga after gently and slowly pushing him off.

Hope whacked Opti and signaled him to get down on his knees.

After deciphering her complex hand gestures, he crouched and frowned.

Hope hopped out from her chair and onto his back. "I apologize for any harm or inconvenience this simpleton has caused you. I am Hope, Queen of the Exps, and this is my residence."

"I wasn't aware we had a queen. Who made you?"

"Deceivant. And you were made by Zenero, correct? He's the first creator of Exps, if I'm not mistaken."

"He is indeed. My apologies I don't pay much attention to the news, so I've never heard of you."

"Your ignorance is of no consequence. Now, as for why you've been brought here: the afterlife is being threatened by Sel, the God of Destruction. We are mobilizing all the Exps we can to fight against him."

"I don't know how to fight, so I can't be of much help," said Durga.

"What is your power?" asked Hope.

"I can transform pleasure and pain from physical states into mental states. I can shape those mental states into captivating dreams. But I only use my powers to help others not hurt them." Durga lifted up her sleeve and showed off a tattoo of a metal heart.

"I wasn't aware you are a member of Deus Ex Machina. Perhaps you will be more useful on Earth than in the Heavens."

"Things were so simple before we breached the afterlife. I wonder if we made the right choice," said Durga softly.

"Atlas is here!" hollered Ada.

"Where's Daddy?" asked Stabby in tears, being consoled by Image as they entered the living room.

"I'm sure Sellum is doing all he can to preserve peace in the afterlife, so stop sniveling. I don't want your snot on my carpets," said Hope, throwing a rag at the dirty girl.

"Wow, you two kind of look like sisters," said D.S., crouching to get a better look.

"Your opinions are as needed as your services," said Hope, sticking her nose in the air.

"Thanks! Come to think of it, where is Dad?" asked D.S.

"Deceivant is supposed to be heading home after an important meeting with progressive leaders, but instead, he's spending the night with his latest catch," said Hope with a dark look.

"Oh, let him have his fun. He's been through so much," said Ada.

"Your carefree attitude is enabling him. You do realize this, don't you?" asked Hope.

"I was very stern with him. I told him that he shouldn't overwork himself and should go out and have fun."

"I stand corrected. You actually encourage his deplorable behavior. I may have to publicly cut political ties with him if word gets out that he hasn't been reformed. Nothing discredits a celebrity like claims of pedophilia, after all."

"Why are you in such a sour mood, sweetie? Oh, I know what will help," Ada rushed into the kitchen and came back into the living room with a tray, "smoothies!"

Hope seized a grape smoothie. "I'm not in a sour mood. I'm frustrated. Seems I'm the only one who takes politics seriously."

The doorbell rang.

"Daddy!" Stabby hopped out from Image's arms and ran to the door. "Not Daddy." Her head lowered.

Senator Jo John entered, a smile stretching across his wrinkled face.

Chapter 151: The Senator Returns

Black suit soldiers marched into the house aiming their assault rifles at the Exps in the kitchen and the living room. They guided them into the closest bedroom and kept watch over them. Only Hope remained in the living room.

Hope glared at the female agent who dared to threaten her but stayed still in her sofa.

Senator Jo John entered the living room. He was wearing a brand-new spiffy tux and his slicked back silver hair shined. The Senator's void-like eyes stared into Hope, searching for a weakness to exploit.

One of his agents pulled a chair from the kitchen before the Senator sat down. He signaled his soldiers to lower their guns.

"I wasn't aware we had an appointment," said Hope before sucking the straw in her smoothie.

The Senator pulled away her drink with his pale veiny hand.

"Hope," said the Senator in a fear-inducing low tone.

"I have a busy schedule. If you have something to say, do so immediately," said Hope, pulling back her drink before taking a sip.

"Who is cloning Exps? Is it the Russians?" asked the Senator.

Hope stifled her laughter by feigning a cough. "Exps are far too complex to clone. Until a capsule can be replicated, duplicating them is impossible."

"Yet, here you are. Your death wasn't staged. Cloning technology is the only possibility."

"I haven't the time for your conspiracy theories," said Hope, wiping her lips with a handkerchief.

"Boss, you heard the report. They came back from the dead," said a female agent.

Senator John slammed his fist against the table. "Only the Lord has the power of resurrection, and he would never grant a boon to abominations!"

"The fact remains that we are here, and we will not bend to your whims."

An agent raised her gun. "Do you have any idea who you are—"

"Silence!" yelled the Senator. "The child is right. The Exps have returned, and the whole world knows it." His smile widened like a fissure in the earth. "The people are afraid."

"You sent an agent to this location earlier today. Were you trying to capture me?"

"Agent Zeta acted without my approval and will be punished accordingly. I apologize for the inconvenience."

"You also kidnapped several of my people."

"My agents seized Deceivant's property, nothing more."

"I want my property returned to me immediately."

"If you cooperate, the property will be returned undamaged."

"Cooperation is a joint effort. I will not submit to you."

Senator John grimaced and then laughed. "If left unchecked, Exps will bring an end to this world. Subduing them is absolutely necessary."

"Conspiracy theories and fairy tales, what other nonsense do you believe?"

"I believe my agent is on standby, and if I don't message him within the hour, Deceivant will be crying blood."

Hope smiled. "Oh my, do I get to watch?"

"Every wall in this house will be drenched in the blood of your people if you dare defy me!" he slammed his fist against the table.

"Mind your temper. You're speaking to a lady."

"You're an abomination."

"I'd rather we work together. You're beloved by both parties and have more influence than any human on the planet. I can already see the headlines: 'Senator Jo John begins peace talks with the leader of the Exps.' Your approval ratings would increase overnight. Our meetings would go down in the pages of history."

"You ruined your chance at peace after the incident in New York. The only hope you had was tarnished by your own actions."

"You underestimate me. Crisis will be publicly disowned by me, and he will be turned over to the authorities. What happens to him after that is of no consequence to me."

"Perhaps we can reach an agreement after all."

"People fear Exps because we are dangerous. If we show we are accountable for our actions, that fear can be diluted," said Hope.

"You've got this all planned out," said the Senator with a toothy grin.

"In return, I want Devlin returned to me," said Hope.

"He was caught collaborating with a member of a terrorist organization. I'm afraid my hands are tied."

"You will return him to me."

"Your kind only exists because I allow it."

"Then why do you allow it?"

Elsewhere: The black suit commander looked out past a gathering of yogis in training, stretching up to the skies while maintaining their balance, and focused his gaze on the calm waters at the horizon.

"Maybe you should join us," said the agent who tortured Devlin, keeping her gaze at a single droplet teetering on the edge of a leaf.

"How has nobody gotten word from her yet?" asked Koshi, leaning his head against a wooden signpost.

The torturer leaves the session after bowing to the teacher. "If I were in your position, I would have stayed at her side," she said, rolling up her mat.

"She gave me the look. My defenses weren't up at the time. She should be here by now. Why isn't she here!?" He paced around in a circle. "Your brother is looking for her, right?"

The agent whipped out her phone. "She's on her way to the main base now. Should be arriving in a few hours."

Koshi checked his phone for messages. "Why were you informed and not me?"

"Because I asked nicely. I'll see you around. Give her a kiss for me when she gets back," said the torturer.

Koshi grabbed her wrist as she walked by. "Where are you off to?"

"Oh, just a girls' night out. You're not invited," she said, slipping out of his grip.

"You're a beautiful woman."

"I know."

Koshi walked past her and stepped in her path. "I wasn't done. Look, I'm in a bad spot right now. I have a date scheduled, but I was thinking doing some overtime might be a better option for me."

"Then cancel."

"I was hoping you could take my place. I can't just let Cynthia down like that."

"Well, since I don't have plans, I guess I could give her a date."

Koshi grinned and he held up his phone to his coworker. "Oh, just a girls' night out. You're not invited."

She glared at him.

"Didn't you just say you didn't have plans?" he asked, tilting his head.

"What I choose to do with my time is none of your business."

"I'm the alpha. Why am I the one in the dark lately? It seems like the toes are less in the dark than the right hand these days," he said in a hushed voice.

"Well, lately the right hand has been more concerned with chasing skirts."

"That's a load of human shit. Kaity is a VIP. I'd be a fool not to see what she was up to."

"My orders were to visit her, and you messed up the mission because you couldn't resist."

"I wasn't having a beach party. I protected her from several Exps. Where were you when we were attacked?"

"I'm not supposed to say, but I'll do it anyway just to see you squirm. I was told to let you reap what you sow. 'If she died, so be it. If you died, then I suppose it was a time for a replacement after all.' I have the audio recorded if you want to hear."

"Asshole!" Koshi slammed his fist into his open palm.

"Remember, you weren't always the Alpha. If you don't get your shit together, you'll be behind bars."

"Whatever you say, Lambda." He snapped his fingers. "Of course! The reason you didn't intervene is because you wanted your target worn down. Not just worn down but isolated."

"Are you quite done? I really do have things to do," said Lambda.

"Then why are we taking the long way around? You know what, you earned your victory. Play the recording; go ahead."

Lambda bit her lip and glared at him. "Leave me alone."

"Well, I wasn't lying about Cynthia. Her life is in your hands, just like Devlin's."

Lambda slammed the murderer against the tree. "You think I care whether your latest squeeze lives or dies?"

"Oho! So now you're going to pretend you don't like her. It wasn't an accident that I introduced you two, and it wasn't a mistake I had you two wait on me at the restaurant. I wanted you to work your magic on her. Cynthia is an insurance policy to me, but to you…I see the way you smile at her."

"I swear when the Boss is done with you, I'm going to mark your body for every innocent woman you've murdered!" she growled.

"Sounds like a fun date, but we don't have time to think that far in the future. Tell me where you're hiding the kid."

"I wasn't the one who decided to keep the information secret. The Boss doesn't trust you, so don't get pissed off at me."

"You are so hot when you get angry." Koshi seized her breast.

She shoved him off. "Only I have access to the room."

"Then lead the way, and don't take too long. Caroline can only last so long."

"What did you do to her?"

"You'll find out in exactly forty minutes," he said, flashing the ticking clock on his phone.

"Why do you care what happens to Devlin?" Her eyes widened. "You must be kidding me! Kaity sent you to rescue her friend, am I right? Why am I asking? I know I'm right."

"It's not your concern why I want to see him. Just bring me to him. If you are right, then congratulations, you can tell the Boss all about my betrayal."

"You should have just worded it that way earlier. Come on!" She raced off and went to a log cabin marked 'Parvati house' on the bleached white door.

"I've been here before."

"Shut it." Lambda opened the door, revealing a modest room with white walls and photographs of a nun. "You owe me, big time."

"For sabotaging myself and handing over my girlfriend to you?"

"That's right. I've given you an opportunity to reform yourself," said Lambda, sliding her hand under a painting.

Koshi smiled as she pulled out a key and opened the closet door.

Lambda pressed against the back wall and slid it to the right, revealing a hidden staircase that led into the darkness.

"I'm giving you the very same opportunity. Maybe after all this is done, I'll give up killing and you'll stop skinning people for fun," said Koshi, stretching his arms.

"It isn't recreation; it's art."

"So is what I do. It's like poetry."

"Every psychopath thinks they're cultured."

"If that's the case, we should be keeping records on people who listen to classical music instead of those who look up books on making bombs."

"Very funny."

They reached the end of the stairs, and she opened a grimy door with the key.

"Did this torture chamber exist before or after the ashram was built?"

"It's not a chamber." Lambda swung open the door, revealing a metal door with a key card slider. "It's a facility."

After inputting a code and getting her prints, the door opened.

A metal hallway, polished and colored with red and yellow paint splotches greeted them.

"You hired cats to paint your walls? Okay, seriously, what's with the décor? Is this a style of art?"

"I get worked up, and sloshing around some paint calms my nerves. Color is so much more important than you realize."

"I have odd hobbies, so I won't judge. Alright, so Devlin got caught. Who else?"

"I'm not supposed to tell you."

"We're both going to be reprimanded for this. Just tell me."

"Exp 8."

"Really? I expected him to put up more of a fight."

"What are you, his fan boy?"

"More like his coach," said Koshi with a grin.

One of the doors on the hallway opened and War approached them. He wasn't wearing his helmet so his face was visible. He had short white hair, sleek tan skin, and gentle tired orange eyes.

"War, where did you put the other captive?" asked Lambda.

"What is he doing down here?" asked War.

"Since we've got two Exps, I decided to bring him along so the interrogation process is sped up."

"The second container hasn't been opened yet. He shouldn't be able to fight in his condition, but best to open it carefully," he said, holding the door open.

Several automated turrets were in the titanium room, all aimed at the box.

"War, lead our guest to Devlin's chambers."

War nodded and walked down the hall. "He talks to you, doesn't he...about the bigger picture?"

"Yeah, and sometimes it's really hard to feign interest," said Koshi.

"When I first let Devlin escape, why did you take the blame?"

"That was years ago. I thought you were done asking me."

"Was it because your sister was involved in the op?"

"It worked out in the end, didn't it? He ended up making several Exps just like we wanted."

"He was released early because of me, and you took the blame for it."

"I was just burying my sister's tracks, that's all. You said so yourself."

"We couldn't have pulled it off without you."

"I get blamed for things all the time. Why tarnish your record when mine's already covered in stains?"

"You're here to rescue him, aren't you? You're just like me, you see a child not a monster."

"That's not it. I'm doing a favor for someone I care about," said Koshi with a small smile.

War smiled at him.

"Not you, someone else. So, is this the room?" Koshi held his finger to his ear.

"Ambush," said Lambda in a whisper from the other line.

Back at Deceivant's home, the Senator and Hope were enjoying some tea brewed by Ada who returned to the kitchen at gunpoint.

"I'm not so certain your agents would win against my subjects. Perhaps you threaten us because you aren't able to contain my people," said Hope, blowing on her tea to cool it.

The Senator popped three sugar cubes in. "You wouldn't put your darling mother at risk."

Hope sipped the tea and smiled. "A confrontation would only bring us both losses. It's best avoided."

The front door swung open, and Exp 8 fired out orbs at the black suit agents near Ada. His recently mangled body was completely healed.

"Stand down, you imbecile!" yelled Hope.

"It's you!" Exp 8 zoomed through the bullet fire and sent an orb at the Senator.

The agent closest to the Senator grabbed the orb with the tips of her fingers, tore it in half, and tossed the halves at Exp 8.

The rebellious Exp jetted up to the ceiling to dodge the blast, allowing the wall behind him to explode.

"Take him down, Beta," said the Senator, fleeing behind a living shield of his agents.

Beta had red and white stripes across her black suit and a blue inscription of her Greek letter. She kicked off the ground and threw a flash bomb. Her star-adorned red, white, and blue bald eagle helmet and one-way visor allowed her to see through the flash. Having blinded the Exp, she dragged her hands around him, coating him in energy suppressors.

Exp 8 hit the ground face first. He hopped to his feet and rushed at Beta, lashing his elbow talons at her.

Four other agents opened fire, pelting Exp 8's back with bullets and poking holes in the velvet couches.

"Why aren't you all fighting?" asked Exp 8, his talons missing their targets due to being shot at point-blank range.

An agent in camo colors broke formation and aimed her gun at Hope. "Stand down or she dies."

Exp 8 stopped his assault and was slammed to the ground by one of the heavy agents.

"Don't get back up," said the camo agent.

Exp 8's head rose up and glared at the Senator.

"I apologize for the trouble, Debbie," said Hope, smiling at Beta.

The Senator turned to his agent with a glare.

Hope got up from her sofa and placed her foot on the back of Exp 8's head. "Do not interrupt my negotiations." Her heel pressed his face into the carpet.

"You should really put a leash on that one," said the Senator, smiling down at the defiant creature.

"Why did you send your minions to capture me?" asked Exp 8, pushing Hope's foot up as he struggled to raise his head.

"You threatened to kill civilians in Israel. I had an obligation to intervene," said the Senator.

"You did what?" asked Hope.

"Stabby went berserk. I had to clear the area to minimize the casualties. I never attacked any civilians," said Exp 8.

An agent whispered in his Boss' ear.

The Senator's eyes widened. "The peace meetings shall begin tomorrow. We can discuss more at that time. Move out!"

The agents raised their guns and walked backward out of the building with their leader.

Back at the government facility, Koshi was running down the hallway. "You free the boy! I have to save her!"

"You're a good man. I'd be a fool to let you die," said War, running alongside him.

They arrived at the door.

"Do you have a key card?" asked Koshi, entirely composed.

"Step back. I have a key to every door in this facility."

"Then why would I need to step—"

War put his palms to the door. "**RELEASE**." The metal door was blasted open. "See?"

Bloody tendrils sprung out from a puddle on the floor and gripped the door.

"I opened the casing and blood spilled out. Koshi, don't try anything heroic." Lambda was hoisted off the ground by tendrils that wrapped around her waist. A blood sickle was poised to cut her throat open at a moment's notice.

"Relax. Nothing to worry about. Let's talk, alright?" asked Koshi, tossing his utility belt to the ground.

"You there," said Demonica, pointing at War. "You said there was another agent who captured Devlin. Was it her?"

"It doesn't matter who it was. Follow me and I'll lead you to him," said Koshi.

"If you try anything, her head comes off. Got it?"

"My name is Koshi, alright? I am the only one who is helping you get your boyfriend back. They aren't involved. War, as your commanding officer, I order you to stand down."

"Then I must obey," said War with a big smile.

"What's he so smug about?" asked Demonica, slowly inching toward the door.

"Don't worry about him. Just follow me," said Koshi, leading her down the hall.

"You know what will happen to her if you attack me, right?" asked Demonica, slamming Lambda against the door.

"I can only imagine," he said softly.

The door opened.

Demonica pulled in her blood and ran to Devlin's side.

"What the hell kind of torture is this?" asked Koshi, gazing up at the gruesome sight.

"It was experimentation, actually," said Lambda, holding her neck in pain.

Demonica's beloved was opened up like a body on an operating table. His wires were strewn out across the wall, stretched to their threshold and held in place by glowing spikes.

"Devlin," cried Demonica. Crimson blades came out from her back and sliced the edges of the wires.

Koshi held his finger to his ear. He mouthed the word 'boss' to Lambda who gave a strange look in return. "He knows," said the agent under his breath.

Lambda gave War a suspicious look but he shook his head. "This was the one place I was supposed to have privacy."

Once Devlin was cut down, Demonica cradled him in her arms, her blood coming out as little hands that reassembled her beloved. "Let me speak to him." Blood shot out from her back as blades. "I want to speak to your boss!"

"Absolutely." Koshi took out his earpiece and cautiously approached, staying away from the blood splatters on the ground.

"I don't care about your little pissing contest with the Exps," said Demonica.

"Who are you to speak to me in such a manner?" asked Senator John.

"A mother defending her child!" yelled Demonica.

"Devlin was never born. He's an abomination—"

"He's the father! The child is within me! I'm only telling you so you realize how serious I am. I was merciful to your agents. I could have slaughtered them all if I wanted to."

"Your mercy is noted." The Senator's voice lost its edge.

"You're in charge. I want to make a deal," said Demonica.

"I'm listening."

"You and your soldiers don't bother Devlin or me, and I won't slaughter them. Truce?"

"And you won't intervene in my pissing contest, as you called it?"

"I don't care what happens to them in the slightest. Do we have a deal?"

"Is it a boy or a girl?"

"I don't know yet."

"Congratulations, regardless. If ever you need a safe place to give birth or any assistance—"

"I want to be left alone. You don't bother my family, and I won't slaughter your family. Deal?"

"Deal. Alpha!"

"Yes, sir?"

"Escort her and the father out of here, and charter them a plane to go wherever they see fit."

"As you command," said Koshi with a salute. The agent walked Demonica out the door.

"I'm here, Boss," said Lambda, her finger to her ear.

"Don't fall behind schedule."

"I'm guessing your informant didn't tell you…. Demonica was in the case Exp 8 was supposed to arrive in."

"I'm aware Exp 8 escaped. He's back at their base. For the time being, we are to let him roam free."

"You told me that I wouldn't be monitored down here. Nobody should see me when I'm like that! Why the hell did you lie to me?" asked Lambda.

"I figured since Exp 8 wasn't where he was supposed to be, there was likely some sort of trap. Turns out I was right. But enough of that; you need to get back to work."

"I'm glad you trust me, but I have no one to interrogate. We're without insurance now," said Lambda.

"Sigma has just arrived on the island with the last captive in tow. You're permitted to practice your craft as you see fit. In fact, I encourage you to damage the captive. Contact Sigma and follow up. I have a call to make."

"Understood." Lambda leaned against the wall and sighed. Her eyes widened. She whipped out her phone and called Koshi. "How much time do I have before Caroline dies?" She pulled the phone away as laughter came from the other line. "This isn't funny! I did what you wanted. Call it off."

"We sure got lucky. Demonica forced us to do what we wanted. Oh, and I lied about my date. She's on vacation in Canada at the moment. You are too easy, you know that?"

Lambda started laughing as she cried.

"You okay?"

"Yeah, just relieved is all," said Lambda, wiping her tears.

189

"Oh, and by the way, you owe me. I could have let you die," said Koshi.

"You just didn't want to get lectured by the Boss," said Lambda, still giggling.

"That's not true." Koshi's jokey voice died out instantly. "You're important to me."

"If I'm so important, I guess I don't owe you anything," said Lambda.

"You got me! But I'm not letting you off the hook. You, me, and Kioshi, let's go see a movie together."

"Alright, but I pick the movie."

"Eh, fair enough. See you tonight."

"Is that all?"

"Nope. On the way back from the movie, I'll pick up some brushes. The walls in your secret cavern are hideous."

"You're a prick, you know that?"

"And you're a bombshell who gets off on torturing people. I think we were meant for each other."

"Screw off."

"See you tonight." Koshi dropped the call.

"I swear if his sister wasn't such a cutie, I'd never willingly deal with his shit. Hmm…I wonder who my new playmate is going to be." Lambda paced around. "I'll just call Sigma!"

Chapter 152: Setting the Foundation

In Lum, the religious leaders were gathered in a violet and pink structure. Energy paintings adorned the walls like neon lights. Each painting depicted a supplementary god or goddess. The entire ceiling was decorated by a three-dimensional energy image of Lum herself, shown as a martyr wearing bandages.

Evol sat among them. To her right was Fatima, and to her left was Rambir.

Having completed her transformation into a Mawali, Fatima's amber eyes were brightened rather than overtaken by Lum's energy. Wings of light came out from the back of her *hijab*.

Rambir no longer had a smile on his wrinkled face. The loss of so many of his people had shaken his spirit.

"First off, I apologize for the delay. A new gathering spot had to be created since Sel removed the last one. Welcome to the Sanctum."

"Violet, you've become a goddess? Where is Efil?" asked Rambir in a wise and friendly old voice.

"The identity known as Violet has been transcended. I am Evol, Goddess of Love. Efil is unable to attend at this time."

The religious leaders whispered among each other.

Fatima released light from her fingertips to seize everyone's attention. "Let's proceed," she said in a gentle voice no longer brimming with joy.

A Christian leader leaned in. "Was she killed?"

"She was taken away," said a woman, stepping out of the light.

The room fell silent.

"Yes. I am who you think I am," said the woman covered by bandages.

"The Great Goddess keeps her wounds as a reminder of the sacrifices she has made for peace," said Evol.

Sefiwah turned around and unwrapped the bandages on her back, displaying the gruesome crimson scars on her otherwise snow-white skin.

"Have you come to kill us? We won't go down without a fight," said a Sikh leader, sitting beside Rambir, his hand on the hilt of his sword.

Lum molded the light from the windows and formed it into a chair before taking a seat. "I've come to join in the discussion."

"Your angels came to our temples and stole our people, and now you want peace?" asked a Buddhist.

"The angels were sent to retrieve the prisoners and to place them in Elysium where they belong," said the Great Goddess.

191

"Your rule is coming to an end," said a female priest.

Lum smiled. "And if it ends, if Sel wins, what do you suppose will happen to you? Sel will turn our realm into a place of fire and ash. This paradise shall become a prison, and all its residents will be made into demons. Each breath you take will burn your lungs. All the bliss you have, the bliss I have given you, shall melt into anguish and create a prison around your soul."

Rambir set his hands on the table. "Where was Efil taken?"

"We successfully retrieved Tcetorp from Absence, but in the midst of the skirmish, Sel's forces abducted Efil. Etaf is fighting demons as we speak, doing all she can to free the goddess beloved by all forms of life," said Lum.

"We are not fooled by your disguise. We know that you can take on whatever form you desire. I will not send my people to the inferno to take back what you lost," said a Catholic priest.

"Defending this realm is not enough. We must take the fight to Sel. Every moment we delay his conquest tips the scales of fate in our favor," said Lum.

The Vedic shaman leaned in. "You've received another prophecy, haven't you?"

Lum's eyes trembled. She folded her hands and lowered her head. "I beseech you for your aid. I cannot save this realm without you."

"We cannot kill the demons. What hope do we have?" asked the Rastafarian who once fought alongside Kanasta.

Lum turned to Fatima and smiled.

Fatima bowed before speaking. "If we wish to defend this realm, we must be able to wield light. Only the light can vanquish demons."

A human angel carried in a demon on a leash.

Fatima approached the demon, formed a sword of energy, and sliced off its head. "If we wish to fight, we must become Mawali."

"Not Mawali." Lum stood up. "Angels. Anyone who fights for the protection of the realm shall be treated as an angel."

"You want our help? Then remove the walls that divide us," said the other Sikh leader.

"Absolutely not. Women are protected by those walls," said a Jain nun.

"If we are victorious against Sel, your requests will be given equal weight as that of an angel's. I cannot force you all to comply, but know that every convert brings us closer to victory…to safety," said the Great Goddess.

"Return to us those you imprisoned and then perhaps we can negotiate," said the Catholic priest, standing up.

"I cannot. They are already undergoing the transformation," said the Great Goddess.

"This world is worth protecting. I'll volunteer for the transformation," said Rambir.

Several other leaders stood up, but the majority of them left the meeting.

The Great Goddess teleported and blocked their exits. "Those who do not fight for this realm will receive no protection when the demons come, and they will come. So, will you comply?"

The leaders reluctantly nodded.

"I'm glad we've reached an agreement. The best way to lead is by example. By becoming angels, you will inspire your people to do the same."

Fatima approached the goddess after everyone left. "What was the prophecy?"

"The death of a realm god in Lum. I must either tempt Sel into my kingdom or find a way to sacrifice Absence in my stead. One can build a moat to redirect lava, but they cannot stop a volcano from erupting," said the Great Goddess.

"Are the prophecies that powerful?" asked Evol.

"They are not to be taken in stride. Evol, you will lead them to the World Tree. I must return to Elysium and create our own army of demons."

On Earth, Deceivant returned to the base along with Kaity.

"You're finally here," said Hope, peering at them from her sofa.

"I picked Kaity up from the airport. What happened to the wall?" asked Deceivant.

"While you were having a sleepover with children, we had some company. Thankfully, I diffused the situation."

Kaity ran up to Hope. "How many did we lose?"

"None were killed, but we still have two missing members. We know Devlin is being held by Senator John's agents, and it seems likely Nina was abducted as well," said Hope.

"Oh no," said Kaity with worry.

"Have you talked to Kanasta about it?" asked Deceivant.

"He chose a path of violence for his own selfishness rather than a path of peace for the good of us all. He is forbidden from returning here, and I will cut any public ties we have with him at today's peace talks."

"You should have told me sooner. We have to save Nina," said Kaity.

"Had you returned on time, you would have been immediately informed. I will bargain with the Senator for her release this afternoon at the talks. For now, we have to make our own plans. Come with me to the round room. I had to postpone an extra half-hour waiting for you two to show up," said Hope.

"I got you something," said Deceivant, reaching into a bag and pulling out a queen bee plushie.

"What I want is your undivided attention and cooperation in our strategy meeting. Now follow me," said Hope, leading them down the hall. The little queen stood up on her tippy toes to reach the door handle.

"I can help," said Deceivant, reaching for the handle.

Hope smacked his hand away. "As the leader, I can't show any weakness." She hopped up and twisted the knob, falling back into Kaity's arms. "There we go."

Everyone stood up from their swivel chairs upon Kaity's entrance.

"You're back!" cheered D.S., joining Opti in a Kaity hug.

"We haven't the time for pleasantries. It is crucial that we make use of every second." Hope motioned Deceivant to lift her up and set her down in her royal, golden, jewel-encrusted chair. "We must ascertain our strengths and find ways to properly utilize them for our cause. If you have any suggestions, raise your hand. Interruptions will not be tolerated. First off, I will be negotiating with Senator Jo John, the greatest threat to our independence. As such, I will be too busy to rally the other groups to our side. Durga, you're a member of Deus Ex. How high are you in the chain of command?"

"As far as they know, I'm human. I don't have much power in the group."

"Very well. After today's peace meeting, you will reveal your heritage. This will give you a sanctified position among the DXM and will likely bolster their membership as well."

"Revealing what I am could end my career."

"If it comes to that, I will fully compensate you."

"That prison is my home. We have the lowest recidivism rate in the country. People are transformed by the time they leave. I can't put that in jeopardy."

"Your prison is one of many of its kind. And with your grand reveal, it's very likely that more prisons will follow suit. We can use this drop in crime to win over approval from Democrats and Republicans alike. If you have any faith in your home, you should believe that your coming out will only bring benefits."

"I'll think it over."

"You must do it! I also demand you make sure there are motivational members of DXM in each yoga prison, not just the ones in this country. We need recruitment facilities to be at a global scale."

"Why take such risks? As long as we look human, Exps can blend in society. What is your end goal?"

"Equality, of course. You've been assigned your mission, so let's move along."

Opti raised his hand.

"Speak."

"I want to join DXM. If one Exp member is good, then two is better. I can also recruit people at the prisons. I want to help in any way I can."

"Very well, you two are partners now. See to it that the other is supported."

Opti beamed at Durga who looked away.

"Moving along."

Toxic, who was coiled around the top of her chair, raised her tail. "How can I help?"

"You can't. You're worthless. Now, let's continue."

"That's not nice," said D.S. "Hope, if you don't have anything nice to say, don't say anything at all." He patted Toxic. "We can guard the base together."

"Actually, D.S., I have an assignment for you." Hope lifted up a business card. "As you all should know, Exps are not seen as people and thus cannot get a job. A few of them bypass this by their keeping their identity hidden, like The Vibrator. Thankfully for the rest, the black market is ripe with opportunity. D.S., you are now a freelance bodyguard who will protect those with the greatest influence. Toxic, you will go with him down to the training room and film his demo tape. You can hold a camera steady, can't you?"

Toxic nodded her head with a sad look.

"Good. Kaity, you will hand over the list of your targets to D.S."

"These are confidential. We need a plan to stop Sel. All this can wait," said Kaity.

"You don't understand. There are likely Exps in hiding, and only when they feel safe will they come out. Sellum will fetch us when it is time to fight Sel, but until that time comes, we have our own battles to manage. You will turn over your list of targets to D.S."

"I thought you said he was going to be a bodyguard," said Kaity.

"Exactly. D.S., you will contact each target, inform them who is targeting them, and negotiate payment for their protection."

"I'm not going to help you sabotage papa!" yelled Kaity.

"Do not raise your voice at me. D.S., as payment for your help, they must openly speak out for Exp equality. Either they do that or you let them die."

"That seems kinda like something a bad guy would do."

"You're protecting others, and all you ask in return is that they petition for your people to be treated equally. You'll be a hero to the Exps. A superhero!"

"Superhero! Awesome!"

"Well, I'm not handing over the list," said Kaity.

"That's fine." Hope sent D.S. a text message. "That's my informant's number. Talk to her for other job opportunities."

"Um, I get kinda nervous talking to strangers," said D.S.

The Captain of Carnage hopped out from his chair and onto the table. "Send those worries into the furnace. I shall assist you in communication and join you as a bodyguard."

"I fully approve," said Hope. "Kitty, you, and BoneSaw will be given a list of targets. I trust you will not leave a trace. This cannot be tracked back to us, is that clear?"

"I don't work for free. It's against my principles," said Kaity.

"You'll be paid through a proxy bank account. I'm sending you the list now."

Kaity looked at the list and then back at Hope. "I'll need to talk to you in private later."

"I expected as much. Wringer, I've created a separate list for you."

Wringer looked over the list, nodding to himself and caressing the necks of his targets with his iron fingertips.

Crisis raised his hand.

"Go on, speak."

"It's worth noting that Wringer, me, and the rest of Atlas' Exps were all once members of DXM. Also, Wringer left once he got what he wanted. I'm not sure how trustworthy he is."

"He sought the necessary power to bring about change in this corrupt world. I have faith in him and feel his talents can easily be put to good use."

"I'm an icon to the Furies. How can I help?" asked Chipko.

"Remain here and convince other members that our cause is a just one."

"I need to be outside, fighting to protect Gaia."

"Your activism is constant fuel for those who want us subdued. We cannot win this battle through force."

"Then put me with Wringer. I've studied his victims and all had a carbon footprint of eight or more Earths."

"Either you stay here or we publicly execute you to show we do not approve of your violence."

"My violence is necessary for the planet. What I fight for is bigger than any social justice movement."

"You will remain here till otherwise stated. Crisis, you will stay behind as well. Contact members of DXM while she contacts the Furies. Let's not forget we've had two security breaches here since we've arrived. We're also counting on you both to keep our most delicate members free from harm. Oh, and clean up the place a bit while you're at it."

Chipko crossed her arms and slouched in her seat. "I'm an activist, not a pacifist. I'm definitely not your maid," she grumbled.

"Atlas, Muffins, and Fusion will go to poor neighborhoods and repair their buildings. Also, I want you to use our funds to create our very own nonprofit organization dedicated to disaster relief and setting up stations that will provide ample food and water to those in need. The logo design and name of the foundation are yours to choose."

"Hmm. How about Unity for the name and a…flock of birds lifting up sticks for the logo. That way we can appeal to the Furies without tying ourselves directly to them."

Hope smiled. "This is why I left it up to you. I'll be sure to have a reporter spread word of your actions. If we want to be accepted, we must show compassion and benevolence to the oppressed."

"I absolutely agree." Exp 8 stood up. "Our people aren't just Exps. They are minorities of all kinds. All those whose freedoms are restricted are my brothers and sisters. If all minorities come together, then we are the majority and freedom is ours to seize!"

Hope clapped with the fingers of her right hand on the palm of her left. The others followed suit. Once Hope was done, she signaled the others to stop. "Your charisma is what this movement needs more than anything. Image, with your knowledge of psychology and his passion, we can do more than gain approval. We can ignite the fires of rebellion." She was so excited she nearly fell out of her chair.

"Ooh! Ooh! I just came up with a great idea," said Ada.

"Share with us, Mother. Your ideas are always welcome," said Hope.

"The problem with human rights movements is that they focus on elevating others to the status of human. We want to be equal but not human. There's only one social justice movement that goes beyond the scope of species: veganism!"

Hope smiled.

Exp 8 looked at Ada. "In order to elevate ourselves, we will elevate the rights of others. Rather than demonize a certain group, we will gain independence by realizing our common ground. All living beings want to be free and we are undeniably living beings. Nice one, Ada!"

"Thanks," said Ada, giving him a high five.

"Mother, your peace schools serve vegan lunches, correct?" asked Hope.

"All vegan. The students also grow their own food, and we learn about religions and cultures of all kinds."

"Durga, what about your prisons?"

"I work there. They are privately owned. They serve lacto-vegetarian food. Dairy consumption is interwoven with Indian religions, and thus it is commonplace to have dairy at yoga centers. It's only been a few decades since they dropped honey, and that was only because of the Global Crop Famine."

"Ada, you too will come out as an Exp, and you will find someone to make a documentary about both Exps and peace schools. Durga, use whatever influence you have to veganize the prisons. The vegan movement is without a doubt our best bet, but we need to show results if we want to be accepted into it."

"Then that's where I come in," said Deceivant. "I'm credited as one of the great vegan leaders of the twenty-first century, second only to Zenero."

"Please, don't say his name," said Chipko, stricken with tears.

"I can rally vegans to our side. More than that, if my queen asks it, I will bring Exp equality into the vegan movement."

"We must be careful. Act too boldly and we threaten to further split the vegan movement. Animal welfarists are less likely to be sympathetic to our cause. I order you to bring Exp rights into the common discourse of abolitionist vegans."

"Your wish is my mission," said Deceivant with a bow.

"You'll be doing more than that, of course. I want every daycare center under your name to have children's books about Exps in them. Mother, that means it's your time to publish a children's book."

"Sounds wonderful!" exclaimed Ada.

"There's still more. Deceivant, you will bring Exps back into public dialogue by building up interest in the scientific community. As long as we are unknown, we will be feared. Only science can bring who we are and what we are capable of to light."

Stabby raised her hand. "What do I do?"

"You'll stay here and be protected. I don't know why Sellum left us with you. Your capture could change the tide of the war if the love I see when he looks at you is genuine," said Hope.

Stabby's face lit up.

"We cannot afford to waste time. If you have other ideas, bring them to Deceivant, Ada, or myself. I must be off shortly. Any final remarks?"

Exp 8 stood up from his chair. "I know that Hope is asking us to perform tasks we aren't sure we can do, and she's asking us to take up jobs we may not want. But I ask you to shoulder this burden. We need to have faith in her. She's been fighting for Exp rights since before I was created. She has sacrificed so much to get us where we are now. If we all work together, utilizing our talents for peace, we will be elevated and all of life will ascend alongside us!"

The room shook as the Freedom Forcers cheered.

"Very well spoken." Hope walked out with a satisfied smile.

"I won't wait. If you have something to say, say it," said Chipko.

"For now we must show the masses we are peaceful. But there will be a time, not long from now, when we must claim our independence by force."

"I'll do as you ask for the time being. We'll see how the peace meeting goes," said Chipko before walking off.

Kaity popped out when Hope turned the corner. "Why are all my targets children?"

"You didn't seem to have a problem with it just the other day."

"I...I couldn't pull the trigger. I don't know what's wrong with me. Maybe the conversation I had with Koshi changed my mind...either way, I can't rationalize it anymore. I can't kill without a cause. I always had my doubts, and I argued with the Viper Squad sometimes, but now...I just don't have it in me." Kaity started sobbing.

"You can't let our enemy sway you. This is important, Kitty. All the children on the list are children of high-standing members of the Furies."

"Then they're our allies," said Kaity with a blank look.

"We cannot publicly align with the Furies until they are seen in a positive light. I can see the news already: feared leaders and known terrorists sobbing at the graves of their children. Create some evidence linking the murders to members of Humans First and we disempower our enemy while elevating our future ally," said Hope.

"They're just kids. Is this really necessary?"

Hope grabbed Kaity's hand. "Chances are I won't be able to negotiate a release for Devlin or Nina. But if we succeed, and success can happen so quick these days, then legally I'll be able to walk in and retrieve them myself. Your mission is of pivotal importance. In order for our mission to succeed, we must have assassins working in the shadows. Your work is necessary for maintaining peace. What are a few lives when weighed against that of the future?"

"I-I understand. I'll do my part."

"Splendid. You hold the future of my people in your hands. Let the gravity of the situation push your finger down upon the trigger of our revolution." She patted Kaity's hand and released it.

"What about Sel? What if he attacks now?"

"Then those who can fight will go to Sellum and those who cannot will remain here."

"What is your end goal?" asked Kaity.

"An eco-ethical revolution," said Hope, her eyes shimmering like stars.

Chapter 153: The World Beyond

Kioshi knocked on a steel-plated door. "Boss, I'm back!"

The door opened and Senator Jo John glared at the incompetent girl. "You attacked their base without orders."

"Yep, I'm being proactive!" she cheered.

"You and your brother are turning out to be more trouble than you're worth."

"I want to be a real Exp Hunter," said Kioshi.

"Hunters know how to follow orders. Obedience is the most important quality of all, Zeta."

"What I lack in obedience, I make up for in confidence."

"Confidence doesn't help me attain my purpose."

"Come on, what do I have to do to prove I'm worthy?"

"You aren't capable of being a Hunter. You may have decent scores in VR training, but you'd never win in a real fight against an Exp."

Kioshi beamed. "Prepare to be amazed!" She kicked open the door behind her.

Inside, the Prince of Pleasure was seated on Absorb.

Senator Jo John blinked several times and looked back at the grinning girl. "You did this?"

"Yessiry! Soooo, does this mean I'm a Hunter now?" she asked, poking his arm.

"You've certainly proved yourself, Agent Pi."

"Finally!" She hopped in the air. "Guess what? I have even more great news. This handsome stud, who's actually my new boyfriend, by the way, wants to make a deal with you!"

The Senator looked at the contorted grin on the Prince's face with suspicion.

"I believe we can help one another," said the Prince, rising up from his seat and approaching the Senator.

"We can discuss more inside. Pi, I will discuss your initiation ceremony at a later time," said the Senator, patting her shoulder.

"Uh-uh. I found him, so I get to stay for the discussion," said Kioshi, crossing her arms.

"This is not up for debate. Leave us," said the Senator.

"You need a bodyguard and the other agents aren't here sooo...."

"Fine. But for every word you speak of this meeting, you will lose a finger," said the Senator.

"I can keep secrets. Don't freak out on me," said Kioshi, holding her hands to her chest.

"Right this way," said the Senator, leading the Prince down the hallway.

"Psst, there's something you should know about my boyfriend," said Kioshi, standing on her tip toes to reach his ear.

"The less I know about your sex life the better," said the Senator, rolling his eyes.

"I'm serious. Energy suppressors don't work on him."

"That is most curious," said the Senator, peeking over his shoulder at the Exp.

"I have exceptional hearing, so there's no point in whispering."

"I apologize for my rudeness. Ah, here we are." The Senator slid his key card and opened the meeting room. He offered his guest a seat in a velour chair and took the seat directly in front of him.

Kioshi sat in her boyfriend's lap and kissed his lips.

The Senator beamed at his guest. "It's a pleasure to meet your acquaintance. I am Jo John, but you may call me John for short. Would you like anything to eat or drink before we begin our discussion?"

"I appreciate the offer, but let's get right into it. My name is the Prince of Pleasure."

"Who created you?" asked the Senator, leaning in.

"I am a demon lord from Sel. I come from the world beyond," said the Prince.

"That's another thing I forgot to say. He's a bit delusional," whispered Kioshi.

Senator Jo John stood up from his chair. "You're a real demon! Ha! They called me superstitious, claiming demons were mere scapegoats for man's actions, but here you are, living proof of the afterlife!"

"Wait, you believe him? What am I saying? Of course you believe him. You think that reptiles are taking over the banks," said Kioshi, holding her forehead.

"Fifth-dimensional reptilian beings, and I am not the only one who has seen the signs. One would be foolish not to be skeptical in a society where misinformation is the greatest weapon!"

"I'll tell you everything you want to know about the afterlife. All I ask in return is that you turn a blind eye to my actions and provide me protection when need be. I'm going to claim every church that worships the devil."

Kioshi hugged her boyfriend. "He's really religious, but he's not preachy about it, so don't worry."

"As a man of God, it is my life's mission to fight against the forces of darkness. I have no doubt that the Seltanic church would expand its rotten roots in your command."

"The greater the darkness, the stronger the light must become to withstand it," said the Prince.

"I should be wary of making any deals with your kind," said the Senator with a honed in glare.

"Come now, I'm sure we can reach an agreement," said the Prince.

The Senator walked behind the Prince. "When I was a lobbyist, my colleagues gave me a nickname. Those who went back on their side of the bargain regretted doing so every day of their lives." He placed his hands on the demon's shoulders. "My enemies know me as Diablo." "Be warned, abomination. Backstabbing me will be the end of everything you hold dear."

"Your surveillance is limited to your own realm. I offer you the chance to learn things no mortal knows. Your only option is to cooperate with me," said the Prince.

"Of course! The Exps did die. They must have returned through a gate of some kind. Heathens, even in the afterlife. They were the ones responsible for causing the global stillbirth phenomena, weren't they?"

"Indeed. It was caused by them forcing their way back to Earth."

"Such selfish creatures. They will pay for what they have wrought. Are there other demons on Earth? Perhaps the new Exps sighted by my agents aren't Exps at all. And what of that hellish crocodile who killed so many Americans. Wait, that's not what I want to ask you." The Senator steadied himself and looked up at the Prince. "What happens to babies who die before being born? According to the poet Dante Alighieri, they are trapped in Purgatory. Is this true?"

"I have your answer, but you have yet to agree to my terms."

"I refuse to make a deal with you. However, that doesn't mean I'm against an alliance. Deals are short term and can lead to conflict. A partnership is the better option for both of us. You and I help each other out, sound good, partner?" asked the Senator, offering his hand.

The Prince stood up and firmly shook it. "The afterlife changes with the times. Perhaps Dante was right back then, but now those with neutral karma, such as the babies you mentioned, are brought to Lum. The realm of Lum is similar to the Heaven you are familiar with."

"What happens to them in Lum?" asked the Senator, his eyes stricken with worry.

"Their ego is weak and their body is frail, so they soon lose their body image and reincarnate."

"Reincarnation is real?" asked the Senator.

Kioshi popped up in between them. "Okay, that I can attest to. I actually met someone who specializes in past-life regression therapy, and I had an experience of when I was a mother possum. I had so many babies; they were so cute!"

"That's right, my dear, reincarnation is currently the way of the afterlife."

"And the babies…the beings torn from their mother's wombs, are forced to reincarnate, aren't they?" asked the Senator, his hands trembling.

"That is correct."

The Senator leaned against the chair after nearly falling over. "Please, leave. I need to be alone."

"What about my initiation?" asked Kioshi.

"Leave me now!" yelled the Senator in tears.

Kioshi put her arm around the Prince and escorted him out. "Sorry about that. He's adamantly pro-life."

"I didn't expect him to be so easily swayed. I'm pleasantly surprised," said the Prince, leaning in for a kiss.

"Wait, does that mean you were lying?" asked Kioshi.

Suddenly a voice came booming from behind them.

"Get away from her!" yelled Koshi, aiming a pistol at the Prince.

"He's an ally now. Actually, he's my boyfriend, so deal with it," said Kioshi before snuggling the Prince.

Koshi lowered his gun. "You know how dangerous he is."

"Things have changed. Don't you trust me?" asked Kioshi with a pouty face.

"Of course I trust you. I just don't trust him."

The Prince released Kioshi's hips. "Perhaps it's best if I leave. I have a lot of work ahead of me."

"You're not going anywhere." Koshi placed his finger to his ear. "Beta, my sister brought an Exp inside the base. He's not an enemy but watch him closely, okay?" He reached into his pocket and pulled out three movie tickets. "Hey, sis, remember that movie I promised you?"

"Why are there three tickets?" asked Kioshi.

"Lambda is coming along too," said Koshi.

"Oh."

"Is that a problem?"

"It's fine. Should I get ready?"

"Yeah. I'm going to report to the Boss once I make sure your new boyfriend is being monitored," said Koshi.

"Let's make it four tickets!" said Kioshi, grappling her boyfriend's arm.

"You're serious, aren't you?"

"Yep, either he goes or I stay."

"Okay then, I'll cancel," said Koshi, walking off.

Kioshi rubbed her face against the Prince's arm. "He's such a jerk."

"Go on, my dear. Have fun. We can make up for lost time tonight," he said, touching her lip while caressing her hair.

Kioshi lit up and shook his pinky with hers. "No taksies backsies now!" She then ran off to meet with her brother.

"Oh, my dear, we'll climb the ranks together," he said, licking a lock of her hair.

Meanwhile back at Deceivant's home, banners with the words "Welcome!" and "Congratulations!" decorated the dining room.

The chairs were scrunched up together to fit as many as possible.

D.S. leaned in as the Captain of Carnage recounted his tale of bravery.

"Leaving behind a trail of my blood from the vicious wound, I stumble down the ashen floor of the city street. My fur stands on end, sensing enemies closing in on me. I whimper as they approach, and once I spot the hesitation in their eyes...I launch myself from the floor. My teeth tear into flesh as I tear out my attacker's throat. As soon as the second attacker is in range, I launch my knife into his forehead. Then, I reel the knife in and my massive foe along with it. With a single kick the knife pierces their brain," said the Captain, gesturing with a knife in his paw.

Chipko sat alone in the corner, petting something in her hands. Muffins came up to her and nestled her leg. The eco-warrior pulled her legs in. "You're certainly friendly."

Opti brought Durga some tea. "You're really pretty. Want to be my soul mate?"

Durga looked at him curiously.

Opti pat his face. "Did I get it?"

"I am complete on my own." She walked off.

Opti sighed. "This is hard."

Exp 8 patted his back. "You're not allowed to be sad. You've got to keep us positive even when things are grim, got it?"

"Absolutely! I'll be the sunlight that scares away the rainstorm."

"That's the spirit. Alright! We have four newcomers here tonight! Let's properly welcome them to the team!" exclaimed Exp 8, raising his fist.

"Is there some sort of ritual you perform?" asked Durga.

"There certainly is. Group hug!" exclaimed Opti, embracing her from behind.

"Welcome back to the team," said Crisis, putting his arm around Wringer.

"Yay! More friends," cheered D.S., hugging Toxic.

The veteran Freedom Forcers got up from their chairs and joined the embrace.

Exp 8 temporarily left and approached the newcomer hiding in the corner. "Come on, it's tradition."

"I don't like hugs," said Chipko, looking away.

Exp 8 grabbed her hand and pulled her onto her feet. "It doesn't hurt. I promise." He wrapped his arms around her.

"Don't touch me!" she wailed, sending a shockwave that pushed Exp 8 off her.

The Freedom Forcers' leader tumbled off his feet and crashed into Atlas' chair.

Stabby ran to Exp 8's side.

"I'm alright. Sorry, Chipko. I didn't mean to upset you," said Exp 8, tickling Stabby to keep her calm.

"Did I hurt you?" asked Chipko, worry in her eyes.

"I'm fine. Don't worry about it," said Exp 8, getting up.

Atlas rose from his chair, holding his wife's hand. "Since the initiation is complete, Image and I are going to retreat for the night."

"Not allowed!" hollered Ada from the kitchen. "Not until you've had some coconut cream fruitcake!"

"We shouldn't be eating anything," said Chipko softly.

"Cake!" D.S. ran off to the kitchen.

"Stabby, dear, won't you slice it for everyone?" asked Ada.

Exp 8 patted Stabby's head. "Go on. I'll be right here."

"Cake!" Stabby ran to the kitchen.

"I wasn't done with the story!" hollered the Captain.

BoneSaw motioned for the Captain to continue.

"Your interest is noted. I'll continue once the boy returns," said the Captain.

D.S. rushed back to the dining room. He approached Crisis and gave him the first slice. "Cake! Just like I promised."

Crisis held his head and laughed. "Okay, you got me." He looked up at D.S. and smiled with teary eyes.

"Are you okay?" asked D.S.

"Thanks," said Crisis, choked up. "I feel like I have a family again." He sobbed in his hands.

Wringer placed a friendly chain on his hand.

Crisis turned to him and nodded, drying his tears.

"That's right! We're all a family! I hereby welcome Wringer, Durga, Toxic, and Chipko to the team! You're all honorary Freedom Forcers!" cheered Exp 8.

"These just arrived this morning. Perfect timing!" Ada rushed in and gave each one of them a bracelet to commemorate their bond.

"Freedom Forcers, eh? I like the name," said Chipko with a small smile.

Hope, lying down in the living room, lifted her head from her freshly fluffed pillow. "Just so we're clear, Kaity is the leader of the Freedom Forcers now, and I am the Queen of the Exps. You're merely a figure head, Exp 8."

Deceivant was massaging the bottom of her feet. "You don't know him. He's so much more that."

"I didn't ask for your opinion. This whole party is premature. I only permitted it because it should boost morale. Come to think of it, where is Kaity? I don't see her," said Hope, poking his face with her big toe.

"She's in the kitchen!" hollered Ada.

Exp 8 left to check on her.

Kaity paced around near the tea dispenser.

"Come on, sit with the group," said Exp 8.

"I can't. If I do…I'll notice who isn't there," said Kaity, her eyes barely holding back her tears.

"Kanasta is safe, you know that," said Exp 8.

"What about Devlin and Nina?" asked Kaity, a few tears leaving her eyes.

"The peace talks are tomorrow. You know Hope will get them back," said Exp 8.

"What are we going to do? We can't stop Sel. We've already lost more members than we've gained by coming here," said Kaity.

"Sellum is strong enough to stop Sel. All we need to do is keep Sel's minions off his back. I know things will work out," said Exp 8, holding her hand.

Kaity pulled away. "Like they did in the fight against Etah? We lost five allies to him alone. When we were talking about political strategies, I kept imagining they were there with us. Matteria would write songs to bolster our popularity. Anthrax would show everyone just how good-natured Exps can be."

Exp 8 smiled. "Kawai would be resting in my lap. Atatasuki…he'd be committing all the most important things to memory. And NoOne would be doubting every idea we put forth."

"Pharma has his own group of friends too. And Tempo…he'd be able to do my mission," said Kaity softly, her head drooping.

"I have total faith in you," said Exp 8, lifting her head up.

Kaity managed a small smile. "That's one of us. I don't think we can succeed without Devlin. If Hope can't bargain to get him, will you help me free him and Nina?"

"Let's discuss that when the time comes."

"Okay. You're right. And Violet! She would be able to reach so many people. She could make her own universalist religion to aid our cause. But she isn't here," said Kaity in tears.

"She's not dead. Violet is doing what she feels she must do."

"I'm scared of losing anyone else to death. I'm terrified of being betrayed again. I just want it all to end."

"Things are coming to a close." Exp 8 embraced Kaity. "Thanks for leading everyone in my absence."

Kaity hugged him back. "Don't die again. I don't want to lead the team without you."

"I'm not planning on dying."

"Hey, if you die in Sellum…what do you think happens?"

"Well, if there's an afterlife, maybe there's an after afterlife."

"A world beyond Sellum…do you think they're at peace there?"

"Yeah, they are."

"You can't say for sure."

"Trust me, they're at peace."

Kaity pulled away from the embrace. She placed a slice of cake on a plate and offered it to Exp 8. "You can't say no."

"Alright. I accept." Exp 8 took the plate. "Everyone's waiting for you."

"Okay…after I finish my slice," said Kaity with a grin.

Exp 8 walked past the dining room, down the hall, and went out the back entrance. He crouched down and picked off a piece of the cake. "I hope you enjoy it." The rebel leader placed the piece by an ant pile. "A small bite for me is enough to feed hundreds of you. Never waste food, that's part of the creed I live by."

"It's a good way to live," said Chipko, leaning against the back wall.

"Thanks. It's good to see you. Sorry about before," said Exp 8.

"I freaked out. I don't do well around crowds. Unless it's a protest or something meaningful. I hate parties," she said, plucking a piece off his cake and setting it near the anthill.

"Do you think Hope will lead us into the right future?" asked Exp 8.

"Don't ask me. I'm not very good with politics," said Chipko, her eyes on the ants joyously carrying crumbs to their queen.

"It's not that I don't trust her. She truly wants Exps to have equal rights. I just…feel like it's a Band-Aid to a much bigger problem."

"If you have a different idea, I'm all ears."

"I shouldn't be hasty. Let's see how the peace talks go," said Exp 8, waving at a bird that flew by.

"I spotted a toad in the pond back here. I wonder if she's still—"

Exp 8 put his arm in front of Chipko. "Careful."

She looked down and noticed a stationary ant on the cement. "I didn't see him. I almost...." She started crying.

"It's alright. I stopped you, just like you would have stopped me."

"But what if you hadn't stopped me?" asked Chipko, holding her small rock to her chest for comfort.

"I know how you feel. It terrifies me how easily a life can be lost. We have to be more than aware of our surroundings. We have to think of the future we are forging. Every action has a consequence," said Exp 8 softly.

"I'll do everything I can for this world, and I'd be happy if you'd support me," said Chipko, putting out her fist.

Exp 8 connected fists with her. "I'm fortunate to have you. Now, what do you say we go see if momma toad is in the pond?" asked Exp 8, reaching for her hand before pulling back. "Sorry."

"It's fine." She gripped his hand. "Yeah, let's go see."

On the other side of the house, the front door opened.

"Everyone! You won't believe who just arrived!" exclaimed Ada.

"If it's Kanasta, tell him he's not allowed in!" hollered Hope from the living room.

"Devlin!" exclaimed Kaity, rushing up and hugging him.

"I wasn't gone that long, was I?" asked Devlin, petting her affectionately.

Deceivant rushed to the front door with Hope in his arms.

"It appears my negotiations have worked after all. Welcome back." Hope smiled at her brother.

"I'll get you some cake," said D.S., rushing off to the kitchen.

"I see a new face. I'm Devlin," he said, offering his hand to the newcomer.

"Durga. Your friends are very welcoming to me," she said with a small smile.

"They're my family." Devlin exhaled sharply. "Okay. Everyone, I need you to promise you'll be extra careful. We can't afford to make enemies with the Senator."

"Already have peace talks scheduled; the first one begins tomorrow. You can rest easy. I'm more than fit to lead us," said Hope, beaming with pride.

"I'm sure you are," said Devlin with a smile.

"Now that you're here, we need to find a way for you to contribute. I'm forging a path to equality for all our people," said Hope, pulling at his shirt.

"You should be super proud of your little sister! She's, like, mega smart," said D.S. with big eyes.

Hope took the plate from D.S. and ate the slice speedily with dignity.

"That was for Devlin!" exclaimed D.S. before rushing back to the kitchen.

Deceivant grasped Hope's hand. "We're going to connect our movement to the vegan movement and spearhead the eco-revolution!"

"That's wonderful. Really, it's just incredible," said Devlin, his eyes shifting around.

"What's wrong?" asked Kaity.

"I'm not going to be joining you...at least not now," said Devlin with an unsure smile.

"Worry not. I'll have Nina safe and secure by sundown tomorrow," said Hope.

"What happened to Nina?" asked Devlin.

"She was captured," said Kaity softly.

"Well, I'm sure Hope can get her free."

"I know I can. But what do you mean you aren't going to join us?" asked Hope with an inquisitive gaze.

Devlin laughed nervously. D.S. joined in till Hope silenced him with a scary look.

"Why not?" she asked, gazing into Devlin.

"I-I I'm going to be a dad." Devlin chuckled. "Demonica is pregnant and I...I have to be there for my child."

Ada smothered Devlin in a sudden embrace. "Our little boy is going to be a daddy!"

"Thanks, Mom. I was shocked when she first told me," said Devlin.

Deceivant smiled at his son. "We understand, son. You have duties as a father."

"Yeah, and I'm not going to just abandon my child like you would," said Devlin with a glare.

"Celebration cake!" cheered D.S., forcing a plate into Devlin's hands.

"Thanks, everyone. I'm sorry I can't be with you all, but that's the decision we've made," said Devlin before taking a bite. "Fantastic cooking as always, Mom."

"You're worried about the safety of your children. That means you won't keep in touch," said Hope, her bottom lip quivering.

"I have a responsibility as a father to keep my children safe. You have to understand," said Devlin before taking another bite.

"I understand," said Exp 8 from the back of the group. "You're running away from your responsibility to us. What about me and Opti? Aren't we your children too?"

"You're grown up at this point. You can decide your own future," said Devlin.

"You're an idiot if you think you can hide. He'll find you; and when he does, you're going to wish you had more Exps around to defend you and your preferred child," said Exp 8.

"Demonica and I will be able to handle ourselves," said Devlin.

"I forbid you from leaving. You can't neglect your responsibilities as my brother," said Hope, pulling at his shirt.

"I've already decided on this. There's no turning back now. I came to say goodbye," said Devlin softly, turning away his gaze.

"You made a promise! You owe me years of sibling bonding!" yelled Hope, shaking his arm.

Exp 8 gripped Devlin by the collar. "This is bigger than just you and your family. If Sel wins, everything is lost! And what about Kaity? Are you really going to leave her?"

"I want my children to grow up in a different world. A world beyond this constant conflict," said Devlin.

"Then maybe you shouldn't have gone off and had kids till the fighting was done!" yelled Exp 8.

"I didn't decide this!" Devlin left and slammed the door behind him.

Opti went to open it, but Kaity shook her head.

"Let me talk to him, okay?" she asked.

Devlin wiped away his tears when he saw Kaity over his shoulder.

Kaity walked up to him. "I think it's great that you're trying to protect your child. Don't worry. Hope, Exp 8, and I will continue to lead the Freedom Forcers."

Devlin seized her in a tight embrace. "I love you. I love you! I love you! I love you! I'll never stop loving you. But I have to stop pursuing you. I know my feelings are a bother to you and that's…."

Kaity kissed his cheek. "I'm honored you feel so deeply about me."

Devlin kissed her cheek in tears. "I can't stop loving you and I don't want to. But I'm a father now. I have to be responsible, for the sake of my child. I don't know when I'll see you again. I don't know anything really." He sobbed on her shoulder.

"We will meet again. Devlin, we've been through so much together. I'm really happy you've been a part of my life annnnd…I look forward to having you be a part of my life in the future." She patted his hand.

"You're so good to me, Katy. Umm, don't tell anyone else…but Demonica…forced herself on me. It's all a blur."

Kaity grabbed his shaking hand. "I'm so sorry."

"I know what Sefiwah did to you. She told me about it when the two of us…had sex. I'm sorry."

"Sefiwah never forced me! And what do you mean you two had sex? When?"

"Back when I first met you. I'm glad it wasn't true. She was probably testing me, like I was her. You won't tell anyone about what Demonica did, right? I don't want them to know."

Kaity held his hand to her solemn face. "I won't say a thing. Thanks for telling me."

Devlin seized her in an embrace. "Thanks for everything! You've brought so much light into my miserable life." He ended the embrace and slipped a piece of paper into her hands. "That's my new number. I'm entrusting it only to you, so don't give it to the others. Call me only if you need me. Emergencies only, okay?"

"I understand. Now come back inside. You haven't said goodbye to everyone yet," said Kaity, turning around.

Devlin grabbed her hand. "Do you…think I'll be a good father?"

"You already are," said Kaity, leading him back inside.

"Sorry, everyone. I'm leaving tonight. It may be years till we meet again," said Devlin, mustering the courage to face his family.

"We can't visit you because it isn't safe. Well then, I'll simply have to speed up the movement. You've given me new motivation to accomplish our goals," said Hope, ruthlessly flicking away any tears that escaped her eyes.

"Goodbye, everyone," said Devlin, turning away as tears welled up.

"I may permit you to leave to care for your children but not before you give me a hug," said Hope, crossing her arms and puffing out her cheeks.

"Yeah. Of course," said Devlin, lifting her out of Deceivant's arms and embracing her.

Hope grabbed his cheeks. "You best not cause any trouble. It wasn't easy cleaning up our reputation after you slaughtered humans at the airport."

"I'll behave. I promise," said Devlin.

"Good boy," said Hope, patting his head.

Opti stepped up. "When everything is safe, we can visit, right?"

"Yeah. We'll meet up sometime down the road," said Devlin, patting his creation.

Exp 8's fists were shaking. "I can't stop you from abandoning us. I fight for freedom, and as much as I hate to say it, you're free to choose to leave. Just remember, once a Freedom Forcer, always a Freedom Forcer. One last group hug. I won't take no for an answer."

"Haha! Alright," said Devlin, putting his arm around Opti.

Kaity grabbed his other arm and put it around her.

The circle was completed when Chipko joined between Durga and Exp 8.

"This is nice," said Chipko, blushing and smiling at Exp 8.

Exp 8 lowered his head. "We are gathered here to honor Devlin."

"Geez, you make it sound like I'm dead," said the scientist with a chuckle.

"Stop complaining. Devlin, you're a powerful fighter, an intelligent leader, and a member of our family. We will sorely miss you, but you can rest assured we will win the fight without you!" exclaimed Exp 8.

"Have you decided what you'll name the baby?" asked Ada.

"Demonica already has a named picked out, but she won't tell me yet. Drives me crazy," said Devlin with a nervous grin.

"Here." Hope handed her reckless brother a cell phone. "It's a secure line. Contact me anytime if you need anything."

"Thank you." Devlin smiled at his team. "Everyone."

"So, is Demonica going to say bye too?" asked Opti.

"She said she'll tell Bob if he manages to find us. We both hope that doesn't happen." Devlin kissed Hope on the forehead. "I'm leaving them in your care."

"I'll do my best to keep them out of trouble," said Hope with a smile.

Devlin turned to Kaity and hugged her. "I'm going to miss you so much." His eyes welled up with tears.

Kaity dried his tears and kissed his cheek.

"Thanks." Delvin opened the door and walked out. "Farewell, everyone! Thanks for everything! Here I go…out into the world beyond!" He waved them goodbye and closed the door.

Chapter 154: Comprimise & Force

Meanwhile in the rocky mountain ranges of Arizona, Lord Sel completed the task at hand.

"Do you feel any different?" asked Riufen to Gladius.

"I feel bereft of freedom. But there's no going back now. Our souls and destinies are intertwined. Looks like I'm stuck with you," said Gladius with a grimace.

Lord Sel created a black portal. "Come along now. We need to discuss our current plan."

The three of them entered the portal and exited into the Core.

"Every moment we spend here is a day they gain to strengthen their forces," said Lord Sel.

"Then we should move out immediately," said Tsul.

"Agreed. Fan out and search for Demonica. I'd rather not storm Absence without her assistance," said Lord Sel.

"You'll never get away with this." Flash Girl shrugged. "No. I'm sorry. Waaay to cliché. How about this?" She cleared her throat. "Your plans will crumble to pieces along with your empire."

"She's got grit. Take her along," said Lord Sel.

"How do we make sure she doesn't try to run?" asked Tsul.

"If she does, start slaughtering humans until she returns," said Lord Sel.

"As you command," said Tsul.

"You guys are darker than the villains I'm used to," said Flash Girl with a nervous smile.

"We're also smarter." Lord Sel formed a portal to Earth and all his minions followed along.

When Devlin arrives at the train station, he is confronted.

"What do you want?"

"I'm not going to let you abandon us," said Deceivant.

"If I kill you, Bob can't use you to make Exps. I wouldn't do it in front of the others, but we're alone now. Don't tempt me." Devlin's wires coiled around Deceivant's throat.

Deceivant slammed Amy into Devlin's head and slipped free of the wire's grip. "Are you really going to leave Kaity behind to be killed by Bob?" asked Deceivant, pressing the blade of the gun to Devlin's cheek.

"What do you care? You're too busy having sleepovers to keep them protected."

"You're the one abandoning all of us," said Deceivant.

213

"Don't you dare accuse me of what you do!" Devlin slammed his knee into Deceivant's crotch. His wires wrapped around the Gravity Gun and pulled it out of his father's grip.

"We need you. Hope needs you!"

"Enough talk." Devlin slammed the Gravity Gun down on Deceivant.

"Be careful, she's delicate," said Deceivant, scanning the gun for loose parts.

"You shouldn't have made me so strong," said Devlin with a smirk.

Deceivant rose to his feet and aimed the gun. "Trust me Devlin; you won't beat me."

Devlin's wires shot out, zooming toward Deceivant.

"Let's see how you fare against my *GRAVITY SHOT*." Deceivant fired a bullet in the middle of the wire mass.

The wires followed the pull from the bullet, redirecting them toward their owner.

Devlin jumped out of the way, almost losing his balance as the bullet sped by his side. "What's this? Can you actually fight?" he asked, poised for battle.

"I defeated Riufen." Deceivant fired a bullet at his son's feet.

"Still lying about that! Just like you lie every time you say you love Mother!" Devlin was pulled to the ground, and his face slammed against the floor.

"I love her dearly! You're the one who murdered her!" Deceivant ran up to his attacker and jumped on his back. He fired gravity bullets backward, using Devlin as a skateboard and riding him down the train tracks.

The humans took out their phones and recorded the spectacle.

Wires shot out of Devlin's back, wrapping around Deceivant's feet.

Deceivant cut the wires with the Gravity Blade and jumped off his son, sending him skidding across the ground.

Devlin's wires grabbed Deceivant in midair. He pulled him up to his face, which was now missing skin in places. "I'm considering killing you."

"Doing so would only send me into Sel's clutches."

They yelled simultaneously as they tossed the condensed explosives.

"*WIRE GRENADE!*"

"*GRAVITY GRENADE!*"

The grenades burst open at the same time.

Wires jutted out but immediately plummeted to the ground once the gravitational increase was released.

Deceivant slammed the back of the gun into Devlin's face and pressed him to the floor. "Stalemate."

"Hardly."

Wires erupted out from Devlin and thrashed around.

Deceivant shielded his face as he was violently slashed.

Devlin rose to his feet, pulled in the wires, ran up and punched his father's face.

Wires shot out the knuckle of his fist and connected to Deceivant's chin.

On the rebound, Deceivant jabbed the Gravity Blade into Devlin's unguarded chest.

Wires came out from the wound and wrapped around Deceivant's neck.

"Why did you ever serve Sel? He's the one who ruined your life!" yelled Deceivant, pressing the blade to his son's throat.

"I joined Sel to protect Kaity," said Devlin with a sweet smile.

"What?"

"My love for Kaity pushed out the vengeance that plagued me. Even as Sel controlled me, I still kept my will to protect her." Devlin pressed Bravery to Deceivant's chest.

"Now you tell me: what reason could you possibly have for joining Sellum? I know you joined him before the rest of us. He has you under his thumb. You can't be so blind that you don't realize he has his own agenda. For all we know, he may be even more of a threat than Sel."

"I can't live without Ada. When she died, I had to do everything I could to revive her. Sellum was the only one who could save her," said Deceivant softly.

Devlin retracted all his wires. "Maybe you're not just a damned pedophile," he said with a smile.

"Maybe you're my son, after all," said Deceivant, retracting the Gravity Blade.

Devlin turned away. "I'm sorry, Father," he said, tears welling up in his eyes.

Deceivant embraced his son. "Please, come back home. I'm sorry for what I did to your experiments. I just didn't want you to end up making the same mistakes I did."

"Watch over Hope for me. I have a feeling she could delve into darkness if you don't support her."

"I will. So…when did you become a father? Who's the mother?"

Devlin turned away. "I don't want to talk about it."

"That's your choice. I'm sure you'll be a great father. And I bet your little girl will be just adorable!"

"Who said it was a girl?"

"I have a sense for these things."

"You better not hit on her," said Devlin with a glare.

"Of course not! She's my grandchild. Hey, do you think Hope will ever forgive me?"

"She's cruel but she's kind of sweet too."

"Hope has really taken a liking to you. I'm quite jealous."

"You're still her father. I'm sure she'll forgive you eventually."

"I hope so. Stay safe, son."

"You too…Dad." Devlin smiled.

Demonica popped out from behind them. "Awww, you two are just adorable." With a snap of her fingers, their wounds had healed.

"Did you get the supplies we need?" asked Devlin.

"Yep. Are you sure you don't want instant travel?"

"If Gimpy knows, Sel could find out. I prefer we go by train."

"Well then, we better hurry. The train just arrived." Demonica changed her appearance to look more human and wrapped her arm around Devlin's. "Let's go, sweetie."

"Take good care of my son," said Deceivant, stepping into the demoness' path.

Demonica smiled and kissed Devlin's cheek. "I'll keep him safe."

Meanwhile at Deceivant's home, Image turned away from the window and planted a kiss on her husband's forehead. "Morning. How do you feel?"

"Rejuvenated," said Atlas with a stretch.

"Exps are always hardwired with energy, so it's hard for them to sleep. Even if they don't need to sleep, it doesn't hurt. Rats clear out their thoughts when they dream. Exps would benefit greatly from sleep just the same," said Image.

"You were right, as always." He puts his arm over her shoulder. "Just in time to watch the sunrise."

"Let's wake the others up. We're a team, so having a morning ritual will only serve to strengthen our bonds and boost morale," said Image, getting up.

"I hope we can continue our nighttime ritual too," said Atlas, kissing his wife.

"Well, not every night," said Image with a blush.

"It's good to be back," said Atlas, following her out of the room. He walked into the living room and tapped Exp 8, who was huddled with Stabby on the couch.

"Etah!" Exp 8 leaped off the couch and prepared for battle.

"We are allies, remember?" asked Atlas with a smile.

"Oh, yeah. You didn't need to wake me, by the way. My internal clock is set to just before sunrise." He leaned over and lifted Stabby up from her floor bed. "Come on. Time to get up."

"Okay, Daddy," said Stabby in a daze.

Exp 8 opened the sliding glass door and sat next to Chipko. "I figured you would already be up."

"Of course. Every morning is a blessing from nature," said Chipko.

Exp 8 placed his hand on hers. "I couldn't agree more."

Hope opened the sliding door. "Deceivant and I are heading out for the peace talks. Exp 8, I'm counting on you to make sure everyone follows the plan, at least until Kaity gets up. Is that clear?"

"Clear as the surface of a lake," said Exp 8 with a salute.

"Good. Then everyone shall start working after the sunrise. We cannot afford to waste time," she said before closing the door.

Kaity, Ada, and Image sat down with the group to watch the sunrise.

"Oooh! It's starting to come up," said Ada, bouncing in excitement.

"Yay! We're not too late," said D.S., pulling Opti along.

Atlas opened the door. "I can't find Crisis."

"He must have gone with Deceivant and Hope. Don't worry. Now sit with me. You're missing it," said Image.

The Freedom Forcers silently watched the sun rise into their view. The early rays of light shimmered as they breached through the foliage and blessed the Exps and animals alike.

Hope raised her chair as high as it would go and straightened out her stack of notes. "I can't even remember the last time I was at a public event."

"There's nothing to worry about, my dear," said Deceivant, massaging her shoulders.

"Who said I was worried?" asked Hope, turning away from his golden gaze.

"Come on, my little queen. Whip that nervousness into submission. Turn it into charisma for your debate," said Deceivant.

Senator Jo John entered the room and took a seat in the large black chair. He leaned over the wide table and smiled at Hope. "On behalf of the President, I am here to speak with you."

"It's my pleasure to be here, Senator. I sent out invitations to many politicians from all three parties, but you were the only one who accepted," said Hope, still a bit jittery.

"Fear leads to prejudice, and what place does prejudice have in the melting pot that is this great country? The only thing I fear is causing America to lose face," said the Senator.

"Indeed. I personally hope my people can coexist with humankind," said Hope.

"That is a lofty desire, but such lofty desires are what have made our nation the place it is today. Hope, you come here representing all of the Exps, am I correct?" asked the Senator.

"Absolutely. I am the Queen of the Exps. This man here to my right is Deceivant. He created me and a number of my people," said Hope.

"And as their leader, I take full responsibility for their actions," said Deceivant.

"Then do you take responsibility for the recent bank robbing incident, an incident that caused the loss of American lives?" asked the Senator.

Hope covered Deceivant's mouth and took a deep breath before responding. "I represent all the Exps, but that does not mean I control them all. I can assure you that Crisis' actions are not in any way connected to me."

"Well, that's a rather convenient claim, isn't it?" asked the Senator with a sly grin.

"If I can get approval, I would like to form a special task force for dealing with rogue Exps. I would like the federal government to recognize me as the sovereign ruler of my people. As such, if they commit a crime, I shall deal with them appropriately," said Hope, folding her hands in her lap.

"Request denied. Your kind may not have personhood, but that doesn't mean they are exempt from federal prosecution," said the Senator, waving his bony finger.

"You misunderstand. My task force shall exist for capturing Exps. My people are powerful, and sending humans to arrest them could lead to casualties. After my task force has captured them, I shall publicly turn them over to the authorities. As far as I'm concerned, an Exp who breaks the law is an enemy to my goal of peace and sovereignty and thus is no longer one of my people. Now I'm quite familiar with the federal laws but would ask that my request be considered."

"Are you asking for accountability to be transferred from the creator to the creation in question?"

"Exps may be regarded as property, but they are capable of independent action. I feel my approach is the best way to manage this very tricky situation."

"What if you are unable to catch them?"

"Then I will step aside and allow the authorities to step in. Though I fear they may find the task quite difficult."

"There's something else bothering me about your proposal. If you aren't accountable for their actions, then you could use your people as sacrificial pawns for terrorism. Need I remind you about the Crimson Bomb terrorist attack of 2080? Your people turned against their own creator!"

Hope closed her eyes and took a deep breath. "Senator, we are a people, not an organization. The actions of separate entities cannot be blamed on the entire people."

"You only want accountability when it comes to capturing the renegades."

"It's quite clear that the purpose of this proposal is to show that I will responsibly deal with Exps who do not adhere to federal laws."

"If this request is even to be considered, a detailed report on every Exp you are aware of must be submitted to the Secretary of Defense. I also ask that you put in place fail-safes for remote detonation of rogue Exps and give that authority to the President's cabinet," said the Senator.

Hope's fists trembled beneath the table. "I shall gladly submit the reports, but remote detonation is a violation of my people's rights and I shall not adhere to it."

"Are you saying you question the moral integrity of the President of the United States of America?" asked the Senator with wide eyes.

"This was a trap," said Deceivant softly.

Hope closed her eyes and took a deep breath.

"Silence isn't an answer," said the Senator with a toothy grin.

"The moral integrity of the President and her cabinet has not been called into question. It is the violation of my people's rights that I reject, and I shan't waver on this matter, Senator."

"Exps do not have rights," said the Senator.

"As living beings, we have a right to live and be free as long as such freedoms do not intrude upon the rights of others."

"Exps are creations of man, not God," said the Senator.

"We are still alive," said Hope, stopping herself from slamming her fists on the table.

"Senator, she is merely asking that you allow her to capture Exps who break the law. Why are you resisting a request with the purpose of minimizing damage?" asked Deceivant.

"The authorities will deal swiftly with lawbreakers. Who's to say how long it will take for this artificial task force to reign in the terrorists? If our hands are tied during an incident, it would likely lead to civilian casualties, American casualties."

"I would not ask for something without merit. Deceivant, show him," said Hope.

Deceivant brought in Crisis from the back room.

Crisis had a blindfold over his eyes and was handcuffed.

"Renegade Exp Capture Task Force Incorporated, or RECTFI if you will, has subdued Crisis for his criminal activity. I now turn him over to the authorities," said Hope.

Two of the guards at the door cautiously approached the dangerous creature.

"You do realize Exps are not citizens and thus do not have the right to a fair trial?" said the Senator.

"I am aware. His fate is no longer in my hands," said Hope.

"Your request for RECTFI approval will be given to the Secretary of Defense alongside the specifications of each Exp, as requested. Meeting adjourned."

The camera lowered and Senator Jo John left the room and was swarmed by reporters.

Hope and Deceivant left through the back entrance.

A single reporter with frizzy orange hair approached, the others watching warily from the sidelines.

"Kelly Reyes, Independent Info Bomb. Can I get an interview with you?"

"Certainly. We're heading home, right now. You're welcome to come with us," said Hope.

Meanwhile, Senator John meets up with Agent Alpha in his limousine.

"How did it go?" asked Alpha.

"Couldn't have gone better. With Crisis in my grasp, I now have control over the weather. Cities that stand against me can be ravaged by hurricanes. I can cause political meetings to be canceled with a lightning storm. Most importantly, states supporting climate deniers can be assaulted till they cave in to the undeniable truth. Claiming this particular Exp is a massive step toward true equality."

"So, does this mean you don't want me to capture Exp 8?"

"If all goes accordingly, Hope will turn him over to me herself," said the Senator, reclining his seat. He sat up and puts his finger to his ear. "You've secured the target, Agent Beta?"

"Yes, sir. They weren't hard to deal with," said Beta in a calm and devout voice from the other line.

"Showing the incompetence of the authorities will only increase my credibility, and Hope's task force shall serve as a stepping stone for the acceptance of our own task force in the future," said the Senator.

"Undermining both the authorities and the Exps; you're so incredibly clever."

"Any event can be bent toward our goal with the proper perspective," said the Senator, leaning back.

"There's a problem. He's unresponsive."

"Not to worry. We can simply bend him to our will. Extract his artifact and hand him over to Lambda when you arrive."

"Sir, there's no artifact."

"What! Are you absolutely certain?"

"As certain as death is inevitable."

"Hope thinks she can make a fool out of me. Your orders remain. Agent Lambda will make an example out of Crisis," said the Senator through gritted teeth.

Alpha tapped his shoulder. "Do you want me to infiltrate and locate the artifact, sir?"

"No need. Call up Chipko. The anti-climate rally has created a blockade on 17th street. Make sure the authorities don't get involved. Let's see how long this task force will take to contain the situation."

"Understood, sir," said Alpha with a salute.

"It's for you," said Exp 8, handing the phone to Chipko.

"Koshi, oh, uh, hi. I mean, can I help you?" asked Chipko with flushed cheeks, fiddling with her hair.

"I wish we had time for chitchat, but the Boss gave me orders. I need you to slaughter some protestors. If you don't, well, I've been told to burn down a forest," said Koshi.

"I won't be threatened anymore. I'm not going to throw away our chance to save this world. If you start a fire, we'll put it out," said Chipko.

The other line was silent. "Hahaha! You're serious?"

"Absolutely."

"Well then, no point in starting a fire if it's going to be put out. Just be careful, beautiful. If the Boss doesn't think you're useful, you could be in danger. I wouldn't want to have to hurt you."

Chipko blushed and hung up the phone.

"Who was it?" asked Exp 8.

"I'd rather not say."

"That's fine. Hey, why don't the two of us go out for a bit?"

"I'm supposed to remain here."

"So, you won't let him boss you around, but you'll let Hope do it?"

"I-I...."

"Look. I'm just saying you should do what you feel is right."

"Okay."

"Okay what?"

"I'll come with you." Chipko smiled.

"That's the spirit."

Stabby hopped around with joy. "We're going on a twip. We're going on a twip."

Meanwhile in Kentucky, Kanasta approaches a ranch. "Should be in and out in no time." He hoists up his shotgun and rams into the door.

Beyond the wooden door was a glossy home with famous paintings and artifacts from a spectrum of human cultures atop the cabinets.

Kanasta rushed into the kitchen.

A man along with his wife and child are seated for lunch. They froze when they saw the gun.

"My apologies. My client has asked for no witnesses," said Kanasta softly.

The father eyed the gun mounted on the wall before his face was blown to bits.

The wife stepped in front of the gun as her kid rushed out of the room.

Kanasta shot her belly, spraying red all over her white dress, and rushed down the hallway. "A few more of these and the Viper Squad will earn back its credibility." He tiptoed into the girl's room and detached a spherical object from his belt. The object unraveled and formed a sonar map of the room, revealing where the witness was hiding. The assassin boss fires a round at the closet door and leaves the room after the agonized whimpering stops. "Mission accomplished."

Agent Beta turned over Crisis to Agent Lambda. "Kanasta, did you confirm all three kills?"

"Yes."

"Good. Get out of there. The co-head of Humans First will be arriving any minute. We'll have the police on him as soon as he arrives."

"And then you'll pay me the other half?"

"That's right. Pleasure doing business with you."

"The feeling is mutual."

Chapter 155: Political Footing

Surrounded by trees in the forest, D.S. was engaged in battle. He ducked under the Captain's projectile blades and countered with his scissors.

"You've left an opening." The Captain's second blade shot out and aimed for someone beneath D.S.

"Not on my watch." D.S. slid his leg into the path of the blade. "You lose!" He pulled on the cord, bringing the Captain right up to his scissors.

Toxic lowered the camera and tapped her tail against the ground. "Great work, and I captured every single moment of it."

"We make a great team. Toxic, maybe you could come and protect people with us," said D.S.

"Um, I'm supposed to stay here. I really don't want to go against orders," said Toxic, hiding her face behind her tail.

"The only reason she didn't want you to join is because she didn't realize how skilled you are," said the Captain.

"I want to stay where it's safe. Sorry," said Toxic.

"As long as it's what you want, it's fine. Can you send my fighting movie to the guys I'm gonna save?" asked D.S., handing her his phone.

"Certainly," said Toxic, looking at the list of targets the Captain of Carnage was holding up.

In New York, Atlas, Muffins, and Fusion confront the men in the orange vests.

"Can I help you?" asked one of the men, approaching Atlas.

"Yes. We'd like to help with the clean up."

"Are you an Exp?"

"I am," said Atlas.

The man lifted up his sleeve to show a tattoo of a metal heart. "I joined back when I first heard about Exp 8's rebellion. Do you know him?"

"I do," said Atlas.

"That is so amazing. I still can't believe you're real. The most advanced androids don't even come close to the emotional complexity of an Exp. I'm in charge here, and I say you're welcome to help. Just, uh, keep your distance from the other workers, okay?"

"As you command."

"Richard. I'm Richard by the way."

"Atlas."

"Condemned to hold up the Earth."

"Indeed, though I gladly accept the role I've been given. The burden is truly a blessing."

"So those little critters with you, are they Exps? I've never seen a bunny that looks like that."

"Fusion is an Exp, and Muffins is a friend. Now, shall we?"

"Sure thing. Can you lift that broken piece? It came off from the building. You can see where if you squint."

Atlas lifted up the fragmented wall. "Come along, Fusion."

Meanwhile, Durga is at a round table assembly with Opti.

Durga rolls up her sleeve and shows the iron heart tattoo. "I'm a member."

"I don't care what religion you're a part of. You do good work here," said the man seated next to Opti.

"There's more." Durga opened her mouth to speak but no words came out.

Opti grabbed her hand. "Come on. You can do this."

Durga nodded. "I'm also an...Exp."

The man's eyes widened.

"Just because we aren't human doesn't mean we are numb to their pain. I've dedicated my life to the recovery of those who are incarcerated and...being an Exp doesn't change that," said Durga, her eyes avoiding the director's gaze.

"I'm an Exp too," said Opti, waving at them with both hands.

"Well, that explains a lot, actually. I assure you that your talents are what we cherish you for. If you're an Exp, then you're an Exp. It doesn't change a thing," said the man next to the cheerful Exp.

Opti placed his aura-laden hand on Durga's and smiled at her.

Durga took a deep breath. "Oh, about that. Something does need to change, Director."

"And what is that?"

"Vegetarian isn't enough. It isn't a spiritual lifestyle. If we want true recovery, real breakthroughs, and if we want these prisons to be places of peace, not violence...then we need to make sure the food is cruelty free."

"I'm sorry, Durga. But changing the menu would alienate a lot of—"

"Excuse me. It wouldn't alienate anyone. Not everyone can eat non-vegan food; everyone can eat vegan food. The prisoners are happy to eat healthy."

"Even so, it's just not realistic."

"Then find someone else with my talents."

"What?"

"I love every prison I've been to. The Samadi Sanctuaries have brought so much positivity to the lives of so many. But if you won't stand with me to bring more peace into the prisons, they aren't something I can support."

The person seated next to him looked at the Director.

"Okay, calm down. I'll...I'll get it done. We appreciate all you've done for us. It's our pleasure to help you."

"Thank you very much, Director," said Durga with tears of joy.

"Durga, I ask that you keep your ethnicity a secret. I don't want reporters coming in and messing up my establishment."

"I'll consider it." Durga walked with Opti out of the room and turned to him. "I really appreciate you coming to help."

"You're so pretty when you smile. Well, you're always pretty."

"You have a way of bringing courage out of people," she said with a smile.

"Ask for me anytime. It's a long road, and I'll keep us motivated throughout the journey," said Opti, skipping along the hallway.

Exp 8 and Chipko were at a park looking out at a lake with ducks swimming in it.

Chipko held a phone to her ear with one hand and clenched her beloved rock with the other. "Yes, would you, um, put in a good word for Exps with the other members? Oh, you will? Uh, thanks a lot. A hottie..." she covered the phone and turned to Exp 8, "he called me a hottie...what do I say?"

"Just say thanks."

"Uh, thanks. Your help won't be forgotten," said Chipko to the phone. She then raised her fist up. "I did it. Success." She cradled herself in a hug.

Exp 8 turned to her and smiled beneath his helmet. "You really have faith in Hope's vision. Don't you?"

Chipko bit her lip. "It was you who made me believe in her. The last time I thought I was part of something great...I was being lied to. Your words gave me hope again."

Exp 8 scratched his helmet. "Well, this is going to be a bit awkward. I don't trust Hope. I feel she has a hidden agenda, and I...I don't really believe what we're doing will work. I do want freedom for our people, almost more than anything. But I don't think dabbling in politics is the way to do it."

"What is your suggestion?"

"When things go south, and they will...I want your help. Will you stand by my side and fight with me?"

Chipko turned away. "So, this was it." Tears flowed down her cheeks. "All those kind words. Holding my hand. It was all just part of your strategy."

"Hey, calm down. I'm only asking you because I trust you." He reached out to touch her.

Chipko knocked his hand aside. "Don't touch me. You act like my brother, but all you want is to use me like my father did."

Exp 8 seized her in an embrace. "I need you! You understand me. You know what must be done. Hope fails to see the bigger picture."

"If I stand by you, if I do what you say…you won't abandon me?"

"It's not just trust. You really understand me. We're kindred spirits."

"Promise?" she asked, on the brink of tears.

"I promise to never abandon you."

Chipko pushed away his arms with a sudden shockwave. "Then I'll help you." She turned to the crowd of people gathering around them. "Stop staring at me!" She hid her face with her gloved hands.

Exp 8 grabbed her hands. "Keep your cool. Pretty sure they're looking at me, not you."

"I hate this body," said Chipko, clenching her hands till they bled.

"It may look human, but you're a full-fledged Exp. You have more opportunities to do good because you look human, you know?"

"I still hate it."

"Help me out and I'll get you a new one. Whatever you want."

"No. Modern conveniences create future catastrophes. The problem with products these days is it's cheaper to buy a new one than fix the old one. We live in a time where everything, even morals, are disposable tools of convenience. I was made with this body so I'll keep it, whether I like it or not."

"Your conviction is strong. It's something I've always admired in you. Never lose sight of yourself," said Exp 8, holding her hand.

Stabby grabbed onto Exp 8's hand. "Hold me too, Daddy."

"Sure thing. When the time comes, you two may be the only ones I can count on," said Exp 8, patting Stabby's head.

Kioshi looked out at them from within the crowd. She held her finger to her ear. "You got all that?"

Hope is in an electric blue car and holding a phone to her ear. "Yes. He's planning a mutiny. Hold on a moment. I'm getting a call." She pulled the phone away from her ear. "Hello?"

"You think you're a clever girl, don't you?" asked the voice of the Senator.

"Indeed. Remarkably so. Any other compliments you'd like to shower me with?"

"You handed over a piece of trash! You don't know the forces you're dealing with."

"I beg your pardon. I turned over Crisis to the authorities. It would have been irresponsible of me to not disarm him first."

"Don't play coy with me!"

"Raising your volume does not increase the validity of your statement," she said, licking a lollypop.

"I want his artifact. Do you understand?"

"Sorry. I've grown fond of it. If you want something from me, it's only polite to give something first." She nibbled on the lolly.

"I spoke with you at the peace talks, didn't I?"

"We both sought to gain from that."

"Give me Exp 8 and I won't massacre every one of you abominations!"

"Doing so would make you look two-faced. We shall discus this later. Farewell, Senator." Hope ended the call and opened the door. "I apologize for that noise."

"Don't worry about it. So, this is where you all live?" asked the reporter.

"Indeed it is. My servant will make us a cup of tea, and then we can chat all you like."

"Can you ask Ada to make it? I've got a call set up," said Deceivant.

"Very well, I permit you to shirk your responsibilities," said Hope, opening the door.

Deceivant waved to Ada and headed up the stairs to his bedroom. He opened his laptop and joined the group video call with three other people. "Thanks for accepting on such short notice."

"It's our absolute pleasure. We hadn't heard from you in a long time," said the cheery woman.

"We thought you were dead," said the somber man with a beard.

"The movement is so fortunate to have you," said a passionate young man with glasses.

"So, what are we going to discuss? Recidivism rates, the Cloning Initiative, a new form of Abolitionist Advocacy?" asked the cheery woman.

"Actually, Shelly, I'd like to discuss Exp rights," said Deceivant.

"Oh. Okay then, go right ahead."

"Well," Deceivant cleared his throat, "abolitionist veganism is about unequivocal advocacy that does not dilute itself. The mere act of dilution or reductionism is speciesism itself."

"You're preaching to the choir," said the somber man.

"Bear with me, Robert. Exps are first and foremost living beings. Just as we do not discriminate between the livelihood of an individual belonging to the mammalian phylum and one belonging to the arthropod phylum, there are no differences with the inherent value of Exps and other animals, at least not from a moralistic standpoint. Like any living being, they seek freedom and cherish their life. Therefore, I feel that to exclude them from our sphere of moral concern is an arbitrary decision. To do so would make us no different than the hypocrites who wish to exclude mollusks because of their lack of pain receptors."

"You're droning on," said Robert.

"I'm done. Now I'd like to hear your thoughts. Gary, what do you feel?" asked Deceivant.

"Well, I don't really have any disagreements with what you said."

"Splendid, and the rest of you?"

"I'll speak," said Robert. "You failed to mention that Exps are artificial."

"Well, the most abused animals of all are genetically distorted for human convenience."

"We don't make hierarchies of abuse. That's what welfarists do. All use is abuse."

"I know that. But surely you realize that—"

"It's irrelevant," said Shelly. "Whether or not someone came from another animal or was created in a lab, our moral obligation to them remains."

"That's exactly right. I propose we bring Exps into the common discourse of abolitionist vegans," said Deceivant.

"I'll vote for whatever amendment helps your inventions," said Robert, "but we need to be realistic. There are many people who distrust Exps. What you're asking us to do will complicate our message. Abolitionist vegan advocacy must remain as logical and simple as possible."

"Robert does have a point. The last thing we want to do is further divide the vegan community," said Shelly.

"So then just because it isn't convenient for you means they're going to be excluded? You're the one who wrote an entire book on the evolution of vegan advocacy and how we must be open to modifications, Shelly."

"I know. I'm not saying no. I'm just weighing the risks here," said Shelly, turning away nervously.

"Don't let him play you," said Robert. "Exps have not been reduced to things. They are not imprisoned or raped so that the masses can steal their flesh and secretions. The day of their execution is not planned the moment they are born. My loyalties lie with the truly oppressed; it lies with the animals. Your Exp crusade is a waste of time and resources. Every second counts, and I won't waste another listening to this nonsense."

"Well, heheh. He dropped the call," said Gary with an awkward smile.

"His heart's in the right place. So is yours. I'm sorry Deceivant, but the movement can't afford any setbacks," said Shelly before leaving the call.

"Gary, come on. Please, help me out. I've done so much for the movement. We all have."

"This isn't about doing favors for one another, okay? I'm going to help you. Every Exp is vegan, correct?"

"Absolutely."

"Then I'll defend them as fellow vegans, not as animals. It's like I said on my essay on vegan rights: vegans need to stand up for their own rights as a group. If we allow ourselves to be silenced, discredited, or discriminated against based on our moral integrity, we won't be able to save anyone. I'll talk with Shelly too, but Robert has his mind made up."

"This means so much to me. You know my daughter is an Exp."

"It's my pleasure. I think we can advocate for multiple causes at once. Francione said we need more peacemakers in this world. If you want to dedicate your life to providing a home for human children or for the personhood of Exps, that's fine. What matters is that when we all get dressed, we don't wear anyone's skin and when we sit down to eat, we eat vegan. I see no conflict with your mission and wish you the best of luck."

"I'll write an article on it. Have it online by the end of the week. Will you give it a review?"

"Absolutely. Well wishes, my friend."

"Well wishes to you too, Gary."

"Did your talk go well?" asked Ada, offering her hubby some tea in her bathrobe.

"Could have gone better. But it turned out okay. You know so many problems in society would be gone if those in power just did the right thing."

Ada kissed his cheek and scooted next to him. She grabbed the mouse and clicked on a file. "What do you think?"

On the monitor was a sketchy drawing of Kawai encircled by animals with the words "Exps are so Cool" in colored crayons.

"D.S. came up with the title," said Ada lovingly.

Deceivant held her hand and smiled. "I absolutely love it."

"I'll get back to it when I come home. I got called to substitute today."

Deceivant seized her in an embrace. "Please, be careful. If something happened to you…."

Ada kissed his lips. "I'll be fine. No darkness can put out this ray of sunshine."

"Hey, I know I've been busy, but maybe tonight we can go out? Just the two of us," said Deceivant, touching her ring finger.

"I'd love that!" exclaimed Ada.

Chapter 156: The Cost of Progress

Kanasta arrives at a theme park in Tampa, Florida. The busy crowds rush along hungering for memories to inscribe and cheap thrills to share. "I'm here."

"Perhaps you should wait for him to head to his hotel room," said the voice of an aged man on the other line.

"I've got a rather lengthy backlog. Besides, I like a challenge," said Kanasta, looking at the image of his target on the phone.

"But how do you expect to find him?"

"I don't need to. I'm the tallest person here. He'll see me." Kanasta maneuvered through the crowd.

A man wearing a flowered shirt saw the assassin and made a break for it.

"Easy enough," said Kanasta, following along at a steady pace.

The man rushed into the spacious jungle-themed playground.

The assassin boss went up the steps near the slide and spotted his target. "Job completed." Kanasta put a cigarette in his mouth and ejected a poison dart from it.

The dart found its way into the muscular arm of Destructus Supplious.

"Sorry, bro, but I'm here to stop you. Hope is willing to pay double whatever they are paying you to ex the guy," said D.S.

"Once a job is accepted, it will be completed." Kanasta rammed into him only to be grappled and brought to the ground. "If you get in my way, I will kill you." He pulled out a knife and stabbed it into his nuisance of a brother's side.

"Just walk away! What are you more scared of, losing a job or getting exposed?" asked D.S., tightening his grip around his jerky brother's throat.

"Why get in my way? This man is not your ally. He's a diplomat. Do you know what that is?"

"Not a clue!" D.S. lifted Kanasta and flung him onto the slide. He then leaped onto him and went all the way down, punching his face repeatedly.

"The only way you'll keep him safe is if you kill me," said Kanasta, spitting blood in his little brother's face. He pulled the knife out and held it to the inexperienced child's throat. "You lost."

D.S. embraced Kanasta. "I...I can't kill you. What do I do?" he asked in tears.

"You get out of my way," said Kanasta.

"Of course. Good guys don't kill." D.S. bit the knife and slammed his hand into Kanasta.

A small metal device latched onto Kanasta's chest.

"What is this thing?" asked Kanasta, trying in vain to tear it out.

"A hero's best friend. I'm bringing you in," said D.S., pinning Kanasta's arms.

The assassin boss slammed his head into D.S. and tore the dagger out from his opponent's teeth, slicing open his mouth. He dug the dagger into his own chest and started to carve out the bit of flesh pierced by the device.

A small knife punctured his hand.

"Not on my watch," said the Captain of Carnage, hidden under the leaves.

"You'll regret this," said Kanasta before D.S. continued to choke him.

The assassin boss lost consciousness.

D.S. looked out at the gathering of kids. "The villain is defeated!"

The children cheered.

"How do we get out of here?" asked D.S., scratching his head.

"In costume. I'll meet you at the changing room," said the Captain of Carnage.

"Okay," said D.S. with a salute. He hid behind a tree and turned to make sure the Captain wasn't looking. "Georgy?"

"Yeah it's me. I need help," said the voice on the other line.

"How's the gang?"

"We're in trouble, man. Some bad folks are after us. This is an emergency."

D.S. took a deep breath and closed his eyes. "Okay, tell me where to meet."

In the rainy streets of D.C., a man in a long trench coat is tailing an old man in a business suit.

The old man stops and turns around. "You're Wringer, aren't you?"

The man in the trench coat freezes in place.

"I'm aware of what you do. You're an Exp, right? I'm in the business of surveillance. If you kill me, you'll be exposed. Come closer."

Wringer stepped up to the criminal.

"On the other hand, if you cooperate, I can offer you protection. It's only a matter of time before your kind is hunted down. I can give you safety and a decent job. You'll still kill corporate criminals, just the ones that I want gone. Do we have an agreement?" asked the old man, offering his hand.

Wringer's chains gripped his hand. They then traveled up his arm and around his throat.

The old man's eyes bulged before his neck snapped.

Wringer hoisted the body up on the nearest lamppost.

Kaity waits outside an elementary school, perched on a hill about half a mile away from the entrance. She wipes a bead of sweat from her head when the bell rings.

"Are you alright? You're breathing heavily," said Hope's voice from the earpiece.

"I'm not sure I…I can do this."

"I'm sure you felt the same way before your first kill. Kaity, politics are tricky. Without assassins, peace cannot be maintained."

"But they're just kids."

"What would your papa think about this?" asked Hope.

"He'd tell me to put my personal feelings aside. What would your father think of what you're asking me to do?"

"There is a cost to progress, and those not willing to pay cannot achieve victory. Nina is counting on you. I cannot guarantee her safety when our political influence is this low. The Furies can bolster our influence overnight, but without positive media coverage, we cannot ally with them. Do you see the target?"

"Yeah. She's a little girl, six or seven, holding a textbook in her hand. She's smiling and chatting with her friend. She has her whole life ahead of her," said Kaity softly.

"If you defy me, there will be consequences. Either cooperate or Kanasta will die."

"You can't kill him," said Kaity.

"Check your phone."

Kaity set down her rifle and reached for her phone. She turned it on. A picture of Kanasta knocked out and with a blade to his throat came up immediately.

"There are only four children who need to die. If they aren't all gone by the end of the day, Kanasta will be. Don't disappoint me." Hope dropped the call.

Kaity clenched her rifle and cried. "Only the first kill. That's the only one I'm allowed to cry for. Just another job." She steeled herself and set up the shot. "Just another body." She wiped her eyes three times before pulling the trigger.

The child's body fell.

Kaity picked up her rifle and left the scene.

"You've done well. I'm sending you the location of the next one now," said Hope on the other line.

"I'm really sorry about this, but orders are orders," said Koshi, aiming his pistol at her.

Kaity dropped her rifle and sobbed.

Koshi approached her cautiously. "Is everything okay?"

Kaity shook her head.

"Look, I'm not going to hurt you. We just need you as insurance," said Koshi.

"Wait." Kaity looked up at him with tearful eyes. She grabbed his hand and pressed his gun to her chest. "Make me bleed. Beat me, cut me, shoot me, make it so I can't fight back."

"W-What!? Okay, seriously, what is going on?"

"Papa is in danger, and you're the only one who can help. If you won't hurt me, I'll do it." She swiped the gun out of his hand and shot herself in the chest.

"You idiot!" Koshi tore the gun from her grip. "If you explain things to me, I promise to help out. Otherwise, I'm leaving. Got it?" he asked, pinning her arms behind her back.

"If I don't kill these kids like I've been told, papa will be killed. They have him captured."

"Who does?"

"That doesn't matter. Wait, where's Nina? You have her, don't you?"

"Okay, so here's my understanding. You want me to beat you so that you have an excuse to not follow this person's orders, right?"

"Yeah. Please, I really need your help."

"Easy enough." Koshi tore out his knife and cut into his hand. He sprayed the blood all over Kaity's face. "Hey, don't smile at me. We got to make this look good." He pressed the dagger against her throat and took a selfie.

Kaity kissed his cheek. "I really owe you one."

"Hey, you can thank me after he's safe. I messaged Gamma to track down Kanasta. Shouldn't take him more than an hour to find him. I'll personally bring him back to you."

Kaity hugged him. "Can you tell me about Nina?"

"I can't. She's alive, that's all I can say."

"What do I need to do to get her back?"

"She's with Lambda, it's outside my jurisdiction."

"I love her," said Kaity, grabbing his hand.

"Well, if you capture Exp 8 for us, we have no use for her."

Kaity let go of his hand and looked to the ground. "Okay. I know where he is. Let's go," she said, walking off.

"Love that look in your eye. You truly are an inspiration."

"Sorry to let you down, but your hero is a failed assassin. I can't kill kids…not anymore."

"You wouldn't be my hero if you could," said Koshi, grabbing her hand.

"Water! Free water. One per person!" hollered Atlas, standing beneath a tent with an uplifting logo in a grimy city.

A line of humans formed.

Atlas turned to Muffins who was watching the crowds vigilantly. "I think this is what Zenero always wanted for me. To extend the blessing he gave me to others. Reconstructing destroyed homes by morning, giving the needy nourishment in the afternoon, and expanding the network by night. Charity is a full-time job."

Muffins signaled to Atlas as a woman with an expensive camera approached.

She saw Atlas but stopped to give a group of emaciated kids the bread in her backpack.

"Muffins, you handle the water distribution. I'll see what she wants." Atlas left the tent and approached the woman.

"Independent Info Bomb, Hope sent me. I'd like to share your story and what you're doing here."

"Leave my story out of it. Do what you can to bring help to these people," said Atlas.

"It will only be a top story if you tell the people about who you are."

"In that case, I'll comply. Ask me whatever you want, just don't expect my undivided attention. There are a lot of thirsty families to help."

"Wouldn't want it any other way," said the reporter.

"Ohm," said Durga, sitting cross-legged in front of a gathering of inmates. "Now, slowly open your eyes."

The prisoners transitioned out of their meditative trance, smiling gently.

One of the guards approached Durga. "Someone is here to see you."

"I can't leave without giving the scripture study session," said Durga.

"It's urgent," said the guard.

"Don't worry, I'll take over from here," said Opti. "I want everyone to write down ten things they're grateful for. Here, I'll pass out the papers."

The guard led Durga out of the mess hall and into the interrogation room.

A red-haired woman in a business suit and black gloves was seated. "Leave us. This won't take long."

"You're the one who is always at the board meetings. I never got your name," said Durga.

"For the purpose of keeping this brief, I'll explain why I'm here. Everything we speak of is confidential; is that understood?"

"I'm actually used to sitting in that chair," said Durga with shaky hands.

"Understood?"

234

"Yes."

"I'm Agent Iota, head of the public relations division for the Senator you're well acquainted with. And you're a valuable asset to him, valuable but not irreplaceable."

Durga turned her head slightly, gauging the distance between her and the door.

"I'm not here to hurt you. The opposite, actually. Hope has given you a mission here, and I've been told to assist you in any way I can."

"That's awfully kind of you. What do you expect in return?"

"You've already helped us. Your presence in these prisons has drastically reduced recidivism rates. You've done your country a great service. The director, the man who made private prisons stand for something more than mere profit...he must do whatever I say." Iota leaned in. "So, how can I help?" she asked with a big smile.

"Deus Ex Machina is a peaceful pro-Exp group. I'd like a recruiter to be placed in each Samadhi prison."

"Consider it done." Iota seized Durga's hand and shook it.

"Just like that?" asked Durga, trying to slide her hand out.

"You have to keep this arrangement between us. Can you do that?"

"Absolutely. Thank you so much."

"It's my pleasure. Now don't cross me," said Iota with a smile.

Exp 8 peeked out to see a massive crowd. "Why am I getting nervous?"

Image grabbed his hands. "Close your eyes, dear. There is nothing to worry about. I wrote down everything you need to say. Just read it with energy and inspire them. They're all so excited to meet you. Feed off the audience and make their spirits tremble."

"You got this," said Stabby with a sharp grin.

"Thanks, both of you." Exp 8 set down the notes. "I got this." He stepped out from behind the wall and onto center stage.

Rather than applause, he was greeted with reverent chanting.

Exp 8 closed his eyes and listened.

The chanting was a *ssshhhsshhh* sound. It was a soothing, flowing sound like a current through a river.

Exp 8 waited for their eyes to be on him and then spoke. "God from the machine, that's what you're all hoping for, isn't it? I'm sorry for the letdown, but I'm no god." Exp 8 stepped down from the stage and walked down the aisles of believers. "Honestly, I'm just like any other animal on this miraculous planet. I want safety, purpose, and, above all, freedom for myself and those I hold dear. If there's any way I'm unique, well then, it's because I wasn't born. Because I have no biological father or mother, I have a unique perspective on what family is. To me a family is made up of those who I understand and who understand me. Anyone who has been oppressed for being different than those who oppress them, I call them brother and sister. Those who fought for freedom and equality, whether they made it to the history books or made their imprint on the individuals they spoke out for, they are my mothers and my fathers. We are all children of Earth, and we can all use the power within us to make a difference for someone else. I ask that you go out there and build sanctuaries for animals. I ask that you write articles bringing modern slavery into the light. I ask that each one of you exercise your right to vote and rally others to do the same. Apathy will destroy everything my fathers and mothers have fought for and everything my brothers and sisters are fighting for right now. Whether we are born or created does not matter, we are united by our thirst for equality. The only way to satisfy this need, and freedom is absolutely a need, is to go out there and make a difference for those who are oppressed. Some may be helpless, others may be fighting in their own way, but we can all lighten the burden on them by uniting and making a difference!"

The crowd chanted with newfound charisma.

Exp 8 turned to Image who gave him a thumbs-up.

"I want all of you to think of ways you can contribute to the fight against systemic slavery. And I want you to share that with me."

Hope is on the phone in the living room getting a foot massage from Kioshi. The TV is muted with subtitles and is giving hourly updates on the recent murder at Grandmark Elementary. "I want Kaity returned to me. Is that clear?"

"It's clearly something I can't help you with," said Koshi from the other line.

"I want to talk to your boss," said Hope.

"He's busy at the moment, but I'll pass on the message. Bye now."

Hope set her phone down. "Your brother has no manners."

"I'm sorry about that, but you shouldn't be concerned; he cares about Kaity, so she's not in danger."

"The more time she spends with him, the weaker my control over her becomes. I need you to bring her back to me."

"Roger." Kioshi bowed, left the house, and entered the sleek black car outside. After setting her navigation point to her brother, she put the car on autopilot and held her finger to her ear. "Boss, I've been ordered to bring Kaity back to Hope."

"She's a fool to trust you."

"Hey, I'm reliable."

"Exactly. Your loyalties lie with me. Right now, you should continue to gain favor with her. Go after your brother and retrieve Kaity as she ordered."

"Roger, sir," said Kioshi before hanging up.

She took out a pink phone and called Hope. "All clear. His orders are to follow your orders for the time being."

"Excellent. Your service will certainly be rewarded."

The call ended and Kioshi leaned back in her chair.

"Ooooh, this is sooo exciting. I'm a double agent! A super spy getting praise from both sides. Brother would be so proud! I can't wait to rub it in his face that I'm better than him!"

Deceivant is seated cross-legged, barely fitting his knees beneath the tiny table. Three grade school girls are seated on tiny stools around the table.

"More tea?" asked the brunette girl.

"Oh, I've had plenty, thanks."

"What's wrong?" asked the blond girl.

"Everything is fine."

"You're lying," said the redhead. "He's lying, right Richard?" she asked the plush seated next to her. "Richard says you're lying and he's always honest."

Deceivant lowered his head. "Well, there's no fooling Richard. I've been lying a lot recently. That's what's been bothering me. I told my wife and daughter I've been spending the past couple nights at a sleepover."

"But that isn't the truth," said the redhead.

"No, Kitten, it's not. There was news concerning a church recently. Ever since I've been searching for someone, someone very important to me."

"Why not tell them the truth?" asked Kitten.

"My daughter doesn't want me to find this person. And…I've had to work with some bad people to find where she is."

"You shouldn't do that. What would she think if she knew?" asked the blond girl.

"Wise, as always, Sunshine. I just don't know what else to do. I need to find her. I'm not going to make the same mistakes as last time, but I am going down that path it seems."

"You know why adults look like raisins?" asked Kitten.

"Nope. Are you going to tell me?" he asked, bopping her nose.

"They always worry. Does he like me? What if I get fired? Am I happy? Worry, worry, worry. You're going to be a raisin if you keep worrying."

"Sunshine, Kitten, Ely, Richard. I'm not sure when's the next time we'll be able to meet like this. Things are getting more and more busy these days. If I don't see you for a while, please keep in mind I love you all very, very much."

Ely poured him a cup of tea and slid it his way.

"Thanks."

"You can't let your daughter bully you. You don't belong to her. If you want to do something she doesn't like, then tough cookies."

"Easier said than done," said Deceivant, taking a sip.

"You gotta stand up for yourself. You're making us all sad here, and this is supposed to be a happy occasion."

"My apologies, Ely."

"You can't come back until you get over this. No worrying allowed."

"You can't do that," said Sunshine.

"It's my tea set so I can," said Elise.

"She's right. You all shouldn't have to deal with my problems. I'll talk to my wife."

"And your daughter," said Elise.

Deceivant looked away.

"Say it."

"And my daughter."

"Good. Oh, and it looks like Steven and Kyle are going to fight over the fire truck so you should probably do something."

"Yeah. I'll be right back."

Ada is at the front of a class with a spectrum of religious symbols behind her. A sprout garden lined the perimeter of the room. Middle school students watched attentively.

"The Ancient Vedics saw sacrifice as a way of bargaining with the gods. The god Rudra was so fearsome that the only thing the worshipers sought from the deity was for him to leave them alone. So you see, not all religions are centered on becoming one with god. In times where humans were more dependent on nature, the gods were integrated into their society. Religion was not a concept; it was seamlessly intertwined with everyday life. There was no separation of sacred and profane. Yes, Marcos, you have a question?"

"The Vedics talk extensively about all aspects of society, but they never talk about suicide. Is there a reason it's never mentioned?"

"Well, Marcos, I don't know the answer to that, but I think you've found a topic for your paper."

The alarm suddenly started blaring. "Code Red. Code Red."

"Get in the corner and keep silent," said Ada, locking the door from the inside.

"Faculty and staff. There is an Exp hiding among you. Turn it over to us and nobody gets hurt. There will be a casualty for every two minutes that pass, so don't keep us waiting," said the chilling voice of a man over the PA system.

"Everyone, keep quiet. I'm going to put an end to this," said Ada, unlocking the door and walking out.

Three men with guns patrolled the halls.

Ada's human skin faded away, and her digitized body came into view. "I'll come peacefully, so there's no need to hurt anyone."

One of the men brought up his walkie-talkie while the other two cautiously approached the Exp. "We got her. Coming your way now."

Ada was escorted out the front where another man was waiting.

A teenage boy was held at gunpoint.

"Sorry, but it's already been two minutes," said the thug.

Ada leaped in front of the gun, shielding the boy from the wrath of the bullet. She turned around, holding up two guns to the criminals and allowing the boy a chance to flee.

"Don't fall for it. Those guns aren't real," said the thug boss.

The two men fired at the guns in her hands, and the bullets went straight through.

Ada rushed toward them, braving bullets. She wrestled a gun out of one of the man's hands and shot him with his own weapon. After taking another bullet, she turned and fired another shot.

A bullet blasted her head open as she pressed the trigger down and aimed at the thug boss. The gun clicked but nothing came out.

Ada awkwardly approached the man and slammed the gun into his face till it caved in. The bloody mess of a body collapsed.

Ada wiped the blood off her face and sobbed into her hands.

Senator John is in a limousine, reclined in his seat and talking on the phone. "This partnership must be strengthened or else everything will fall apart. There is a cost to progress. Truman ended a great war by sacrificing civilians. The Bush administration sacrificed American lives for the sake of overseas conquest, keeping America's empire alive. And it's not just the leaders; civilians sacrificed their freedom for a sense of security, and they sacrifice their sense of justice for cheap affordable products. Sacrifice must be voluntary. Take away a man's freedom and he will revolt. The trick is to get him to hand it over willingly. A true visionary, a great leader can accomplish many things at once. I just turned Exps into heroes, fed the fear machine, and tarnished the names of our enemies in one fell swoop."

"Next time you should ask me before sending armed goons into a school," said Hope.

"I wanted to surprise you, like you surprised me when you handed over Crisis. It's a pleasure doing business with you."

"The pleasure is all yours."

"Hahaha. I helped you out and you won't even thank me. You're a challenge. It's been a while since I've had a real challenge. Keep in mind I hold all the cards. If you want your Exps to have freedom, they must give up their independence to me. Something so dangerous must either be controlled or annihilated."

"Dangerous? I'll keep the Exps in check, and you'll get the votes you want."

"Please, this isn't about votes, and it's not about independence either. Let's be real. We both want control. The peace talks are just decoration, an early step on the path to our true goals. Which reminds me, given the recent developments, I think it's time we had another meeting."

"If you want to get on my good side, you should return Nina to me."

"She will be released soon enough. Working with me is an opportunity. You don't want to lose it. See you at the peace talks."

"Good day, Senator."

"It is indeed."

Chapter 157: Opportunity Lost

Nina was shocked to her senses, waking up on a hospital bed. Metal binds held her limbs in place.

Lambda stood above her bound patient. "Today has been a busy day for me, but now we finally get to relax."

"I'm no use to you," said Nina.

"I hope you'll reconsider that," said Lambda, wheeling in a tray of her favorite tools. "I'd hate to ruin such a lovely figure."

"If you let me go now, I won't kill you when I escape."

"Such confidence. I love it when they're confident. Makes breaking them more fun. You've been completely disarmed, so you can't threaten me. Agent Alpha performed a particularly thorough strip search on you."

"Nothing I know will be of any use to you."

"We'll see about that," said Lambda before gripping Nina's finger. "You have such beautiful hands. So soft and strong. I wonder how resistant they are," said Lambda as she suckled and nibbled the Exp's right index.

"I hope you enjoy this because all you'll get from this is pleasure."

"Oh, I do enjoy it. My job is to find out what you know. That's all. Even the smallest bit of information speaks volumes. According to the documents turned over by your friends, your body is ultra-sensitive. Playing with you is going to be such fun! First question: are you aware of an Exp named Abyss?" asked Lambda, slowly sliding energy needles under her doll's fingernails.

"He was mentioned once. Hope said he wasn't worth trying to recruit," said Nina, not responding to the pain in the least.

"Well, she's right about that." Lambda removed Nina's shoes and socks. "I've never seen legs quite like these. I wonder how flexible they are."

The bed expanded, stretching Nina's legs to their limit.

"Who are you loyal to?" asked Lambda, dripping a single drop of hydrochloric acid on each of her doll's toes. She then lightly brushed them with a metallic brush as if painting them.

"Devlin. You can stop hurting me. I don't know anything important, so I'll gladly share what I know."

"I would stop, but that stern face you make when you're trying to hide the pain is just too cute. Also, today's special; I'm not just performing for myself." Lambda slowly pried off Nina's fingernails. "Devlin left the Freedom Forcers. Knowing this, are you planning on staying with them?" She pressed a nail into the Exp's bloody fingertips and attached a node to it. "You can scream a little. I won't judge." She flicked a switch on her console, sending electricity into the conductive nails.

Nina breathed intensely, struggling not to scream. "I-I won't leave them. Protecting Kaity and his family is my mission. Is that all you've got? I thought you were an expert."

Lambda smiled and used a scalpel to remove Nina's shirt. "Oh, I'm just getting started. There's something about you I just don't get. You have enchanting breasts, so why cover them?" She sliced through the wraps, cutting a thin line into her toy's chest.

"They get in the way of me eliminating my enemies," said Nina with a killer's glare.

"You are just adorable," said Lambda, pinching the Exp's cheeks. "What is Hope's endgame?" She punctured the its nipples with energy needles. "Oooh, so responsive."

"She keeps that to herself and torturing me won't get her to tell you. It won't accomplish anything," said Nina through clenched teeth.

"You and I both know it will get Kaity to come to your rescue. You were egging me on so I would kill you. So dedicated and loyal. Kaity is lucky to have someone who loves her so dearly." Lambda glided her scalpel across Nina's breasts, savoring every bit of pain in her prey's eyes.

"I don't love her. I can't." Nina closed her eyes.

"Giving up your life for her isn't love?" asked Lambda, cutting off Nina's skirt.

"I'm doing it so Devlin can be happy."

"Devlin left her for Demonica. Kaity is no longer a part of his life. So, you still want to die for her?" said Lambda slowly pushing more energy needles into her most receptive areas.

"I-I don't know." Nina sobbed.

"Love is so painful, isn't it? I'm going to give you so much love," said Lambda as she lovingly flicked the needles inserted into her toy's pressure points. "Yes, Boss. I'm interrogating her right now. The other one? It's restrained too. Just haven't gotten around to its interrogation. Okay, I'll get right to it." She puts her phone in her pocket. "Well, I have to go for a bit, but I'll be back soon. Feel free to share anything else you know."

"Just kill me."

"Why? Are you afraid for Kaity's safety?"

"If Devlin is with Demonica, he's beyond my reach. I have no reason to live."

"You truly are pitiful. Just admit you like her." Lambda pushed a switch to raise the bed up vertically. "Did you know that pain can be activated without visually damaging the body?" She turned on a switch that bathed Nina in purple light. "Incredible, isn't it? If you don't talk, I'll increase the intensity. See you later." The agent left and went past two doors before entering another room.

"Why did you keep me waiting for so long? I've been using my body as a flute to stave off the boredom," said Absorb, whistling a tune with his pores.

"Well, I had three dates today—lovely women, all of them—and some other business. But I promise I'll give you my undivided attention."

"Good. I'm Absorb. Are you with the government?" asked the sponge.

"I ask the questions, but, yes, I am," said Lambda.

"I am the god of this world, the holy talking crater," said Absorb.

"I know you're an Exp and a sponge," said Lambda.

"Do you plan on killing me?" asked Absorb.

"Maybe."

"I think you should reconsider. I have something you'll like very much."

"Oh, really? What's that?"

"A burning hatred for Deceivant and Hope. I want them both dead, and I assume your boss does too."

"What we value is loyalty. Will you serve us in exchange for your life?"

"My life isn't worth much. How about this? I'll help you in exchange for three things."

"You're not really in a position to bargain."

"Don't shoot down my proposition until you've heard it. One: I want my safety and the safety of one other Exp guaranteed, only one, mind you."

"Which one?"

"Toxic."

"Who?"

"She's a metal snake. Sweet and innocent."

"What else?"

"Two: if your boss wants Deceivant dead, I get the kill. Lastly: I am to be treated with respect. If all my conditions are agreed to, I'm yours to command."

"Will you assist us in capturing more Exps?" asked Lambda.

"Absolutely."

"I'll forward your proposition to the Boss."

"Pleasure doing business with you," said Absorb.

Deceivant drives Ada home, holding her hand the entire ride. They arrive at base and he opens the car door. "Come on in. Lay down and I'll get you some tea."

"I don't belong."

"Yes you do, Sweetie. This is our home. It's not home without you."

"The children, they could have been killed because of me."

"They were saved because of you. We need to tend to your injuries, so come on, follow me."

"I was scared and I killed them. How can you still look at me?" She turned away from his gaze.

Deceivant grabbed her quivering hands and pulled her into an embrace. "Getting rid of scum like that doesn't tarnish my image of you at all. You're still a sweet, innocent girl. You're still my beloved wifey no matter what happens."

"What if this is just the beginning? If you got hurt because of me...." Ada sobbed in his embrace.

"This won't be an easy road. Without your sunshine, I'm not sure I can bear the coming storms. We need you, Ada. You're so much more important than you realize." The loving husband kissed her forehead and smiled at her.

Ada looked at her hands. "There's no going back now, is there?"

"All we can do is move forward." Deceivant opened the front door and led Ada to the living room.

"I saw what happened," said Exp 8.

"Keep her company," said Deceivant, running off.

"I killed them," said Ada softly.

"Yeah. And everyone thinks you're a hero because of it. Everyone but you," said Exp 8, massaging her shoulders.

"Aren't you scared?" she asked with teary eyes.

"What frightens me isn't what the humans are capable of doing. I know that, and I'm not afraid of dealing with it. There's something else bothering me. Do you think Hope knew what would happen? Do you think she set it up?"

"Hope is a sweet girl. She would never do that."

"We were the talk of the town earlier this week, but this incident has given us a positive image. I'm not even fully against it. Freedom takes sacrifice. What scares me is what comes next. We're on a slippery slope. Crisis is gone and Hope had something to do with it. I can't trust her, but for now I don't have a better option than to follow her orders. For the time being we need to keep climbing, but we also need to be aware of the rocks that fall with each step."

"I'm scared," said Ada softly.

"Don't say that. If you're scared, we're all going to freak out. You've always been the one who keeps us calm."

"I thought Deceivant was just being nice, but you feel the same way."

"We all do," said Exp 8, patting her hand. "I have to go prepare for my next speech. Get some rest, okay?"

Ada nodded and tried to smile.

Koshi is driving on the freeway, and Kaity is in the seat next to him, her eyes glued to the rearview mirror.

The young assassin cocked her pistol. "We're still being tailed. The windshield is one-way only, so no way of knowing who is following us."

"Wonder if they're after me or you. Let's get off at the next exit and find out." Koshi sped past the car from the rightmost lane all the way to the exit on the left, nearly causing three accidents in the process. "You impressed?"

"Eh, I've seen Ego drive, so not really," said Kaity with a cheeky grin.

"Well, I'm impressed. They're still on us." Koshi sped into a shopping strip and went around to the back parking lot. "Empty. The perfect place to take care of things. Stay in the car. I'll handle it. If things get dicey, leave without me."

Kaity twirled her pistol with her tail, tossing it up and switching out the clip before catching it with her foot. "Who do you think you're talking to?"

"Fair enough. Just stay low and give me cover fire if things go south." He took a sharp turn and parked. "Just like old times." After patting Kaity's head, he exited the car. "Okay. Come out slowly," said the agent, aiming his gun at the car parked next to them.

The door opened and Kioshi emerged, holding two guns.

"Sis, what are you doing here?" asked Koshi, lowering the gun.

Kioshi cocked both guns by pressing them against her arms. "I'm here for your cargo."

"Heheh. Sis, stop trying to be cool and just talk to me, okay?"

"You don't realize how high up the ladder I am, do you? This mission was given to me by the Boss. Now hand her over."

"Wait up. The Boss told me to capture her and bring her to base."

"Yeah, but the base is the other way," said Kioshi, pointing with a gun.

"True. But I already explained to the Boss that Kaity and I are going after Priority One. It makes no sense to send you to stop me from following orders."

"In the business of spies, things are complicated."

"There's complicated and then there's stupid. Hold up, I'll see what's up. Boss, you there?"

"I am. Have you completed the mission?"

"Sis wants me to hand Kaity over to her. Any reason why?"

"Just hand her over and don't think about it too much. I'll send you some back up to retrieve Priority One," said the Senator.

"Understood."

"How does it feel not being in the loop for once?" asked Kioshi, sticking out her tongue.

"I'm not happy." Koshi whacked the guns out of her hands. "There's only one reason he'd send you to retrieve Kaity from me. You're a double agent."

"Heehee. Impressed?"

"I'm worried. Sis, you're just starting out as a spy. Working as a double agent puts you in great danger. As your brother, I forbid it. Go back to base."

"You're not the boss of me. Hand over Kaity."

"The deeper you dive, the more dangerous it becomes."

"I'm not afraid of dying."

"Well, I'm afraid of losing you."

"Urgh. I'm not a toy. I'm my own person."

"That's right." Koshi embraced her. "You're my sister."

"If you love me more than Kaity, hand her over."

"I love you more than anyone, and that's why I refuse."

"Then I'll fight you for her." Kioshi slammed her knee into his crotch.

Koshi slid behind her and restrained her arms and legs. "Love the new shampoo. Is that pineapple?"

"You're such a creep."

"Look, there's really no reason for us to fight. After Kaity and I retrieve Priority One, I'll let you take her back. Sound fair?"

"Fine, but only if you take me along."

"You can come along for the ride but not the fight."

"Deal, now let me go," she said, struggling in his grip.

Hope finished her tea by the time the Senator arrived. "Greetings, Senator. May I ask the purpose of this meeting?"

"The President has entrusted me with handling the situation, and I deemed it necessary to have another discussion."

"Then, by all means, proceed."

"Let's go over the most recent developments. Humans First leader Derrick Donovan was killed along with his entire family. The current evidence leads to Michael Kormac, the next in line and the more violent of the two. Since he has taken charge, Grandmark Middle School was put in a hostage situation by members of Humans First. The Exp known as Ada was substituting there at the time and was a teacher just a few years before she quit and fled to New Mexico. Are we on the same page?"

"Everything you said is exactly as I know it."

"Good. Now hopefully Humans First will see the folly of putting the lives of American children in jeopardy for the sake of their illegal crusades against the Exps, but realistically, things may get worse. Exp presence, whether renegade or not, is posing a risk to this nation's real people. I'd like to discuss ways to lessen the risk or, preferably, remove it entirely."

"Well, realistically, it cannot be removed. Lone wolf attacks, such as what took place at Grandmark Middle, are something that existed before Exps were created. They are something that can only be minimized, and I'll gladly discuss ways to minimize them with you. The issue of terrorism cannot be easily uprooted, and I don't exaggerate when I call this an act of terrorism."

"Absolutely not."

Hope looked beyond the Senator with her golden eyes. "Violence creates more fear, and that fear gives those terrorists more opportunities to recruit others to their cause. Attacking Humans First risks giving them the image of martyrs. To defeat terrorists, one must take away their ammo, but they must do so in a way that does not appear as a compromise, else they risk encouraging not only more attacks from that group but also further terrorism in general. Thankfully, I've come up with several ways to mitigate the issue at hand. I believe a public statement from respected political figures, such as yourself, that Exps are not enemies of the state nor of humankind would weaken the fires of hate that Humans First has been stoking. There may not have been casualties but there has been damage. The psychological trauma of being in a hostage situation is not to be understated, and I shall personally pay for any and all psychiatric help the victims need. The fight against terrorism cannot be won by the passing of laws or by strategic assemblies of government officials." The Queen of the Exps turned to face the camera. "It can only be won with the support of the citizenry. I ask you aknowledge that Exps seek only equality and will reach that goal through peaceful means. These Humans First members are just terrorists hiding behind a message of hate to gather the fearful to join their cause. Their goal is the same as any group of radicals; they seek power and will do whatever it takes to gain that power. If you let go of the fear in your heart, the fear that Exps will harm you, your loved ones, or your nation, you've disarmed them of their only means of manipulation. I thank you all for participating in our collective mission for a peaceful world."

"It's just as she said. Our true enemy does not belong to any race, religion, or species. If things were so simple, that enemy would have already been dealt with long ago. Toxic ideas can come from anyone, and it is our civic duty to detoxify this nation."

Hope turned back to the Senator with a satisfied smile. "Well then, is there anything else?"

"Have you heard of the Metal Pact?"

Hope nodded.

"Russia, China, and other nations not allied with the American people are concerned about what they call a secret alliance between Exps and the United Nations. Some even go so far as to claim the United States of America is willing to collude with Exps to perform actions against the UN."

"Oftentimes giving the fear mongers attention creates the idea that their nonsense has some clout. I assume that these statements are just that and that no solution has even been presented."

The Senator smiled. "Nonsense when spoken by top officials is worth addressing, I believe. I assure everyone on behalf of the president that the Exp threat is to be contained, not appropriated."

"Perfectly stated."

"Thank you, but I feel more should be said. Studies show that over ninety percent of Exps are currently in America. Can you confirm the Depot theory based on your knowledge?"

"Well, if I'm to keep them from acting up, I need them close by. Exps were created in America, so it's only natural that we remain here. There are no wars, so there's really no need to fear. We only seek citizenship and equality."

"As long as the President is monitoring the Exp threat, we assure you there is no reason for concern. Those countries that harbor these fears are showing they do not have faith in the President, and America will not tolerate it. I thank you for your time," said the Senator, getting up and shaking her hand.

"You're most welcome. This wouldn't be possible without you or the President."

"I must go. Have to try to convince NRA enthusiasts that firearms regulations aren't a slippery slope to a dictatorship. Till we meet again."

"Safe travels and best of luck." After leaving the room, Hope is joined by her newest pet.

"That was absolutely fantastic," said the reporter.

"I take terrorism very seriously. Well, this is a nice surprise," said Hope after turning the corner.

The reporters who once feared her were now lined up, hungry for the slightest quote to add to their story.

"You'll have to excuse me for a moment." Hope held up her phone. "Captain, is everything alright? I told you not to call me at this time."

"D.S. was here a moment ago but now he's gone. He went inside the candy shop, and it has been three hours. I tried contacting him, but he left his phone here. What do I do?" asked the Captain of Carnage.

"Do you have Kanasta with you and is he restrained?"

"Yes to both."

"Kaity has been captured, so be on your guard. They may come after you next. I want you to head back to base with Kanasta. Take him down to the lab and keep him sedated there. I'll contact the others to return to base. We'll form a search party for Kaity and D.S. once we're all together. I hope for their sake they were captured. If they openly defied me, I shall take it upon myself to ensure their obedience."

"I'll round everyone up."

"Good. I won't allow the Senator or my own subjects to ruin this opportunity. Captain, you've performed exceptionally and have earned my trust. I'll be sure to put your new weapon on higher priority."

"My loyalty is with Atlas. He is the one who told me to follow you."

"Interesting, and why is that?"

"He believes in you."

"Well, you have your orders. I have some business of my own to attend to. Till then," said Hope.

D.S. was waiting by a bus stop in D.C., practicing his skills with a paddle ball. "You only win if I give up. Ten is my goal, so I'm not stopping." Six bounces were followed by a sudden miss. "Oh, the bus."

The doors opened and a man with a Mohawk stepped out, followed by four men with shades and bad attitudes.

"Georgy?" asked D.S.

"Yo, D.S., how ya doin', man?"

"I'm doin' a fine," said D.S. with a bad Italian accent. "But you guys are having trouble, right? That's why I'm here."

"Always a brother. See? The other guys were wrong about you. They said you would be nothin' but trouble. But here I am, in a heap of trouble, and you come to help out."

"Friendship is forever, right?"

Georgy grabbed his big buddy's hand. "That's right, but family is even stronger than that. You're family to me. To all of us. Guys, ain't he like family?"

"Absolutely." "Sure thing." "Blood is thicker than water." Georgy's followers responded.

D.S. smiled. "So, what's wrong and how do I help?"

"The Rocky Reef. You probably never heard of them before because they showed up after you, uh, took a break."

"I didn't take a break. I left the Empty Hand. We were hurting innocent people."

"Yeah, yeah. That's true. I want you to know, and I'm saying this from the heart, that we reevaluated everything after you left. We became more forgiving of debts, more cautious about who we picked a fight with, and we took our civic duty more seriously. Problem is, we got too soft and these Rocky bastards come up and start taking territories. We've lost three cities in the past year."

"We only had one city back when I was with you."

"Well, yeah, we were just starting up, you know. Anyways, we're part of something bigger now. Got some funds from an anonymous donor, and we made some alliances with some groups on the East Side and the West Side."

"Can they help you then? Georgy, you're a friend to me. But I don't want to do this stuff anymore."

"Hey, hey, it's a-okay. If you want to come back to the Hand, you can, but the Hand isn't pushing you. Look, bro, we need to show our partners that we can stand on our own two feet. If we come begging for their help, we lose cred, ya get me?"

"Ya get that it's a one-time thing, right? I help you guys get out of danger, then I'm out."

"Of course, brother."

"Good. So what are we doing?"

"Taking back our turf. These Rocky bastards took over the police station up town. Local big wigs are too scared to make a move. They need us, man."

"Not sure if I can do this. Hope wants me out of trouble, and this sounds like a lot of trouble."

"They have been terrorizing the neighborhood, demanding blood as payment. We may have cut some fingers and got rid of some stingy bastards, but we never targeted their families. These Rocky assholes have become the law for this city, and they ain't got no sense of responsibility. The Hand needs its scissors. We need you."

"But rock breaks scissors, and the Hand is basically paper, so you guys will do just fine," said D.S. with a grin.

Georgy frowned. "This ain't a game, bro. We lost Collin to those sums a bitches."

"Hey, I'll help out, okay? I should dress up though. If someone finds out, it could be bad."

"Sure thing, bro. I'll take you to my girl's place. Angie can hook you up with a smooth look. Hey man, I know we weren't always doing the right thing before, but now we're the good guys."

"I know that. Otherwise I wouldn't be helping you guys out."

"This is a golden opportunity, my brother," said Georgy with a slug.

"Just hope it isn't fool's gold," said D.S., slugging his friend back and toppling him over. "You okay?"

The goons held up weapons to D.S.

"Chill, bros. He's just strong is all. One of you gonna help me up?" asked Georgy.

Chapter 158: Civil Dispute

A black car drives up to a junkyard.

Kaity signals the others to stay behind before exiting the vehicle. She soon spots Exp 8, who is lying in a pile of discarded appliances.

"Everything I do is to keep my people from ending up here. I came as soon as you called. Let's talk."

Kaity forced a smile. "I'm really happy I can count on you."

"Of course. You're family to me, and I hope we can work together when things get rough." Exp 8 sat up. "I could hear your fear from the other line. Who's threatening you?"

"I need your help. Nina is captured, and the only way to get her back is an exchange. Will you come with me?"

Exp 8 stood up from the trash and approached her. "We have a responsibility. Devlin already shirked his duties to his people, but I thought you really cared about us."

"I do care. I care about all of you."

"I have an important role in this. Things are already unraveling. My people need me and they need you too. Damn it, Kaity! You can't give in so easily."

Kaity turned away and tossed him her phone. "Watch it."

Exp 8 stared at the screen for two minutes, watching holes being drilled into Nina's tan skin and hearing her muffled screams distorted by the speaker. He tossed the phone back to the terrified girl. "Do you trust me?"

"Of course I do, but right now she needs me. I love her," said Kaity, breaking down into tears.

"If we aren't strong, then we fail everyone. Not just the Exps but everyone. Consider her a martyr and fight all the stronger for her."

"I can't believe you. We aren't playing pieces. We're alive; she's alive. It isn't your choice to sacrifice her."

"But it's my choice to sacrifice myself and I refuse. You ran away from Hope's orders, and you're still running now. I know it's hard, but we have to be strong," said Exp 8, tears leaking from his helmet.

"Her orders were to kill children. And if I didn't follow them, she'd kill Kanasta!" yelled Kaity.

Exp 8's eyes widened. "I-I didn't know. I'll talk to her."

"No…you won't. I'm bringing you in," said Kaity, engaging her plasma claws.

"I won't let you make that mistake," said Exp 8 before taking to the skies.

Kaity disengaged her rifle and took aim. An energy bullet erupted from the gun before bursting into her friend's back.

"Is this really what you want?" asked Exp 8 before noticing an incoming missile. He wrestled the missile while searching the skies for the attacker. "You're willing to work with them to take down your comrades. Nina values loyalty. What would she think of you if she saw this?"

"Don't care," said Kaity, lining up her sights before triggering the missile to burst.

Alpha, standing atop a trash hill, aimed a rather bulky weapon at Priority One. A magnetic rope burst from the gun and coiled around Exp 8's legs. "I'll bring him down."

Exp 8 fired a slow orb and then a slightly faster one. These orbs combined as they went toward their target, creating a shadow over the entire hill.

"Exp Hunters specialize in energy manipulation. You don't stand a chance," said Alpha, rubbing his hands to create a coating of energy. Pressing both hands together, with the added propulsion of a jet of energy from his back, he pushed the massive orb.

The force was so strong it sent the wrecking ball back to its creator.

"I gladly accept the gift." Exp 8's wrists detached and pulled the orb up to them. After connecting the orb to the magnetic field, he swung it around, destroying two incoming missiles. "Let's test the strength of the government's greatest errand boy." The poles reversed, propelling the orb into Alpha in a mere second.

"Oh shit!" Koshi dived into the trash and hardened his suit.

As the orb burst, Exp 8 noticed someone running up the metal rope.

Kaity sliced through incoming orbs and braced turret fire, focused solely on her target.

Once in range, Exp 8's tail slammed into her.

The young assassin's tail grabbed onto his and she swung herself behind him, clawing open his jetpack.

Exp 8 grabbed her hands as the two of them fell, doing his best to keep her plasma claws from slicing him.

Kioshi searched through the burnt trash for her brother.

She was suddenly gripped by her ankle and pulled into the heap.

"I told you to stay in the car."

Kioshi embraced her brother and broke out into tears. "I thought I had lost you."

"Wait, seriously? I live for this shit. Now stay low," said Koshi, peeking out to see that Priority One had a rough landing.

Exp 8 ejected Kaity off him with an orb and shielded his eyes as she furiously unloaded her clips into his face as she was carried through the air.

Alpha approached from behind, pelting his target's back with machine gun fire.

Exp 8 pulled the orb that launched Kaity back in and then turned and launched it at the government's errand boy.

Agent Alpha kicked the orb back at Priority One.

"Let's see if this works." Exp 8's tail wrapped around the orb before slamming it into the agent. "Thanks again, sis!" The Ultimate Exp turned and fired his turrets at Kaity's feet.

"*Surprise Spy Attack!*" Kioshi hopped onto Exp 8's back and pressed ten energy suppressors, one on each finger, into him.

"Well played. Alright, you win," said Exp 8 before toppling over.

Koshi stood up, holding his sides. "Not done y…who beat him?"

Kioshi waved at her brother and then stood atop the strongest Exp.

"Well, Kaity and I softened him up for you…a lot," said Koshi with a blush, keeping his magnum aimed at the downed enemy.

Kaity turned away.

"So, brother, we make a great team. Don't we?" asked Kioshi, poking his arm.

Koshi grabbed Kaity's hand. "Yes, we do."

"I'll put him in the back," said Kaity softly.

"Hey Boss. Priority One has been captured. You can call off the reinforcements."

"Hey, hey! Tell him I captured Exp 8!" whined Kioshi.

"Sorry, sis. Just ended the call."

Kioshi kicked her brother. "Jerk! You're stealing my glory. You don't love me at all."

Koshi grabbed her hand and pulled his sister into a deep kiss. "I love you more than anything."

Kioshi covered her flushed face and squealed, nearly falling over.

Agent Alpha slammed his fist into Kaity's chest.

She spit out blood and fell to the ground.

As she fell, he lined her back with energy suppressors. He held her arms as she struggled until she collapsed. The agent then flung her over his shoulder.

Kioshi peeked out from her hands. "What happened?"

"If the Boss knew you took down Priority One, he'd send you on missions that would likely get you killed. No more renegade missions and you're no longer a double agent. You think Kaity means a lot to me and she does. But she means absolutely nothing to me compared to you. You're going to drive her and Exp 8 back to base."

"You don't get to order me around," said Kioshi, crossing her arms.

Koshi seized her hands. "Actually, I do. I'm your commander now. You're officially an Exp Hunter and I accept that. That means you follow my orders. The two of us are going to go on a lot of missions."

Kioshi bounced up and down. "You mean it? You really mean it?"

"That's right. Now bring Kaity in, sever your ties with Hope, and I'll see what our next job is, partner." He ruffled her hair and smiled.

Kioshi hopped into his arms and kissed him. "Hey, there's a lake nearby. Want to go skinny dipping?" She pulled on his collar while kissing his neck.

Koshi stripped out of his suit and kissed her passionately. "You're the only one I need."

"You know I really like the sound of Agent Alpha. It's just so cool."

"Thanks," said Koshi.

"I might just take it!" Kioshi dragged her hands along his bare chest.

Koshi looked up at her with wide eyes.

She stuck out her tongue.

Koshi collapsed, his chest lined with energy suppressors.

Kioshi held her finger up to her ear. "I have retrieved Kaity, my queen."

"Excellent work."

"Annd I also took down Exp 8 annnd my brother."

"Your contributions will always be remembered. Bring them all here. Atlas has created a makeshift prison for those who defy me."

"Roger," said Kioshi with a nod.

Koshi suddenly gripped her hand, causing her to jump. "I'm not stupid. But you are. You're a total idiot."

"How are you still?"

"I have three capsules not one. I'm a super weapon, sis. I don't go down easy."

"I know all about your special perks, but you should still go down!" Kioshi kicked him in the face.

"I wanted to see what you were planning, and I'm not happy," he said, sitting up while pinning her down with one arm.

"I don't need the Boss' approval. Hope has believed in me from the start," said Kioshi, wiggling around in his hold.

"She's just using you, moron."

"You're wrong. She values me. I'm more than her ally. I'm her friend."

"Do you have any idea what the Boss would do if he thought you were defying him?"

"I'm not afraid of dying."

"Oh, he wouldn't kill you. He'd hand you over to Lambda, and she would take great pleasure in torturing you."

"Stop. You're scaring me," said Kioshi, shivering in tears.

"This isn't a game. Now get in the car. We're going back to base," said Koshi.

"Were you lying about being partners?" asked Kioshi, bobbing side to side nervously.

"Absolutely not. But if you can't behave then—"

"I'll behave. Let's take them back, together," said Kioshi, grabbing his hand.

"You're driving. I'll make sure they don't escape. No funny business, got it?" asked Koshi.

"My initiation is tonight! You'll be there, right?"

"Wouldn't miss it if it was noon on the doomsday clock," said Koshi with a grin.

Hope is in bed, resting in her father's arms. "You've done well. Not only was your scientific article well-written analytically but it also had real emotion. You're making your queen very happy." She rolled over and smiled at him.

Deceivant stroked her hair and smiled back. "I'd do anything for you."

Hope put her hands on his cheek and sat up on his chest. "I was hoping you'd say that." A smile as wide as her ambition spread across her puffy cheeks.

"Of course, you're my little queen," said Deceivant, poking her belly.

"Well, no need for these anymore." Hope reached into her dress and removed the pads.

"Why were you padding your chest? My little girl should be proud of her wittle boobies," said Deceivant, pinching her cheeks.

"I was only padding my boobies to spite you. And they aren't wittle; they're petite," said Hope, shielding her chest.

"Does this mean you're accepting me as your father again?"

Hope smiled and then grimaced. "You're going to give up your search."

"What search?"

"For Mika."

"Oh. Kioshi told you…didn't she?"

"It wasn't hard to get her to talk. You should know better than to keep secrets from me. You also used my agent for your own desires. You've forgotten your place," said Hope, digging her heels into his stomach.

"Oww. Look, I can multitask. I've done everything you asked for. It won't slow me down."

"We can't afford to be unfocused. I forbid it. There's no discussion to be had."

Deceivant looked into her eyes. "Okay. I'll stop searching."

Hope's eyes became fearsome. "You're lying to me."

"I can't just abandon her," his voice cracked.

"You must. She's going to drive you mad, if she hasn't already."

"There's something I need to know. You didn't have anything to do with the attack on Grandmark…did you?" asked Deceivant, turning away from her.

"Don't change the subject. And no, I didn't. The Senator orchestrated it every step of the way."

"I believe you."

"I'd rather not resort to threats. You're going to stop looking for her."

"I can't do that."

"Get out." Hope clenched her fists and hid her tears by lowering her head.

"This is my room."

"Out," said Hope with a tone devoid of love.

Deceivant got out of the bed. "Just because I love her doesn't mean I don't love you. You're my daughter."

"Leave!" yelled Hope, her entire face drenched in sadness.

"I'm sorry." Deceivant left the room.

Hope dried her tears. "I swear when I locate the little siren who stole his heart and turned him against me…I'll turn her into a limbless doll." She took a deep breath. "Let's see how my approval rating is at the moment. TV on."

"…assault on the police station," said the reporter. "It's hard to confirm the casualties at this time, and special forces are on their way to end this skirmish."

Hope's eyes nearly popped when she spotted one of the gunmen. She slid out of bed and went to the living room. "Emergency meeting. Now."

Deceivant and Ada scrambled to bring everyone in the house together.

"What happened?" asked Ada.

"D.S. is at a police station right now murdering cops with his gang buddies. Atlas, I know you're powerful, but have you the heart to end him?" asked Hope with intensity.

"Sweetie, calm down. I'm sure your little brother is just confused," said Ada.

"I don't care why he's doing it. D.S. must be killed. If we capture him, he'll end up in the Senator's hands, and he doesn't need an artifact to be a force to be reckoned with. Now, who is willing to kill him?" asked Hope.

"You can't hurt D.S.!" exclaimed Ada.

"I'll go," said Atlas. "Captain, I'd like you to come along as support."

"Surely you can handle him. You must have confidence."

Atlas lowered his head. "I need you by my side. It won't be easy to end someone I'm fond of."

"As you command," said the Captain, saluting with his tail.

"This is absurd. We aren't killing anyone," said Deceivant.

"That's right!" exclaimed Ada.

"Do not talk back to me. Atlas, take the Captain and leave now. I'll prepare a speech to try and salvage this mess," said Hope, running off.

Ada blocked the front door. "I'm not letting you leave."

"Neither am I," said Opti.

Atlas grabbed them and tossed them into the kitchen. "I'll be back soon."

D.S. was in a spiffy shirt and had on a curly blond wig. He stood up from behind cover, taking a stream of bullets and allowing his friends to get in shooting range. He raised his own assault weapon and fired near the bad guys but didn't hit them. "I'm not killing anybody. Big sis Hope is going to be super proud."

"Yo, bro! Calvary is here! The cowardly bastards called in some of their friends," said Georgy.

"I'll keep them busy. You guys go on ahead," said D.S., throwing Molotov cocktails at the armored trucks.

"Ignore the big guy. He's an Exp. We don't have authorization to engage. It would be a waste of bullets anyway," said the SWAT commander, signaling his men to rush in.

"Hey! Don't ignore me!" yelled D.S., watching the bad guys open fire.

Georgy took a bullet from behind and tumbled before reaching the front door.

"No!" D.S. ran into the line of special policemen. He wrestled a shotgun out from one of their hands before opening fire. "Don't kill him!"

"Split up! Do not engage. I repeat, do not engage!" yelled the commander as his men were blasted off their feet.

D.S. fired at the SWAT team, picking up new guns rather than reloading, and made his way to Georgy's side. "Are you okay?"

"Yeah. Told you they were ruthless. Shot me from behind. Good thing we came prepared," he said, showing the Kevlar vest beneath his jacket.

"Everyone! Stand down. As a member of RECTFI, I will take it from here," said Atlas.

"Hold him back. Man, the people are gonna love you for this. You'll be a hero," said Georgy, patting D.S.'s back.

D.S. opened fire at the bad guys as he approached Atlas. "Are you here to help?"

"We're here to kill you," said the Captain, zooming by and slicing D.S.'s legs.

Atlas lifted up a police car and hurled it at D.S.

"Shockwave Burst!" Chipko's fist collided, projecting an aura that deflected the car.

"They can't see us fight. Stand down, sister," said Durga.

"If we don't do something, they'll kill my friend," said Opti.

"And if you get in my way, I'll kill you as well," said Atlas.

Muffins hopped out from behind him and sprayed needles at Opti.

"Muffins? What are you doing?"

"She understands that Hope must succeed if all beings are to be treated equally. If there must be a sacrifice, so be it," said Atlas.

"I don't want to hear about sacrifices!" yelled Toxic, shooting into the Captain as he launched toward the troublemaker.

D.S. stood in front of Opti. "What is going on? Why are we fighting?"

"You're killing policemen, and Hope doesn't want you in the government's hands. She thinks killing you is the best option. I won't let them do it," said Chipko, waiting to deflect the coming attack.

"You guys don't get it. The police station was taken over by bad guys. These Rocky jerks killed all the cops. Now they are the law here," said D.S.

"Don't waste your breath. Stand aside. There's no need for this to escalate," said Atlas, taking a step forward.

"We shouldn't kill each other just to keep the humans happy." Chipko slammed her foot against the ground. The resulting shockwave launched four police cars into the air. "Shockwave Cannon!" Her fists released her aura, which sent the cars smashing into Atlas.

The ex-god summoned up the Agony Axe and sliced the incoming cars. He took another step forward and then stopped. Something gooey was stuck to his foot.

"Nice one, Fusion," said Opti, flying around to dodge Muffins' needle barrage.

D.S. lifted up a shotgun. "We're both bald, so we shouldn't be fighting. But if my friends are fighting for me, then I'm gonna fight. You're also my friends...but they're better friends!" He opened fire on Atlas.

The hulking man of muscle shielded his face from the assault and summoned up the Woeful Whip. The weapon cracked and sliced D.S.'s front.

"Tears aren't gonna stop me!" yelled D.S., wiping his eyes while shooting.

"If you give up your life, everyone will be safe," said Durga.

"You're on the wrong side!" yelled Opti, trapping Muffins beneath the sawed-off hood of a police car.

Another car pulled up, and the remaining Freedom Forcers came out.

"Stop fighting!" cried Ada, running into the fray before Deceivant stopped her.

"I'm sorry. But Hope's right. We don't have many options," said the troubled inventor.

Hope was lifted from her chair by Image.

"If this keeps up, D.S. won't be the only casualty. They won't back down and let you kill him. You have to end it," said Image.

Hope hopped out of her arms. "You're right. Atlas, this cannot continue. Your orders have changed. Bring D.S. in; don't kill him."

"Understood," said Atlas, firing arrows at Chipko.

"You think that will change anything? We don't even know what happened to Crisis! I'm not going to let my fellow Exps be used by you any longer!" Chipko sent a powerful shockwave toward Hope.

Ada broke out from Deceivant's grip and stood in front of the blast.

She was knocked off her feet and sent crashing into a burning police car.

"Ada!" yelled Deceivant, running to her aid.

"This was not supposed to happen!" yelled Hope, stomping her foot. She was lifted into the air. A chain was wrapped around her throat. Her hands gripped the chain, and she used all her strength to keep her lungs from collapsing.

"Hey! What are you doing?" yelled Opti before a spray of needles shot into his wings.

"Wringer, set her down. You don't realize how important she is," said Atlas, sending a chain at Wringer.

"I don't want anyone to die because of me! I surrender, okay?" D.S. was in tears. A fortified metal projectile zoomed by. Destructus Supplious' head slid off his shoulders and rolled to the ground.

BoneSaw popped out from behind a police car and hopped with joy.

Lord Sel suddenly rose out from the ground, clapping with great enthusiasm. "So, this is what you've all been doing while I've been busy. Oh, don't mind me. Please continue killing each other. I won't interfere."

Atlas tossed the Searing Sword, cutting the chain suspending Hope.

"You miserable wretch!" Hope turned to face Wringer with intense loathing.

Opti picked up D.S.'s head and placed it back on. "You're okay, right? Say something, buddy," he said in tears.

"As long as she lives, our people won't be safe," said Chipko, keeping Atlas' staff at bay with her shockwave punches. An extra strong punch sent the staff flying.

"You're not ruining everything Zenero worked for!" Atlas' fists became coated in a shadowy energy. The energy tightened, forming dual gauntlets with white frowny faces around his fists.

Chipko reinforced her hands with a continuous shockwave and punched his fists but it wasn't enough.

Atlas broke through and pummeled her.

"Stop! Don't kill her!" yelled Durga, grabbing onto his arm.

A light suddenly came from the center of the Exp battlefield. Lord Sellum emerged from the light. He looked out at the fragmented Freedom Forcers. "This must end." His raised hand shot out beams of white energy.

The healing beams mended the wounded warriors of both sides.

"You always spoil the fun," said Sel before vanishing through a black portal.

Sellum created a portal and Kaity stepped out. "I believe you have something to tell everyone."

"Hope captured Kanasta and she said that if I...I didn't kill children, she would kill him." Kaity broke down into tears.

Deceivant crouched down and embraced her. "It's just a misunderstanding. Hope would never do that."

"You haven't a clue what I would or would not do. Atlas, get me out of here now. We've accomplished what we claimed for. As for the rest of you, anyone with any sense will flee the area before the Senator's attack dogs arrive," said Hope.

Atlas lifted her up.

"Our time is running short. The species that threatens us all must be dealt with. There will be no going back anymore. Things must move forward," said Sellum before vanishing.

Sellum reappeared inside the amphitheater where Exp 8 had given a speech to DXM. "I know you're all gathered here for your idol's words of encouragement, but he has been captured and thus cannot attend. You all are likely wondering who I am and what I'm doing here." Lord Sellum gently moved his hand above the stage.

Flowers sprouted out, blooming and shooting light up into the air. Soon the entire amphitheater was blanketed in a rainbow of flora.

"I'm God and I'm here to ask for your aid." The flowers opened, releasing beams of light that brought vitality to the devotees in the audience.

The humans in the crowd froze in place.

Sellum watched stoically as they slowly came to, and when they did, they got up from their chairs and gripped their tattoos, showing their devotion.

"Exp 8 is merely a vessel for my message. In a sense, all Exps are. I am God, but I wasn't always God. I first incarnated as an Exp, and I seized godhood with my own power. I could not bear the feeling of helplessness as I watched oppression pollute this world. We are in the midst of the sixth great extinction, the first ever caused by a single species. Mankind claims monopoly over divinity, yet when faced with the consequences of their actions, they claim God controls the weather. They use God as a scapegoat for their crimes against nature. Yet even God should not judge the living; so I will not judge. Who am I to decide who should and should not die? It's irrelevant anyways. We must focus on who must die, not who should die."

Sellum took a deep breath, taking in the fear brewing in the audience. "For a while, I thought humans were negotiable. As frugivores, they lived within the system of nature, but that all changed after the ice age eleven thousand years ago. The lack of fruit led them to the consumption of animal flesh. Their denial of their biology began to affect their minds, and they soon believed they were the superior race. A title wasn't enough though; they played as gods. They planted seeds in the ground to later be cut down and farmed their fellow animals just for the sake of killing them a mere one thousand years after the end of the last ice age. To validate their actions, the ruling class always upheld the ability to reason as the sole determining factor of worth, claiming that every other animal, along with those of their own species with disabilities, a different color, or a different sex lacked this crucial ability. Their special ability wasn't reason, of course. After all, what they claimed was the most absurd theory ever postulated. How could living beings function in such a complex world without the ability to think, predict, and conceptualize? If they have no sense of self like humans claim, they would never eat, as self-preservation would be a concept beyond their understanding. And what reason would they have to live if they were unable to experience love, enjoy family, and cherish freedom? Sentience is a word used to oppress others; in truth, it means nothing at all. Humans simplified and demonized instincts as something mechanical simply because their own instincts had weakened. Instincts are feelings, but they are worthless without the ability to freely choose whether to follow them or to ignore them. What separates humans from the other animals isn't the ability to reason; it's the ability to rationalize anything. And this ability is something I have no way of overcoming. Humans can rationalize the greatest atrocities: the genocide of entire cultures, the destruction of land for profit, and the systemic slaughter of animals for the sake of palate pleasure."

Images flashed like fragments of a horrifying memory. Forests were made barren by machines, ocean reefs were torn apart by trawl nets, fish were suffocating as they are taken from their home, human and non-human animals were in cages, and those chained up were being whipped by their self-proclaimed masters.

Tears gushed from Sellum's helmet. "Mankind's atrocities are entirely bereft of reason and compassion. The ability to rationalize such atrocities makes humans the most dangerous species on the planet. This belief in superiority is given even more weight by mankind writing itself into godhood. I speak, of course, of religion. They write books and claim they are written by God. These books are then used by those of ill will as a transforming and evolving tool of rationalization. Using God as a scapegoat, they slaughter their own brethren. Their anthropocentrism is so deep-seated that even the Eastern religions that believe in animal reincarnation claim that only mankind can reach liberation. These scriptural hierarchies are devotionally charged tools of rationalization that serve as catalysts to the preexisting assumption of human superiority. And even those who claim to uphold science as truth fail to realize the most basic of scientific truths and its moral implications. Humans are animals. Thus any divinity we have is due to what traits we share with our fellow animals, not with what differentiates us from them."

The massive screen showed an image of several animals in a circle: a chicken, a frog, a cow, a human, a bee. The screen took a moment to show the eye of each animal.

"The issue of mankind's oppression of others cannot be solved simply by removing religion. Religion is merely the tool exploiters use to convince others to give up their lives for what they desire. Few wars are actually fought over religious differences. Religion is a political tool, and as such, is not the core of corruption, despite what many humans claim. The infinite search for land, money, power, and, worst of all, knowledge is far deadlier than any scriptural text. Humans will never be content with what they know. While rationalizing is their greatest weapon, discontent is the force that brings them to use that weapon. The root of their discontent is a mental separation from God. Must humans forever live in conflict with the other species? They raze forests, pollute the air, and butcher the seas while claiming to be God's favorites! The animals live in God and thus are content within nature. Yet humans act like they are nobler, when they slaughter the innocent. The other animals, they have a linked consciousness, a oneness in God. Humans drift further and further away, ironically claiming to be the sole species able to reach liberation. Is liberation a loophole then? Why else would animals who have been on Earth for millions of years not be able to attain it? If liberation is so central to existence, why would only one species be able to attain it? I had hoped that when humans saw the global consequences of their actions, things would change. But instead, they paint the effects of their greed as conspiracies. My last hope was that Exps could lead them into deconstructing their anthropocentric worldview, but instead, my people have been demonized and abducted."

Sellum created a visual portal displaying Nina's bloodied body. The image shifted to that of Exp 8, broken and bloodied.

"Mankind has existed for over 200,000 years, a small amount when compared to that of the other animals who call this their home, but a rather large number when we consider that roughly 15,000 years ago was the fall of man and the dawn of civilization. The descent of mankind has been swift and irreparable. I see no way of salvaging this lost animal. I see only one way to cure this planet of the discontented rationalizing disease that infects it. Extinction. When a species brings about an extinction so massive that it rivals that of Earth's greatest calamities, that species must be removed. As I said before, I am not here to judge nor be an executioner. You all aren't like the others; you are like me…purposeful pacifists. But pacifism and inaction must not become one in the same else our pacifism shall fail the oppressed and encourage their oppression. Humans are not intrinsically evil, but they are systemically bound to a culture of greed and ignorance. I declare that 2100 is the last century of mankind."

Sellum bowed his head to the crowd. "I ask of you now to stand with me and make the necessary sacrifice for a fair and just world. I ask that no blood be shed and no lives be taken. You all believe that God's next incarnation will be that of an Exp, and I tell you with absolute certainty that your belief is correct. The question remains whether or not you will help your god. I cannot accomplish this task alone. Will you help me cure this planet?" He reached out to them, his voice as firm as a mountain range.

Chapter 159: Human Extinction

Previously: D.S. was killed in battle. He awakened on a flowery bed in Lum. The big kid held his head as he slowly stood up. "What happened?" he asked, removing his wig.

A portal appeared and a woman with blue skin, clad in thin pink armor emerged.

"Violet, is that you?" asked D.S. in a daze.

"Sel's forces are attacking several of our temples. They seem to have gotten wind of our plans for invasion. You have two options; either I end you or you join Lum and fight with us."

"The second one, duh!" D.S. embraced his dazed friend. "Let's go beat up some bad guys, buddy!"

Devlin and Demonica were at a convenience store.

"Oooh, I like this one," said Demonica, pointing to a black crib.

"What are you doing?" asked a man in a nasally tone.

"Minding our own business," said Devlin.

"Demonica, you really think I'll just allow you to run off? Efil has been captured, I'm so close to attaining victory!" exclaimed the man.

"How did you find us, Bob?" asked Devlin with a glare.

"And you, what are you doing? Didn't you see the news?" asked the possessed man with a sly grin.

"No. We're trying to be off the grid," said Devlin.

"Hope's leadership has split up the Exps into two groups. D.S. was murdered by Hope's side. Oh, and Sellum declared he's going to wipe out humanity."

"D.S. is dead," said Devlin softly.

"Yes. All because his little brother, that's you, ran away," said the man, wiping his eyes.

"None of that is our problem," said Demonica, grabbing Devlin's hand.

"I raised you, so at least give your father the courtesy to fight with him in his time of need," said the possessed man.

"We should check up on the others. If only briefly," said Devlin.

"Now more than ever we need to stay hidden. Father, I'm not going to be involved with your struggle any longer. I'm pregnant," said Demonica, touching her slightly bloated belly.

"My little girl, pregnant. Oh, I'm going to be a grandfather! Of course you are free of obligations," said Sel cheerfully.

"Don't act surprised. You're the one who used my body to impregnate her," said Devlin upset.

"Don't remind me. Let's pretend it never happened. To think it actually worked. I wonder if the kid will be an Exp," said Sel with a wide smile.

Demonica gave Lord Sel a peace sign.

"Well, I best be off. I'm so proud of my little girl," said Sel, rubbing Demonica's head before walking off.

Devlin grabbed Demonica's hand. "We should check up on the others."

"Kaity is an assassin; she'll be safe."

"It's not just Kaity I'm worried about."

"We don't even know where they are. Looking for them will only cause trouble." Demonica put his hand on her belly. "You have other obligations."

Devlin smiled. "You're right."

"Naturally," said Demonica with a smile.

Agent Alpha and his sister were outside, looking up at a California warehouse.

"You sure you're up for this, sis?" asked Koshi, grabbing her hand.

"They're just humans and they're pacifists," said Kioshi, screwing in her silencer.

"Exactly why I'm the only one who needs a gun," said Koshi, confiscating her weapon.

"Hey, no fair."

"Honestly, we don't know if they have Exps inside. After the Police Station Skirmish, the Exps split up and vanished. It's not unlikely they took refuge with DXM."

"Hey, so what do you think about that super Exp?"

"He was just employing scare tactics. Most likely he said what he said to get the Exps to end their fight against themselves. Think about it, if Hope has no chance of success, there's no need for her to show credibility by taking down renegade Exps. If mankind becomes the enemy of Exps, that could unite Exps. Nothing brings people together like a common enemy."

"I'm confused."

"Don't worry. It's just my theory. Oh, and I also think he's the one who snatched Kaity and Exp 8 from us. What's got me worried is that some of these religious nuts may have taken his speech seriously."

"Didn't think you cared about human extinction."

"Of course I care. Say what you want about the species, but they make the best food." He poked his sister's cheek.

"You're horrible!" exclaimed Kioshi, slugging him as she giggled.

"Charles David, the branch leader for the New York DXM was in a meeting with the head of the Furies about the God Exp's speech. The meeting was innocent enough, but what worries me is that several DXM members were scoping out the building during the meeting. Not sure what they were looking for, but it could be problematic."

"Ow!" Kioshi smacked a mosquito on her arm. "Oh, sorry. It was just a reflex," she said, looking at the bloody stain on her arm. "Hey, brother. Look at this."

"She attacked you, so I'm not upset. I don't swat mosquitoes off me, but I wouldn't hesitate if they hurt you."

"It's weird-looking. See? I mean, the blood is red but the body is…it looks like metal."

"Shit. Could be a bio-weapon. Get back to base; get an immediate medical exam. I'm going in," said Koshi, cocking his gun.

"Hey, we're a team. I'll get an exam after the mission. I'd rather die than ruin my chance at a promotion," said Kioshi.

"You really need to take your life more seriously. I'm ordering you to head back to base!"

"I'll kill myself if you don't let me help!"

"Enough! Here, take it," he said, handing her a gun. "I took out the bullets, so it's only good for intimidation. No need to get our hands bloody if we don't have to. Follow me," said Koshi, crawling out of cover through the tall grass.

"This is so exciting," said Kioshi, trailing behind him.

They rose out from the grass when they arrived at the side of the warehouse.

"I'm setting some charges," said Alpha.

Kioshi beamed at him.

"That means you should back up."

"Oh yeah." Kioshi pointed her fingers like a gun and mimicked firing when her brother pressed the trigger to blast open the wall.

Koshi signaled his sister to stay in position before rolling into the warehouse. He shot three guards and checked the rest of the room before welcoming his sister in. "The room's secure, and don't worry, they were tranquilizer rounds."

"Why not give me one?"

"Well, you might shoot yourself by accident."

"Don't be a jerk," said Kioshi, kicking him.

"Okay, fine." He took her gun and loaded it up. "Only shoot if you need to."

"Roger, sir."

"Gamma, a power outage would be great right about now," said Koshi, holding his finger to his ear.

"Sure thing," said the voice of a kid from the other line.

"Night vision and stay directly behind me," said Koshi, adjusting his sister's visor.

They slipped past the fumbling scientists on the stairs.

"Why are scientists here? I thought DXM was religious," said Kioshi.

"It's a science-based religion. Exp 8's rebellion was what created the idea of an Exp messiah. Before then they worshiped the Big Bang. Deceivant was a member but left after it got too devotional. We're almost there." Koshi shot the two guards by the door and covered them in a camo blanket.

"Wow, they turned invisible."

"Yeah, pretty handy, right? Now, be warned, things might get ugly soon." Koshi removed the lid from the key pad and set a robotic spider in the mesh of wires. "Or there might not be anything here at all. We'll find out soon." Once the door was unlocked, he collected the spider and flung the door open.

"Not a word," said Alpha, pointing his gun at the three men in the room.

By the time Kioshi entered the room, only one man was standing.

"They're just sleeping, but we're not above violence."

"Who sent you?" asked the man.

"We came here to take back what you stole from us, Charles."

"Well then, you're already too late."

"What did you steal from us again?" asked Kioshi.

"You're going to tell me where it is, or I'm going to skin you alive," said Alpha, taking out a knife and slicing Charles' arm.

"Go ahead make me a martyr," said Charles with a smile.

"Our Boss thought about what you said at the meeting. He may have come up with a solution."

"This is the only peaceful solution. Your Furies are terrorists. We will never see eye to eye."

"Still, he needs to know what you did."

"Well, it's too late anyway. No harm, I suppose. They've been released," said Charles with a smile.

"We're only here to get back what you stole. Our boss didn't give us the whole rundown."

"We stole the bio bomb, and we created an effective way of delivery. The Zika Prime is a modified form of the Zika virus. The Furies have threatened to release it before, but they didn't have the stomach. The Zika Prime is non-lethal. It ensures sterility for males and makes females barren. Our god asked us to save this world peacefully, so this was the only way. Mosquitoes are seen as only a nuisance to man, how fitting that they be what brings about their end. This is the last generation. Once mankind dies out, the Exps shall become the stewards we never were."

"Boss, are you hearing all this?" asked Alpha.

"I am," said the Senator in a ghostly whisper. "Kill him and make it painful. Kill everyone in the building."

"Hey, I wouldn't have brought my sister along if you hadn't told me this was a clean job."

"That man said Zika Prime is harmless, but it's not. The Furies have used it before by means of injection. The wife of an oil lobbyist miscarried later that week. It isn't harmless. It robs babies of their chance at life. Now kill him and everyone in that building!"

Alpha shot the man in the legs with his sidearm and wrapped taped around his mouth so he wouldn't scream. When the man tried to remove the tape, he shot his arms. "Okay, Boss. I get that you're freaking out, but shouldn't we worry about the mosquitoes first?"

"I can't think clearly while those involved in this atrocity draw breath," said the pained voice of the Senator on the other line.

"Okay. Understood. Sorry, sis." Koshi fired a tranquilizer round into her. "Things are going to get messy," he said before plunging his dagger into Charles' throat.

Senator John, who was seated at the edge of his bed, ended the call and sobbed in his hands.

"What do you need me to do?" asked Agent Beta, putting a hand on his.

"You were the one who spied on the meeting? How could you let this happen?"

"It was taken during the meeting. The discovery of the missing bio-weapon was only just yesterday."

The Senator turned to her and gripped her throat. "You promised me the threat would be contained!"

Beta grabbed his arm and made him release her neck. "I only know what the Furies know. It's not too late. The mosquitoes were likely released earlier this morning. That means they couldn't have gone far. If we cleanse the city they were in, it should be enough to contain this."

"No, that isn't good enough. We need to be thorough. The whole state has to go. We cannot let the public know about this threat. No mistakes will be permitted."

"What are your orders, sir?"

"There are two things that must be done. Firstly, every member of DXM must die. Every last one. As for who killed them, let's just say a rogue Exp from the Furies was sent at them."

"But where's the motive? California is one of the greenest states."

"Then chalk it up to an orchestrated Exp attack."

"On their own followers?"

"We can figure out who to blame later."

Agent Beta nestled his head to her bosom. "You aren't like this. You're usually so clear-headed."

"If we can't contain this, no baby will ever have a chance to live. It will be abortion on a global scale. Send out our Exps to attack the city. We can then bomb it after I get the president and the rest of the Senate to agree."

"Do you think they'll listen? You're not just bombing civilians. These are Americans."

"The severity of the situation is enough to gain their approval. I'll be off at once. Send out the Exps, and get the energy bomb ready for deployment."

"Yes, sir."

"Damn it all. California is a blue state. Why couldn't it have been Texas?" asked the Senator under his breath.

Agent Beta saluted and then left the room. "Codename Famine, get to the hanger immediately."

"Alpha told me what happened, but count me out," said a sad and angsty voice from the other line.

"You say that you're going."

"I don't want to do this anymore. Please don't make me."

"I know where your little sister is."

"How long have you known?"

"Not important. I'll bring her to you once you've completed the mission."

"What's the target?"

"Well, it starts with the DXM lab in California. But from there it will just spread."

"I'm en route."

"That was fast."

"Alpha already called me over to talk with me."

"About what?"

"Not a clue."

Famine landed the jet in the tall grass outside the warehouse. The green suit soldier removed his lime green insectoid helmet. The 5' 11'' toned agent had greasy and messy grey hair the covered his weary topaz eyes. When he opened the door, he was met with a friendly face.

"I'm here on a mission. Sorry, no time to talk," said Agent Alpha.

"You called me here. Hey, is Mom okay?" asked Famine.

"Just sleeping, don't worry. I called you 'cause I needed a ride. Is it alright if I use your jet to get out of here? The Boss is sending me out on a kill spree, and I want to get a few supplies."

"Go ahead. Hey Dad, when this mission is over…Beta promised to bring my little sister to me. Can you believe it?" he asked, hugging his dad.

"It's been over two decades. I'll believe it when I see it," said Koshi, starting up the jet.

"Yeah, good point," said Famine, walking inside the building. He crouched down to the first body he found. "Let's get this over with." After using a knife to cut out a piece of flesh, he put it in his mouth. "I'm sorry everyone, but I need to do this." His fingers grew mouths and began chomping on the body.

Sellum arrived before Kaity, who was hidden inside a shed.

"How did you find me?"

"Are you coming with me to defend Absence?"

"Why haven't you found Nina yet?"

"I don't know where the Senator's base is."

"You should have waited till we arrived. I let Koshi capture me so I could break her out."

"I'm not sorry for saving you. I promise once the war is over, I will find her."

"Every minute we spend up there is months on Earth. I can't go without her."

Sellum gripped her. "Kaity, you're the next in line. You have to see the bigger picture."

"D.S. was killed! He was just a kid and now he's dead." Kaity said with a cracking voice. "Maybe you need to see the smaller picture."

"I can't convince the others without you."

"Why can't Exp 8 give them a pep speech?"

"He's decided to stay and keep the others safe. I told him they were safer in Absence."

"So, you lied to him?"

"If Sel gets his hands on Zenero, he can go anywhere. I cannot allow that to happen."

"Is Stabby going?" asked Kaity.

"Of couwse I am!" cheered Stabby, popping out behind the couch.

"Look, this isn't even just about Nina. For all I know, Hope has Kanasta and—"

"Hope released Kanasta after Deceivant found out about what she did. He hasn't talked to her since."

Kaity looked up at him in silence.

"I speak the truth."

"I know so little about you. All the gods have used us, just like the Senator, just like my father. How am I supposed to trust you when I know nothing about you?"

"Kaity, as the next in line to be Sellum, you're my only chance at distracting Sel."

"And what if I get captured? What then?"

"I won't let that happen."

"We have a mess to sort out on Earth. I don't think now is the time to try and get involved in a fight between gods."

"You forget that every advantage Sel gains is an advantage over your mother."

"Fine! I'll go! Can't let him be the one who kills her," said Kaity. "BoneSaw, are you coming too?"

The eager robot saluted with a saw.

"Right this way," said Sellum, creating a portal.

They arrived at a log cabin in the woods of Melbourne, Florida.

"Yay! Kaity's here!" cheered Opti, seizing her in a big hug. He froze once he saw BoneSaw. "What is that friend killer doing here!?"

"BoneSaw felt that killing D.S. was the only way to stop our quarrel. It was only trying to protect us. At least, that's what I hope," said Kaity softly.

"If you say so, then I trust you," said Opti, shaking Kaity's hand.

BoneSaw offered a saw shake but Opti ignored it.

"I wasn't sure she'd come," said Chipko, punching the air.

"Well then, it's settled." Kanasta walked into the room, hoisting his suitcase over his shoulder. "I'll be staying here."

Deceivant approached Kanasta. "Are you sure? Even I'm planning on going. We could really use your help."

"I have work that needs my attention," said Kanasta, messaging clients with his free hand.

"I'm going. Won't you protect me, brother?" asked Toxic with a sad look.

"I won't change my mind," said Kanasta softly.

"I just want to get away from all this. We can't even hold a funeral for my son because of all the Exp hate going around," said Deceivant, biting his thumb.

"I will personally locate him once Absence is deemed safe," said Sellum.

"He's strong but he's also innocent. I don't want anyone to take advantage of him," said Deceivant with a solemn tone.

A woman came in and offered drinks to the Exps. She smiled at Kaity. "Welcome. A friend to the Exps is a friend to DXM."

"Thanks. I really appreciate you letting us stay here," said Kaity with a bow.

"Have you all seen what is going on in California?" asked the woman.

"I know all about it. He's the last one we need," said Sellum.

Senator Jo John was in the midst of a debate with the Senate.

"I have the President's approval, but still you all remain hesitant."

The Senator in front of John smiled at him. "I'm surprised with all your Exp fear mongering that you haven't managed to create some sort of deterrent."

"I'm a Senator, my battlefield is politics."

A woman leaned in. "Senator Ross' rudeness aside. You're asking us to okay a missile launch on our own city. Do we have a cover up?"

"An excellent question, Senator Eva. Perhaps we can claim Humans First caused the attack."

"You're wrong there, Ricardo. That would mean the US government allowed terrorists to steal weapons from us. We cannot lose credibility over this. I'm sorry, John, but your request is denied. We will send in the military to defeat that creature."

"Wait. It's more severe than I stated earlier. The Furies unleashed the Exp as revenge against DXM for stealing from them. What they stole has already been unleashed. It's a bio-weapon."

"What does it do?" asked Senator Ross after everyone else fell silent.

Senator Jo John leaned in and waited for all eyes to be on him. "I have absolutely no idea."

Senator Ricardo took a deep breath. "I agree with John. We aren't left with many options. If the publicity is too strong, we can say the President passed it through legislation with a veto."

"Actually, she told me she would do just that if you did refuse."

"Does anyone disagree?" asked Senator Ricardo.

Silence.

"Well then, let's blow it to hell," said the Senator with a smile.

Agent Gamma looked up from his computer console at Agent Sigma. "His request passed. Hey, come to think of it, how is Famine going to get out of there before the missile hits?"

"Perhaps this is his final mission. Though he be a demon, I shall pray for his soul to have a smooth ascension to the inferno. Will you join me?" asked Sigma with a benevolent smile.

"Sorry, no time. Alpha, are you there?"

"Yeah, what is it, squirt?" asked Koshi from the other line.

"The missile got approved, and Famine is in the area. Is there any way to get him out?"

"There sure as hell better be! Can you reroute the missile?"

"Of course I can, but that would be treason, so no luck," said Gamma with a shrug.

"He's my son and he'll die! Imagine if Lambda were out there. Wouldn't you do anything to save her?"

"I can delay the launch but that's it. You need to bring him to his senses," said Gamma.

"That's going to be hard without the Boss' help, but I'll figure it out. Thanks."

Sellum approached a naked man in his late twenties in a pile of flesh and debris.

"What are you doing here? And why did you stop me? I wasn't done," said Famine, struggling to stand.

"I need your help."

Famine burst out into laughter.

"This isn't just about me. It would greatly benefit Stabby if you would join us," said Sellum.

"That's not her name."

"Will you join or not, Abyss?"

"That's not my name either! Look, I'm already a part of the government; you think they would like it if they saw me working with the one who is trying to cause human extinction? They already have a hard time trusting me," said Famine with a grimace.

Sellum leaned in. "Have they fooled you? Do you really believe all those lies they told you? How Exps are demons?"

"I will gladly follow them if it means killing you," said Famine with a cold stare, smacking a device on his chest. The device expanded, forming into his green skin suit.

"Your rage won't change anything. We both know the best way to protect your sister is joining me," said Sellum.

"You don't have the right to talk about her!" Famine's fist slammed into Sellum.

"You do want to protect your sister, don't you?" asked Sellum, unfazed.

"More than anything."

"Welcome aboard," said Sellum, offering a handshake.

"Hey, you. Get away from my son," said Koshi, pointing a gun at Sellum. A barrier of dark energy rose up, blocking the agent's view.

"Why would I ever help you?" asked Famine.

"Because I know where your sister is."

"I'll believe it when I see it."

Sellum created a portal and Stabby peered out from it. "Hi, Daddy," she waved innocently.

"Hi there, my little vampire," said Sellum monotone, waving joyously back.

Famine fell to his knees and cried.

Sellum lifted him to his feet. "Come along. It's about time you two were reunited." He pulled Famine into the portal.

"You…you haven't aged a day, sister," said Famine, embracing his dear sister in tears.

"Sister?" asked Stabby with a curious tilt of the head.

Sellum motioned everyone to grant the siblings a moment.

"We're never getting separated again. Never." He clenched her tighter.

"Who are you?"

Famine released her from the hug but kept a steady grip on her hand. "It's me, Chris. Your brother. I know it's been years, but it's really me."

"I don't have a brother. I do have a daddy though!" cheered Stabby with a hop.

Famine turned to Sellum, his eyes intensely gazing into the monster.

"She missed you dearly after the separation, so I erased you from her memories."

"You're despicable."

"I did what I felt was best."

"You want my help? Then you're going to have to put back her memories," said Famine, still gripping her hand.

"It isn't that simple."

"Daddy, who is he? And why won't he wet go of me?" asked Stabby, trying to free her fingers from the man's grip.

"He is someone you once knew," said Sellum.

"You're going to fix her!" yelled Famine in a hushed tone. "You wouldn't have come to me if you didn't need me."

"I can show her my memories of you two, so at the very least, she'll believe you."

"That's not good enough. If I'm going to join you, I want something in return," said Famine.

"Let me guess, after all this is over, you want me to turn myself over to the government. Or do you want money? Power? Knowledge? Land? Please tell me when I'm getting close," said Sellum, tapping his chin.

"I want the truth," said Famine.

"The truth can be a very painful thing," said Sellum.

"You have no grasp of the pain I went through," said Famine enraged.

"Be a little more specific," said Sellum.

"Show everyone what you did to me."

"Without proper context, that could ruin the team's synergy."

"Then give it context!" yelled the furious brother.

"And in return you'll serve me?" asked Sellum, tilting his head.

"I won't even consider it otherwise."

Sellum stared at him in silence.

"Fix her! You owe it to her, damn it!" yelled Famine.

"Regrettably, this is the only bargaining chip I have, and I do indeed need your help."

"Fine then. Tell everyone what you did to me and to my little sister and then I'll go with what the majority decide."

"This could end up hurting me more than it helps. I've decided that I will return you to the government," said Sellum with a smile.

Kaity dropped down from the ceiling in front of Sellum. "If you want us to trust you, you will show us," she said firmly.

"Secrets can be kept with good intentions," said Sellum.

"If I'm going to kill my mother, I want the whole story."

"That is only fair." Sellum exhaled sharply. "Must I show everyone?"

Famine and Kaity glared at him.

"It's all or nothing then. With these limited options, I must give in. Very well. Gather the others. It's time you all learn more about who you're following."

Twenty-four Exp Hunters gather in a church to welcome their newest initiate.

Sigma wore a priest's robe over his Hunter suit, and motioned Kioshi to the pews. "We welcome our newest Hunter."

Kioshi, completely naked, blushed as she smiled and bowed to the audience.

"Why aren't you smiling? You should be proud of her," said Lambda, nudging Alpha.

"There's no going back from here. She'll never be safe again."

"You will be reborn in service to our great Messiah." Sigma doused his fingers in holy water and pressed it to Kioshi's forehead.

"Is the Boss going to show up?" asked Kioshi, covering her chest.

"He's too busy, but Beta is keeping him company," said the shortest agent.

Sigma placed a custom-made possum-styled helmet with a one-way visor on top of Kioshi's head. "The Messiah's will is imbued into this helmet. When you act, you act in service to our Lord." He placed a device on Kioshi. "To fight against the demons that plague the Lord's domain, you must offer every inch of your body to his divine protection. This is now your flesh." The device expanded into her officially designed Exp Hunter suit with her Greek letter inscribed at the chest.

"My little sister finally has her own flashy, lewd, external, slim Hunter suit," said Koshi.

"Did you forget the name, or is that your attempt at a joke?" asked Lambda.

"Fortified lean electro-absorption shifting hazmat," said an agent behind Koshi.

"I like my name better," grumbled Koshi.

Sigma pressed his energy-laden palms to Kioshi's Flesh, lighting it up with energy. "Agent Pi, you are now one of the Messiah's warriors," said Sigma with folded hands and a smile.

"Thank you!" exclaimed Kioshi, repeatedly shaking his hand.

Hope is seated in a comfy sofa in a living room with newspapers lining the walls.

The Info Bomb reporter stood at the doorway. "I need to head out. Best of luck on your call."

"Your hospitality is saintly, Kelly," said Hope with a smile.

"It's a pleasure to help in any way I can. Atlas and the Captain will be back from their training soon. Kioshi is in the kitchen."

"Stay safe," said Hope, waving her ally farewell. The little queen pulled out her phone and dialed the Senator.

"John, are you there?"

"I am far too busy to deal with the likes of you."

"I have a solution."

"To what?"

"To the outbreak. Now that the dreadful monster is gone, you can't launch the missile, can you? Oh, how I'd love to see you squirm like a little worm."

"My patience is lower than your current approval ratings. How can you solve the outbreak?"

"Well, I can't say how until my demands are met, but I'll make the decision very easy for you. Adhere to my demands or I'll release documentation showing your ties to the California monster. I believe Abyss is the name the media coined for him; apparently, it's not the first time Abyss has gone on a rampage. I wonder if you were behind the other attacks as well. Oh my, you're in quite the pickle jar."

"You dare blackmail me?"

"Not without rewarding you for complying with my demands. That would be rude," said Hope, stirring her tea.

"What are your demands?"

"Three things. One, you'll abandon your plan to create an Exp kill squad. Two, you'll cease the order to wipe out DXM. And, lastly, I want you to make it so Exps can run for state government positions."

"I'll cease the order to wipe out DXM once their bio terror attack is put to a stop. As for your other demands." The Senator's frustrated breath could be heard from the other line. "I'll agree to them."

Hope perked up and took a sip of delicious tea. "And you'll agree to giving me the credit for stopping the outbreak?"

"Why do you want to save humanity? Was this whole disaster your idea?"

"Watch your tongue. That Exp who ordered humanity's extinction has absolutely no ties to me. I know very little about him. You'll be happy to know he won't be around for a while, leaving us with ample time to salvage what we've built together."

"I'll choose to believe you. You realize the only way I'll get your third demand to pass is if you succeed in wiping out the bio attack."

"That's why I needed the blackmail, you see. Well, Senator, I see this partnership as something that will only strengthen with time."

"So, how do I stop the virus?"

"You use the antidote, which only I possess," said Hope with a smile. "I'll bring my reporter to where our peace meetings first began. But I'll only turn over the antidote if you tell the public the truth about the threat that faces them."

"I don't have the authorization."

"It will continue to spread then. What's more important, saving face or saving lives? I want everyone to know who saved them. This isn't negotiable."

"I'll make the announcement today."

"Wonderful. I'll hand over the antidote by the end of the week."

"We need it now!"

"Come now. A little death and panic will make the moment when we reveal the cure, our moment, all the more effective," said Hope, rubbing her mittens together.

"Politics are irrelevant! Babies will die!"

"A leader must deal with incidents, not individuals. Saturday is as soon as I'll turn it over. A few days of fear won't bring this country to its knees, Senator." She took another satisfying sip.

"Don't force my hand."

"Any attacks on me or my people will result in the elimination of the antidote. Oh, and be sure to bring Nina along when you come to fetch it."

"I accept your terms."

"Compromise is such a wonderful thing, isn't it?" asked Hope, ringing a bell for her afternoon foot rub.

"I can go in and retrieve it. It won't take me long to pinpoint her location once I'm done here," said Beta, closing her hybrid car's door.

"There's too much at stake. We have to stomach these intolerable deaths. But once we have the antidote, Hope will regret threatening Diablo," said the Senator with fearsome eyes.

"You salvaged the two-party system after the Carbon War. Things will work out, sir."

"Even Christ was tried in the desert. This is truly a hopeless desert."

"Stay strong, I'll be back shortly." Beta went down the alleyway and found Wringer in the midst of propping up its latest victim.

"Changed your hours of operation, but I still found you. Don't make this difficult," said Agent Beta.

Wringer sent a chain her way, shaping it into a chainsaw rail and swinging it around.

Beta coated her hands in energy, creating claws that tore through the chains. "I can either kill you or capture you. Your choice."

Kioshi crouched down to Hope. "Do you want strawberry-scented or pineapple-scented lotion?"

"Just water will do. Not sure you know this, but the washing of the feet of a great sage is the honor of the highest order."

"Oh, I'm definitely honored. Now more than ever."

"Why more so than usual?"

"Well, because we're both members of the itty-bitty titty committee," said Kioshi, patting her own chest.

"If you use that to take away my father, you will regret it." Hope pushed her foot in Kioshi's face.

"Did he come back?" asked Kioshi, removing the little queen's Goth boots.

"No. I...I don't know if he'll ever forgive me."

"Do you forgive yourself?" asked Kioshi, removing Hope's socks.

"Do not presume to know my thoughts. They are the ones at fault, not me. All this could have been avoided if D.S. simply followed orders."

"He's dead now...right?" asked Kioshi softly.

"To think a single death was all it took to shake my empire."

"And saving ten billion lives is what will fix it!" Kioshi left and then brought a washtub from the kitchen.

Hope smiled.

"How did you get the antidote made?" asked Kioshi, massaging Hope's feet.

"You tracked down the ones who modified the Zika virus. I simply changed their mind, and now they're slaving away at creating an antidote."

"Then you aren't just letting people die? Why didn't you tell my boss?"

"I am your boss. Obviously, I'm trying to coax him into making an error. I finally have the greatest enemy to my people under my boot," said Hope with a satisfied smile.

Sellum's Warriors sat in a circle on some pillows in the living room, having moved the furniture to the kitchen.

"This won't take much time, correct?" asked Kanasta, playing two handhelds at once.

"A couple of seconds to show you everything, but I'd like to answer your questions and put your doubts at ease once we are done," said Sellum.

"Alpha likely already reported that I'm missing. Let's begin immediately," said Famine, looking over at his sister who was seated in the monster's lap.

"Roughly thirty years ago, July fourth, year 2080. That's where I'll begin my story."

Part 19
Sellum's Ascension

Chapter 160: Carbon Tax

The area around the Freedom Forcers faded away as it was overtaken by a new environment. The sun set over a lake. Grass grew out first, followed by trees, until the image was fully visible.

I looked at Chipko, who was wearing an outfit fashioned out of newspapers, all of which chronicled pivotal moments for environmentalism. Despite her intense conviction, her facial features had a softness to them that always put me at ease.

"You seem uneasy," I say, offering my hand to her.

"I'm disappointed, and yes, I am concerned," said Chipko, crossing her arms and slouching a bit.

"I will keep him safe."

"Why didn't he ask for me?"

"You don't like crowds."

"Yeah, but he could have still asked."

"How long will you cling to this? He married Casey; you must let go."

"I just want to be at his side for every special moment in his life."

"True love requires a detached state of mind."

"You're right. I should just be happy with what I do have and be in the moment." She put out her fist.

We knocked fists together. "That's the spirit."

"Well, you best get going. Don't want to be late. Plus, I hear there have been earthquakes in the area," she said with a grin.

"Do you think the myths you create will be enough to protect this place?"

"I think if they learn to fear nature again, they will start to respect it."

"Respect isn't the issue. It's the idea of humans being independent from nature that has brought about the eco-crisis."

"The issue has to be tackled from all angles. This isn't a simple war."

"It's not a war, it's a struggle."

"Semantics."

"It is so easy to become desperate and try to take the violent route, the easy route. I implore you, hold on to your faith, dear sister. Zenero has helped usher in a new age of eco-accountability, and I feel that tonight may bring that age to the next level."

"I'm heading back home. You should go too."

I reached out and grasped her hand. "You are dear to me."

She smiled and pulled her hand away. "As are you to me."

With a snap of my fingers, a portal to our home was created.

Chipko stepped through.

Another snap and that portal vanished only to be replaced by another.

I walked in, stepping out into the back of a truck.

Atlas was fidgeting in his tuxedo. Not only was it too tight for him but I could tell he didn't like dressing like a civilian. My brother looked up and smiled at me, though I could feel the worry weighing down the sincerity of the gesture.

"Last week's incident in Paris is over. Everyone will be extra vigilant. Zenero couldn't be safer," I assured him.

"We're in the midst of an internal war. Coming out here is asking to be killed."

I placed my hand on his shoulder. "This may be our only chance at stopping this war."

Zenero approached his creations. Every step he took was imbued with purpose. His golden eyes captivated and motivated us all at once. The charismatic man's long flowing silver hair was as beautiful as his dream. "If we live in fear, the oil barons win. To keep this planet healthy and safe, I will gladly put myself at risk. But Atlas, you must relax. This isn't the battleground of Michigan; it's a public stage in Maryland," he said in wispy, uplifting and regal voice, his every word filled with poetic passion and intent.

"Exactly, and we have those who will protect us." I turned Atlas to show him the open crowd of humans and the enforcement watching the crowd for suspicious activity.

A human in a suit was speaking to the crowd about sacrifice and progress and other political jargon used to gain approval.

"Well, this is the moment of truth," said Zenero, noticing the man had finished his speech.

Zenero stepped up to the podium. "We live in times of unprecedented crisis. While we all are gathered here, war is raging in this very country. Civil wars have also erupted in France and Germany; it seems likely that more countries are soon to join this three-year bloodbath. The UN's Carbon Tax Initiative, and the enforcement thereof, caused a split we have felt since. Some even credit the tax for the crisis we face, as countries began buying and selling accountability in return for export cuts and other benefits in a brand-new market. Even though it has thus far caused more negativity than positivity, I in no way regret my support of the Carbon Tax Initiative; doing so would betray the pure intent behind my decision. Before carbon and methane emissions were externalities and as such had no economical weight, but now human-caused climate change is an economical reality. By changing them from externalities into realities, there can no longer be a denial of mankind's hazardous effect on the planet's life-systems. In this war there are those who have much to lose, but we are not them. We are not the oil barons, the lobbyists of Big Pharma, or the

Animal Agriculture investors who seek profit over progress and put a dollar value on everything they can. We have nothing to lose and because of that many of us have chosen to be martyrs. But what good are we to this planet if we are dead or imprisoned? And what message are we sending if we use terrorism and violence to force humanity to change their consumerist ways? We vote with our dollar; every purchase is either a step toward a better world or a step toward ecological crisis. Fear is a weapon, but it is not our weapon. The only way we can win this war is to stop fighting. Violence is a habit we must absolutely break out of. To end the ecological crisis requires an evolution of ideology. Exps are the peak of the evolutionary process; blending qualities of animals, plants, and minerals into an ecological marvel. For those of you who are not up to date on the technological breakthroughs I've made, please pay extra attention. Exps are photosynthetic artificial beings. They are not androids, and they are not to be feared. They are nomadic by nature, see Earth as their nation, and carry a strong will to change the planet for the better. Since they are not human, they are not bound by the weight we give human constructs and thus can introspectively discern the most ecological way of living. Exps are free from the habits that plague us; every choice they make is marked by intentional moments of decision. With them, we have new idols to aspire to become and we can reexamine everything we see as truth. Today marks the day that Exps will be known throughout the world. Everyone please put your hands together for my creation and dear friend, Atlas!"

Atlas stepped up to the stage, staring out at the crowd.

Zenero smiled. "Exps are organisms that do not need to eat or sleep. They are free from necessity and connected to nature. They clean the air, purifying it of pollution with each inhalation, yet do not need oxygen to breath. Look at Atlas; he is the picture of health. My dear friend is powered by a complex device known as a capsule, an energy conductor that converts solar rays into potential energy with unprecedented efficiency. This is not mere photosynthesis; the capsule absorbs the sun's rays on a grand scale, cooling our planet in the process. Mechanics aside, Atlas is stronger than any human, and the same holds true for most of my creations. I created Exps to serve humanity, not in an economic way but in an ideological one. After this day, I will release my Exps as a war deterrent. They will enter the warzones and disarm both armies. My creations will bring an end to this war without a single casualty! Exps will serve as ideal planetary citizens, reminding us all that we can break free of the artificial constructs that bind us. If we deconstruct harmful technologies and worldviews, we can emerge from this age of crisis into an age of planetary flourishing!"

Someone in the crowd started clapping, and like a virus, the acceptance spread. Soon there were hundreds clapping.

Zenero's smile dropped and he collapsed. Blood leaked from his chest.

My whole body froze.

Why is it so easy to destroy?

My vision became blurry with tears.

Humans ran out in a panic, trampling each other and struggling to push through the enforcement agents. Once the humans reached the exit, a bomb activated, and they exploded into bloody bits.

Atlas grabbed Zenero and held him in his arms, tears falling out of his eyes uncontrollably.

I watched as they left, scanning every one of them for the weapon that took Father away from me. The fleeing humans who survived the blasts were shot by the police force sworn to protect them. The political corruption was more widespread than anticipated, but at the moment I wasn't concerned about the possible reasons for the mutiny.

I had to find him. He must die by my hand.

After the civilians broke free from the initial shock, they began wrestling the guns out from the enforcement agents. That's when I spotted him: a human male with the rifle slung over his shoulder.

The rage nearly consumed me.

I raised my trembling hands to my face but kept my eyes on him.

DIE!

My mind went blank as it was overtaken by a potent dark fury.

I came to in a world of smoke and silence.

My eyes were drenched with tears, and my throat was heavy with grief.

My sadness must have saved me from being consumed. But I must move beyond it, else I'll be broken.

I teleported outside the smoke cloud. Peering down from above, I spotted only a single survivor.

Atlas is alive. My brother survived, so I must become happy.

Metal ropes dropped from helicopters, followed by soldiers that slid down them.

I vanished and reappeared in front in Atlas, who was already being assaulted by gunfire.

Escape. We have to escape.

I grabbed Atlas' hand and tapped into the artifact situated in my capsule.

We emerged just outside our home.

Atlas kicked open the door, covered in Zenero's blood and his own tears.

A dark-skinned youthful Exp saw the body and froze in place.

I grasped her hand, and for an instant, we shared our grief. "June. Please…tell the others."

She dried her tears and sped off, informing our brethren of the tragedy.

After I laid a blanket on the ground, my brother set down the body.

"Don't leave us," said Atlas, holding his father's hand.

Zenero gasped and spat out blood.

He didn't have much time.

A tan woman with cream-colored hair entered the room.

"Tranquil, I failed him," said Atlas.

"What happened?" asked Tranquil, her caring eyes polluted with grief.

I never wanted to see her like this.

I grasped Tranquil's gentle hand. "The murderer is dead," I said, shaking with a mix of rage and misery.

She's here. She'll keep me balanced.

"Why him? Why are the best people the ones who get shot?" asked June, turning away from the tragic sight.

June held her sporty hat over her eyes with her fingerless gloves. She buried her hands in her cutoff shorts.

"It only takes one selfish bastard to destroy the peace of the world," said Bob, seething with added anger to mask his misery.

"We have to save him!" cried Casey, shivering in Chipko's embrace as they entered the room. My distraught sister was dressed in all white. I look forward to the day where she no longer feels it necessary to hide her face beneath the shadow of a hood.

August slammed his fist into the wall, making a hole. "We can't. Look at the where the wound is. You can't fix a punctured heart."

"Then we must replace it. May, can you replicate it?" asked Casey, turning to her sister.

May grasped her chest. Her amethyst eyes were overtaken with tears. Those tears dropped down her tanned cheeks and landed on her Egyptian sandals. She shook her head after wiping her tears. "It won't work," she said in a timid, trembling voice.

"It's worth a shot," said Chipko, trying to bury the despair by clenching her bare fist.

"Yes! We have to try!" wailed Casey in tears.

"Casey, keep hold of his hand. He…he loves you more than anyone. You have to keep him with us," said Chipko, blasting away her tears.

"We're going to save you," said Casey, touching Zenero's cheek.

"Bob, give Zenero energy," commanded Chipko.

"Understood." He shoved the Atma Blade into Zenero and the spectral spiral reversed direction, filling the man's body with spirit energy.

"Tranquil, I need you to pray. Even the slightest grace could give us the chance we need," said Chipko, before turning and noticing that her sister was already praying.

My sister's body emanated a pink aura, no doubt from her Love Artifact.

"August, soften his skin so we can get to his heart," ordered Chipko.

"*SURFACE PERMEABLE*," said August, and the skin above Zenero's chest became like a cloud.

"June, we're going to need to exchange his heart. Can you do it?"

"Can I get suited up first? I'm terrified," said June.

Chipko embraced her sister and caressed her short, curly hazel hair. "You can do this, June. We all believe in you."

"Why do I have to do it?" asked June, holding the capsule in her trembling hands.

Durga grabbed her sister's hands. Her hair completely covered her eyes. "We need to steady your hands. Close your eyes and concentrate on your breath."

"No time. I have to do it now," said June, a bead of sweat dropping down her cheek.

"Then concentrate on the pain, not the fear."

"O-okay," said June about to cry.

Red hooks came out from Durga's fingertips and tore the pain out from the frightened girl.

"Sister, you shouldn't hurt yourself for me," said June.

"Your hands are steady," said Durga, smiling despite the relocated pain.

June exhaled sharply and then…it was done.

Please, let Father live.

"August, return his skin to its normal state. Now, February…where is he?" asked Chipko, turning around.

"He decided to stay in his room. He was afraid of seeing what happened," said Flash Girl.

"He's the only one who can close the wound."

"I'll get him." Atlas tore down the door and lifted the crying creation up from the bed.

"February, get over here and heal the wound," said Chipko.

My frightened sibling put his hands to Zenero's chest and got to work.

"October, I'm going to need you to hold him steady," said Chipko.

My brother followed her command without a word.

"What can I do?" asked Atlas, his shoulders drooping.

"If you know CPR, you can help," said Chipko. "Give him air after each compression. One…two…three…clear!" She hit her beloved's chest.

Directly afterward, Atlas gave Zenero air.

"One...two...three...clear!" yelled Chipko, hitting him harder with the shockwave this time.

Atlas put his ear to Zenero's chest.

"I think I heard it!" exclaimed Atlas.

"June, I need you to accelerate the energy circulation rate," ordered Chipko.

My siblings continued the routine, more tears flowing and more hopelessness weighing all of us down after each failed attempt.

Zenero's body started shaking from the blows.

"One...two...three...clear!" Chipko punched Zenero's chest with all her might, putting all her power into it and jumpstarting the capsule.

Zenero started coughing up blood.

Blood, that which had led to our despair, now renewed our hope.

We all gathered around him, relief washing away our pain.

"I'm...here," said Zenero weakly. He turned to Tranquil. "I heard your prayer. It helped me find my way back."

Chipko beamed at him. "Zenero, you have given us life and purpose. We are honored to be able to do the same for you. You are no longer human; you are an Exp now...just like us." She grasped his hand.

Zenero broke down into tears.

"You know, you could thank us," said Bob with a shrug.

Zenero weakly smiled up at them. "My family," he said softly.

"Yes, we'll always be family," said Casey before kissing his forehead.

After a few hours, Zenero was back on his feet and watching the news for updates.

"As you can see, the explosion not only consumed the convention building but also spread out for a mile before finally fizzling out. According to our sources, the attack was not committed by the conservatives or the liberals. The Exp known as Pathos lost control after his master was killed. If the obedience they show is linked to their creator's life. Then with the creator dead, the Exps have gone rogue. Hold on, we're getting an estimated death count." The reporter turned pale. "Seventeen thousand. My God, what are we going to do?"

Seventeen thousand humans is one thing, but how many other animals lost their lives because of me?

I was brought to tears. "Why aren't they talking about the enforcement agents who shot unarmed citizens?" I asked, my rage coating my words.

"The cops were obviously on the other side of the spectrum. There's nothing to even wonder about. You're a TV star. You should be proud. So many dead...all because of you," said Bob, grabbing my face.

Zenero turned to me in tears. "You lost control because of me. I shouldn't have brought you along."

He always shoulders our burden...but I'm the one to blame.

"What do we do?" I asked.

"Well, we could paint you as a rogue and publicly execute you," said Bob with a chuckle.

"How am I supposed to raise a child in a world like this?" asked Tranquil, tears dripping from her gentle eyes.

"I want to make this right in any way I can," I said, dropping to my knees and bowing my head.

"I...what we can do? Exps were supposed to be idolized not demonized."

"You've really put us in a bad spot. Congratulations on being a miserable failure," said Bob, patting my shoulder with genuine pride, making the insult all the more unsettling.

"Do we know who ordered your death?" asked Chipko.

"With so many enemies, it's impossible to know," said Zenero.

"Then you can't risk letting them know you're alive," said Chipko.

"You're right. The government is likely already setting up a program to eradicate Exps. None of us are safe here."

"So, what is the plan now?" asked Sellum.

"We have to consider our options. Yes, of course. Hand over the Teleport Artifact," said Zenero, opening his palm.

"A quick escape won't ensure your safety," I said, passing the traveler's stone to him.

"There's only one man who hates Exps enough to do this. If we all work together, we can track down John and kill him," said Atlas.

"That will only harm the public's image of Exps further," said Zenero.

"Further than this?" asked Bob, showing a short clip on his phone of humans being gunned down on suspicion of being Exps.

"In the end, we can't prove John was behind this. Let's not forget he showed support for the Carbon Tax Initiative. Either way, we don't know his story or his thoughts, and I believe everyone is innocent until proven guilty. There will be no more violence. This must be solved with pacifism!" yelled Zenero.

"How utterly boring. If there's no going back, why don't we just seize control? Then we can forcibly put an end to the war and make ecological harm a crime," said Bob.

Chipko raised her fist. "If that's what it has come to, I'll gladly fight. We are your family, but we're also your army."

"A new route has opened up for us. We are not safe on Earth, but there is still somewhere we can go," said Zenero with a smile.

"I will not flee to the moon or another planet while the animals of Earth are enslaved. If mankind wants us as an enemy, we can take them down. Exps could be the law enforcement. We could maintain peace," I said calmly, my fists quaking with intensity.

"There is no need for that. With the power of the Teleport Artifact, we can instantly travel to any place I've been before. I've been to over a hundred countries, helping those in need while creating an eco-accountable network of activists," said Zenero.

"Yes, of course. We just need to find a place where we will be welcomed," said Tranquil.

"Just recently, I was brought to a new domain entirely. We're going to Heaven," said Zenero, raising his arms to the skies.

Tranquil's face lit up. "You saw it?"

"With this artifact's blessings, we can go to the heavens themselves. Even the greatest misfortune can pave the way to new opportunity," said Zenero with divine confidence.

"Are we going to ask Allah to aid us?" asked Tranquil, her white pupils shimmering.

"Heaven and Earth are connected. That's what you told me," said Zenero, smiling at Tranquil.

"From Heaven, Allah watches us all."

"Observation is not enough. The mission on Earth has failed. We must go to the heavens, so we can save Earth," said Zenero with a hope-laden smile.

"You mean conquer the heavens, right? What a splendid plan and so true to your pacifistic nature!" cheered Bob.

"Can you be certain it will work?" asked August, leaned against the wall.

"It must work and therefore it shall. **Portal to the Heavens!**" exclaimed Zenero.

A portal appeared before them, leading to white grassland.

I caught Tranquil in my arms after she nearly fainted.

"Am I worthy?" she asked, looking up at me with those enchanting eyes.

"There is no one worthier," I said, moving her hair away from her face with a smile.

"Everyone, we march onward into a new frontier. Stay together and we shall unite the heavens for our cause," said Zenero.

One by one we walked through the portal, following the will of a man who created us and inspired us to be planetary agents of peace.

Chapter 161   A New Frontier   Book 4: Part 19

Chapter 161: A New Frontier

"It's real! Heaven is real!" exclaimed Tranquil, dancing through the white grass.

She truly is a living blessing.

Bob smacked me to bring me back to my senses. "Stay focused. We're here for a reason."

"The whole land emanates joy," said Casey, snuggling up to Zenero.

"Indeed it does. I'd like to share something with all of you. This paradise is not the only world beyond. Before I was pulled into the white portal, I saw two others: a black portal and one that was clear. There is likely a ruler for each of these realms," said Zenero.

Atlas stepped in front of Zenero. "Stay behind me."

Etaf approached the new arrivals. "I've seen all manner of creatures here but never something like that," she said, eyeing Bob.

"Are you in charge of this world?" asked Bob.

"I'm in charge of keeping the peace and the energy you're emitting is…."

"Godlike?" asked Bob.

"More than anything I've witnessed," she said softly before drawing the Destiny Sword. "What are you?"

"I'm not sure you would be able to comprehend my answer," said Bob with a grin.

"We are peaceful beings hoping to put an end to the conflict on Earth," said Tranquil.

"It will never end. In this world the only option is surrender," said Etaf.

Zenero stepped out from behind Atlas. "Surrender is against the core of our being. We'd like an audience with the god of this world."

"The Great Goddess is unreachable, for you at least. I'm taking you all in for processing. If all goes well, you will transition into your new life without delay," said Etaf.

"Hold on! We aren't dead. We came here with our own power. His power," said June, pointing to Zenero.

"Hmmm. Perhaps it is best I speak to Lum, after all," said Etaf before vanishing.

"Bob, how powerful was she?" asked Zenero.

"Strong enough to take all of you down, but I can handle her," said Bob with a grin.

"We aren't fighting the goddesses. They are doing the work of Allah. We should help them not harm them," said Tranquil.

Another portal appeared and a new goddess emerged.

"So, you must be in charge," said Zenero with a smile.

290

"Her aura isn't even as strong as the goddess before. They're redirecting us to the lower echelons of their management," said Bob with an irritated look.

"Greetings, visitors! We actually call all occupants visitors, since this is a place of transit, but you came here without dying. Is that really true?" asked Efil with wide eyes, leaning in.

"Ah, that look in your eyes. It's hope, isn't it?" asked Zenero.

"I'm a bit concerned. The workings of the afterlife must remain a secret," said Efil.

"And why is that?" asked Bob, circling around her.

"Well, because...I'm not sure. But it's the way things have always been."

"Can you send your friend back? I don't have time to waste with simpletons," said Bob before sinking into the ground.

"We need access to the other realms. Will you help us?" asked Zenero, bowing to the goddess.

Efil was taken aback by the gesture and twiddled her thumbs. "You don't need to bow. It's my duty to help out as long as it doesn't go against the will of Lum. Why do you need to go to Sel and Absence?"

"We want to do all we can to help those who suffer on Earth. The more we learn about these worlds the better," said Zenero with a disarming smile.

"The only ones who can bring you there are the ambassadors. Working alongside them, we've been maintaining balance between the realms," said Efil.

"What about Earth?" I asked, my fingers tightening into a fist.

"What do you mean?" asked Efil with a curious look.

"The afterlife is balanced, but Earth is in absolute chaos! Countless living beings are suffering from your refusal to intervene on Earth!" I yelled, my body heating up.

"Says the observer," said Bob, rolling his pupil.

"Lum and the goddess' duties are to maintain peace in the afterlife. We cannot interfere with the incarnated," said Efil.

"Cannot or will not? The greatest sinners are those who have the power to act but refuse to do so," I said, channeling my conviction.

"I shall return with the ambassador if Lum permits it. Please, stay put," said Efil before vanishing.

"That means we should split up, right?" asked August, playing hacky sack with a white rock.

"Pathos, I would like to speak with you alone," said Zenero, turning to me.

"Whatever you have to say to me can be said to everyone here," I said, putting my hand on Tranquil's shoulder.

"I wouldn't have asked if it wasn't of pivotal importance," said Zenero, taking my hand.

I suddenly found myself on a hillside. We were at the edge of the horizon. I could see my family in the distance, all specks on a white landscape. The moment seized me until he stepped in front of me. "What is it you wish to speak about, Father?"

"We will be unable to negotiate with these gods. They have lived in this world far too long and have become distanced from the turmoil of the incarnated. Routines are followed without reason. We must seize control," said Zenero.

"You want me to convince the others to take up arms against the gods, don't you?" I asked.

"You know me well. Pathos, if not for me being human, you would be the ideal prophet to lead humanity into the ecological age. I had hoped to dispel that bias in my lifetime, but it's all fallen apart. We are both pacifists at our core, but we know what must be done," he said, gazing into me.

If we fight against the gods, we will not be able to avoid casualties.

"We have not exhausted all our options. We've only just arrived."

"If the time comes for us to act, will you promise me you'll convince the others to fight with us?" asked Zenero, outstretching his hand.

His eyes betrayed his firm words. Father was feeling helpless.

I seized his hand. "I will do what must be done."

Zenero embraced me. "Thank you. No matter what happens, I can always count on you."

"What about Casey?" I asked.

"You are the only one who is my equal," said Zenero, grabbing the back of my head and making us bow to one another. "That will never change," he said with a smile.

"Thank you," I said, feeling bliss coat my body.

"You're forever welcome," said Zenero with a joyous smile.

The next moment we were back with the others in the grasslands.

"Had a romantic encounter behind our backs?" asked Bob, nudging me with his spectral arm.

"Brother, are you jealous? I care about you, don't worry," said Durga, patting Bob.

"Your inability to perceive the feelings of others amazes me. I was clearly mocking him," said Bob with a glare.

"We shared a special moment," said Zenero softly.

Bob leaned up against me and whispered. "Okay, so seriously, what happened?"

"Nothing to be concerned about," I said, patting him.

"Urgh." Bob sank into the ground.

"Do we have a game plan or not?" asked August, bouncing a boulder up and down with his springy fingertips.

"We wait, as the goddesses asked of us," said Zenero, smiling at Tranquil.

Chipko stepped up to Tranquil. "I don't get it. Doesn't this place go against what you believe in with its multiple gods?"

"Scripture is but a window into truth. Here, the truth is in everything we see," said Tranquil with a look of pure contentment.

I must keep her safe. I will keep her safe.

A portal appeared and a crystalline figure emerged.

Bob popped out and read the being's aura.

"What's the verdict?" I asked.

Bob's pupil grew and shimmered. "This one is special."

"I am Crystal, emissary of Absence. Who is the leader amongst you?" it asked, scanning us.

"I am," said Zenero, taking a step forward.

"Hmmm." The god walked past Zenero and stopped when it was in front of me. "What is it you seek?"

Words escaped me. This being's presence, its emotional body was as complex as the cosmos.

"I seek control," said Bob, floating in front of me.

"You seek approval," said the being, keeping its gaze on me.

"You can read me. Ohohoho! I was hoping to make something fun happen. Looks like things are going to get very fun indeed," said Bob with a twirl.

"I seek to end systemic suffering on Earth," I said with absolute firmness.

Space twisted and a portal leading nowhere appeared.

"Come," said Crystal, beckoning me.

"We all go together," I said.

"I'm staying here," said Tranquil.

"We don't know if it's safe here," said Chipko.

"You can't change my mind."

"Not to worry…Flash Girl will protect you!" exclaimed the super girl, all suited up.

"I'll stay too then. The goddesses may be dangerous but the environment is nice, except the lack of color," said Chipko.

"The white color is the purified aura. It's beautiful," said Tranquil.

Leaving three of our sisters behind, we ventured into the unknown.

The ground was gone but we were standing. Each step we took seemed absolutely meaningless.

"This is the place where change begins," said Crystal, leading us along.

"We wish to speak to your leader. How can we gain an audience?" asked Zenero.

"True gods do not exist anywhere. They are everywhere and nowhere," said Crystal, its gaze never leaving me.

"There is one more place. The black portal. How do we reach Sel?" asked Zenero.

"I feel so foolish. You're Zenero, aren't you? You've arrived sooner than expected," said Crystal.

"You've been watching me?" asked Zenero.

"Not since I left you. Had more pressing matters at the time. Do you remember me?" asked Crystal.

"Should I?" asked Zenero.

"It matters not. You want access to Sel, correct? I'll take you there. We have a lot to catch up on." Crystal fired a mineral into the sky.

Needle emerged from a clear portal.

"We need access to Sel. I'm giving an old friend a tour," said Crystal.

Needle nodded and created a black portal.

Bob popped out from Zenero's side and grabbed his hand. "You're going to need an escort to keep you safe."

"Then I'll come along to provide protection," said Atlas.

Zenero turned to me. "Talk to them," he said, before leaving with Bob, Atlas, and Crystal into the darkness.

"Talk to us about what?" asked October.

What do I say?

I took a deep breath. "Zenero believes we must take over the afterlife by force."

"'Bout time he started thinking straight," said August, cracking his knuckles.

"That's why I felt uneasy around him. I'm entirely opposed to it," said Durga.

"I absolutely agree," I said. "We don't know what will happen if we disrupt the system of this realm."

"We know what will happen if we don't disrupt it," interjected Casey.

"Do you really want another war?" I asked.

"Come now. You all know Zenero. He wouldn't suggest this unless it was absolutely necessary," said Casey.

"All options must be considered before taking action. It's how we've always lived," said May.

"He's going to need one of us to rule over each realm, right? I choose this place," said October.

"You can't be serious. Zenero may have created us, but we are individuals. We can't let his desperation tear us apart," I said.

"What do you suggest we do?" asked Durga.

"If Zenero makes a move against the gods, I say we take him down. That will give us leverage. We can work with them, and once he's cooled down, he can help us," I said, imbuing my words with bliss for extra persuasion.

"You're using him to forward your agenda. I won't allow it," said Casey.

"I said 'if' he makes a move. I'm trying to avoid conflict, not start it."

May stepped up to my side. "If it comes to that, I shall help you."

A portal spawned in front of us and Zenero appeared.

"My love, you must know what Pathos has said about you," said Casey.

"That must wait. Bob is locked in combat. Whoever wishes to protect him must come with me," said Zenero.

"Yeah, I think I'll stay here," said February.

"I'll come along," said August. "And I know we don't have time, but Pathos here said he'd take you down if you tried to attack the gods. Even tried to get us to join in on it."

"Bob's life is in danger. We can deal with mutiny once he's safe," said Zenero.

Could be a bad decision, but I can't abandon my brother.

I went into the portal, followed by August.

We ran out into a scorched landscape. The air was thick with ash, and even the sky was buried under a blanket of black fog.

Zenero teleported into the battle, creating a portal to protect Bob from the incoming ray of darkness.

"Watch out!" yelled August.

The dark beam coiled around the portal. August leaped into the beam, sparing his benefactor from harm.

"Keep Bob safe," said Zenero to me before vanishing along with his injured comrade.

"I don't need your protection," said Bob, phasing through a black sphere before firing his lasers at the foggy figure attacking him.

His pride won't allow me to help. The only thing I can do is watch.

The dark fog changed shape and became spherical.

It spoke to Bob in unintelligible whispers as its tendrils extended and chased him.

"Who started this battle?" I asked when Bob was within shouting distance.

"I was bored!" yelled Bob, his eye glowing with energy. He disappeared into the ground and popped up behind the deity.

The dark entity dispersed into fog and then formed behind Bob.

My brother dug into the earth as dark energy ate away at it.

"No point in hiding from you, I see," said Bob, before sending spectral arms into the dark amalgamation.

The being of darkness shot up into the sky, avoiding its enemy's clutches.

"Very fast. This is turning out quite exciting!" exclaimed Bob, speeding after the being.

The dark god entered the blanket of dark energy above.

"Hmmm. How am I going to find it now?" asked Bob, randomly firing lasers.

The black blanket of energy fired out an armada of tendrils.

"Is that fear I sense?" asked Bob, focusing energy in his pupil. "*Eyeball Laser!*" he yelled, ejecting a beam larger than his own body.

The sky parted to dodge the attack.

"Oh, so you are the energy now. I understand."

As he sped through the tendrils, Bob released souls and shaped them into the Atma Blade.

If he fails, I lose a brother. If he succeeds, he may become too powerful to contain.

Bob sped across the living ground of the realm, taking in the souls of the enslaved residents all the while increasing the size of the Atma Blade.

"With such a feast, I'll never go hungry again," said Bob, before aiming his weapon at the skies. "*Atma Blast!*"

A massive collection of soul energy was projected into the air, splitting off and gaining speed before piercing the skies.

A black figure fell from the sky.

"Not going as planned?" asked Bob, following the falling god.

Black tendrils came out from the cloudy entity.

"I win," said Bob, shooting a condensed laser beam.

After a direct hit, dark energy gushed out from the deity. It spread out along the ground before erupting and creating a dome around its master and Bob.

Time seemingly froze as I waited for a victor to emerge.

The moment the dome collapsed and the being of darkness shot toward me.

"You're next," it said, pointing at me with a black tendril. The deity then fell to the ground and rolled around. "Ehehahahahahahaha!"

That laugh is unmistakable. Always makes me so uncomfortable. Never thought I'd be so happy to hear it.

"Brother, is that you?"

Bob absorbed the dark energy covering his body and smiled. "As if I would lose. By the way, I'm no longer Bob. I defeated the god of this realm. Its power is mine. I am Sel!" he exclaimed, coating his body in a black aura.

Zenero's faith in him was not misplaced. Even gods could not compete with my brother's power.

"Why aren't you clapping?" asked Sel, rolling his eye.

"Do you see that?" I asked, pointing behind Sel.

A pink bunny shook off some residual dark energy and approached me.

"Don't worry. You're safe now. Is he what you were fighting?" I asked, picking the bunny up.

"Perhaps. Must have been so afraid I'd vanquish him that he turned into a harmless little bunny," said Sel, patting the little rodent's head.

"I'll bring him to Lum as soon as Zenero arrives," I said.

"Oh, he must think I'm still fighting. I'll send him the signal," said Sel before firing an assortment of lasers into the sky.

Zenero emerged from a portal with August. My injured brother's body was being consumed by the energy. "Can you save him?"

"Hmm. I could if he swears loyalty to me," said Sel, circling around August.

"This is no time for jokes! He is dying!" yelled Zenero.

Perhaps I was too hasty to judge him. Zenero hasn't changed after all.

"Stop whining." Sel gripped the dark energy and pulled it off before absorbing it.

August's flesh was partially consumed, but at least he was alive.

"We should take him to Lum. The gods can heal him," I said as the bunny nibbled my finger.

"That's where I went. But they refused. They said doing so may be seen as intervening in Sel," said Zenero with a grimace.

"Maybe February can help," I said.

"Good idea." Zenero teleported with August into Absence.

"Bob, don't you think there will be consequences if we take over these realms?" I asked.

"These realms are collectively known as Sellum. I'm not worried about the consequences. I'm more than fit to rule this realm," said Sel.

Zenero reappeared in front of us. "I dropped off October, but we have a problem. I don't know how, but the goddesses know you have become Sel. They are not pleased."

"Worry not. I'm the god of this world now. It's as if a database of information has been uploaded into me, granting me instant comprehension of every bit of lore this realm contains. You can't imagine how incredible this feels. I'll send out my army to attack Lum. If the goddess surrenders, my warriors will stop slaughtering her people. Shouldn't take long," said Sel with a mischievous grin.

"Zenero, you have to talk him out of this. He'll listen to you," I said, grabbing my creator's arm.

"If Lum is worthy of leading, she will surrender her throne. If she does not surrender her throne, she believes in acceptable losses. Should that happen, we will kill her and seize her power! Ah, a perfectly, morally sound outcome either way," said Zenero.

"You two have already plotted this out?" I asked.

"I trusted you, Pathos. You betrayed that trust. I assure you that this takeover will involve as few casualties as possible."

"Zenero…by your own logic, you aren't fit to rule." I rushed toward him, ready to snap his neck with my clenched fist.

Can I really kill him?

"Yet by my own logic, I will win." He created a portal and closed it as soon as I was inside.

"Brother, you look shaken up," said Tranquil, grasping my hand as soon as I arrived.

"Zenero is going to force Lum to surrender the throne. We have to do something!" I exclaimed, causing the bunny to hop out of my hands.

Sister grasped my fist and smiled. "Violence didn't work out for you, did it?"

"I don't know what to do," I said, tears pouring from my helmet.

"Zenero still loves us, doesn't he?" asked Tranquil, pain blooming in her pure eyes.

I smiled. "He does. I saw the concern in his eyes when he saw August's injury."

"Look at this place. Have you ever seen a tree so massive and vital?" she asked, gazing up at the World Tree.

"I want to protect this place."

"I have an idea, but I'm going to need you to promise me something beforehand."

"What do you need?"

"Don't use what I'm about to do to rally the others. I fear if you do, our family will become divided."

"You have my word. What are you going to do?"

"I'm going to meet with Zenero and inform him that if he attacks Heaven, I will end my life. That declaration will no doubt bring him to his senses," she said, petting a tortoise that nestled against her leg.

"What if it doesn't?"

She turned to face me. "Then you can't turn me into a martyr to encourage rebellion. Try to find a peaceful route to reach your goal."

"My only goal right now is keeping Zenero from ruining Sellum," I said softly.

"A peaceful goal needs peaceful means to achieve it," said Tranquil.

"I hope one day I'll be as wise as you," I said, walking up to her and embracing her. "I have faith in you, and I still have faith in Zenero."

"Look, it's glowing," she said, gazing up at the tree.

"I sense light in you, overflowing light," said the tree in a soothing tone.

"Me?" asked Tranquil, her cheeks red like roses. "You're Lum, aren't you?"

My sister likely didn't even notice it, but her body emanated energy from her artifact. Her kind and giving nature meant her Love Artifact was almost always active.

"I am Lum, but I fear my time is near its end."

"No. I know I can stop Zenero. I'm not afraid to die," said Tranquil.

"What about your child?" I asked, grabbing her hand.

"I…" Tranquil burst into tears. "Will you look after her for me?" She wiped away her tears and smiled. "No. Zenero won't go through with it. He wouldn't put my life at risk."

"What if he does? Will you give up your life to end the conflict?" asked Lum.

"I…I can't. If it comes to that, we'll find another way," said Tranquil.

"I can think of another way." The World Tree stretched out its branches. "I've watched over this world since it was entrusted to me. Now it is time for me to pass on the responsibility. I've watched you since you came here, Tranquil. And I see the determination in Zenero as well. He will not stop until his people rule this world. If I surrender my throne, I protect you and my people," said the World Tree.

"I'm not a leader. I'm merely a vessel for Allah's vision," said Tranquil.

"Lum can only be maintained by a mediator, not a ruler. Are you certain my surrender will protect this world?" asked Lum.

I grabbed Tranquil's trembling hands. "It will. I know it will. And you have my word that I'll do all I can to keep Sellum safe with my own power."

"Well, dear one. Do you agree?" asked Lum.

"Perhaps you should let me try to reason with Zenero first," said Tranquil.

"Sel has already fallen. Either I surrender my powers or I will be killed. I'm fortunate to have a worthy successor appear before me now," said Lum.

"I'll keep this world safe, no matter what. And I'll never forget what you've done for me," said Tranquil, reaching out and grabbing a branch.

"I will never regret this decision," said Lum.

"I fully accept your gift," said Tranquil with open arms.

A cloud of white energy left the tree and entered my sister.

The energy coated her skin, changing her complexion to that of snow.

"Are you okay?" I asked.

"This world is a paradise," she said, her eyes glowing with newfound wisdom.

"Well, there's no reason for Zenero to attack. You're Lum now. The battle is over before it began," I said, grabbing her hand.

What's going on? She feels distant.

"They've arrived. Let's go," said Lum, forming a white portal.

I grasped her hand as we entered, hoping to breach past whatever barrier was diluting her joy.

Zenero smiled at us once we arrived. "All that remains is Absence."

"You killed Lum? Didn't know you had it in you," said Sel, staring suspiciously at Tranquil.

"Call off your attack," said Lum.

"There is no need for you to attack Lum," I said.

Sel burst out into laughter. "It's just like Zenero said. You are so gullible. I couldn't assemble an army that fast. We expected you'd find your crush and tell her all about the impending attack. Looks like Tranquil isn't the pure angel you make her out to be."

You're wrong this time, brother.

"The protector of this realm surrendered to keep the peace. I did not harm her," said Lum.

"What? That wasn't supposed to happen," said Sel with a snarl.

"As expected of you, dear," said Zenero with fatherly pride.

"Exps rule both Sel and Lum now. Let's stop before we cause any more damage," I said.

"Not yet. We must go to Absence. Follow me," said Zenero, creating a clear portal.

What is he planning? He knows I won't allow him to harm the gods.

Lum waved me farewell. I followed Zenero and Sel into the portal, unsure of what was to come.

Once we arrived, we met up with October who was seated on a clear throne.

Crystal appeared behind us and spoke. "You've arrived. The god of Absence has spread out through everything in this realm. October is in a meditative state, trying to overpower the god."

That's why Zenero brought me here. To make me feel powerless.

"There's only one thing that remains," said Zenero, putting his arm on my shoulder.

"To return to Earth and take over by force?" I asked, grabbing his wrist.

"Once this is over, we won't need to. Bob spoke of a god who watches over all the realm gods. I shall take its place," said Zenero with a smile.

"How do we lure out the Omni God?" asked Sel, rolling around in deep thought.

"Well, assuming that God is omniscient, it should be rather simple. Sellum, I seek your throne. Either accept my challenge or watch as your demigods are killed one by one," said Zenero.

If I know he's bluffing, does that mean Sellum knows it too? If so, does that mean Zenero will have to change that bluff into a reality? Given that becomes a reality, can I do anything to stop him? Love. Love. Love.

My worries left me the moment Lum sent her energy my way.

"They cannot harm Sellum without my help. As soon as I became Lum, Zenero lost," said my sister with a contagious smile.

The impossible has happened. She's even more majestic.

A portal appeared in front of Zenero.

"Looks like Sellum did hear you," said Sel, rushing into the portal only to be bounced off.

"I challenged Sellum, so the god is permitting only me to enter. Fret not. I shall return with all the powers of the afterlife," said Zenero, entering the portal.

The portal stayed open and I entered.

It closed behind me, leading me to a realm surrounded by the Milky Way galaxy.

"Welcome to the Microcosm," said a booming, godly voice.

"Before you make a move, I should warn you that if I don't return, the new Sel will lay waste to your worlds," said Zenero.

The deity laughed. "Zenero, you've arrived sooner than expected. I am Sellum now, but you may have heard of my last incarnation, Xholk."

"A prophet of the twenty-first century. I read your scripture; it's not bad. So, you were a human and you became a god," said Zenero.

"Humans have such incredible power! Look at what we've achieved."

"My human vessel would never have been able to reach this place. I come here as an Exp," said Zenero proudly.

"You have a capsule, but you're not an Exp. Nothing inside your mind has changed, so deep down you are still human."

"What does it matter? I'm here now and I challenge you to your throne."

The cosmos around us split and a foggy figure dropped down.

Sellum's body was flowing like clouds. The being's form expanded, shaping itself into a dragon. The Omni God's golden eyes came into view when the foggy white energy concealing them dispersed. "Don't think your success in taking over the afterlife is from your own willpower. Your apotheosis has been preordained," said the God of Gods in a wise, intense, and bored deep voice.

"Then you know you won't be able to kill me," said Zenero with a confident smile.

"Such arrogance. But you misunderstand entirely. You are my salvation. I've waited for you to take my spot. Now that you're here, I can step down. I can…become mortal again."

"This is almost too easy," said Zenero softly.

He's right. We only just arrived recently. How is everything just falling into our hands? Is it this god, did it will us to win? Is this some sort of trap?

"I surrender my divinity, my perfection, to you. I look forward to witnessing how you and your evolved perfects will change the afterlife," said Sellum with a grin.

A black, white, and clear cloud of energy left the dragon and entered Zenero.

My creator closed his eyes as the power of Sellum took over.

It was over. He had won. Zenero had become the supreme god. Whatever he wished was now within his grasp.

Zenero created a portal to Absence by channeling his energy.

"Why do you think Xholk allowed me to enter?" I asked.

"If he knows me, he knows you're my equal. You had every right to come here. Now, let's return to our family," he said, offering me his hand.

I seized his hand,

The man who created me, who raised me and my family, was alive.

Chapter 162: Balance of Power

Time zooms by; days pass in an instant. When time resumes, I am standing alongside my family in Absence.

October's eyes opened. "I felt a sense of nothingness. I mean, I didn't feel…it was a void…a profound emptiness. I could feel the weight of nothing for an instant. I think I have become a god," said my brother, his eyes lax with contentment.

It's hard to measure time here, but it's been a few days. Now every major god has been replaced. Are the demigods next?

"Welcome back, my son," said Zenero, smiling at his new god. "Everyone, pay respects to the new god of Absence."

"Thank you, Father. What are we going to do now?"

"We have achieved victory over the gods! The old council has been destroyed, and its ashes have formed the new council, Renaissance. The rebirth of the heavens has begun! I'd like to discuss the next step as soon as possible. Casey, Chipko, Durga, come with me. We shall return in a few moments," said Zenero, leaving with them in a portal.

"Things are really going to get interesting now," said Sel to himself.

I turned to him. "What do you mean by that?"

"Oh, did I say that out loud? Pay it no mind," said Sel, his eye arching into a smirk.

He's toying with me. What more could he have planned? Ugh, I'm going to regret this.

"Tell me what you know," I said, towering over my little brother.

Sel floated up to meet me eye to eye. "Zenero has always been thorough. He plans to get rid of any threats to his kingdom, with the purest of intentions, of course."

"You're still speaking in riddles. Please, brother. It's important I understand what you're saying."

"It's not my job to paraphrase things for simpletons. If you want to learn more, you need merely wait," said Sel with a wide grin. My cunning brother then dropped into a black portal.

"Does anyone know what he's talking about?"

"Eh, I say ignore him. He's just trying to stir up trouble," said June.

"Don't you trust Zenero?" asked Atlas, looming over me.

"When Zenero made me, he told me my mission was to keep you all safe. All I'm trying to do is look out for all of you," I said, grasping my brother's hand.

Atlas pulled away. "Zenero is watching over us. All we must do now is await his command."

Zenero reappeared, along with my three sisters.

"How did it go?" I asked.

"Fine," said Casey, smiling at me.

Durga looked mortified.

"She's just a bit overwhelmed," said Chipko, patting Durga's head. "Come on, let's go figure things out," she said, walking off with her sister.

Zenero approached me and created a portal. "August, you come along too."

We arrived at the Microcosm.

"This isn't going to go well," said Sel, creating a seat out of his dark energy.

"Zenero, you'd like our thoughts on what to do next?" I asked.

"How long before we can return to Earth? We are going back, right?" asked August.

"Once we've secured our kingdom here, we shall return," said Zenero.

"And what do we do once we return?" I asked.

"One thing at a time please," said Zenero.

"Yes, we need you to kill your siblings first. Well, at least the rebellious ones," said Sel.

Even as a joke that was in poor taste.

Zenero ignored Sel and turned to face me. "We are so close to our dream of a world of equality. The politics of men are inconsequential to a god. A divine intervention could overturn global politics overnight."

"So, you want us to take down some high-risk targets on Earth, right? Just say the word," said August, tipping his straw hat.

"That is one possible route. Let me ask you all, what is the most important quality in any relationship?" asked Zenero.

"Trust," I said.

"Loyalty," said Zenero, pacing around. "Loyalty transcends trust. Both parties must be loyal to one another. Sadly, some of my creations have been disloyal as of late. Regrettably, I feel my own loyalty to them has been shaken by their actions."

"Stop beating around the bush. Tell them what you want," said Sel.

"I don't trust Sel. But that matters not, for he is loyal to me; therefore, I can return the same sense of loyalty to his wellbeing and ambitions. I was unsure at first of what to do about our group's diminishing loyalty, but he offered me a solution. A way to test the loyalty of those I trust and a way to deal with those who are likely to turn against me. August, you've proven your loyalty."

"Then why test me?"

"We live in trying times." Zenero stopped pacing and faced me. "Pathos, you were once my most trusted creation. It wounds me to say this, but you've corrupted our family. My children, who once followed my word as god, questioned me because of your actions. But you're too valuable to simply throw away. We need you for what's to come."

This isn't the Zenero I know. Becoming a god has changed him. There's no warmth in his voice.

"I won't attack any of my family. How can you even consider this?" I grabbed his shoulders and shook him. "You're a pacifist! Think about what you're saying!"

"Pacifism has failed us again and again. The carbon tax bill was done with peaceful intentions, yet it led to widespread war. I've already got blood on my hands. I will make any sacrifices I need to. Think of what's at stake. What are a few lives compared to everlasting peace and equality? You know who I am. My vision has not shifted even a millimeter. What's changed is my conviction to do what must be done."

"If you walk down that path, I'll stop you."

"That's the thing. You won't be able to stop me." Zenero vanished along with August.

"Hehehehahaha! You look so helpless," said Sel.

"What are you laughing about? Our family is in danger!" I yelled, gripping onto my mischievous brother.

"That's right! And you're stuck here. Oh, wait. There is one way you could escape. You'd need the help of a god, and there's one right here."

I released him and fell to my knees. "What do you want?"

"Oh, I could really get used to this. Let's start with some pleading and see where we go from there."

"Please! Brother, you're the only one who can save them."

Sel grabbed my face with his tendrils. "So pitiful. I suppose I could help you out if you swore eternal loyalty to me." His eye widened.

"This isn't a game! Every second wasted could be the difference between life and death."

"You're right. It's not fair for them to suffer from your apprehension. Tell you what; I only want a single favor. But you won't know what it is until I decide it's time to collect."

"Does that favor involve violence? If so, I refuse."

"I assure you it's as peaceful as a prayer. Oh no…I think I just felt a soul leaving this world." Sel turned away once I noticed his grin.

Is this really what he's like? My brother has always been tricky but never cruel…not to us.

"I agree to the deal."

My arms were seized and crossed as they were excitedly pulled up and down.

I felt my body sinking into a portal.

I fell onto the ashy floor of Sel. After rising to my feet, I noticed a gathering of demons.

August leaped out from the horde with our littlest sister in his arms. He landed in front of me.

"I thought you were with Zenero," I said with a suspicious glance.

"The moment he targeted us, he became an enemy. Have you seen May?"

"I haven't but she's more than capable of defending herself."

A clear portal appeared and Absence stepped out.

"Are you with Zenero?" I asked, raising my fists.

"The real question is, why are you against him? Have you forgotten who gave you life?" asked Absence, his hands coated in a clear energy.

"He seeks now to take that life away!" yelled August.

I grabbed his trembling fist. "Get our sister out of here. There's a portal somewhere in each realm that leads to Earth. Find it. I'll keep him busy."

"I'll be back as soon as she's safe."

"There's no guarantee they won't hunt her down on Earth. I'm counting on you to watch over her."

"You better punch Zenero for me! A really tough punch! That asshole needs a wakeup call."

"Sure thing!"

At this point I'm going to have to try hard to not kill him the next time we meet.

"You do realize I can end you merely by touching you, right?" asked Absence, stepping up to fight me.

"Your loyalty was what I admired most about you, brother," I said.

"You called my loyalty a massacre in the past. You never approved of my way of resolving conflict."

"Come to your senses, my brother!"

"Enough talk. Neither of us can be swayed by words. Our minds are made up," said Absence, before his arms vanished from sight.

I kicked off the ground to dodge the sudden swipe.

Shit! I can't see his movements. I've got to keep my distance.

I sidestepped to dodge another jab and slammed my fist into his back.

Absence toppled over and condensed his body into the size of a marble. The marble vanished.

I have to run!

Unsure where he was going to strike next, I sped off. I broke through a blockade of demons and kept running.

Absence reverted and tossed a handful of marbles on the ground around me. "**Revert.**" The balls were all weapons and sliced against my armor. "**Compact, Revert, Compact, Revert.**"

The weapons vanished and reappeared but were unable to pierce my armor.

A figure suddenly leaped onto October's back.

"**Surface Spike.**" August's body shifted into spikes that pierced my attacker.

"Where is June?" I asked, slowly rising to my feet.

"Didn't like being a damsel in distress. She's searching for the portal as we speak," said August before he was torn off Absence.

Another portal appeared and Chipko emerged.

"Thank goodness you're here. We need your help to take down October," I said, approaching her.

Chipko's hands pressed against my chest.

"Shockwave Pulse."

No. Not her too.

I gripped my chest as the shockwave barraged my insides.

August sprang out of the way of Absence's fist.

"October, Zenero wants you to destroy the portal. You know where it is, right?"

"You think I'm just going to let him do that?" asked August, trapping Absence in a sticky trap.

"I'll make sure you don't interfere," said Chipko.

"Come on! You're smarter than me! Why are you letting yourself be used by Zenero!?" yelled August.

Chipko smiled. "It's a contest. If I kill more of you than Casey, Zenero will take me as his queen."

Absence nodded before running off.

"Are you kidding me!?" August pulled out a small metal rod from his back strap. "Don't think I won't fight back."

"You love me, don't you?"

"Of course I do, you're my sparring partner," said August.

"If you want my happiness, lay down your life for me." Chipko rushed in.

Should I try to help? No. I need to trust him. Wait, the portal is still open.

A figure clad in black armor emerged and immediately rushed me. Despite being attacked, my focused stayed on my siblings' bout.

"*SURFACE EXTEND.*" August slammed his weapon into Chipko. The consistency of the staff changed on impact, bouncing her away with each strike.

I deflected the sword strikes with my arms, but the enemy left no openings.

"I've got more range than you. Now come on, let's join up, find Zenero, and knock some sense into him."

"I'm not just fighting for myself. Zenero is wiser than all of us. If there was any other way, he would have found it. We've run out of options. You have to die!" Chipko slammed her hands against the ground, causing the fleshy ground beneath August to erupt. She rushed in only to be bounced away by the staff.

"You know me better than that. I'm not going to get distracted so easily," said August.

"I'm aware."

As Chipko rushed in, a jet of flame shot up.

The fire scorched August's face, giving her the opening she desired.

I have to get up. I have to stop this.

Chipko leaped up and kicked the rod out of August's grip. "Now die!"

"Damn it!" August dodged her swipes and grabbed her arms. "You think having our blood on your hands will make you happy? You're not a fool! Why are you letting Zenero use you?"

"I've made up my mind!" Chipko slammed her leg into his stomach. She twisted her arms out from his grip before slamming them into his chest.

He fell to his knees, coughing up blood.

"You won't kill me," he said, beaming at her with a bloody smile.

"I'd do anything to save this world." Chipko lifted him up into an embrace. "Thanks for all the good times."

I finally knocked the sword out of my opponent's grip.

No!

"Get away from her!" As I yelled, my opponent released its aura.

August was in tears.

"*Death's Embrace.*" Chipko's entire body released a shockwave.

Bones broke and organs ruptured.

My brother fell out from her embrace, choking on his own blood.

He's going to die!

I dodged the sword's swipe, but somehow it pierced me.

"Who are you!? And why are you working with Zenero?"

"I've been tasked with taking you down," said the warrior in a detached and firm voice.

I gripped the sword, keeping it from slicing me.

Chipko whipped the blood off her hands and turned to me.

A white portal appeared between us. A ray of light shot out from the other side, blinding us.

When my vision cleared up, I smiled.

"You're safe," I said, gazing at my sister.

Lum did not smile back. "Am I too late?"

"It's over. Casey doesn't have it in her to kill anyone. I've won. Zenero is mine," said Chipko.

"He isn't dead yet," said Lum, pooling energy into her hands.

The beam shot past Chipko and into August.

A beam came my way and mended my wounds. Another beam blasted the black helmet off the warrior who assaulted me.

"Etaf, stand down."

"I don't take orders from you," said Etaf, pointing her sword at Lum. She left into a white portal.

Isn't Etaf a Lum goddess? Who does she work for if not Lum?

June suddenly sped up to August. "I've located the portal. Who's coming along?"

"I'll go!" Sel popped out from the ground and fired at June.

Chipko ran into the blast. "If you love me, get her to safety!"

"Oh, being defiant, are we?" asked Sel, lifting Chipko as his energy pooled into her.

Lum split the beam with a blast of her energy and Chipko fell.

"I've failed," she said, stricken with tears.

"Indeed you have," said Zenero, approaching from behind me.

I sped up to him with my fist ready.

If I kill him, will it end?

Casey stepped out from behind him and raised her hands.

A clear prison suddenly formed around me, stopping my fists just inches from his face.

"If you want us dead, kill us yourself!" I yelled.

"If I must," said Zenero, raising his arms as portals spawned endlessly above him.

Lum condensed and transmuted her energy into a focused stream of water.

The water parted when it crashed into a clear case, making it miss Zenero entirely.

"Where is May?" asked August.

"She's dead! And what a painful death it was. Oh, I can still hear her screams," said Sel with a maniacal grin.

They'll pay. I'll make them regret this!

June sped off with August.

"Let them go. We have more important enemies to deal with," said Zenero.

"Is it true!? Did he really kill May?" I asked, slamming my fists against the casing.

"Sel is just trying to aggravate you. May is safe on Earth with Atlas and Durga. I sent them off to start the foundation for the Renaissance," said Zenero.

"Why must you spoil my fun?" asked Sel, with an annoyed glare.

"It was Casey's idea and such a splendid idea it was." Zenero pulled Casey into a kiss.

"Why don't we go back home? Our children are waiting for us," said Casey.

"Not yet." Zenero vanished and reappeared behind Chipko. "Why did you allow them to leave?"

"I underestimated August's capabilities," said Chipko, her head lowered.

"She's lying. She stepped in the way of my attack. You can tell by her wounds," said Sel.

"Bob attacked me! He's lying to you!"

"Whether he is or isn't, one thing is clear. You've failed me." Zenero turned away from her.

"Wait. I'll kill August. I was only trying to save June. She's just a child."

"You admit to lying to me."

"Please, just give me another chance."

"Alright. Kill Pathos for me," said Zenero.

With a snap of his fingers, Chipko was teleported inside the case with me.

"Sel, escort Tranquil to safety and then return to me," said Zenero.

"And miss out on all the fun?" asked Sel with googly eyes.

"Do it," said Zenero.

"Alright," said Sel, leaving with Lum into a black portal.

Chipko approached me.

"Do your worst. I won't fight you, sister," I said, opening my arms.

"Damn it. Damn it. Damn it!" Chipko pounded against the walls.

"Please, my dear. This is the only way for us to seize the future we've longed for," said Zenero, transmitting his voice through a tiny portal near her ear.

"Why him? Why do I have to kill him?" asked Chipko in tears.

"His beliefs are too strong. He split our family apart. He abandoned me when I needed him most. Ask yourself this: who do you love more, me or him?" asked Zenero.

"If he dies. If I…kill him. You'll make me your queen? You'll love me?" asked Chipko in tears.

"What is she talking about?" asked Casey. "I'm your wife, not her."

"Don't worry yourself. It was an empty promise. I must say I am disappointed in Chipko. I thought she would be more useful. How about this, dear? Kill Pathos or you die. How's that for a proposition?"

"He sent Atlas away. We can take him down together," I said, grabbing her hand.

"No. I'll prove I can do it! I'll show him my love!" Chipko turned and slammed her fists into me.

I gripped her arm before being sent back. Once we hit the ground, she was pinned down.

"I've seen enough," said Zenero.

With a snap of his fingers, Chipko was outside the cube.

"Without loyalty, you're useless. Your worth has been used up; it's time to dispose of you," said Zenero, pooling dark energy into his hands.

"Zenero, I can't hurt you. I love you," she said, beaming at him through her tears.

"If your love is as worthless as you are, I have no need for it."

Portals encircled Chipko.

"Wait. She doesn't need to die. Only Pathos does," said Casey.

"Chipko's presence puts everything in danger. Family and loved ones are so trivial compared to the survival of Earth. If I must sacrifice a few lives to save trillions, am I not just?" asked Zenero, pulling her into his arms.

"I am sorry for doubting your judgment. I will eliminate the Exps for you, Lord Zenero," said Casey bowing.

"Do not apologize for doubt. Doubt is what makes us question our actions. Doubt is the first step in a revolution." Zenero created a portal and dipped Casey into it. "I shall join you once it's done."

"You've changed so much. I'm afraid there will be nothing left of the man I love when I see you again," said Casey.

"I assure you this experience will only refine my character."

A crack. Finally.

The case shattered.

I was free.

Casey turned to me as more of her vanished into the portal. "We have children back home, waiting for their father. Promise me you won't kill Zenero."

"I can't do that," I said before she vanished completely.

Zenero smiled as he approached. "Before you strike—"

My fist finally connected with that self-righteous smile.

311

Damn that felt good.

The punch sent him tumbling across the ground.

"You were saying?"

"Before you strike me…again, consider this. You're the only one who must die. Your life is all that stands in the way of everlasting peace and equality. Are you so selfish that you'll throw it all away?" asked Zenero.

This all happened so fast I haven't had time to think. If I'm really the only one who needs to die, why am I fighting? I'm not protecting anyone but myself.

"You promise?"

"I swear upon my mother's soul," said Zenero with a bow.

"He's lying. I know what the plan is. Tranquil has to die. Casey is her replacement," said Chipko.

"You've interfered for the last time!" Zenero turned to her with a murderous gaze.

Portals appeared around my sister.

Zenero formed a metal spoke in his hands and thrust it into the portal in front of him.

I was too late.

The spoke emerged from the portals around Chipko. They were repelled by her shockwave and came together as a single spoke that zoomed out from the central portal.

Zenero gasped as the spoke impaled through his stomach. He fell down to the floor, helpless.

Chipko rushed up to him, pulled back her fist, and cried. "You used me, yet I still can't kill you. How can I still love you after all of this? Why must my fist be weaker than my heart?" she asked, her fist shaking violently.

Zenero pulled a rock out from his pocket and tossed it.

The stone hit Chipko across the face, mixing blood with tears.

My sister picked up the rock and held it to her chest. "We are both so easily used. Our spirits are too fragile."

"I'll end it. Zenero, you expected your subjects to turn against the king, and therefore they did. You provoked us; we merely acted," I said as I approached.

Zenero pulled the spoke out of his stomach, healing the wound in the process. "I am God!" Beams of light blinded me, followed by dark energy that barraged my body.

No. I can't die now.

Zenero put thrust his Absence-coated hands into the portal.

I avoided his grip and plunged my hand in. I pulled him out of the portal and slammed him into the ground.

Before I could follow up, he sank into another portal and popped out above me.

"You're a tool made for my vision! You never should have defied me." A spray of black bullets hit the floor around me.

Several large portals appeared at my sides, firing the combined bullets as a beam of concentrated Sel energy.

He's using my artifact against me. I have to get in close to finish this.

I leaped over the blasts, but more portals formed around me.

"Zenero, come to your senses. You think if I die, we'll somehow have peace. You told me to correct you if you ever fell down the wrong path. Well, you're deep in the ditch now! But don't worry. No matter what happens, I'll keep fighting for your vision. You chose me as your successor; well, it looks like I'll be taking the throne by force."

I sped through the dangerous labyrinth with diminishing luck.

How long before the dark energy enraptures me.

"I...I truly am lost...aren't I?"

Tears flowed down his cheeks.

I finally reached him.

"Go on. End me. Show you're willing to make the necessary sacrifices for a peaceful world." Zenero teleported in front of me and stretched out his arms, welcoming his death with a smile.

It's over. He's finally back.

A dark portal appeared in front of me and Sel emerged.

Oh no. Why now?

"Don't fall for his lies. Sellum can only be dethroned by the combined power of all the gods." Sel gravitated the energy from the portals and absorbed them.

"What is going on?" asked Zenero before he was suddenly pulled to the ground by vines.

"Do it now!" yelled Sel.

Lum and Absence sent out their energy into Zenero. Their beams were soon followed by Sel's reinforced dark beam.

Something ethereal encircling Zenero shattered.

"Now he is mortal!" Sel's spectral hands permeated Zenero and tore out his artifact. He tossed the traveler's stone to Tranquil who absorbed it.

Tranquil fired Lum blasts while teleporting around, encasing Zenero in vines of light.

"You betrayed me?" asked Zenero, looking hopelessly at Sel.

"You were just a stepping stone. I'm sure you understand."

"Wait. Casey made me promise not to kill him."

"That's fine. I'll do the honors," said Sel.

Lum turned to Absence.

"Can you imprison him?" she asked.

"Absolutely. If I compact him, he'll be unable to escape," said Absence.

"Ugh, fine. It's foolish to bury your problems, but I suppose it could lead to some interesting twists down the way." Sel turned to me. "Wait! I can't become Sellum as long as he's still alive."

Why is he so obsessed with becoming Sellum?

"You're already Sel. Pathos should become Sellum. You don't need to kill our father out of spite, but you do need to end him," said Absence.

"Wait. I've lost. I concede. Take my powers. Leave me with my life," said Zenero.

"No deal! Pathos, I told you I'd collect a favor down the line, and now it's time to pay up. Tell him to make me Sellum!" exclaimed Sel.

The cloud of energy left Zenero's body and entered me.

Wisdom from every god that preceded him pooled into my consciousness.

Will becoming God put an end to all the problems? Will I change like he did?

"Damn it! Hand it over! It's mine!" yelled Sel, shaking me around.

"Let go. I need to be alone."

"Rrrgh!" Sel vanished in a portal.

I turned to Absence. "Compact Zenero and keep him imprisoned. Also, what made you change your mind?"

Absence lowered his head. "I saw your fight with him. I heard what he said." He beamed up and smiled at me with the same belief he always gave Zenero. "You're his successor now. You will lead us to our goal. I'll gladly follow your orders as they are his will."

I placed my hands on his shoulders. "I need my family to work with me, not for me. We're a team. Now, what do you think we should do next?"

"Once Zenero is secure, maybe some of us should try and find the others," said Absence.

"That's a fantastic idea. Can I trust you to watch him?"

"Absolutely, my lord," said Absence with a nod.

I need to prepare for every possible outcome. Zenero entrusted me with leading the others, and they're counting on me to keep them safe.

Chapter 163: Familial Responsibilities

The world of Sel faded. Sellum's Warriors were back in the cabin.

"I was such a fool back then," said Chipko, turning away from everyone.

"I don't get it. Zenero seemed like a nice guy at first," said Opti.

"He was desperate, and he became too powerful far too quickly," said Sellum.

"You really like my mom, don't you?" asked Kaity with a smirk.

"Your mother was so different back then," said Sellum.

"Yeah," said Kaity softly to herself.

"Why did we stop?" asked Famine. "You aren't getting any help until you show them everything."

"I'm aware. There's something I noticed that I think we should discuss. It was so long ago, I seem to have forgotten about it altogether," said Sellum.

"You mean about Etaf?" asked Kaity.

"Precisely," said Sellum.

"If she wasn't working for Lum or Zenero, that pretty much leaves only one person: Bob," said Deceivant.

"Wait. Why would she work for Bob?" asked Opti.

Sellum looked at Deceivant. "I came to the same conclusion. Etaf's actions have become more and more suspicious, but could she have been his ally all this time? My brother had only been Sel for a few days, what could he have offered her to win over her loyalties."

"The most logical assumption is that she was already loyal to Sel. When Bob took the title, her allegiance remained," said Deceivant.

"That's not good. Lum is in danger!" exclaimed Opti. "We have to tell Muffins!"

"Muffins is with Hope at the moment. I…don't want to talk to her," said Deceivant.

"For all we know, she has a search party to hunt us down. It would be unwise to contact her," said Chipko.

"We need to tell Lum then," said Opti.

"No. Etaf has attacked us, but she's also saved us many times. I know I said I wanted her dead for having Napkin spy on us, but those could be Lum's orders. I will confront her first before talking to any of the goddesses," said Kaity.

Abyss clapped his hands to get everyone's attention. "Alright, mystery solved. Now, let's continue the story."

Sellum turned to Kaity. "The next part is about you. Do I have permission to show everyone?"

"Yeah. I've got nothing to hide," said Kaity.

"Don't skip over anything important. I'll be paying close attention," said Abyss.

"Stop picking on Daddy!" yelled Stabby.

"It's alright." Sellum patted her head. "Now, let's continue."

The area faded away before shifting into the Microcosm.

"Brother, I trust Zenero is placed under guard," said Sellum.

"Absolutely," said Absence.

Lum approached me. "I'm placing Evol in charge for the time being. I need to go back to Earth. I've been gone for over a week. I don't want my daughter to worry about me."

"I'll accompany you. We can search for Durga, May, and March there. Zenero gave them a task, and they could use our help to accomplish it. I've already sent the other non-gods to Earth. Bob is still nowhere to be seen, but the Sinful Sorority is managing the realm without him."

"Without our powers, he can do nothing to you. All three gods must attack at once to destroy the Ultimatum that protects you," said Lum.

"As far as we know, but as long as he lives, he will seek out a way to end me. In case of my demise, I should select an heir."

"But if you select one of us, Sel will simply kill them," said Absence.

"True. We need someone he will never find out about. That's why I've selected Kaity as my heir," said Sellum.

"You can't; she's just a little girl. Sel will kill her if he finds out," said Tranquil afraid.

"She's your little girl, dear sister. She's the only one pure enough to rule Sellum. I would have chosen you but you're Lum. Besides, like it or not, a human has more political influence than an Exp ever could," said Sellum.

"Doesn't she get any say in it?" asked Tranquil.

"I have decided. We leave at once," I said, forming a portal.

When we stepped through, we arrived just outside her home. It was a two-story log cabin nestled in a forest of pine trees.

"It will be nice to see Kaity again," I said.

"I want to be alone. Is that alright?" she asked.

"I'm sorry, but we don't know when Bob will strike next. I'll mask my presence," I said, turning invisible.

"Very well. Don't make any noise, okay? I don't want Kaity to get startled." Lum smiled and knocked on the door.

A 5'4" man in a white lab coat, wearing rectangular glasses answered the door. His tired black eyes widened when he saw Lum.

"You're finally back," he said in shock, smiling as he hugged her.

Lum kissed him on the cheek. "Yes. You look so tired, Konton. Have they been working you hard?"

"Yeah, it hasn't been easy without you here."

"How about we go out tonight as a family? I hope Kaity hasn't been too much trouble while I've been away."

The man gripped her tightly and sobbed. "I thought they had killed you. We both did. What happened?"

"You didn't hear? Zenero was assassinated."

"Well, yes, but that was nearly a decade ago."

What, how could...? Of course, time in Sellum flows differently.

I turned to my sister to see the same revelation had dawned upon her. When we became gods, we linked to a collective archive of information about the afterlife. Sadly, that knowledge remained dormant in our subconscious until it was needed.

"How could I have been gone so long?"

"That's what I've been wondering! You went away on a religious journey, but that was only supposed to be for a month!" exclaimed Konton.

Please. Don't say a word.

"After he was revitalized, my father found a way to go to the afterworld," said Lum.

"You have quite the religious troupe," said Konton with a smile.

"That wasn't part of the trip. It was unexpected."

"I'm sorry, dear, but I'm almost out of a job. The government is saying my designs are ridiculous. It hasn't been easy looking after Kaity without you. It was difficult to pool hours into my work like I used to."

"I'm so sorry. I promise I'll make it up," she said, hugging him tightly.

Sister has such a gentle spirit.

"Do you want to see the designs?" he asked.

"I'd love to, but right now I need to see Kaity."

"Kaity is still at school. The bus will drop her off any minute now." Konton sifted through some files on the living room table. "Here we are. Take a look."

I peeked over Lum's shoulder as she looked over the design.

They were schematics for plasma claws. There were around twenty different sketches, most of which had been crossed out.

"You know I don't like looking at weapons," she said softly.

"Then why did you marry a blacksmith?"

"Maybe I just needed a nice man to give me a beautiful daughter," she said before kissing his lips.

He thinks she's joking, but from what she's told me, she really has no interest in men, or women for that matter. My sister has always wanted to be a mother. And now she's missed out on it...I can't help but feel responsible.

"Well, dear, my client sees a war on the horizon, and the money we'll make if he buys the product will be enough for us to live off of for the rest of our lives."

"Who is your client?"

"Government type, don't know his name or political affiliation. He always sends in a different person to discuss my projects. I think they're special ops, or something, because they really like my work. They bought the design for the energy suits, you remember those?"

"Yes, but I thought those were for labor, not violence," said Lum.

"These men and women are defending our country. I'm proud to give them extra defense. All they told me is, they will use my equipment to keep the peace between the two warring parties. Thankfully, there hasn't been a war, and who knows? Maybe I'm partly to thank for that."

"I'm so proud of you, Konton," said Lum with a sweet smile.

"So, about the claws...apparently their boss thinks they look silly. I told him, of course, how cats are the ultimate hunters, but he would hear nothing of it. I've almost got them sold on the energy rifle. It's solar-powered just like you and your family. How are they doing, by the way?"

"We've been through a lot, but we all made it out okay."

Konton placed his hands on hers. "You weren't kidnapped, were you? Did they torture you? I'm aware there are many critics of my work. Did any of them hurt you? Is that why you were missing?"

"I told you. I traveled to the afterlife. Zenero used the Teleport Artifact to bring the whole family."

"I don't understand those artifacts at all. They brought you to another world?"

"Yes, and it's a beautiful world. Time there must flow differently. That's why I've been gone so long. Would you like to go?"

"Dear, of course I believe you, but the unknown frightens me."

"Then I won't pressure you." Lum searched through the sketches. "Ooh, I really like this. The ears make the wearer more aware, and the tail serves as an extra appendage. You're so clever."

"Thanks. But practicality isn't good enough if the buyer doesn't like the visual design. My best bet is to sell a few sets at a lower price as part of a night mission package."

"Well, I think they look adorable!"

"They do. That's the problem. Well, there's one more problem. In order to function properly, they need to be melded with the user. See that's why I thought selling to special agents made sense."

"It's a wonderful idea. Now that I'm back, I'll go looking for a job. I want to support you. How about a vegetable garden? With my new abilities, I should be able to set up a permaculture in no time!"

"I'm sorry, dear. I know I'm supposed to support you. I've been going on business trips. Kaity loves them, but I haven't been able to sell much."

"We support each other," she kissed his lips and rubbed noses with him.

"*Tadaima!*" exclaimed the voice of a girl by the doorway.

Konton gently pulled Lum toward him. "Dear. There's a chance that Kaity won't recognize you. It's been so long. I just want you to be prepared, alright."

Lum nodded and opened the door.

Kaity was wearing a purple shirt with a smiling kitty cat. Her green eyes radiated with childlike energy. As soon as she noticed Tranquil, she jumped into her mother's embrace.

There she is: the next in line. Tranquil will keep her safe even if I do perish. I can rest easy.

Kaity's eyes were full of tears and her nose was dripping. "Dad said you were dead. I was so scared."

"It's alright. I'm here and I'm not going anywhere."

"I missed you so much," said Kaity with a sniff, hugging even tighter.

"My little girl has grown up to be so beautiful."

Someone is outside.

I left the house and peeked out from the right corner. I saw Absence and released the energy keeping me invisible.

Absence noticed and approached me, holding some stapled papers.

"Is there an emergency?" I asked.

"No emergency, but it is important. This is Zenero's will!"

"Not so loud. What does it say?"

"I don't know yet. I wouldn't read it without your permission," said Absence as he handed me the papers.

He isn't dead, but nevertheless I feel I should see what it says.

"I don't understand. His possessions are evenly distributed, but he's giving me the responsibility of raising his children."

What was he thinking when he made this? Does he truly have that much faith in me?

"I thought he'd give Casey that task," said Absence with a curious look.

"I'm as confused as you are."

"So, what are you going to do?"

"I'm going to take care of them. He may have become a terrible father, but that doesn't mean I should."

"Should I inform Casey you're on your way?"

"Wait a minute. How did you learn he had a will?"

"Bob came to me, but he wasn't the one who discovered it. Durga did. And then she left. She wanted time to think."

I can't think of anything Bob could stand to gain from giving me ownership of the kids, but I best be wary regardless.

"When will you be coming by?"

"Let's go right now."

Absence bowed to me. "His will lives on in you."

I grabbed his hand and brought up his chin. "It lives on in all of us. And in him. We should discuss our future plans with him when things have calmed down a bit."

"You're a wise leader."

"A wise leader is useless without those who help him achieve his goals. We must act immediately." I created a portal to Zenero's house and we stepped through.

"Oh, one more thing, my lord. As far as they know, their father died. If they discover he is in prison and you put him there, it will only cause tension," said Absence.

"I understand. Are you coming along?"

"I must maintain Absence. Best of luck," he said before leaving into a portal.

I opened the door to see a little girl coloring in a book with cartoony vampires. She had short blond curly twin-drills and a toothy smile. She looked up at me with wide topaz eyes. "Cool, another Exp! Are you one of Daddy's friends?"

"Yes, your father made me."

"You're so tall!" she exclaimed, jumping up as high as she could.

I'm the reason their father isn't coming home.

"What's wrong? You look sad," she said, tugging at me.

A young boy came running in from the other room. He had messy blond hair and a look of anger in his topaz eyes. He hoisted up a shotgun and aimed it at me. "Stay away from my sister!"

"I mean no harm. I'm a friend of your father's."

"My father was killed for defending your kind! You don't belong here!"

I will not stand for slander.

I crushed the shotgun in his hand using only my mind.

"Your father fought for us with all his strength. He died a hero."

"If it weren't for you freaks, he'd still be alive."

"Stop it!" yelled the little girl. She smacked her hand against my leg. "Stop it." She then went to her brother and bonked him on the head. "Stop it."

A mediator, just like her father.

"It's nobody's fault that Daddy is…is…." The little girl broke down into tears.

The boy embraced her. "Hey, it's okay. I'm here. I'll keep you safe. And Mom's here too. Do you want me to go get her?"

The girl nodded.

The boy gave me a glare and then ran off.

The girl was still crying in her hands.

Alright, time to be a father…no, a guardian.

I crouched down to her and started humming.

She peeked up from her hands, no longer crying. "You have such a pretty voice."

I continued humming and the girl became happier and happier.

Oh yeah, I've got this.

"I felt that everywhere!" she exclaimed with an excited spin.

The boy entered alongside his mom. "Do you know this guy?"

Casey turned away from me, shaking. "Chris, run along with your sister. I need to talk to him."

Chris nodded and grabbed his sister's hands. "What are you so happy about?"

The girl responded with a playful birdlike chirp.

Casey looked at me and exhaled. "I need to sit down." She formed some small cubes for us to sit on.

"Is everything alright?" I ask.

"I…need to know what happened to him…but I'm so scared," she said, shivering in her own embrace.

I approached her and crouched down. "Zenero is alive."

Energy burst throughout her body. Casey lit up like a firefly in the night sky.

"I couldn't promise you at the time because I didn't know what would happen. I take my word very seriously. If I'm to lead the Exps, I must—"

"Where is he?"

"That, I cannot say."

She grabbed my hands. "Please. I need to know."

"He vanished after our battle, after making me the next Sellum."

"Why would he give up?"

"Perhaps he realized he had lost control."

"What about you? Has the power affected you?"

"If you ever feel that I've been compromised, I beg you to tell me."

"I miss him already. It's hard for Chris to adjust. Can you imagine? One day his father's here and the next day he's gone. It's a good thing I returned to Earth after Zenero became Sellum. The poor boy had to raise his baby sister on his own."

"Sadly, Tranquil was away the entire time. Her five-year-old daughter is now twelve."

"I'm sorry, but I don't want to be a part of the revolution anymore. I just want to stay home and take care of the kids. If human society hates us, why don't we just live in the shadows?"

"I refuse to live like that, but I will gladly defend your choice to do so."

"They love it when we go out to a nature preserve. I do too. When there aren't any humans around, I can relax. The birds and the insects don't judge me for the way I look."

"Casey, I'm sorry."

"I'm the one who should apologize. I was scared. I couldn't let Zenero be alone. I wanted to support him. I…was afraid that if I didn't, he'd kill me. No. I was afraid he'd say he doesn't love me."

Casey embraced me and cried on my shoulder. "Can you ever forgive me?"

"It's in the past. Let it go and seize your future," I said, gripping her hands.

Even now his words inspire others.

"He really was such a wise man. Is! He's alive. Thank God he's alive!"

"You're welcome," I said with a grin.

We both chuckled.

Casey smiled at me. "So, what brings you here?"

I hand her over the document.

"No. No. No. No. This can't be right. Why would he want you to raise them? I'm their mother. I've already been raising them!"

"I think I understand now. Casey, there's another reason Zenero fled. Bob tried to kill him. He must have already been skeptical of Bob's allegiance."

"What does this have to do with you raising my kids?"

I looked at her with firmness. "Zenero must have been worried that Bob would go after his children to get to him. I can't call his fear irrational. The truth is, we don't know what Bob is capable of. It terrifies me."

"Poor Amy. She's barely seen her father. She was only a few weeks old when he was killed. Please find him. She needs her father."

I'm sorry for lying to you, sister.

"You've done a fine job yourself. My priority at the moment is to locate Bob. And until he is detained, I think I should watch over the kids."

"Zenero is no longer Sellum. Why would Bob go after the kids now? That threat is no longer an issue."

"At the moment. You're not safe, let alone the children. I'm the only one strong enough to oppose Bob. Sister, I promise I will keep them safe."

Casey stood up and paced around. "First Zenero and now the kids. No. I won't let you take them from me!"

"Calm down. It's summertime. They're off from school. I'll have them back to you before the school year begins."

"Why is it your decision?"

"It's not. It's in Zenero's will."

"He made me, but I've raised both children. I should have the last word."

She's right.

I bent down. "Will you entrust your children to me? I promise to keep them safe and return them as soon as the threat has been dealt with."

Casey turned away, her eyes watering up. "They're the only joy left in my life. Can't I come with you to watch over them?"

"Absolutely. When do we leave?"

"Ask the kids. Amy is a delicate girl. If you can convince her, then…I'll allow it."

"Thank you," I said softly.

Amy suddenly ran into the room, her brother following close behind.

He tackled her and tickled her on the rug.

Amy broke free and smiled. "Mommy, mommy. Is he going to stay with us?" she asked with shimmering eyes, pointing to me.

"What?" Casey looked bewildered.

"*The bird flies free. Free through the sky. Dives through the clouds. Whoosh, see it fly!*" sang Amy as she ran around me.

To think she derived the lyrics from my humming. How is that even possible?

"Sit down, my dear. Mommy has something important to say."

Chris ran off to get a comfy pillow. He came back, lifted up his sister and placed it beneath her. "What's the situation?"

"You're going to be staying with your uncle over the summer break. Is that okay?" she asked, her voice cracking.

"No freaking way am I staying with him!"

"Yay! New Daddy," said Amy, hopping off her pillow and into my arms.

"Okay, what gives!? Did you drug my little sister!" exclaimed Chris with daggers in his eyes.

"Son, watch your tongue. This is my brother. You may not know him, but he's very dear to me," said Casey.

"Well, he's a stranger to me!"

"Your father asked him to look after you."

"He has pretty eyes! Pretty!" cheered Amy with a hop.

Well, at least I have one supporter.

"We haven't had a father for seven years, and we don't need one now," said Chris, pulling Amy off of me.

"I only want to protect you," I said.

"I can protect Amy just fine! You're trying to take our mom away from us!" yelled Chris upset.

"Do not yell at my brother!" yelled Casey.

There was a sudden knock at the door.

"I'll get it," said Amy, rushing to the door.

The door opened and Deceivant stood there, looking as youthful as ever and beaming at Amy.

"May I help you?" asked Casey, smiling.

"Who the hell are you?" asked Chris.

"That is not important. What matters is who she is. It is an honor to finally meet you in person," said Deceivant as he lightly kissed Amy's hand.

"Get away from my sister before I rip your pedophilic eyes right from their sockets," said Chris enraged.

"Brother, you think everyone is a creep," said Amy, rolling her eyes.

"Get away from my daughter. Do you know him?" asked Casey, turning to Amy.

Amy shook her head.

"Pardon my rudeness. I've come to ask for your permission to date your daughter. Her beauty has captivated me," said Deceivant, passionately.

"What is your name so I can report you?" asked Casey, stepping in front of her daughter.

"I'm Deceivant."

"The one caught in that scandal?"

His shoulders drooped. "Yes, that and the brilliant scientist."

"You mean the one who was found with a knife in his chest?" asked Chris, whipping out a blade.

"Protective as ever, I see. That's good." Deceivant stood up. "Very well, I trust Amy with you. May she always be happy at your side," he said as he backed off.

"He's lucky I didn't gut him," said Chris.

"He seemed nice," said Amy, sucking on a lollipop.

Chris grabbed the candy from her and licked it.

"Hey! That's for me," said Amy, reaching for her treat.

"He probably poisoned it," said Chris, licking it fast.

"Is he always like this?" I asked.

"Let's all head inside," said Casey, closing and locking the door.

"For your information, wannabe dad, I make all of her food because I don't trust people," said Chris, now nibbling on the lollypop.

"He's a sugar addict," said Amy, crossing her arms.

"That may be, but I understand his concern. You can never truly know someone. However, don't ever let your suspicions endanger your sister," I said, looking into his eyes.

"I could never do that," said Chris softly.

After I notice they are shaking, I grab my sister's hands.

"Thanks. I'm just stressed out. That creep showing up didn't help."

"Talk it over with your kids. I'm going to see how Tranquil is doing."

"Send her my regards," said Casey with a smile.

"I certainly will."

Chapter 164: Designated to Die

I returned to Tranquil's log cabin. Immediately, I could sense something was wrong.

"Hello, dear brother. What brings you here?" asked Sel, swinging open the door and welcoming me in.

"What are you planning?"

"You're being very rude. I was just thinking about the promise you made to me. You do remember, right?"

"Have you seen Kaity around?" I ask with a calm voice.

He can't know she is my chosen successor, can he?

"Oh, she's helping her father with something. Why do you ask?"

"Brother, I know you feel slighted, but I need your help to maintain balance. Sellum is a combination of all the gods. Your assistance is mandatory. I will not rule on my own. I need all of you at my side."

"You stole my kill and now you expect me to help you out?"

"You know I've imprisoned not killed him. Brother, please. I don't want to be your enemy."

"The girl's soul changed rather recently. Tell me who's Sellum after Kaity dies?" asked Sel with a sly grin.

So that's how he figured it out? I was careless. I've got to find some way to distract him so I can check on Kaity.

"Well, brother, if Kaity dies, I choose Atlas's grandchild as the next Sellum," I said with joyful gestures.

"Atlas doesn't even have a wife yet, let alone a grandchild," said Sel with a grimace.

"Well then, you better help him find someone."

"I'm going to kill you!" exclaimed Sel, bursting with fury.

"After you've killed me, you still have to kill Kaity, Atlas's grandchild, and Nibbles."

Wow. That is a really cute name.

"Who?"

"Nibbles, he's a pink bunny and the next Sellum after Atlas's grandchild."

"You'd choose a fluffball over your own brother?"

"What's wrong? I thought you liked bunnies."

"You're a fool to test me"

"You're a bigger fool to upset me when I can make as many successors as I want."

"I hate you!" yelled Sel.

"And where has that hate gotten you? Face it, brother, you'll need to convince both Absence and Lum to attack me if you hope to gain my powers. Then you'd have to convince Tranquil to end her own daughter. Realize how impossible the task is. Realize the title isn't worth all this conflict."

Hopefully I can reach him through logic.

"We incarnated for a reason, brother. Nothing will stop me from seizing that which I have earned!"

"If you continue down this path, I will destroy you," I said with tears in my eyes.

"When your world is coming apart at the seams, remember it all could have been avoided had you let me kill Zenero. Remember it was your greed that led to all that pain and bloodshed."

"You only have words to threaten me with."

"I only wish you could be there when I achieve my ambition," said Sel, sinking into the floor.

Wait, the basement. He's going to the basement.

After the panic took over me, Casey stepped out from the living room.

"You lied to me," she said softly.

"I don't know what you're talking about, but Kaity is in danger."

"You mean the little girl you forced your burden upon? You've been lying to all of us. You said it yourself. Zenero was imprisoned by you. Where is he?"

"Bob is setting us against each other."

"Where is my husband?!"

"We can discuss this later," I said, erasing the ground beneath me with Absence energy.

Sel peeked up at me after I landed.

"I wonder what Tranquil would do to get her little girl back," he said, twirling Kaity's ribbon with his telekinesis.

The brother I knew is no more. Sel must have taken over him entirely.

I grabbed Sel and slammed him into the ground.

"Oh, losing your cool, are you?"

"Where is she?" I slammed him against the wall.

He phased through and popped out the ceiling.

"Tranquil is on an important errand in Lum. You should find her soon. Every moment Kaity gets further and further away," he said, his eye turning a sadistic red hue.

I arrive in Lum.

I need to find her! If I don't, I'll be consumed by loathing.

My body fires out beams that decimate the forest in front of me.

Angels swarm to my location. "Stand down, demon. Else prepare to be cut down!" exclaimed a flying shark.

"Where is Lum? I have to talk to her. It's urgent."

"More urgent than crushing Allah Jannah's uprising?"

"Her daughter is in danger."

The shark's eyes softened. "I shall fetch a goddess at once," she said before flying off.

I closed my eyes and tapped into my divine archive.

Of course.

I teleported to the Observatory, but Lum was not there.

Where is she?

I close my eyes again, visualizing the layout of Lum. After locating Lotus, I teleported just outside it. My sister was crouched over an injured angel, sending her energy into him.

"Have you come to help? The humans have turned against the angels who protected them. Do you think this is Bob's doing?" she asked.

"It doesn't matter right now. Kaity is missing. Bob took her away."

"Then why aren't you searching for her? Every minute we spend here is hours on Earth." Lum created a portal to Earth and pulled me in.

"Because I need you." I embraced her tightly. My tears fell onto her neck.

My rage is gone. She's truly the greatest blessing in my life.

"We need to find her," she said, looking into my eyes.

I can't bear to fail her. I have to keep Kaity safe. It's my fault she's in danger.

Sel collided into my sister with a face full of tears. "Thank goodness you're here! Your mortal partner went crazy. He's experimenting on Kaity." He held up the phone to her ears, but there was no need. I could hear her desperate screams from where I was standing. Sel turned to me with a glare. "Why did you just leave? Don't you care that Kaity is in danger."

"Where is she?" asked Sefiwah, fear entering her watery eyes.

"Sadly, I don't know. But he does. He's Sellum. He knows everything, right?"

I closed my eyes and asked my inner self for her location.

Why isn't it working? Am I just too inexperienced to tap into my omniscience?

"We have to hurry. I know. If I were Sellum, I'm sure I could track you down. Let's kill Pathos so we can save your daughter!" Sel seized her hand and raised it triumphantly.

Pathetic. My brother's tricks used to have much more tact. There's no way she would fall for his trick.

"You must think me a fool. As long as he is alive, my daughter can't die."

"But she can suffer. Listen, she's calling for her mommy." Sel pressed the phone against her ear. "I can't bear to think of how traumatic this must be for her," he said, wiping away his tears.

"You know Konton. Where would he take Kaity?" I asked.

"That doesn't matter. Bob's the one who hid her. He's the one torturing her." My sister fell to her knees and sobbed.

"I'm trying to help you find her. I wouldn't harm your daughter unless I absolutely had to," he said, patting her back.

Tranquil said something softly.

As I tried to process her words, something struck me from behind.

Before I knew it, a Sel, Lum, and Absence beam came crashing into me.

The ethereal shield that protected me shattered.

Sorry. She said sorry.

"Splendid work," said Sel, patting Tranquil on the head. "I'll kill him later. Let's go save your daughter!"

Tranquil walked with him into the black portal.

Tears flooded uncontrollably from my entire being.

I feel so helpless.

"Brother, why are you working for Bob?" I asked, unable to look him in the face.

Absence lifted me back to my feet. "I was following your will, my lord. You told me I must do everything I can to keep my realm safe. Bob threatened to annihilate my world if I did not attack you." He bowed down and lowered his head. "I know he's our brother, but he must be put to an end. Now that he's made an attempt on your life, you must strike back."

I will. I will kill Sel and free my brother!

"Will you stand with me?" I asked.

"Absolutely, my lord," said Absence on his knees.

"Thank you, brother." I lifted him back to his feet. "And stop calling me your lord."

I'm not alone. I can do this.

"As you wish, great swami."

"We have to track down Bob. Once Kaity is safe, I'll end him."

"Oh, Bob told me where to meet him after I attacked you. Dragon Labs, do you think that's where she is?"

I close my eyes, scanning Earth for the location.

"It's about ten minutes away," said Absence, showing me the location on his phone.

Outperformed by a device...am I really up to fighting Sel?

I created a portal and entered it alongside my brother.

Tranquil was just outside the lab; she was shaking. She approached me, nearly falling over.

I caught her in my arms.

"I thought you didn't know where she was," she said, her voice weighted with sadness.

"I told him," said Absence.

"Kaity's inside. I'm going to save her," I said.

Tranquil grabbed my arm. "It's too late."

I'm terrified to ask her, but I have to know.

"What do you mean?"

"She's already well into the surgery. If we stop now, it could lead to her death."

"That's not possible. As long as I'm alive, Kaity is immortal."

"Then leave. Go where Bob can never find you."

"I'm going to save Kaity."

"I'm sorry for attacking you."

"I forgive you," I said before teleporting inside.

I was nearly blinded by the bright lights in the room.

Kaity was on the operating table with nothing on but a blindfold and a white towel that was splotched red. Her father was using sharp devices to meld a metallic tail to her backside.

"It hurts! Stop!" screamed Kaity in tears.

How can Bob be cruel enough to use her father to mutilate her?

"If you move an inch or say even a single word, she will be punished," said Konton, pressing the knife to his own throat.

Of course. He knows she can't die. I have to plan my next move very carefully.

"I won't let you hurt my daughter!" Tranquil slammed into Konton, getting stabbed in the process. After she screamed in agony, she flashed a smile at me.

She is planning something. If I trust her, I must play along.

Konton turned to Sellum, hate engulfing his eyes. "Nothing will get in the way of my goals!"

"Mommy!" wailed Kaity, writhing in desperation.

"When you chose Kaity as Sellum, you designated her to die!" said Konton, glaring directly at me.

Tranquil leaned over Kaity and removed her blindfold.

Why fake her death? How will any of this trauma help her daughter?

Lum grabbed my hand, burying my doubt under her devotion.

Kaity opened her eyes, completely horrified.

"M…" she said, her bottom lip quivering.

"I thought I told you not to open your eyes," said Konton in a crazed voice. He tossed Kaity to the ground.

I stepped up to approach Konton. He raised the blade and I stepped back.

I should be able to disintegrate the blade, right? Damn it. I can't concentrate.

Kaity stood up. She was bare naked other than the blood. She had robotic cat ears cropping out of her bleeding scalp. A mechanical tail was connected to her spine. Her wrists were bleeding from the plasma claws embedded into her skin.

That power emanating from her. I chose right.

"Thank you, sweetie. Thanks to your sacrifice, we'll never have to worry about money again," said Konton, petting Kaity.

Kaity crouched down to her mother, holding her loving hands while sobbing.

I want to tell her that she's alive, but I have to trust Tranquil.

Her mother's eyes closed and her body went limp.

Kaity tried to take the claws off of her hands, but it was no use.

"Let's start the tests." Konton grabbed a shotgun and aimed it at Kaity.

I collected each bullet he fired and stood in the pathway.

I won't allow Bob to hurt Kaity anymore.

I grabbed Konton's hand and shattered his arm.

"This is all your fault," he said, spitting in my face.

If I stay, I could be killed by Sel. If I leave, he'll torture Kaity until I return. I need to get her out of here.

Konton grabbed a gun from his vest and shot Kaity's back.

With swift reflexes she sliced the bullet with her plasma claws.

She turned to her father with tears in her eyes. "Why," is all she could say to him.

Konton raised the gun again. As soon as he pulled the trigger, a card shot through the gun. The gun backfired, sending Konton smashing against the floor. He scurried over to Sefiwah's body and tore out the knife; he then turned to Kaity.

He's trying to scare Kaity off. I figured it out. He wants to control her.

A youth with hair colored like a checkerboard dropped from above between them. He smashed Konton's hand, causing him to drop the knife. The boy tossed the knife upward with his feet, shooting it up straight through Konton's jawbone. Kanasta ripped the knife out, slitting Konton's throat before snapping his neck. "First target neutralized."

What is going on? Is this Sel's doing?

Before I could process everything, the boy aimed his gun at Kaity.

A bullet hole pierced her forehead.

He took the purple suit on the table and dropped a smoke bomb.

I ran to Kaity to heal the wound, but it was already closed.

I reached my hand out to her, but she knocked it aside.

"Leave me alone!" she exclaimed, her catlike gaze piercing me,

I turned to Lum for an answer of what to do, but she was still playing dead on the floor. I looked at the miserable girl. "I'm sorry." I walked out of the room drenched in tragedy.

Chapter 165: Legacy

I nearly collapsed before I could exit the lab. I teleported to the Microcosm, sat on my throne, and cried.

I feel so helpless.

Tears flowed uncontrollably from my face. I felt something in my lap and dried my tears. It was Nibbles.

He nuzzled against me, trying to snuggle away my woes.

I placed my hand atop his head. "Thank you. I know what must be done."

If Bob is willing to harm Kaity, who's to say what he'll do to Zenero's children? I'll do what I have to.

I teleported to Casey's home and swung open the door.

"What are you doing here? Come to tell me where you're hiding their father?" asked Casey, stepping into my path.

"It's only a matter of time before Bob comes here. I'll take them where he can't find them," I said, walking right past her and up to the kids.

"Don't you dare!" she yelled, throwing herself at me.

I grabbed her before she could topple over. "Hate me if you want, but I'm doing what I know is best."

I have to keep them safe.

"You said I could come along," she said, looking at me with motherly anguish.

"You absolutely can. I'll come by and pick you up. But first there's something I have to do that you won't approve of."

I created a portal, picked up Amy, and walked in. Chris rushed in to save his sister as I closed the portal.

"Wow," said Amy, gazing up at the forest that popped out from nowhere.

"What did you just do, freak!?" asked Chris, punching my legs with his tiny fists.

I crouched down. "You weren't safe there. I'm going to need you two to stay hidden until everything calms down."

Amy's stomach growled. "I'm hungry," she said, holding her tummy.

Oh yeah, non-Exps need to eat. I nearly forgot.

I focused my Lum energy and created an assortment of fruit.

Not bad for my first try.

"Oooh, raspberries!" cheered Amy, reaching for the berries.

Chris grabbed her hand. "You can't trust him."

I watched the two children bicker.

Am I doing all I can to keep them safe? Who's to say Bob won't find a way to get here? If he frees Zenero, he can go anywhere he wants. I can't make them immortal, but I can certainly make them more resilient.

"Ow, you bit me," said Chris, pulling out his finger from his sister's mouth.

"My raspberries," she said with stuffed cheeks.

"Amy, I'm going to need you to follow me. I assure you that what I'm going to do is for your safety."

Chris stepped up to me and puffed out his chest. "I've been protecting my sister on my own. She doesn't need your help."

"There are people who might want to kill you."

"Don't pull this crap with me. We are not your kids, and you're not our father," said Chris.

"He is! Anyone who takes care of you is family. Yay! I have two daddies," said Amy as she embraced my leg.

I lifted her into my arms and created a portal.

Chris leaped onto my back. "Get your hands off of her!" He punched my helmet repeatedly.

I pulled him off and tossed him in the portal before entering.

We arrived in the same lab where Kaity was.

Chris saw the blood on the operating table and ran for the sharpest object he could find.

"My dear friend's daughter was tortured here by my maniac brother. I fear he will come for you and your sister next. Now calm down. I'm going to make you stronger."

"You mean you're going to make me a freak like you," he said, raising the jigsaw.

I stepped up to him and crouched down. "Don't you want to be able to defend your sister?" I asked, disintegrating the saw in his grip.

Fear overtook him. "Do what you want to me. Just promise me you'll leave my sister alone."

Strong conviction, just like his father.

"The two of you will help me continue what your father started," I said before putting him to sleep.

I teleported back to the forest and brought Amy back to the lab.

"Where are we?" she asked.

"Don't worry," I said, willing her asleep.

With a clear mind, I can do anything. With the powers of Sellum, I will fulfill Zenero's legacy.

I teleported to Zenero's home, the place where I was raised. I rushed up into the attic and search for the capsules.

I hope Bob hasn't already taken them.

I found them hidden inside the wall. The last two capsules.

His children will be the final Exps.

I teleported back to the lab and set Amy on the operating table next to her brother.

Let's spruce this place up a bit.

I released a pulse of Lum energy, making flowers and grass bloom inside the room.

"I am going to evolve you into something greater." I closed my eyes and channeled the expertise of the greatest scientists.

Sellum is more than power; it is perfect knowledge. The records of all that is known can be accessed through me.

When I opened my eyes again, the transformation was complete. Their outer appearance was unchanged but beneath their human skin was the body of an Exp.

"Chris, Amy. It's time to wake up. Welcome to the movement," I said softly.

Chris got up in a daze. "Something seems off."

"Your powers can be triggered. I took traits from your personality and framed your Exp traits around them. That way you have more compatibility and opportunity for growth," I said with a bit of pride.

Chris looked up at me with worry. "And my sister. She's the same, right?" he asked, shaking her to her senses.

"I feel funny," said Amy, holding herself.

"What did you do?" he asked, his eyes gleaming with intensity.

"You're both Exps now. You'll be able to defend yourselves and continue your father's legacy," I said.

"I don't care about his legacy. You made my sister a freak! I'll kill you!" exclaimed Chris, rushing at me.

"Hate me all you like. It won't change anything," I said, turning away from him.

"You're dead!" he yelled, trying to stab me with a scalpel.

"You shouldn't say those things lightly. You are an Exp now. You've transcended the need to consume. In time, you will thank me for your transformation."

"Shut up! Stop acting like you know everything. I'm going to kill you…just like this ant." Chris slammed his foot down on a small black ant.

No.

335

"Look at you weep. You're pathetic. Crying over a stupid little bug," said Chris, sticking out his bottom lip while stomping a line of ants.

My tears left me and my entire body shook with rage.

Murderer!

Chris squished another ant. "And like that one too."

"Stop fighting," said Amy, getting up in a daze.

"Sister, are you okay?"

If I don't do something, I'll lose control. I have to get rid of him.

"Chris, you will never again take a life for granted! Your new body will teach you this as you carry the guilt of your victims inside you." I teleported him away.

"What did you do?" asked Amy with shock in her eyes.

My anger left me and my emotions became balanced.

"Amy, as his father it is my duty to set him on the proper path and teach him right from wrong."

"Bring my brother back," she said, her eyes watering up.

"I will as soon as he's learned his lesson."

"I miss him."

Her memory of him will only hurt her right now.

My eyes widened.

That's it!

I picked her up and placed my hand atop her head.

As long as I focus, I can do anything.

Once the memories were erased, I brought her to the Microcosm and set her down.

I'll do everything I can to give her a proper life.

Amy is safe for now. I need to check up on Kaity.

I found Kaity by tracing the bond that connected us.

I pray that Bob doesn't have the ability to find her.

She was in a park wearing a hoodie and a long sleeve shirt. I approached her and sat down.

"Get away from me," she said in a whisper.

"Please, just come with me. I'm a friend of your mother's. I can keep you safe," I said, tears flowing out from my helmet.

"Get away from me!" Kaity swung her plasma claws at me.

"As you wish." I walked off and masked my presence.

I will protect her.

Night came and Kaity eventually fell asleep.

"Mommy!" exclaimed Kaity as she awoke from a nightmare. She gripped herself and sobbed. When she stopped crying, she stood up. I stealthily followed her down the street and into a bank.

The owner of the bank was an enemy to Zenero. I felt treacherous just being inside it.

Kaity looked up at the cashier. "Give me all the money."

"Have you lost your mom?" asked the cashier.

"Give me all the money," said Kaity, louder this time.

"I think you're too young to go to juvie," said the cashier with a playful smile.

Kaity's stepped away. She approached the ATM machine and cut it open with her plasma claws. Money shot out of the machine and Kaity caught it, stuffing it in her clothes. A man in the crowd handed Kaity a bag.

"Here you go. You can fit a lot more money in here, trust me," said Deceivant, patting her head.

"Thanks, mister," she said as she shoved a whole wad of cash in the bag. She ran out the door before anyone could react to the situation.

I followed her back to the park.

The boy with the checkerboard hair was seated on the grass, with a picnic all laid out. "It really is you." He stood up and approached the immortal girl.

I had nearly forgotten about this kid.

Kaity dropped her bag and rushed at him.

Kanasta grabbed her arms and kept her plasma claws from reaching him.

"Robbing a bank is a serious crime. Give me the money, and I'll give you some food. Deal?" asked Kanasta.

Kaity squirmed in his grip, trying to bite him.

Kanasta spun her around and pressed her to the ground, pinning her down.

He doesn't know who he is dealing with.

"You have the instinct to kill; that's good. Sadly, your reasoning is clouded. I'm Kanasta; what's your name?"

"You killed my father."

"He was my target. There was no other option."

"Die! Die!" Kaity squirmed in his grip but was unable to escape the hold.

"I'll only let you go once you've calmed down."

Kaity gave up on escaping and started sobbing.

"Alright, now why don't you sit down and eat so we can talk?"

As soon his grip loosened, Kaity turned around and rushed him. She sliced his leg as he jumped back. "I won't let you kill me too."

"You're no longer my target. I told my client you weren't worth the amount of money he offered me. He kept raising the amount, but I stood my ground."

"Then why are you here?" she asked before rushing at him on all fours.

"I search for people with special skills. You have exactly what I'm looking for. Be realistic. Do you think you can find work anywhere else?" he said, dodging her advances before kicking her aside.

Kaity slowly stood up and retracted her claws. She sat down and started feasting on the picnic.

After he set the sack of money on fire, Kanasta sat down next to her and waited for her to finish.

"My dad was hurting me and you…stopped him. You saved my life, but I can't forgive you," said Kaity softly.

"My business is hardly about saving lives. Kaity, that's the last free meal you'll ever have. Nothing in this world is free. Now, if you want, you can come with me and get a job. Or you can stay here and wait for the authorities to find you." He stretched out his hand.

Police sirens rang in the distance.

Kaity stood up but did not take his hand.

Kanasta smiled.

I followed invisibly until they arrived at an apartment complex.

"Another successful mission?" asked a youthful Tempo, playing a game of Poker with his buddy Ego on a wooden table in the center of the room.

"There were some unforeseen complications," said Kanasta.

Tempo looked up and stood up from his chair. "Rookie mistake, Boss. You've been followed. You're going to have to kill her now that she's seen our base," said Tempo, pointing at the girl.

Kaity hid behind Kanasta.

"No need. She's with me," said Kanasta.

"If you're stuck babysitting, do it somewhere else. Being here compromises us and her," said Tempo.

"I found her robbing a bank. Decided that I'd teach her the importance of a job," said Kanasta.

"You can't just recruit some cosplay girl who robbed a bank. Think about how crazy you're acting," said Tempo.

"Dude, take a closer look," said Ego. "She's not cosplaying. The metal is a part of her. Wicked."

Kanasta opened up the closet and pulled out a body bag. "Her name is Kaity and she has great potential." He put a knife in her hand. "I want you to stab the bag."

Kaity looked at the knife and then back at Kanasta. She dropped it and shook her head, too terrified to speak.

Kanasta, Tempo, and Ego started clapping.

Kaity looked at them confused and afraid.

"Well done," said Kanasta, patting her head. "We only kill if we are being paid, and I didn't offer you any money. We are businessmen, not murderers. There are lines we mustn't cross."

"First try; maybe she's not so bad. Took me three times to pass that test," said Tempo.

"Alright, now on to business. I'm offering you two thousand to end the life of whoever is in that bag. Do you accept?"

"I don't want to kill anyone," said Kaity, starting to cry.

"Oh yeah. She's definitely assassin material," said Tempo, holding his forehead.

"Maybe you should let her rest, boss. She looks traumatized," said Ego.

"Why don't you take her outside for a walk?" asked Kanasta.

"We're in the middle of something," said Tempo, picking up his cards.

"I'll finish when we get back," said Ego, walking outside with Kaity.

Should I follow them or stay and see what these people are like?

Kanasta sat down on the couch. "She's a smart girl."

"Maybe, but she isn't cut out for killing," said Tempo.

"You couldn't be more wrong."

"You expect her to be able to kill without hesitation?"

"Assassins must respect the life they are taking. Killing without hesitation can lead to the process becoming mechanical. This is a business, but it's a social business."

"Who was that in the bag?"

"Just a manikin."

"My first kill wasn't a manikin," said Tempo, his eyes softening.

"Different assassins need different tests. Kaity requires a more gradual approach."

"You chose her for her software, not the hardware," said Tempo, his voice rising in revelation.

"I chose her because I had no other choice." Kanasta reflexively looked at the gun in his hand.

"Well, if she happens to fail you, I got you covered. On the job I met a competitor."

"Was she skilled?"

"I never said anything about her sex."

"I know. I was merely guessing…and I guessed correct."

"Ha, you really do make everything a game," said Tempo.

"You were impressed with her professionalism and offered her a job. She got the target before you."

"Okay, now you're freaking me out."

"It's all in the way you speak. I pay attention."

"The shot she made was impossible. The bullet curved midair. I think she has been augmented, like us," said Tempo, turning his tea into an ice pop with his finger.

"When is she arriving?"

"I wouldn't have her come here. Why did you bring Kaity here, anyway?"

Kanasta twisted the gun around in his hand. "I couldn't kill her. There was nowhere else I could allow her to go."

"Don't talk like that. You're an assassin. Can't go soft because of some kid."

"I do not discriminate by age. You know that. Kaity is special, how special has yet to be determined."

"Boss, you know it's my job to tell you when I think you're straying off the path."

Kanasta set down the gun and set both hands on Tempo's shoulder. "Do you trust that I know what I'm doing?"

"Yeah…I do, Boss."

The two of them grabbed their guns when they heard a knock at the door.

"Too obvious for an assassin. You think it's some high and mighty government dog?" asked Tempo.

"I'll take care of it," said Kanasta.

As soon as he opened the door, the room was flooded with smoke.

I was suddenly swept off my feet and brought to the ground.

The intruder cuffed Tempo and held a dagger to his throat.

"I see you've found the place," said Kanasta, lowering his gun.

"Yeah, but not sure I'm interested. You two didn't realize someone was in camo," said a cold feminine voice.

"How the hell did she find this place?"

"Any good assassin does research." She released Tempo, dropped her knife and grabbed it with her toes. The knife was now pressed at my neck.

I should be invisible. How can smoke reveal where I am?

"It's nothing to be concerned about. It's just an Exp," said Kanasta.

"Boss, I don't think we're equipped to fight Exps," said Tempo, hoisting up his shotgun to my face.

"As of now, there is no need to be. This Exp has been by Kaity's side since I first found her. It's likely tasked to keep her safe, an extra precaution made by her father."

"Fair enough," said the woman.

The smoke was pulled into a container.

The woman's entire face was covered by a burka.

I recognize those eyes. It's Tranquil.

"I hope I made a good first impression," she said, burying her radiance with a cold persona.

"Told you she's good. Much better than the kid you picked up."

Kanasta turned to face Tempo. "You've already spoken with her. Anything I should know?"

"I think her skill speaks for itself."

"Skill is fine, but what of her character?"

"She's got her shit together, what else matters?"

"Why do you want to join us?"

"Skill can only get you so far. I want to expand my opportunities. Right now, I'm my own agent. The workload has been too light as of late."

"See, Boss? Professional. She followed me here and I didn't even notice."

Kanasta looked into her eyes as if interrogating her soul. "I leave the decision to you, Tempo. Should she be allowed to join?"

"She can come along on our next gig. Need to see if she's a good team player before I decide on it," said Tempo.

"A cool head as always. For the sake of communication, I'd like a name," said Kanasta.

"Sefiwah," she said softly before flashing me a smile.

She's here to watch over Kaity. I need to trust her.

Kanasta lifted me up to my feet, gripping my hand hard. "Give her the rundown of our next mission. I'm going out for a quick walk," said Kanasta before leaving. He shut the door.

"Can you talk?" asked Kanasta.

Should I answer? I need to know if I can trust him with Kaity.

I released my Absence coating, becoming visible.

"Very impressive," said Kanasta.

"I am Kaity's guardian," I said.

"Not anymore, I'm taking care of her. You're an Exp, aren't you? Did Deceivant make you?" asked Kanasta.

No use lying to him.

"I was created by Zenero."

"Nothing to hide. That's good. We're taking Kaity along on the next mission. You're welcome to come and witness her first kill," said Kanasta.

His lax tone makes me sick.

"Is Kaity safe with you? I know you shot her," I said.

"Ah, so you saw me kill her. Yet she lives. Why are you concerned about the safety of a girl who cannot die?"

"I've failed to protect her so many times. I don't want to fail her more than I already have," I said, shaken by my own honesty.

"I shall treat her like a daughter," said Kanasta.

"Thank you," I said, bowing to him.

"You're free to go. Oh wait. One more thing, how does Sefiwah know you?" asked Kanasta.

This guy can see right through me. If I can't lie, I'll only tell him a partial truth.

"She wants to keep Kaity safe," I said. "I need you to trust her."

"I trust you both."

"You do?"

"I trust those who conceal their identity."

"Why is that?"

"They know the importance of secrets," said Kanasta with a slight smile.

He's wise. I hope he will mentor Kaity properly.

I grabbed his hand. "I am entrusting you with Kaity."

"You won't regret this decision." He firmly shook my hand.

Being an assassin will keep Kaity hidden while training her to defend herself. He'll mold her into a warrior who won't hesitate to strike down her enemies. It won't be easy for someone so compassionate, but it's what must be done. Maybe I'll find a better solution once this fight is over. For now, Kaity's safe. Time to find Bob and end this.

He released my hand. "I hope one day in the future, you're my target. Fighting an Exp would elevate the Viper Squad to new heights," said Kanasta.

Overconfident human.

"If you did, you'd end up dead," I said with a grin.

"I doubt it. You wouldn't kill Kaity's father, after all."

"I'll come to check in on her every so often, so you better do a good job mentoring her."

"Well, if I fail as a father, there's nothing to stop you from killing me. Ah, a new game to play," said Kanasta with a smile.

I bade him farewell, vanished in the trees, and teleported to the Microcosm.

"Hi, Daddy," said Amy, waving at me upon arrival.

"We were wondering when you would return." Zenero was standing right in front of me. "You must be wondering how I managed to escape."

Impossible.

"Daddy, how do you know new Daddy?" asked Amy.

"He's the man who created me. Zenero, have you come to your senses?"

"Indeed I have. I've decided you aren't worth the trouble. I heard how you stole my children. And I want you to explain why she doesn't remember her brother."

"Amy, I need you to get out of here. Find a Lum goddess and ask for protection." I created a white portal.

"But I don't wanna go," whined Amy.

"Don't worry, dear. You're perfectly safe with me," said Zenero.

"Can we talk?" I asked.

"How long have I been imprisoned? You made me miss my daughter's upbringing," said Zenero with a solemn tone.

"What are you planning to do now that you're free?"

"Absence released me after I convinced him you weren't worthy of being Sellum. Naturally, I'm going to kill you."

"If you somehow managed to succeed, that would only put Kaity at risk."

"Yes, I know all about your heir. It may take some time, but I will become Sellum once more," said Zenero, sharpening a knife in his grip.

"Bob is a greater threat than I am."

"Sel and I made a deal. He will be my advisor. Together we will keep the afterlife in order. To think you, who had such great judgment, allowed family to get in your way. We once thought alike and valued everything equally. If I had to kill my daughter right now to save this world, I would, but you wouldn't—"

"Wha...?" Amy pulled away from Zenero and hid behind me.

"You would let Earth crumble because of your obsession with freedom," said Zenero, shaking his head. "A god mustn't be an observer. You've already squandered your time as Sellum. If I had killed the Exps who posed a threat, you would have felt true loss. I had hoped you would realize that your selfishness only endangers those you love. Once you lose everything you love, you realize every life is the same. A spore in the air and your mother have the same worth. You realize you must put aside the lies that say life has more value based on size, abundance, relation, threat, and expectancy. Only those who take this to heart can truly be leaders."

"You don't have your artifact, and you don't have any god powers. Do you really think you can kill me?"

"You shouldn't assume." Zenero tossed a spear into a portal he created in front of him. The spear reappeared inside me, piercing my capsule.

I fell to my knees.

He can bypass my defenses.

"Daddy!" yelled Amy.

I pushed her into a Lum portal. My gaze then turned to Zenero. "Tranquil took your artifact. How did you get it back?"

"I'll let you figure that out. Now go on, attack me."

"I refuse."

Did he strike some sort of deal with her? Damn it, what the hell is going on!?

"You've already committed yourself to killing Bob. Why are you afraid to kill me? It would be so easy for you, like snapping a twig."

"We can still work together," I said, rising to my feet.

"Without power, goals are meaningless. I have no need for a false sense of faith. Hoping the world is going to change does nothing; you have to act. I acted and I was imprisoned for it. I had hoped that an evolved species would have been able to sacrifice themselves for the greater good. I was wrong; you all needlessly fought for survival. Ironically, it was Casey who convinced Absence to free me. Casey valued my life too much, so she freed me. Not so I could save this world, but because she loved me. She may have committed a great act, but her intentions were selfish. You need to cast aside your love of all things living if you hope to save them," said Zenero as he tossed yet another spoke in the portal, causing it to shoot out of my hands.

"If you had just trusted we wouldn't kill you, you wouldn't have been imprisoned," said Sellum. "

"Don't be naïve. You all disobeyed me once, and I'm well aware of the strong ambitions Exps harbor. Sel would have eventually tried to overthrow me. I would have expected you would have as well, but you imprisoned me for the wrong reason. Oh, if only you had done it for the sole purpose of saving this world. If that were the case, you would have had the ambition necessary to rule."

"When you let suspicions control you to kill your family, no one is safe. Without compassion for those closest to you, how can you expect to spread kindness to others? You realized your folly before. I don't know what they told you, but you cannot let your fear change who you are."

"You accuse me of suspicions, yet you assume I would become controlled by fear. I have no fear anymore! I've already lost all that I love."

"You don't love us?"

"Exps are a means to an end. You all were never able to fill the gap left after I lost my family." He fired more spokes into me.

I have to stop him even if it means killing him. Die!

My armor fell apart, revealing lasers that locked onto Zenero. "Give up and I won't kill you."

Zenero created a portal in front of him and another behind me. "Those lasers continuously fire mines; you can't stop them, can you? I spent my time in Absence thinking of how to beat you, while you just assumed you'd never have to fight me again."

I created a portal to Lum, but Zenero whisked it away.

"You needn't worry; I will save this world," said Zenero.

The mines went off inside me, destroying my insides.

"Die!" I yelled, firing a massive Sel beam at my attacker.

A single massive portal absorbed the blast.

Portals appeared all around me and flooded me with dark energy.

I lost?

I fell to the ground as I was consumed. "I hope you can save this world."

"Hope is meaningless," said Zenero.

A clear black and white portal appeared and headed toward Kaity.

"I am above the laws of the universe," said Zenero as he teleported the cloud inside him, making him Sellum once more.

Everything went black.

"Freedom is a shackle." These words repeated fervently in my mind. When I opened my eyes, my body was floating freely in a gelatinous fluid. Everything went dark. The cabin slowly came into focus, along with the Freedom Forcers.

Part 20
Battle for Godhood

Chapter 166: Identity

Once the flashback finished, all the information was absorbed in an instant.

Ada looked at Sellum in amazement. Kaity looked at him with anger. But the bulk of the rebels were beyond words.

"Why is everyone so quiet? Are you disgusted that he turned me and my little sis into killing machines? Wait, how are you even here if you died?" asked Famine.

"Did you plan my whole life? Why can't you just leave me alone?" exclaimed Kaity in tears.

"I have no idea what is going on!" announced Toxic, raising her tail.

"I knew it was you," said Chipko, smiling at Sellum.

"We were duped," said Kanasta.

"I can't believe I didn't recognize you. There were so many similarities," said Ada with a smile.

"Similarities to what?" asked Opti.

"Sellum is our dear friend Exp 8!" cheered Ada, hugging the god.

Deceivant approached Sellum with fire in his eyes. "You played us the whole time. The entire thing was just *lila*, a god putting on a show for us mortals. But what do you stand to gain? Did you plan on faking your death?"

"Abyss made me realize that I can no longer hide anything from you. I decided to show you the truth of my own volition. Keep that in mind."

"Already trying to turn things in your favor." Famine crossed his arms.

"Was it supposed to be a secwet?" asked Stabby, tugging on her daddy's arm.

"Secwet?" asked Famine.

"You know what I meant," said Stabby, crossing her arms.

"Hey guys, this means Exp 8 has been by our side this whole time! Isn't that great?!" cheered Opti.

"Yeah, he stood by and watched as the bystanders he manipulated were persecuted. Not only that but he forced his will onto children. I knew never to trust a god. They're all selfish," said Deceivant with contempt.

"Allow me to explain my intentions. As Sellum I could not intervene and stop Sel directly. Exp 8 was my way of bypassing this limitation. I needed loyal warriors to stand by my side if I was going to keep the afterlife safe. I thought that even Tranquil had betrayed me."

"All I hear are excuses," said Kaity.

"After I died, Stabby gave Deceivant my blueprints so I could be reborn."

"I couldn't resist the request of a lonely little girl who missed her father." Deceivant seized his chest. "Regrettably, I was unable to create a body able to handle the ex-god's energy. Devlin overcame that obstacle and created a proper vessel to serve as your avatar. Exp 8, the power of a god…I should have figured it out. There were many feats that Exp 8 accomplished that no other Exp could."

"I'll list them for you," said Sellum with a proud voice. "The ability to weaken the power of artifacts, which Exp 8 used in his fight against Devlin. An impossibly fast energy production speed and an energy mass that far exceeded its container. The teleportation of Devlin, Exp 8, Nina, and NoOne to the Liminal Space, which I triggered upon Exp 8's self-destruction. And most importantly, the godlike charisma Exp 8 utilized to turn foes into comrades."

"Why are you saying Exp 8? Is my friend just a persona?" asked Opti, raising half a white drama mask to his face.

"Exp 8 is a separate consciousness I created to rally the Exps. Just as Vishnu incarnated as Rama in the ancient epic, I created a new persona that would be apt for the task."

"How can we trust anything you say?" asked Kaity.

"It's your decision whether or not to trust my words, but at least hear me out. Exp 8 was unaware that he was once Sellum. In fact, he only began to regain awareness when he entered Sel, becoming fully aware in the battle against Etah. That's when I took the helm. I teleported to Lum to meet with Tranquil. She explained that Bob stole the Teleport Artifact from her and handed it over to Zenero. She did not betray me. In fact, we went to the Macrocosm together. Using Exp 8's power, along with Tranquil's assistance, we subdued and imprisoned Zenero, forcing him to give up the power he took from me. My god powers never fully abandoned me since Zenero's seizing of them was illegitimate to begin with. Thankfully, I was able to remove his artifact without destroying his capsule."

"Yep! And Daddy twusted me with the important rock!" cheered Stabby. Sellum lowered his head.

"What? I thought we weren't keeping secrets anymore? Did I mess up?" asked Stabby, looking worried.

"It's fine. After Zenero killed me, he gave Stabby the Teleport Artifact. She gave it to Deceivant and Devlin stole it. When Devlin tried to absorb the power of Exp 8, I seized the artifact. Using its power, I made it to the Microcosm and took down Zenero with Tranquil. After that I entrusted it to Stabby, but the artifact is now safely in my care. Once Sel captured Efil, I felt having Stabby hold onto it would only make her a target."

"I don't care how you came back! You, Bob, and Sefiwah were manipulating all of us from the start," said Kaity in tears.

"Why didn't you tell me the truth, brother? Don't you trust me?" asked Chipko with watery eyes.

"I'm sorry. I decided to keep it a secret from everyone, but you saw through my guise." Sellum turned to Kaity. "And it's as you said, Bob was definitely pulling the strings."

"We were all just pawns in their game. I must admit, I'm impressed," said Kanasta.

"Shut up! You only recruited me because you couldn't kill me. I thought...you cared about me," said Kaity before succumbing to her tears.

Kanasta reached out to comfort her, but BoneSaw stood in his path.

"I'll give you some time," said Kanasta before leaving the room.

Sellum turned to Kaity. "We weren't all working together. The three of us each had our own reasons for what we did."

"You forced me into this whole mess! My life would have been fine without you!" yelled Kaity.

Opti grasped Kaity's hand and channeled his energy into her.

She pulled away. "I don't even care what Sel does anymore."

"I made a grave mistake," said Sellum. "I felt that making you the heir would make Bob give up. His only option if he killed me would be to either kill your mother or convince her to attack her own daughter. I didn't know he would actually try to murder his own sister." He lowered his head to the ground. "I apologize with all of my being."

"Your words are empty," said Kaity.

"But wasn't it his words that made you his heir?" asked Ada.

Kaity burst into tears.

"There, there, sweetie," said Ada, nestling Kaity in her bosom.

"There's no proof that anything he's told us about Exp 8 is true," said Kaity.

"Remember when Exp 8 had amnesia? A part of me became aware then. That's why I recognized you."

"Even if Exp 8 didn't use me, you did!" yelled Kaity in tears.

"That's right. You were all just tools to this high and mighty god," said Famine with a sneer.

"I don't know how to apologize for everything," said Sellum without tone, tears flooding from his helmet.

"You can't," said Kaity with a dark look. "I can't believe my mother was with me all that time and she never told me. I am tired of being used," she said, wiping her tears as they came out.

"But Daddy didn't mean to huwt anyone," said Stabby in tears.

"Hey, you saw the truth. He manipulated your memories."

Stabby nodded. "Yeah. He didn't want me to be sad."

"And what about what he did to me?"

"I don't know. You were being a meanie. Daddy was just trying to help."

"Good intentions are never enough. Zenero will never understand that. It is true that no good deed goes unpunished. Abyss, my son, I am sorry for what I did to you. I wanted to teach you that life is precious," said Sellum lovingly.

"By turning me into a killing machine, which you conveniently skipped over, I might add!"

"If I show them, then will you forgive me?"

"I will never forgive you! And the only way I'm helping you is if they agree to help you. Face it; you just lost all your allies. All that hard work manipulating them has gone to waste," said Famine with a big grin.

"They know what's at stake. The decision has yet to be made." Sellum stood up. "What happened in the past is over. Now we must stand together. However, I will not force you. It is up to you to decide if you want to join me and stop Sel. Right now he is in Absence, seeking to free Zenero. Will you join me in protecting the balance of Sellum?" asked the God of Gods.

The Freedom Forcers fell silent.

"I'm still trying to process everything. We don't want to make a hasty decision," said Ada.

"The answer is obviously no!" exclaimed Deceivant.

Opti stood up. "Come on, friends. We were hesitant about working for Sellum because he was a stranger. Well, now we know he was our dear friend all along. If Exp 8 was asking us to help, would you really turn him down?"

Fusion spun in place.

"She agrees too!" exclaimed Opti.

"I fully trust Exp 8," said Ada.

"I certainly don't. For all we know, Sellum just made him up and is lying to us," said Deceivant.

"Whether he used us or not, we can't just abandon our friends in Sellum. If we can help people, then we should!" exclaimed Opti.

"I couldn't agree more!" exclaimed a sarcastic nasally voice.

Everyone turned around to see Sel.

"Why are you here?" asked Kaity, glaring at the murderer.

"Killing the army of Absence was getting boring. I was hoping you all could join in and up the difficulty."

"You've already begun the attack?" asked Sellum.

"That's right. I went to Hope's team already. Most of them came to help out; you wouldn't want to abandon them, right?"

"Everyone, I need you to decide now."

"Come on, Kaity!" Opti grabbed her hand. "They need our help. If you go, I'm sure the others will too."

"I don't know what to do," said Kaity, burying her face in her arms.

"Oh, did I miss something interesting?" asked Sel, turning upside-down.

Stabby climbed onto the sofa. "We need your help! When Daddy died, did I cry? Uh-huh. I cwied a lot. But after I cried, I got to work. I helped the angels fight demons. And was I captured? Well, yeah, I was. But that didn't stop me! I found the nice demons. The ones who knew Sel was a bad man! And I helped them all get along! I was the mediator. I didn't even know that word when they asked me to do the job, but that didn't matter! I've helped a lot, even after Daddy died. A nice demon brought me to Earth. Then I asked a nice man to make my daddy. I returned to Sel when I realized my daddy wasn't coming back. But every day in Sel I prayed. I pwayed a lot. And look! Daddy is alive now. And he wants help. So stop arguing and help him!"

Sel was the first to clap, followed by Ada and Opti. "What a speech! Even I'm motivated to fight the tyranny of Sel!" The eyeball's pupil intensified. "Jokes aside, I really am getting tired of waiting. Right now, decide if you're going or not. Keep me waiting too long, and I might accidentally disintegrate you. Deceivant, you're up first."

"I know what I said before, but I've decided to stay here with Ada. We fought hard to make it safely to Earth. We'll continue helping out the Exps without Hope," said Deceivant, holding his wife.

"You're right. I'd hate to be a burden," said Ada softly.

"Alright, Chipko. What about you?" asked Sel, popping out beneath her.

"After that heartfelt speech, I can't say no," said Chipko, looking at Stabby with a smile.

"Very, very true. Opti already said yes," said Sel, searching the crowd.

"Yeah, Sellum is Exp 8. Of course I'm helping my friend," said Opti.

"Oooh, so they know now," said Sel.

"Wait, you already knew?" asked Opti.

"Well, I can see souls. That makes it pretty easy. Didn't bother to check Sefiwah's. No offence, but she was very underwhelming."

"You kept his secret for all this time!" cheered Ada. "Oh, that is just the sweetest thing!"

"What!? It's not like I was doing him a favor. I just didn't want to have you all to think God was on your side. Religious motivation is a powerful weapon, after all."

"Aww, he's being shy," said Opti, smiling at Ada.

"I am not! Rrgh! Alright, final roll call. Go in the portal if you want to try and stop me from freeing Zenero. Or if you want to help me free him," said Sel, eyeing Chipko.

"I never want to see that user again," said Chipko with pain in her voice.

"You look so adorable like that!" exclaimed Sel, pinching her cheeks.

"True as that may be, we need to stay focused," said Deceivant.

"I'll go," said Kaity.

"Really?" asked Sel, his pupil enlarging.

"I didn't ask to be the heir or to get pulled into this conflict, but it doesn't matter. I am the heir and I can't just let you get your way!"

"Oh, I'm so happy I could motivate you," said Sel.

"Hey! I motiwated her!" yelled Stabby.

"Don't push your luck, kid," said Sel with a glare.

Kanasta entered the room. "Best of luck to you."

"What luck? I've probably died dozens of times. There's nothing for me to lose," said Kaity.

BoneSaw raised its saw.

"Thanks, but you really don't need to come along."

"Alright, step up everyone. On the other side of this portal is a warzone. Be prepared or else you may lose your life," said Sel.

Gimpy appeared and created a portal to Absence.

"Sorry, Bob, but I don't really trust you. Exp 8, can you make a portal?" asked Opti.

"We can't trust either of them, and we're wasting time." Kaity rushed into the portal.

Chipko, Opti, Fusion, and BoneSaw followed.

"How about we go on a date?" asked Deceivant, holding Ada's hands.

"That sounds great!" cheered Ada.

"Enjoy your date. And remember, if you don't get in my way, I won't have to kill you," said Sel, waving as he floated backward into the portal.

"Abyss, are you coming along?" asked Sellum.

"My sister's going so of course I am! But you better restore her memory once this is done."

Sellum crouched and placed his hand on her head. "I may not get another chance. I'm sorry," he said with a solemn tone.

"I don't want your apology. Did her memories return?" asked Chris.

Sellum shook his head. "I used Absence energy merged with my power over memory to wipe her mind. What has been erased by Absence cannot be brought back."

"When all this is over...I'm going to kill you," said Famine with a deadly glare.

Chapter 167: Battles for Zenero

The Freedom Forcers arrived at a battle-torn landscape. Unseen bodies were strewn across the invisible field, visible only from their blood and scorched flesh.

"Spread out. Find the strong enemies and engage," said Sellum.

"Don't you have the power to stop them all?" asked Kaity.

"Sel is my priority. If he falls, they will retreat."

"You heard him; split up. If you need help, retreat and regroup!" hollered Kaity.

"You'll be a fine leader."

"Not like I have a choice."

The Absence gods were already keeping the strongest of Sel's forces busy.

Crystal slowly approached Pesi as he was assaulted by depression bullets.

The Baroness sliced Tsul's whip before the ground beneath her burst.

The Führer had accidently led some of his best warriors into the Duke's string trap.

Occupy, Void, and Loyal were fighting Gimpy who was teleporting around to keep them busy.

"Everyone who is fighting armor-plated fodder, I want you to focus your attack on Stabby. Kill her and take the artifact she's carrying!" hollered Sel.

"I won't let you touch her." Sellum sent out a light orb. It fired out its contents, each one homing in on the dark god.

"Is that all you've got?" asked Sel, seeping into the invisible ground to dodge the barrage.

"None of you are getting near my sister!" yelled Famine, picking up a demon before tearing it in half.

"Yay!" cheered Stabby, standing under the demon with her mouth open. "Bwood!"

Riufen approached, hoisting up his living sword. "I apologize, but I have my orders."

"Tell you what, we'll only kill the girl once you're sliced to pieces," said Gladius, his teeth shimmering.

Famine bit into the demon. "Keep your distance from me. I'm surrendering control! *STAGE 1!*"

"Let's bweed 'em dry!" exclaimed Stabby, blades pushing her teeth out of her mouth.

Chipko approached August. "What do you think you're doing?"

"Haven't seen you in a while. How ya been?" he asked, bouncing Limit's lance off his fist.

"You're fighting on the wrong side. Sel wants to free Zenero."

"Once Absence comes out of hiding, we'll make him reveal Zenero's location. That's when I'll kill him." His hands turned sharp like blades before he engaged Limit.

"You can't!" yelled Chipko.

"What, don't think I'm strong enough? I've grown a lot since you've last seen me." The lance clenched between his hands, he shot off the ground, disarming the knight.

"Think you can stop me?" asked Chipko, knocking her fists together.

August was pushed back by the shockwave. Once he regained his footing, he kicked off the ground. His body became like a bullet as it tore through the air before slamming into her.

Chipko lost her footing and tumbled over.

"Don't cry after I beat your ass," said August, tossing his hat in the air.

"Stop right there," said the Captain, intercepting Yvne's path.

"You must have such courage to stand in my way," said Yvne as her body shifted shape.

"I'm an assassin. We aren't known for our courage."

Clear needles shot into Yvne's back.

"We are known for our efficiency though," said the Captain with a grin.

Kaity rushed in front of Casey. "What are you doing? She's your daughter, isn't she?"

"After what Pathos has done to her, I'm not sure how much of my daughter remains. But you can relax; I'm going to capture her. I wouldn't kill her even if it was to free Zenero. She just needs to hand over Zenero's artifact," said Casey, running past Kaity.

Kaity fired a round into the Exp's legs. "I'm not letting you free Zenero. Don't you get that he's just been using you since the beginning?"

"What do you know about him? It matters not. Zenero will need you dead to reclaim his powers. I might as well capture you now. 𝕮𝖔𝖘𝖊 𝕮𝖔𝕷𝕹𝖊"

Opti flew up to the top of the pillar. "Why is a pretty lady like you working for Sel?"

"You're right, I am gorgeous. As for why I'm helping him, well, it's simple really. I want Lum to become a scorched wasteland. A lifeless realm of fire and ash!"

"If that's really what you want, then as a defender of animals, fluffy and scaly, feathery too, I will strike you down!" exclaimed Opti, pulling a sword of optimism out from his chest before thrusting it back in.

"And boom!" Cheered Regna, blasting a squad of armored Absence residents. She lowered her head. "Ugh, it's hard to get excited when I'm not slaughtering angels." She fired out her arm at an approaching squad.

Fusion leaped up and connected to the arm.

"Yvne? Is that you?" asked Regna.

The arm disengaged from Fusion and shot into Regna before exploding.

Sel's dark beam clashed against Sellum's light beam. "You're only as strong with Lum energy as the Great Goddess, whom I nearly killed under your omnipotent gaze."

Chains suddenly wrapped around Sel. His dark beam weakened before it was overpowered completely.

"Then perhaps he could use a bit of assistance," said Atlas, gripping the Chaos Chains tightly.

"Keep killing till Absence comes out from his hiding spot! Hold nothing back! Annihilate our enemies!" yelled Sel.

"Easier said than done!" yelled Pesi, flying to dodge a mineral barrage from the lay-about Absence guard.

"You flew straight toward me. Do you have a death wish?" asked Crystal.

"You mustn't have been paying attention! I chose you as my opponent!" exclaimed Pesi, sticking out his tongue.

"Really? And why is that?"

"Because you have a fatal flaw!" Pesi fired a beam of pessimism at Crystal.

The Absence god took the beam head on. "Is that all you've got?"

Pesi blinked rapidly. "You're a depressed lounger! There's no way that didn't affect you!"

"The last time your leader attacked, he captured a goddess. Where is Efil?" asked Crystal, his arms enlarging as mineral spikes jutted out from them.

"I don't know!" yelled Pesi before being shot out of the air.

Crystal loomed over Pesi with a sharpened mineral blade. "I'll ask you one more time. Where is she?"

"I honestly don't know! I wouldn't keep it a secret while my life's on the line."

"Whatever." Crystal stabbed the blade into Pesi's arm, pinning him to the ground. "I'll ask someone else then."

Kaity was trapped in a multi-layered case. There wasn't a strand of light to be found. "Of course. That's why Bob invited us here. He wants to wipe out his enemies in one fell swoop. I'm the only one on my team who can't die. I've got to get out of here and provide support."

"Talking to yourself is a sign of loneliness," said Casey, shrouded in the darkness. "I'll level with you, dear. It's a shame you've been selected as Sellum, but there's nothing we can do about it. Oh, but wait, there is! Once Pathos dies, you can willingly turn over your power to Zenero. Nobody has to get hurt. Sound good?"

"Sounds great. So, does that mean you'll let me out of here?"

"Sorry, dear, but I can't really trust you till the time comes. You understand?"

"I hope you understand that I'll kill you if you get in my way. I will drench myself in your blood to protect my allies." Kaity released her plasma claws, giving her enough light to spot Casey.

Her first strike was blocked by a box. Another box was kicked into her foot. A third box was promptly summoned above the girl.

Kaity jumped up, stabbed her claws into the falling box, and swung into Casey. "Get rid of this cage or I'll separate your head from your body."

"Do you have any idea how long I've been searching for Zenero? I love him like fish love the water. All these years I've been suffocating, and now I finally have a chance to return to comfort. You're probably too young to have been in love. It's an incredible feeling. Takes over your whole body."

Kaity sliced off the woman's arm and clenched her purple scarf. "I have experienced love. And every moment I spend here is a day that the woman I love is being tortured."

"Surrender now and I'll take you to Earth myself to see your lover."

"I'm not abandoning my allies, not even for her."

"Then you aren't in love."

"That's not true. If I did that, I wouldn't be worthy of loving her. She'd be ashamed of me. Now get rid of this prison!" Kaity pierced the woman's other arm.

"I don't feel pain. Oh, and if you kill me, you're stuck here."

"That's why you entered," said Kaity with wide eyes.

"That's right. Only I can enter the case freely."

"Please, let me out." Kaity sobbed.

"Powerlessness is an awful feeling, isn't it?"

"That's a sharp toy you've got there. You should be careful," said Tsul, making the ground burst around her opponent.

"You've forgotten your responsibility to uphold the balance," said the Baroness, sidestepping through the assault.

"You're the one who fled to Absence," said Tsul, sending her whip-like arm at the mortal.

The Baroness unsheathed her sword.

After the whip was sliced, it expanded and burst, spraying Tsul's aura over the swordswoman.

"I'm in Absence to uphold the balance," said the Baroness, trying to swipe the aura off her as it expanded.

"There's no point. It's already too late for you."

"It's a good thing I'm a god now." The Baroness' sword fragmented and sliced the aura blobs.

"What did you just do?" asked Tsul with wide eyes.

"Explaining would put me at a disadvantage," said the Baroness, her sword fragmenting and slicing the whip to pieces.

"I'll take care of him. Why don't you go help your allies?" offered Chipko to the knight.

"Apologies, but I've already selected him as my foe," said Limit.

"Then don't get in my way." Chipko pressed her hands to the knight's armor. "*Shockwave Pulse!*"

Limit grunted before falling to his feet. "There's a storm inside me!" he yelled in anguish.

Chipko turned to August. "Are you sure you want to get in my way?"

"Sounds like you're afraid to hurt me."

"Quake." Chipko sent a shockwave beneath the ground.

August was blasted into the air before being pulled back by a sticky substance. "There's not much my artifact can't do."

"Then I'll test your limits firsthand," said Chipko, tightening her glove.

The Duke of Deception sliced the head off a bound Absence soldier. "Go on, keep sending more soldiers my way," he said, ending the life of its captives on by one.

"The title of Fifth Guardian is not merely a namesake. You've become stale following the whims of a tyrant. I, on the other hand, have grown far more powerful." The Führer's spider-like legs brought him just outside the Duke's trap.

"You could have expanded your rule beyond Avarice, but instead you fled and joined the pacifists."

"With proper politics there is no need for anything but pacifism. However, we are demons! Violence and sin shapes us into who we are!"

"Spare me your hypocritical speeches. Come closer if you dare."

"The guard's job is to protect the guardian. The guardian's duty is to be of service to the people of Absence. With my ascension, Absence can now grow in ways not possible before."

"You made a mistake in thinking I was wasting my time bowing and chanting. I've refined my weapons, not merely in sharpness."

The strings split and unfolded, slicing away the troops behind the Führer.

"You failed to protect your people!" The Duke pulled a string, which brought the severed bits of Absence warriors together around the Führer. "If you have a trump card, now would be the time to reveal it."

"Stay away from me!" yelled Regna, firing her fingers at the approaching sticky ball.

As soon as they connected, the fingers stopped blinking.

"How can you defuse my parts! I'm a god and you're a ball!" yelled Regna, her body steaming. "Fine then! I'll make you go mad with rage!" She fired her aura into the sticky ball.

Fusion continued to roll after her.

"Does nothing work against you?" Regna's eyes shimmered. "That's it!" She fired off her newly grown fingers into the ground in a circle around Fusion. "Oh yeah! You're trapped now!"

The sticky Exp was blown to bits.

Regna looked down to see her feet stuck in muck. "Ugh, I can't move! Think you trapped me, huh?" She sliced off her legs and fell to the ground. "You only delayed me ten seconds."

"Crumble under the weight of your own insignificance!" cheered Edirp as four insult arrows pierced Opti.

"You've been living the wrong way. You've got everything backwards." Opti's aura flooded into the arrows. "Feeble" became "Strong", "Ugly" became "Beautiful", "Glass Boned" became "Bones of Steel", and "Insignificant" became "Highly Valued".

"What did you do?" asked Edirp, shrinking in horror.

"Wow! I feel better than ever! Come on, let's hug it out!" He exclaimed before embracing her.

"Get off me!" she cried, piercing him with more and more arrows that were swiftly corrupted by his contagious idealism.

"These insults...are they what people said to you?"

"What?" Edirp's face becomes flushed.

"You pull them out of your body, so they come from you. You know you don't have to lower people to feel good. Instead, you can lift yourself up!" Opti hoisted up Edirp and spun her around like a baby playing airplane.

"Teamwork...I'm so jealous. Nobody ever teams up with me," said Yvne, drooping a bit. She shifted and became an armor-plated but not particularly fluffy bunny. That bunny then split into two bunnies. "Good thing I can be my own friend."

"You can copy our appearance but never our soul!" exclaimed the Captain, readying his dual blades.

"You're right. What kind of pathetic goddess am I?" asked Yvne in tears. She ziplined out of the way of a needle barrage before firing out her own needles.

The goopy needles screamed as they shot through the air.

The Captain blasted them with his blunderbuss but was still pierced by several of them. "Steel-tipped...I'm impressed," he said, wincing in pain.

"Oooooh, a compliment! I'm used to seeing other people get those, but it's a rare treat when I get a feast of them!" she exclaimed, wriggling with joy.

The Captain sped past her, having hooked onto a needle placed by Muffins. He grabbed onto his tethers and crossed them, pulling the two armored bunnies together.

Muffins fired a single massive needle at the two bunnies.

Yvne grew as quickly as possible before the Absence needle pierced her. "I can't win! If I try, I'll die! I'm a failure!" she screamed as she fled the battle.

"Well done, soldier," said the Captain of Carnage to Muffins.

The chubby bunny looked out at the devastation and her eyes watered. She then steeled herself before rushing headfirst into a hoard of demons.

Sel, still attached to the Chaos Chain, was firing lasers at random.

"Keep him tethered like that and we can win this," said Sellum, pumping the Sel god full of Lum bullets.

"Why can't I phase through it!?" Sel released a fog of darkness from his body. He then shot into the air, hoisting Atlas off the ground.

Dark energy materialized over Atlas' hands.

"It may have taken time to digest this soul, but now its full power is mine to command." Atlas pummeled Sel with the shadowy gauntlets. "Feel the despair of the Grief Gauntlets!"

"That grief is a mere breeze when faced with the strength of my ambition!" Sel fired a laser into Atlas.

"How dare you make my comrade depressed!" yelled Atlas before crashing to the ground.

"Look, I don't want to waste my time. Can you even do anything against me?" asked Sel with a yawn.

"My comrades are ethereal and physical! You will die today by the arsenal of souls I've rallied against you!" exclaimed Atlas, tossing the Torture Trident at his nemesis.

Sel caught the Trident with a spectral hand just as it was launched. He twirled it around before piercing Atlas with it. "Ha! Not able to control your chains now, are you?" The dark god slipped free.

"**LIGHT CORE ORB BOMB**!" Sellum sent a massive orb into Sel the instant the scheming deity broke free.

"No use!" Sel fired a beam through the orb.

"As expected," said Sellum.

The beam burst the orb, sending light energy crashing into Sel.

The god slammed against the ground. "That was a cheap trick!"

"I know. I thought you'd be proud," said Sellum.

"Don't get cocky!" yelled Sel.

"Exp 8, take it from here. You've fought him more than me anyways." Sellum collapsed and jumped back to his feet.

"What game are you playing at? You shouldn't underestimate me!"

Exp 8 dodged the incoming beam.

Sel crashed into him and impaled the Atma Blade into Exp 8. "If this is a trap, you better spring it soon!"

"Good morning to you too." Exp 8's turrets popped up and pumped Sel full of energy.

"Arrrgh!" Sel went into his phase form and backed away. He then fired a laser.

"I know what I'm capable of now." Exp 8 created a light orb that absorbed the laser. He fired the orb back at his old ally.

Sel phased through it only to have another one come his way. The dark god dodged the entire armada of orbs. "Is that all you can do?"

"Not even close. **CONNECT**!"

A line of white energy connected the circle of orbs. The supercharged spheres closed in on Sel, creating a huge explosion.

"I sure beat your ass!" yelled Exp 8 triumphantly.

"Not quite," said Sel, appearing in front of Exp 8 with spirit drills all around him.

Exp 8 tried to create an orb to protect himself, but Sel was too quick.

The orb exploded as the drills penetrated it. The drills pressed onward and ripped Exp 8 open. Without the power to sustain his levitation, the Exp's limp body fell. Sel fired a laser downward, hitting Exp 8's wound as it regenerated. The laser sent Exp 8 crashing down.

"You are just a minor obstacle in the way of my ambition. But no more. I'll be sure to make Kaity suffer in your place!" exclaimed Sel with a glowing red pupil.

An arrow shot into Exp 8's arm and pushed Sel away.

Sel turned to face Atlas. "Oh, so you want to die first?"

"Who's dying?" asked Sellum, his wound already healed.

Atlas clenched the Torture Trident, his body shivering. "I will take it from here. All souls bound to me, take form and destroy my enemy!"

Famine looked at his sister with watery eyes. "He really did turn you into a monster."

"Don't say that. I'm not a monstuh," whined Stabby.

"What are you waiting for? Strike the boy down," whispered Gladius.

"Patience. They are going through something right now."

"Well, that's a crying shame for them! They should be focused on the battle!" yelled Gladius.

"Brother. I'm so…" Stabby hugged his leg. "I'm so sorry I forgot you!"

Famine blushed. "Hey, don't apologize. It wasn't your fault. Sis, I need you to keep away from me. When I transform, I lose control."

"Uh-huh! Me too," said Stabby with a toothy grin.

"I'm tired of waiting!" Gladius freed himself from Riufen's grip and rushed after Stabby.

"Stay away from—"

Gladius slammed his tail into the enemy. "Foolish boy, you left yourself open."

"Like I give a damn!" Famine grabbed Gladius' tail and slammed him against the ground.

Stabby pounced on the blood buffet. Her fingers split open as blades shot out. She pierced the big lizard's belly. "Wook, I freed your dewicious bwood," said Stabby with wide eyes. "I'll free all the bwood!" Knives shot out of Stabby's back, ripping off her skin.

Famine was paralyzed in horror, giving Riufen the opportunity to slice his throat.

The samurai's blade stopped at his opponent's neck. "Shall we start our battle?"

"Aaargh!" screamed Gladius as his entrails were yanked out.

Famine grabbed the blade with his hand.

The tip of the sword fell.

Riufen hopped back to create some distance.

"As long as I don't go past Stage 4, I can stay in control."

"Then I shall get you to five!" Riufen tore out two spines and thrust them at his fellow combatant.

The mouths inside Famine's palms bit onto the blades. "The Boss sends me out when he needs to cause an unnatural disaster. You don't know what you'd be unleashing."

"Now I must see it!" Riufen sliced the hands open as he yanked his swords out. He merged the blades into a single thick sword before thrusting them into his opponent's chest.

"Nasty little imp!" Gladius' tail grabbed Stabby, getting sliced in the process, and tossed her away from him. "Hurry up and finish him off so you can help me end the girl!"

"My blade is stuck," said Riufen.

"You're mine," said Famine.

Riufen let go of his sword as it was pulled into Famine's stomach.

"That's Stage 3," said Famine with a glare

"Just two more left then," said the samurai with excited eyes.

"You're only seeing up to three." Famine's hands spit out bone fragments at the samurai's face. He slammed his hand into his chest, piercing him with an energy suppressor.

"What's this?" asked Riufen.

"I'm an Exp whose been trained to hunt down his own kind. With the other Hunters, we're going to wipe you all off the face of the planet!

 !"

Bone Fragments shot out from his stomach like a shotgun blast.

Riufen was blasted to pieces.

Famine clenched his hands and covered his stomach back up with his Hunter suit. "The boss is going to freak if I tell him the afterlife is real."

Riufen's arms crawled to each other and clapped. His body then reformed. "Splendid! Immobilizing me before unleashing your finishing attack. And you haven't even entered Stage 4 yet!"

"How are you still alive!?" exclaimed Famine, slamming Riufen to the ground.

"You want to keep her safe. Your loyalty to your sister is why you're holding back against me. I appreciate the honorable burden you are carrying. It pains me that I'll never have a chance to witness your final stage." Riufen kicked his respectable foe off and leaped to his feet. "C̶E̶R̶T̶A̶I̶N S̶E̶P̶P̶U̶K̶U!" He used a small bone dagger to pierce his chest.

Famine gasped in pain.

The samurai dragged the sword up to Famine's throat.

Famine's shocked eyes fell to the ground along with his severed head.

Chapter 168: Zenero's Will

Crystal approached Regna. "Do you know where Efil is?"

"Who cares about some high and mighty goddess?" asked Regna with a shrug.

Crystal fired out a line of minerals.

Regna caused an explosion to create smoke and then jumped onto her enemy from behind. She pierced him with her arm, kicked off, and triggered her arm to burst.

Crystal was unfazed. "Tell me where she is."

"Not even a dent!" yelled Regna, grinding her teeth.

"So, then you're really a goddess of Absence now? Well, well, it may be fun to play with you after all," said Tsul with a grin.

"I'm not the warrior you faced before. I have a true cause to uphold," said the Baroness, closing the distance.

Tsul created a whip from her aura and cracked it against the ground in front of the Baroness. "You lust for battle. Don't try and fool yourself."

The Baroness paused, but her legs were trembling. She rushed in.

"You just can't help yourself," said Tsul, triggering the ground to burst.

The Baroness kicked off the ground as it burst and used that to jettison herself into Tsul. "*IGNITION*"

The goddess screamed as the Baroness sliced her in two.

The new Absence goddess' sword fragmented once more, slicing at the aura mixed in the Sel goddess' blood.

"Your cause is empty. That is why you lost," said the Baroness.

"Lord Sel seeks to uplift our realm! He seeks to wipe out those who oppress us!" Tsul's aura became whips that assaulted the Baroness.

The sword sliced through the aura but was unable to stop the assault.

The Baroness raced around the area, cutting down friend and foe alike while moaning in ecstasy.

"You never stood a chance. Drown in your own bloodlust," said Tsul, using her aura to reconnect her body.

Chipko rushed in to take down August. She held firm as he punched her, allowing her to slam her fist in the ground.

The floor trembled before bursting.

August shielded his face, allowing Chipko to get three consecutive punches to his exposed stomach.

The punches bounced off as if hitting jelly.

August's fists became super hardened before he slammed them against the sides of Chipko's head. While she was in a daze, he lifted her up and brought her down on his fortified knee.

Chipko gasped in pain and her eyes teared up.

August hesitated for a moment, allowing her palm to slam into his chin.

While his brain was rattling, she swiped his feet.

He fell to the ground before being assaulted by kicks.

"It's no use. Your ability doesn't work on me," he said, his body bending at each hit.

"That's fine with me!" She lifted him up with her foot and slammed both fists into him. "Shockwave Blast!"

The incredible force of her attack sent him flying into the sky of Absence.

Chipko bit her bottom lip and cried. "Nothing has changed. We're fighting again because of Zenero."

The Führer was tied up in the Duke's trap. "This is difficult."

"What is? Coming to grips that you've lost?"

"No. I'm trying to formulate a plan for victory that doesn't involve you dying. Hmm, most difficult indeed."

"Don't mock me!" yelled the Duke.

The Führer escaped the strings, or rather, they were shed from his body.

"What did you just do?"

"Oh, I must have forgotten to share the good news with you. I'm a guardian of Absence now."

The Duke was tied up in his own strings. "I don't understand. What's going on?"

"Come now. A leader must be vigilant. I've forged new paths; your strings have merely followed them."

Ethereal arrows appeared, showing the direction that the strings followed to free the Führer and capture the Duke.

"My death will not hinder Sel's plan in the least!" yelled the Duke.

"Precisely why I don't seek your end."

The strings tightened, slicing off the Duke's limbs but not his head.

"The rules of Absence are different. Your death would have been permanent here," said the Führer.

"I apologize, Gladius, but I do not have it in me to kill the girl. Her brother, however, has been dealt with!"

"Wha!?" exclaimed Stabby, her blood red eyes softening.

"Oh, that look of fear in your eye! I hope you'll keep it as you slide down my gullet," said Gladius, fully healed and rushing after her.

"W̶A̶Z̶O̶R̶ W̶A̶I̶N̶!" screamed Stabby.

The knives on her back shot far into the sky.

"You'll be digested by the time they land!" Gladius's tongue shot out and pierced her legs. He then reeled her in.

"Bwother killer dies!"

Knives burst out from Stabby's sides, forming metallic spider-like legs. The legs pierced through and lifted Gladius off the ground. The knives rained down, shooting into the murderer.

Gladius' body was tossed aside.

"Bwother is dead," said Stabby in tears as she embraced herself.

Riufen approached her. "Hand over the Teleport Artifact and I won't cut you down."

"I don't have it! Daddy said so and Daddy doesn't lie."

"Very well then." Riufen sheathed his spine. "I shan't dishonor my weapon with the blood of a child." He reached for her.

"Hands off my prey!" exclaimed Gladius with his mouth full. He gulped Abyss' body and then smashed his head. "You didn't want to help, so I won't let you steal my kill."

Riufen gazed at Gladius with shimmering eyes.

"Umm, is there something you want to tell me?" asked Gladius with an uncomfortable look.

"You're volunteering to end her to preserve my honor. Has there ever been a more noble blade?" asked Riufen, moved to tears.

"It's ignoble. Ugh. Your sweet talking is hurting my stomach." Gladius said with a frown. "What is that feeling? Agh! Agggghhhhh!"

"What ails you, my valiant blade?"

Gladius cried in pain. "My insides, he's eating my insides!"

Abyss burst out of Gladius, his hands morphed into mouths, and devoured Gladius's body feverishly. "It has been too long since I've tasted flesh," said Abyss maniacally, mouths covering his whole body.

"Is this Stage 4?" asked Riufen, his eyes sparkling.

"What was that, flesh bag?" asked Abyss, his mouth filled with extra rows of teeth.

"Why hasn't Gladius resurrected yet?"

"Oh, you want to see your delicious sword? His scrumptious flesh and crunchy metal has become one with me," said Abyss, his iris now shaped like mouths. The addict's arm morphed into Gladius.

"So, you are a swordsman after all," said Riufen, pulling his spine out with a smile.

Gladius opened his mouth. "That's what I'm talking about! This host has so much power! I won't need to be a parasite; a mutual relationship will more than suffice."

Riufen rushed in and countered with his spine.

Gladius sliced straight through both the spine and its wielder.

"Are you leaving me? After all we've been through?" asked Riufen with hopelessness in his eyes.

"Leaving you? He's already left!" exclaimed Abyss, rapidly munching on the meat bag's flesh.

"Oh, wake up already! I was a parasite latching onto your power. Just like a hungry flea, I joyfully hop to a new host once I've got my fill," said Gladius, taking a bit out of Riufen's side.

"We bonded. Our souls are one. You can't abandon me."

"That's just an insurance policy. Abyss has been around a lot longer than you. He's the more experienced warrior!"

"Maybe you should have latched onto this host a little longer before deeming it useless," said Riufen, standing up while being devoured.

"Shut up! Die and become a delicious meal for me!" yelled Abyss.

Riufen shoved his spine into Abyss' stomach, which promptly devoured his bony sword.

"Useless!" exclaimed Gladius and Abyss together.

Riufen thrust his hand into the open mouth.

"Your arm is mine!" Abyss' stomach teeth clamped down, severing the flesh bag's arm.

"Victory is mine alone. ZERO ARM SWORD-STYLE," said Riufen with a tinge of melancholy.

Abyss was cut in two from within.

Riufen's severed arm leaped out from the stomach wound and sliced off Abyss' sword-wielding arm.

"I shall not be divorced from my blade," said Riufen, grabbing Gladius' hilt before slicing Abyss in two.

"Perhaps I was a bit hasty," said Gladius, averting his gaze.

"You were just testing me, right?" asked Riufen with a broken voice.

"Don't make me feel guilty! Ugh, I wasn't testing you, but you earned me back. Give yourself a congratulatory pat, and let's pretend this never happened," said Gladius, slapping his tail against Riufen's back.

"I would never have left you for another sword," said Riufen softly, cutting Abyss down once he regenerated.

"Don't get all gooey on me. That's only because there is no better sword. Well...maybe one."

Riufen's eyes lit up. He smiled. "Well then, once I find that sword, you can find some other tree to perch on."

"But you just said you'd never leave me!" whined Gladius.

"That was before this incident. Now you're a temp blade," said Riufen sternly, slicing off Abyss' legs and walking off.

"Why are you being so difficult. Oh, I almost forgot. We need to kill the...where is she?"

"You mean you weren't paying attention? The ultimate blade should be sharper."

"Are you mocking me?"

Riufen patted his fickle sword. "Don't get heated. We must find the girl or else face the dishonor of loss."

"I didn't lose her, you did!"

"Haha! You attacked me, allowing her to escape! Did you forget?"

"You're really irritating me, you know," said Gladius with a glare.

"So, what is the name of the actual ultimate blade?"

"Joke's on you! I made it up!"

"Ultima, Ragnarök, Excalibur, Masamune, Sakura, Sparda, Hrunting, Amaterasu?"

"Ugh, I said I made it up. Stop being annoying."

"Perhaps I should ask Sel about Amaterasu."

"Don't do that!"

"Because it's real?" asked Riufen with shimmering eyes.

"Ugh, fine. It's real. But you wouldn't like it."

"I bet I would."

"You wouldn't even be able to carry it," sneered Gladius.

"Then I must grow stronger."

Kaity was still sobbing inside Casey's prison when Stabby appeared. "What are you doing here? You should run!"

"Are you...my little Amy?" asked Casey before breaking down into tears.

"Momma?" asked Stabby with watery eyes.

Stabby ran into her mother's embrace and cried.

"I'm here now. Honey, I need your help. The only way to free your real father is with the special rock you have. It's the one you used to get here. Just hand it over to Momma, and I'll take care of the rest," said Casey, caressing her daughter's hair.

Stabby shook her head. "If I do that, Daddy will be upset with me."

"Oh, you poor girl. I promise I won't let him punish you anymore."

"Daddy doesn't punish me. I just don't want him to be sad," said Stabby.

"He is not your father."

"Yes he is! A Daddy is someone who takes care of you and wuvs you wots and wots!" whined Stabby.

Kaity approached the girl. "Stabby, can you get me out of here? I need to protect my allies. You should hide your magic rock on Earth. If you get captured, everything will be ruined."

"Don't listen to her! Your fake father is wrong. Zenero is a good man. He deserves a second chance!" exclaimed Casey.

A figure in a clear cloak permeated through the case.

"A pleasure to finally meet you," said the figure, bowing reverently to Kaity.

"I won't let you touch her," said Kaity, standing in front of Stabby.

"I'm just as interested in you as I am in her," said the figure in a wise voice that changed intonation midsentence.

The figure's radiant rainbow aura permeated through its disguise, overwhelming Kaity with the powerful mix of auras. Kaity took a closer look to see a shimmering face under the hood. Though it couldn't exactly be called a face, the figure had a collection of stones beneath its cowl, along with a cranial protuberance reminiscent of a Buddha statue. It had a stone of grey gypsum in place of a left eye. There was only a crevice for the other eye. A violet blue Lazurite stone was placed above the figure's eyes like a tilak.

"You're the emissary of Absence who used Etaf all those years back. What do you want, Crystal?" asked Kaity.

The figure pointed to her chest with a crystalline finger. "Your artifact. It is calling out to return home. I must oblige it."

"Amy, dear, I need you to get us out of here. It isn't safe," said Casey.

"She's right. Go. I'll handle him," said Kaity.

"You'll handle me?" asked the ex-god.

"This artifact was given to me by someone precious to me. I won't let you have it," said Kaity.

"Ah, and who do you think gave it to your mother's creator?"

"What do you know about my mother?" asked Kaity, releasing her plasma claws.

"Never once pondered upon where artifacts originated from, have you?" The figure released an icy aura, freezing the area.

Kaity's claws emitted extra heat, keeping her from being captured. She whipped out her pistol and fired at the figure's chest.

The bullets slowed down and were blasted aside by a sound burst.

Kaity's ears quickly adjusted. She kicked off the ground and disengaged her rifle from her pack.

Claws emerged from the figure's sleeves but missed their mark when her bullet hit its arm. "Well played."

"You want it so badly. Let's see if you can handle it. *BULLETS, LOVE, TARGET.*" She fired her rifle in various directions. Each shot converged on the ex-god.

Slowing down the bullets did nothing to stop them from making contact. Despite every shot hitting its mark, the figure was unaffected.

"I will free you soon." The figure increased the temperature, melting the case and Kaity's body. It froze the immortal girl as she regenerated. "Your comrade Tempo never created a heat this powerful. That is because you're all using artifacts rather than channeling them." The figure shoved a hand into Kaity's chest and tore out her capsule. "So inefficient." It removed the artifact and carelessly dropped her capsule. It clawed open a hole into its robe and placed the Love Artifact into the center crevice in its chest. "You've been through many an ordeal, but now you've returned to my *Anahata*," said the figure, petting the pearl at its heart center. "Now to find the little girl."

Exp 8 nodded to Atlas before flying off.

All of Atlas' tattoos lost their luster as they materialized in front of him. His soul arsenal was wrapped with the Chaos Chain, combining into a warrior with weapons for its many arms.

"What is that?" asked Sel with a curious gaze.

"I am Unity and I am your end," responded the collection of weapons in a wispy voice that resonated with great charisma. The Agony Axe shot out, attached to the Chaos Chain.

"Prepare for a short battle, Sel," said Atlas before collapsing.

Sel fired beams as he dodged the assault.

The axe swept past him but was suddenly pulled back, slicing his side.

The god cringed in pain, allowing Unity to wrap its foe in the Chaos Chain.

The Agony Axe, Torture Trident, Woeful Whip, and a muscular hammer continuously assaulted the God of Sel while it desperately shot lasers and Sel beams in all directions.

"Another realm god shall be added to my arsenal. You are the first threat to my world that shall be repurposed." Unity reeled in the helpless god.

Sel screamed as his doom neared.

The center weapon of Unity, the Misery Mace, shifted in place. The mace split in two, revealing the ethereal soul-crunching teeth within.

"Please don't kill me," begged Sel.

"You aspired for too much," said Unity.

Sel was dragged into the mouth before being promptly devoured.

"A new soul has joined my arsenal!" exclaimed Unity.

Chapter 169: Hidden Agenda

Meanwhile in Absence, Opti set Edirp down after spinning her around like a child.

The Sel goddess was knocked out cold.

"Oh, maybe she got too dizzy. I hope she feels better when she wakes up." He flew off and joined up with Crystal.

"Damn it! Why won't you go down!" yelled Regna.

"Just tell me where Efil is and I'll let you go!" yelled Crystal.

"I'm here to help! *OPTIMIST!   LAST* !" Opti fired his aura into Crystal.

"Hey, two on one! No fair!" yelled Regna.

"I won't lose her again! **CRYSTAL PRISON**!" Extra reinforced minerals erected out around Regna.

"It didn't work last time! Why would it work now!?" exclaimed Regna, firing out her limbs and triggering them to burst.

The prison was unharmed.

"How?" asked Regna, banging her head against the walls.

"He just needed to believe in himself," said Opti, patting Crystal's shoulder.

"Thanks, man. I really appreciate the help."

"I'm not failing!" Regna's aura pooled into her new limbs. *CLAWS OF WRATH*!" Her aura solidified into crimson claws.

The fire in her body gathered in her arms.

The Sel Goddess stabbed her fingers into the diamond fortress. "Boom!"

The crystalline structure was blasted to bits.

"I shouldn't have underestimated you," said Crystal, taking a step back.

"Yeah, no shit!" yelled Regna before piercing him with her claws.

The mineral man was blown to bits.

Opti screamed as he flew off.

"Come back here!" yelled Regna, racing after him. She bumped into an invisible figure. "Out of my way!" The furious goddess thrust her arms at the invisible obstacle.

The figure became visible as its Absence coating was shed from its body. "This ends here." The God of Absence erased her claws in his grip.

"The big boss finally showed up!" Regna kicked his chest, getting her foot eliminated in the process.

Absence grabbed her with both hands. "**compact**." The furious goddess was shrunken down to the size of a marble.

"My lord, why have you shown yourself?" asked Occupy, teleporting around to capture Gimpy.

"Sel has fallen. The threat is over," said Absence calmly.

Gimpy screamed out illegibly before being pinned down by Loyal.

"Return to your realm. You've lost, demon," said Loyal.

Gimpy vanished beneath the claw.

"Brother, remember me?" asked Chipko, approaching the ruler of the realm.

"I could never forget. Is August alright?" asked Absence.

Chipko scratched her shoulder nervously. "He's fine. Hey…I want to see him again. Sel's gone, right? Then there's nothing to worry about."

"I cannot oblige you. I have my orders."

"What about your loyalty to Zenero?"

"He chose Pathos as his heir. I am honoring him by following Pathos' will."

"Look. I…I need to kill him. I won't be free of him unless he dies by my hand. Pathos let him live twice. Zenero is too dangerous," said Chipko.

"Perhaps, but now isn't the time."

"No! We have to do it now before they free him! If he gets his artifact back, who knows what he will do!"

"You're absolutely right, but I have my orders, and I will follow them as instructed."

"You're a coward. Fine then, I'll just take you down myself," said Chipko, entering a fighting stance.

Something sped by her and swiped her off her feet.

"Sister?" she asked, looking up at the familiar figure.

"You appear to be mistaken. I am Flash Girl. And I'm here to stop you from making a terrible decision."

Gimpy appeared in front of Stabby.

Casey was holding her daughter in her arms. "Don't hurt her. I'll get the artifact. I just need more time. An intruder is here. Don't you think you should deal with that thing first?" she asked, pointing to the approaching figure in a clear cloak.

Stabby leaped out from her mother's arms and sprouted blades from her sides. "Get out of here, Momma."

"I'm sorry, dear. **Case NΕΕₒΕΕΕΕ**

Stabby's back flattened out like a box.

Casey swung it open and pulled out the traveler's stone inside. "Don't just stand around. Subdue Absence! We're nearly there!"

Gimpy nodded before vanishing.

Noticing that Chipko was preoccupied, Gimpy appeared in front of Absence and fired black bullets at the realm god.

"Your master is trapped, yet you still fight to carry out his will. I respect your loyalty. Very well, I shall not hide. If you want the artifact, you'll have to defeat me."

"Allow me to assist you, my lord," said Limit, having recovered from Chipko's attack and finished off a squad of demons.

"Hold nothing back. To do so would be to disrespect our enemy and would bring shame to this realm," said Absence.

Sellum materialized in front of Gimpy, followed by Unity. "If you want Absence, you'll have to take us down first!"

Gimpy removed its helmet, revealing long flowing blond hair and an androgynous face. "Where is Sel?"

"Your master has been devoured by me. You no longer have to follow its whims," said Unity.

"Spit him out!" yelled Gimpy, rushing at Unity.

"Give it back," said Stabby under her breath.

"Your mind has been twisted by that monster. I can't believe I ever thought of him as a brother!" yelled Casey.

"Give it back now," said Stabby, turning around.

Casey held Zenero's artifact to her chest and absorbed it.

"*Ee Ee Ee Ee Ee* She didn't budge. A knife had been pierced into her foot, keeping her in place. "Are you really willing to fight your own mother for that kidnapper?"

Stabby's fingertips split open as blades shot out of them.

"I won't fail Zenero!" exclaimed Casey, forming a prison around her daughter.

Stabby screamed inside the prison, scratching it with her knives.

"I believe you have something that belongs to me," said the figure in a clear cloak from behind Casey.

"This belongs to Zenero, and I will return it to him! **Case No Ee Ee Ee s Ee Ee** Casey trapped the figure in larger and larger cases.

"Zenero is very important to me as well," said the cloaked being, exiting the prison.

Casey sent a flurry of boxes at the figure.

The shadowy individual formed a shield that deflected each projectile. It then sent out a sound wave that crippled Casey. "Anything that is borrowed should be returned." His chest glowed with a white light.

Casey grabbed her chest as her artifacts burst out of it. She grabbed onto them as they magnetized to the figure.

Evolution clasped its hands atop of hers.

A case crashed down from above her. She lost hold of the artifacts, and they tumbled along the ground.

The two artifacts were magnetized to the ex-emissary of Absence. "Welcome back."

"My old friend, is that you?" asked Occupy.

The figure in the clear cloak nodded.

"I wasn't sure you were still alive. Welcome back."

"I see I've been replaced," said the figure.

"I hope you aren't offended. Oh, what name do you go by now?"

The figure approached, leaving a dip in the ground with each Absence-coated step. "I am the enemy of stagnation and the hope of the incarnated. I am Evolution."

"I'm sure we can find a new job for you."

"Regrettably, I must to reject your offer. I have only returned to claim your leader's artifact."

"You seek to free Zenero as well?"

"What I seek is not something so simple. Either way, the artifact will be mine," said Evolution, freezing Occupy in place.

The warrior monk ignored the cold and stepped into Evolution's path. "Something is different about you."

"I am no longer lost," said Evolution.

"Gods, offer me your aid. We must work together if we seek to bring down the old emissary!" hollered Occupy.

The Absence gods appeared in a circle around the intruder.

"So many old faces. Ah, and some new ones. Hmm, what lessons do you have for me, I wonder," said Evolution, bowing to the gods.

The ruler of Absence was the last to appear. "If there is a threat, I must face it head on. Together, this foe will fall!" he exclaimed, thrusting his arm in the air.

Htols, who had an entire battalion of demons and the Baroness of Blades frozen in place, looked over at the gathering of Absence gods and decided they could make do without her help.

375

Evolution was encircled by Absence gods. "You appear to be surrounded."

Cloaked figures appeared in a circle around the gods.

"Mere illusions; pay them no mind," said Occupy.

"This battle ends now. **compact**!" exclaimed Absence.

Evolution was unaffected. "In order to use your power on living beings, you must be able to assert your will over them. You cannot sway me." The ex-god pressed its hands together.

A powerful gravity pressed down against the other gods.

"Hey! Brother, I want your artifact. Fight me! No holding back!" yelled August, standing just outside the gravity field.

"Go, my lord. We will take out the intruder," said Loyal.

Absence bowed and vanished.

Absence reappeared in front of August. "I cannot allow Zenero to be freed."

"Well then, good news, I only want to free him so I can kill him," said August with a grin.

"All the more reason I cannot allow it." Absence reverted a marble into an extendable staff. "Come at me!"

"You know, there's something I never understood. If you're loyal to Zenero, why are you following the guy who imprisoned him? Are you afraid of Pathos? And why did it take you so long to show up?" asked August, keeping just out of range.

"I only hid to keep my realm safe. So many lives were lost. I shall never make that mistake again. If anyone challenges me, I shall meet them head on and strike them down." Absence's staff elongated and tripped his attacker.

August grabbed Absence's feet. "*SURFACE BIND*."

Absence's feet fused with the ground. With a rapid series of jabs, he pushed back August.

The expert bounty hunter changed his entire body into steel. "You're like a punching bag now. And I'm going to need to warm up if I'm going to kill Zenero," said August, rapidly punching his brother. "What's wrong? Afraid to use your Absence powers? Afraid you'll kill me. You really are a coward, after all."

"**compact torrent**!" yelled Absence. The single marble he tossed into the air de-compacted into hundreds of compacted balls.

August punched Absence before getting pierced by the god's clear fingers.

"Shit. That was a good hit." August fell to the ground.

"You want to die, don't you?" asked Absence.

August smirked.

"Very well then. 𝐑𝐞𝐯𝐞𝐫𝐭." The compacts unfolded into a hailstorm of weapons.

"I'm steel-plated; don't you get it?" asked August, weathering the storm.

"Indeed." Absence grabbed a spear, coated it in his energy, and pierced August before shooting him in the leg with a clear-tipped arrow.

August fell to the ground. "Just a little rain, is that all you have?"

"Any more wounds and you will die, brother," said Absence as he walked off.

"Flash Girl confronts her sister to stop her from making a great mistake."

"It's not a mistake, June. The mistake was letting him live," said Chipko, sending small shockwave blasts at her speedy sister.

"Flash Girl takes off her mask, revealing her true identity to her sister! Hey look, I know you already know who I am. But in the comics, you don't know my secret identity. The whole reason my comics are in first person is so that nobody knows my face. Sooo, if you could just give me a live reaction to this grand reveal, well, that would be super," said Flash Girl with a smile.

"This isn't a game, June. I need him dead, and I need to kill him!"

"Our mild-mannered comic enthusiast knows that she can only reach her sister as long as she keeps her alter ego hidden beneath her mask," narrated Flash Girl as she put on the mask.

"Flash Girl is the alter ego not the other way around, Juniper." Chipko punched the ground. It instantly rose up, sending Flash Girl flying. The environmentalist jumped up and grabbed onto her sister. As soon as they hit the ground, Flash Girl was behind her.

The super speedy girl swiped her sister off her feet and took off her mask. "Honestly, I'm terrified about this whole thing. I mean that dark cloud eyeball thing captured me, but he let me go so I could, and I quote, 'keep things interesting.' That means he must have known you would try to do this, July. Are you sure you want to fall into his scheming hands?"

"You know how much this means to me," said Chipko, causing a minor tremor to destabilize her sister.

June leaped over the incoming shockwave. "Sorry, sister. I'm not the helpless little girl you once knew. I'm a superhero now, and if you don't stop, you're going to become a villain."

"Seems to me, superheroes make more villains than they stop." Chipko jumped up and grabbed her sister's legs.

"July, don't do it!" yelled August, looking exasperated and beaten.

Distracted for an instant, Chipko met a flurry of kicks to the face by her younger sister.

"Ugh, I feel awful." June slipped her mask back on. "If you're going to be a villain, then I will stop you as a hero!"

"Hey, June, lay off her!" yelled August.

"For those of you who haven't read issues number sixty-seven through seventy-two, Flash Girl's brother is a top-class bounty hunter known as Crimson August. She faced him in the past but lost. However, that was at a time when she had yet to make her secret technique."

"Goddamn it, June. Just play dead so we don't have to hurt you," said August.

Flash Girl took off her mask. "Okay, so I'm seriously confused. Weren't you fighting July earlier?"

"Yeah, but now she gets that Zenero has to die! You were on Earth at the time. Zenero ordered Bob and...May is dead."

"It's true," said Chipko softly.

"Stop! He did what? Nobody told me about this. Oh, I'm definitely not letting anyone free that villain," said June, putting her mask back on.

The floor sunk under the heroine's feet before sending her up.

"Sorry, but we're going to have to cripple you if you don't stand down," said August, propelling himself up while raising his steel-plated fists.

Flash Girl rapidly kicked his arms, avoiding direct contact with her brother's reinforced hands.

A shockwave hit her from behind before August's fists crashed into her chest.

Flash Girl fell to the ground, coughing up blood. "Shit, are you kidding me? There's not supposed to be this much blood in my comic." She struggled to get back to her feet. "Secret Technique: *FLASH FINISH*!" The super girl sped up to her sister and used her fingers on her pressure points. "Before you call plot device, please read issue number ninety-four where I was trained by a pacifistic assassin."

Chipko fell to the ground. "I can't move."

"That's right! Flash Finish is a completely painless immobilization move deemed boring by my fans. Now I only use it in a pickle, and this sure was a big jar of pickles."

"You should pay attention!" yelled August, sending his fist her way. With a look of utter bewilderment, he was knocked off his feet by his own fist.

"By using Tai Chi alongside my incredible speed, I can make my foes attack themselves. Read the next issue, which will be a double feature, explaining how Flash Girl learned this ancient martial art," she said with a smile before immobilizing the veteran bounty hunter.

"I'm sorry, sister," said Chipko softly.

Chipko embraced her dear sister, wrapping her arms and legs around her. She brought the stubborn girl to the ground.

"Our hero would have escaped already, but her head is dizzy because her secret move failed."

"I may have been immobilized, but my capsule still circulates, so I always have a pulse. I amplified that pulse to reconnect my joints. Here's a special technique. I made it just for you." Chipko slammed her foot down harshly.

The ground shot up, boxing both of them in a long clear chasm.

"Flash Girl is in danger! Come back in three issues to see what her fate will be!" The super girl took off her mask. "Okay, seriously? Are you really going to hurt me, July? I'm your little sister!"

"I know you're a tough girl, Junie. **Shockwave Amplifier!**" Chipko punched the wall violently. Her shockwave ricocheted off the wall, knocking her sister off her feet and becoming more powerful each time it bounced. "Now you're mine." She placed her hand on her sister's chest. "**Shockwave Burst!** I'll take over narration for you, little sis. Our mighty heroine was downed by the reinforced shockwave." Chipko crouched down and thrust her arm into her sister's chest. "What will our brave heroine do without her artifact?" asked Chipko with tearful eyes, clenching her sister's Amber artifact.

The ground fell back down revealing Chipko to be victorious.

Gimpy was suddenly choked by a whip and pulled in, keeping it from being sliced by the Agony Axe.

"Your master isn't here right now, which means you need to follow my orders, got it?"

Gimpy shook its head.

Tsul kicked its back and pulled on the whip, strangling the wretch. "How about now?"

Gimpy nodded with a dazed smile.

"Good puppy," said Tsul, stabbing her heel into the slave's back.

"Sel is dead. The conflict is over. I will not fight you," said Exp 8.

"Fine with me." Tsul pooled her aura into her whip-like arm. It expanded and transformed into a red whip with pink fluids dripping from its spikes. "Tremble in excitement for the Whip of Lust!"

"If you won't fight, then move," said Unity, firing the Appalling Arrow at the goddess.

The arrow shot into Exp 8's back.

Gimpy vanished and reappeared, standing atop the rebel's head. The slave kicked the enemy's face.

The Torture Trident plunged into Sel's servant before it was pulled in.

Gimpy moaned in ecstasy as its body was bombarded with pain.

"You haven't earned your reward yet!" yelled Tsul, tearing out the trident with her whip.

The Woeful Whip coiled around her Whip of Lust.

"That's one," said Tsul.

The Woeful Whip uncoiled and turned on its owner.

Unity blocked with the Searing Sword, but the blade overheated when wrapped by the whip.

"My whip is so potent that even souls can become slaves to its power!"

Exp 8 fired a massive orb at Gimpy.

The slave pointed above Exp 8 with a curious look.

The rebel's eyes widened when he saw his attack come down upon him.

"Now that's a good boy. Come here for your reward," said Tsul.

Gimpy teleported up to her.

She lashed her whip against the lustful slave's back, slicing it and filling it with her aura.

Gimpy's muscles expanded, and its body became coated in her aura.

Exp 8 jet boosted up to Gimpy. "Let's see how you handle this!" The rebel blinded Gimpy with one hand and slammed a wrecking ball of an orb, held in place by a gravity field, into his foe.

Gimpy was sent flying, and then it was sent flying the other way toward Exp 8.

"What the hell?" asked Exp 8.

Gimpy kicked off the orb and slammed its reinforced legs into the rebel leader.

Exp 8 was unfathomably sent back into his own orb.

Tsul strutted up to Unity, who was too busy battling its own weapons to counter attack. "Having trouble, are we?"

"I shouldn't have used Kawai to attack you," said Unity.

"Well, it's too late for regrets now. Don't worry. Soon all you'll know is carnal lust," she said, releasing pink smoke from her mouth.

"I'll at least take down one of you!" yelled Unity.

The Agony Axe swung at Gimpy.

The slave closed its eyes while it stood with trembling legs.

Exp 8 appeared in front of it and bore the brunt of the attack.

Gimpy then hopped onto the axe, joining in the pleasure ride.

"Stop messing around! We might still be able to save Sel!"

After gasping with its tongue out, Gimpy reappeared on Unity. With reinforced arms, it pried the god's mouth open. "Master, I'm here to rescue you." Its eyes went hollow.

There was nothing inside.

Evolution teleported behind Loyal and froze its tail, causing it to shatter upon impact. The ex-emissary created a shield inside Loyal and expanded it.

"Cease your attack at once!" exclaimed Limit, piercing Evolution with an Absence-coated lance.

The lance combined with whatever was beneath the cloak.

"𝔄𝔟𝔰𝔬𝔩𝔲𝔱𝔢 𝔏𝔦𝔪𝔦𝔱!" yelled the knight, binding the enemy with ethereal chains.

"Such passion, yet it only serves to keep things as they are," said Evolution.

Muffins fired an Absence-coated needle barrage at the bound intruder.

"I hardly recognized you," said Evolution, liquidizing the incoming assault.

"If I win, you all have to recognize me as the strongest god! ⒸOPYRIGHT!" exclaimed Plagiarism.

Loyal's wounds were healed as his body shifted. Once Plagiarism had become Loyal, the original Loyal completed his transformation as well.

"I may need an actual spell for this to work. 𝕊𝕀ℤ𝔼 𝔻𝕀𝕊𝕋𝕆ℝ𝕋𝕀𝕆ℕ!" exclaimed Evolution.

The two dragons shrank down to the size of lizards.

Separate made circles around the intruder and fired itself into Evolution like a machine gun. The amoeba was suddenly trapped inside a bubble, stopping the assault.

The smaller amoebas died before making contact, corrupted by an unseen illness.

Evolution emitted sound waves that swerved upward, avoiding contact with the gods. "Most peculiar."

Ethereal arrows appeared, graphing the readjusted trajectory of the sound waves.

"I suppose my attacks are worthless now," said Evolution.

"With enough force, he should break apart!" Occupy, kicked Void at the intruder from above.

"And so, it ends." Evolution overpowered Void's will and enlarged the enlightened rock, having it crush the gods below. The visionary shrank the stone and flicked it aside.

No longer bound by Limit's chains, it stood before Absence, having merged the other gods with the ground and frozen them solid.

"Why do you want to free Zenero?" asked Absence.

"I'm not sure I do," said Evolution.

"Then why do you want my artifact?"

"Does the answer matter, if you cannot stop me?" asked Evolution as his heart chakra let out a powerful light.

The golden artifact came out from Absence's chest and into Evolution's open hand.

Absence smiled. "You'll never find Zenero."

"Everything your artifact knows, I know." Evolution shoved its hand into Absence's eye. "A very clever place to hide the prison."

Absence coated his hands in his aura and reached out to grab hold of the thief but Evolution had vanished.

In the distance, Unity fell apart.

Sel opened up the Misery Mace from within and exited the mouth. It immediately rushed to claim the Compact Artifact but the figure had vanished. He glared at Absence. "Just so you know, I was playing dead so you'd come out of hiding. After seeing the old emissary, well, I decided to watch a bit longer. But now I'm free again and soon Zenero will be as well." The God of Destruction seeped into the ground.

"Well then, you should know that I never trusted you or Lum. I feigned ignorance at the Council Meeting to avoid confrontation," said Absence.

"Heheh. A lot of good that did you," said Sel, snickering under his spectral hands.

"Hey everyone, Sel's forces are retreating!" hollered Opti, keeping the Absence warriors motivated as they held back armadas of demons.

Evolution appeared in front of Chipko. "I believe this is yours," it said, offering her the gold nugget with one hand and the condensed prison with the other.

"What do you expect me to do?" asked Chipko.

"Your choice is inconsequential to me. Zenero won't stay imprisoned forever."

"I don't want it," said Chipko in tears, tossing the compact away.

Gimpy appeared and grabbed the compact.

Sel swiped the Compact Artifact from Chipko. "You were so busy trying to free me that you let some has-been take the spotlight! You were ordered to do three things. One, take the Teleport Artifact. Two, keep Occupy busy until Absence appeared. And three, claim his artifact when he showed up! You're a miserable failure who didn't have faith in its master!" The furious realm god teased Gimpy with spectral drills, making them phase through rather than pierce the wretch.

"Shockwave Cannon!" Chipko blasted Sel while he was distracted.

Gimpy caught the Compact Artifact and activated it.

Exp 8 grabbed Chipko as he flew by, keeping her from getting buried under the unfolding prison.

Tens of thousands of compacts were released from the prison compact.

"If you want to redeem yourself, you're going to find Zenero! Get to work!" yelled Sel.

Gimpy reverted each compact and then tossed them into a Sel portal.

"Why not just bring all the compacts to Sel so we can look through them in peace?" asked Tsul.

"Ugh, you understand so little. Half the fun of a breakout is seeing the warden's reaction," said Sel.

Absence appeared in front of Sel. "If you like fun, let's play a game. If Pathos and I end you before your minion goes through all the artifacts, you lose. As long as you live, we won't interrupt your minion."

"Are you sure about this?" asked Sellum.

"I must redeem this failure. Eliminating Sel is the only way I know how," said Absence, coating his fists in clear energy.

"It sounds fun enough. Just keep in mind I'm not trying to kill either of you. There will be time for that later," said Sel, firing a beam of darkness.

Sellum was hit by the beam but redirected it without suffering damage.

"That's a rather peculiar move," said Sel, creating spectral drills to assault his opponent.

"You will meet your end now!" exclaimed Sellum, creating a flying whale of Lum energy.

The whale opened its mouth, releasing a barrage of light.

"I only need to hold you off long enough to break Zenero out," said Sel, swerving out of the way of the barrage while shooting dark beams into the whale.

"If you can pin him down, I can finish him off!" hollered Absence.

Sellum appeared behind Sel. "At this point, I want to end him myself." The armor plating along Sellum's arms fell off, revealing lasers.

The lasers instantly locked on to Sel.

"Give up now or I will shoot," said Sellum.

"I'm not going to fall for your ruse," said Sel.

A line of Jiva appeared, held up by Sel's telekinesis.

"Have a taste of your own violence." Sel created a massive spectral hand that closed on Sellum and his minions.

Sellum escaped the hand. "That's why you didn't block," he said, coated in an armor of light.

"As if I ever need to!" Sel's eye shrank, increasing his focus.

Each mine sent Sel's way was knocked back by a spectral tennis racket.

Sellum zoomed around Sel in an attempt to avoid his own attack.

"Damn it, I can't concentrate," said Sel as he deflected the mines and fired Sel beams at the whale's incoming light rays.

Evolution grasped Chipko and placed a compact in her hand.

"You found him?" she asked, her face going red.

"You could crush him right now. It would be our secret."

Chipko shook her head. "I want him to know it's me. I want to see the look in his eyes as I tear out the capsule I once gave him."

"To be in love must be so mystifying," said Evolution.

"But we need the Compact Artifact. I...shouldn't have lost it."

"Regrets will not serve you. Just say the word and I shall reveal him."

"I'm scared," said Chipko, holding herself.

"Understandably." Evolution placed its hands on her shoulders. "You're out of balance. You of all people understand the importance of vibrations. Close your eyes and Ohm with me."

"O-okay." Chipko shut her eyes.

"Ooooooohmmmmmmm," they chanted together three times.

Evolution released his arms from her shoulders. "There. Now, are you ready?"

Chipko set the compact on the ground. "Do it."

Evolution snapped its fingers.

Zenero appeared, trapped behind a clear wall.

"Wait. I don't need this anymore. Give it back to June," she said, handing Evolution the Flash Artifact.

"Your gift is well received. I'm sure your sister will understand."

"I hope so."

"Only a matter of time before the others notice," said Evolution, handing her the Teleport Artifact.

"Thanks," said Chipko, placing the traveler's stone in her chest before teleporting inside the prison.

"You came for me," said Zenero in awe. His golden eyes softened upon seeing her. The once legendary man was a scared and naked wretch.

Chipko stiffened her fist as she stepped up to face him.

Zenero touched her fist and cried. "I've missed you so much."

The anger in her eyes vanished. Chipko embraced him and sobbed.

"That's it, let me take in all your sorrows," he said, caressing her head.

"Did you order Bob to kill May?" asked Chipko, her voice trembling.

"Oh, you poor dear. I never got a chance to tell you. She's on Earth with your brother Atlas and your sister Durga."

"I've looked for her and she's nowhere. How can I trust you?"

Zenero interlaced their fingers and kissed her hand. "Is this a gift?" he asked, grasping the traveler's stone in her palm.

Chipko pushed him off. "No. I won't let you use me again."

"Calm yourself, my dear. It must not have been easy finding me. Did Bob help you out?"

"Yeah…he's the one who staged this breakout."

"As expected. His deceitfulness ironically makes him quite dependable," said Zenero with a slight smile.

"Casey convinced him to. I don't know what she told him, though."

"She would willingly give up her life just to keep me alive. Her faith in me comes from love, not understanding. This pointless infatuation brings her to believe whatever I say is right."

"But, you still love her…don't you?"

"Not once during my duration here did I think of her. Blind love no longer interests me. Still, I suppose she deserves some appreciation."

Chipko clasped his hands; her cheeks became rosy. "You thought about me? Are things going to be like they were before?"

Zenero slid his arm behind her and pulled her into an embrace. "I couldn't stop thinking about you. And no…things aren't going to be the same."

Their lips met. When they parted Zenero looked pained. "I must know, why would you help me? I crushed your heart and yet its smashed remains still pulse for me."

"I wanted to see you…so I could kill you," said Chipko, trembling.

Zenero smiled. "You look more beautiful than ever."

"I love you," said Chipko, kissing him as tears ran down her cheeks.

"Let's combine our power," said Sellum, coating his fist in a clear aura.

Absence pressed his head to the ground and sobbed. "They found Zenero. I've failed you!"

"Not yet you haven't. I'll keep Sel busy. You need to kill Zenero," said Sellum, creating a portal inside the prison.

Zenero vanished, leaving Chipko kissing the air. He appeared in front of Casey, fully adorned. He wore a red and gold robe that draped over his body like theatre curtains. His golden eyes shimmered beneath his glasses. "I need you to die for me."

Casey took a step back. "What?"

"We haven't time to waste. It's the only way I can save this world. Will you do it for the man you love?" he asked, offering her a metal spoke in his open hands.

Casey teared up as she grasped it. "Will you hold me as I die?" she asked, shivering as she pressed the spike into her chest.

Zenero teleported the spoke away. "It was a mere test. I'll meet with you shortly." He pushed her into an open portal, closed it, and vanished when Absence showed up.

"I won't fail!" yelled Absence.

Zenero appeared before August.

"You're free again?" asked August, motionless on the ground.

"You've seen better days."

"When I'm back at full strength, I'm going to kill you."

"Will that make you feel better about being attacked by the woman you love?"

"You ordered Bob to kill May!"

"May is alive on Earth. Oh, but we'll discuss your pointless vengeance at a later time," said Zenero, teleporting August away.

Absence grabbed Zenero's arm. "I haven't failed yet."

"You won't kill me."

"I don't really have a choice anymore."

"You fear responsibility. Why don't you just curl up in a ball where time no longer holds meaning? Oh, my apologies. You've lost your artifact, haven't you?"

"What are you waiting for? Do it!" yelled Sellum, holding Sel back by pooling his energy into a light cage.

Zenero slipped out from Absence's grip and appeared in front of Sellum. "If you want to save this world, you will have to make sacrifices. If you hesitate, all you love will be destroyed by your misplaced sense of self-righteousness. This world needs a truly selfless leader who would cast aside their beliefs about justice to do what is right," said Zenero.

"As crazy as before, I see," said Sellum.

Zenero vanished just as Absence appeared to grab him.

The Exp inventor appeared directly in front of the white bars that kept Sel at bay. "Why did you free me?"

"You are the only one who has ever killed Pathos. Let's work together to end him again," said Sel.

"Hmm. What exactly do you plan to do once you are Sellum?" asked Zenero.

"I will take over Earth, and then I will go to all the other destinations and kill their gods. I will then be the supreme Sellum, and I will unite all realms. Everything shall be fair and just under my rule!" exclaimed Sel, firing reinforced dark beams against the light walls.

Zenero clapped four fingers against his palm. "That is a worthy reason to save me." He appeared in front of Sellum. "You heard what he said, right? He wants to save the world, yet you deem him a villain because of the extent of his ambitions. Is the line between a hero and a villain so thin? It would seem that heroes are too self-absorbed to be able to cast aside petty beliefs and even their integrity for the greater good."

"He's over here now!" yelled Sellum, once Absence appeared.

"I need some time to think things over." Zenero vanished and reappeared, holding Chipko bridal style.

"So, she's the one who rescued you. As expected," said Sel with a grin.

"You shouldn't discredit your own work. I'm truly thankful," said Zenero with a bow. He snapped his fingers and created a portal that Casey dropped out from.

"Wonderful! Casey, tell him the terms of his release," said Sel.

"What he does when he's released is up to him. I hope you and Pathos both end up killing one another."

"You think you can just back out on our deal!?" exclaimed Sel.

The light prison shattered.

The three gods rushed to grab Zenero.

"I wish you the best of luck. Teleport," said Zenero, vanishing along with Chipko.

Sel stared blankly into space, baffled by the betrayal. "Casey betrayed me. I was the pawn of my own pawn. Here I thought she wasn't paying attention! Oh, I'm so proud of her. Deception spreads like peanut butter, after all."

"You sure seem happy about losing," said Sellum.

"Zenero would have made things easier. But he is by no means necessary. I have all that I need," said Sel, snapping his spectral fingers.

Gimpy appeared, holding onto Stabby. He then vanished.

"Let her go!" yelled Sellum, zooming toward his cruel brother.

"We'll discuss the terms of her release once you've calmed down!" exclaimed Sel, seeping into the ground.

Sellum blasted the ground of Absence, searching for his treacherous brother.

"It's time I take my leave," said Evolution, looming over Kaity. The figure melted the ice around her.

Kaity gasped as she awoke. Her chest wound healed, recreating her heart in the process.

"When the time comes, I hope you'll stand at my side." Evolution vanished.

Chapter 170: Bargaining Chips

Meanwhile on Earth, the day of the exchange had arrived.

Hope sat patiently in a comfy chair. She was where her peace meetings with the Senator had begun.

"I'm nervous," said Kioshi, combing Hope's hair.

"Don't be or you'll mess up my hair. The Senator should arrive any moment. The man would have to be a complete fool to attack me when I hold the key to saving his species," said Hope, taking a sip of tea.

The space in front of them distorted into Agent Beta.

"What are you doing here? It goes without saying that if he wants the antidote, he'll have to meet with me in person. Leave and go fetch your leader," said Hope, shooing away the agent.

"I'm not here for the antidote. Your allies have all abandoned you. You've got nothing with which to bargain. I've come here to take your last possession," said the agent, ejecting energy and shaping it into claws.

"Get behind me," said Kioshi in a whisper.

"If you kill me, you'll never get the anti—" Hope's eyes shrank in horror.

"Your power to read people has left you wide open." Agent Beta pulled out a gun.

Kioshi shielded Hope from the ensuing bullet spray, her Flesh absorbing most of the impact.

"Stand down, Agent Pi, unless you're willing to die for her. Your mission as a double agent is over, so there's no need to defend her."

"No way am I standing down." Kioshi rubbed her hands together, forming energy blades.

"So, she's already broken you," said Beta, reloading the gun.

Kioshi shot the gun out from the agent's grip. "Hope hasn't broken me; she's pulled me together. She believed in me when nobody else did! She's my friend, and I won't let you kill her!" She ran toward Agent Beta and thrust the energy blade.

Beta grabbed the blade with her claws, twisting Pi's arm. She was suddenly behind the traitor and brought down her claws.

Kioshi kicked off the ground and dropped a smoke bomb.

"All you've done is blind your friend," said Beta with an intense gaze, appearing above her enemy. Her claws dug into the traitor's back before being pulled out, spraying blood.

Hope approached Agent Beta without fear. "Debbie, you have let fear inspire you ever since you were a child. Your benefactor found you in the trash in an alleyway in Italy after your parents discarded you."

"Hold your tongue, demon," said Beta with a crazed look. "Where did she go?"

Agent Pi stabbed two metal prongs into Beta's back and fried her with a powerful electric shock. "Bzzzt! Oh yeah, I'm a real agent now!"

"That's not a Hunter device," said Beta, slamming her elbow into Pi before kicking her aside.

"Ever since, you always felt inferior. Yes, your boss gave you life, but you never felt deserving of it. You tried to overcome this weakness by dedicating yourself fully to everything you did. Even your obsession with America fuels this inferiority because you know you're not American-born. You served the Senator diligently to become his top assassin, but you never could quite reach there, could you? I wonder why that is," said Hope with a cruel smile.

Pi leaped onto Beta's back. "You're going down!" she yelled, punching the agent's face repeatedly.

"Shut up! Shut up! Shut up!" yelled Beta, her hands shaking as she fired at Kioshi.

"You failed to reach your goal, and you'll always fail to reach it because deep down you know you aren't worthy! You sabotage your ascension by throwing a wrench in your benefactor's plans. You've done it many times in the past, and you're doing it right now," said Hope.

"Die, Exp," said Beta, struggling to fire as Pi wrestled her for the gun in her hand.

Pi sent the gun away with a gust. "Zapitty zap!" She grabbed Beta and violently electrocuted her.

"You! She gave you Crisis' artifact!" yelled Beta, slamming her head into her attacker.

Hope leaned over Beta. "It doesn't have to be this way. If you join me, if you stand by my side, you shall be known as Agent Alpha. You're far more skilled than the other Exp Hunters. The only thing holding you back is your own lack of self-worth." She offered a hand to the pitiful agent.

Beta sobbed and then smiled. "Kshkshksh, you think you've got me all figured out! I'm not dumb enough to fall for your trap! You've given me no reason to trust you."

"Right you are," said Hope with a smile. She moved her open palm to her follower. "Give me the Geo-Hazard Artifact."

"What are you…?" Kioshi looked at the confidence in Hope's eyes and placed her hand to her chest. "Okay. I trust you." She placed the green Olivine into Hope's open palm.

"I give you the power to end us both not out of trust but out of respect," said Hope, placing the Geo-Hazard Artifact into Agent Beta.

Debbie's eyes widened beneath her helmet.

"Get away from my daughter!" Deceivant entered the room, aiming Amy at the murderous agent.

"What are you doing here?" asked Hope.

"I came here to stop you myself," said Deceivant.

"Stop me from what?" asked Hope, taken aback.

"I know we're a despicable species, but killing all of us is wrong! I won't let you harm the children of this world. Come home with me and let's put an end to this."

"Stop it! Don't look at me with that wretched look. I have done nothing to deserve your fury," said Hope with watery eyes.

"You have a room full of scientists who you enslaved to make a virus to wipe out all humans! It's all over the news! They discovered them this morning. If you tell them where the other labs are, maybe we can still fix this. I won't let them execute you, but you need to surrender," said Deceivant.

Hope fell to her knees and sobbed.

"Kshkshksh, you've lost Hope. Agent Pi gave us the location. We have the antidote now. You can't outfox us. Thanks for the artifact," said Agent Beta, patting the stupid little girl.

"They didn't tell me this is what they were going to do! I just wanted to get the antidote to the people as soon as possible! I didn't set you up!" whined Kioshi.

"There's no need to pity her. Come with me and I won't tell the Boss about your treachery," said Agent Beta, offering Agent Pi her hand.

Hope wiped her eyes and mustered up all her strength. "Let me speak to him. Put your boss on the line," she said, her hands trembling.

"Still trying to salvage things even now. Your tenacity is hilarious! Kshkshksh!" Beta held her sides.

Kioshi called the Senator and gave Hope her phone.

"You've won," said Hope, trying to steady her hands. "I became overconfident. I take full responsibility for creating the virus. That means you must cease your attack on the Hero's Militia. None of them nor the Exps are to blame. I brainwashed them all."

"I hope you have that speech memorized. You can make that public statement when you're in handcuffs," said the Senator.

Hope dropped the phone.

Beta hoisted up the girl who didn't even bother struggling.

"Stop! I won't let you take my daughter away from me," said Deceivant, aiming the Gravity Gun.

"I must always take the best path for our independence. Do not try to stop her. I'm choosing to go with her," said Hope, unable to look at her father.

Deceivant fired a bullet that sent the agent off her feet. "I don't care what you chose! You're my little girl. I'm going to save you!"

Beta sent a wind gust that disarmed Deceivant. The next wind blast sent him out of the room.

Deceivant ran after them as quickly as possible but lost sight of them. He ran outside, but couldn't find Hope anywhere. "Kioshi, you have to find her!" he yelled, grabbing the agent when she stepped outside the building.

Hope was in handcuffs in the back of Beta's limousine.

"That was fun," said Beta, taking off her helmet.

Dramatic streaks of red decorated the agent's short white hair. Her eyes were black and her face was rough with scars.

"Don't speak...please," said Hope, her charisma as dry as a desert.

"You said a lot of really hurtful things about me. But you got one thing wrong. Guess what? Come on, guess," said the agent with a manic look.

"I guessed about the American obsession," said Hope.

"Oh, I'm definitely obsessed! America is an empire sowing chaos by enforcing order worldwide."

"You're insane. Do you have two personalities?" asked Hope, her throat dry.

"Well, you guessed wrong, buuut I'm going to tell you anyway! I don't self-sabotage because I feel inferior. I just really hate it when things go according to plan!" Agent Beta swerved off the road and went on to the highway on the other side. "Showing up and fighting you, part of the plan. Framing you for the outbreak, part of the plan. Turning you in to be executed, all part of the plan. It's all sooo boring!" She looked at the miserable girl from the rearview mirror as she drove backward through traffic. "You know what was fun?" Her eyes lit up with stars. "Fighting Agent Pi, you attacking me mentally, you giving me that artifact, your father fighting to save you...none of it was scripted! I sabotage my boss not because I feel unworthy of success. I do it because winning is boring, and he's too good at winning. You're the first challenge we've had in soooooo long!"

"Are you done gloating? I don't want to hear anything else."

"Aww, don't cry. I took a gamble. If you bored me, I would have killed you myself before you could make a public statement and then revealed the incident online via Wikileaks. Buuut you didn't bore me. So, I won't let you die. See, I moved the antidote before I got Pi to tell me it's location."

"I thought the Senator was my smartest foe," said Hope, a look of fear in her eyes.

Beta smiled a wide, almost inhuman smile. "Only I know where it is. You're going to expose the truth to the world, and my boss is going to have to make amends for his treachery. Exps running for governmental positions, that's going to make things quite interesting," she said with a deranged look.

Hope laughed through her tears. "The reason you're helping me is because it's fun?"

"You betcha!"

"You'd be wise not to reveal all your cards to your enemy," said Hope, drying her eyes.

"I know you won't turn me in to the Boss. You've got nothing to gain from it." She tossed Hope a red, white, and blue handkerchief. "Now clean your face up. You want to look good when you save humanity from extinction."

Meanwhile in Absence: once Sellum calmed down, Sel came out with his hands raised. "Let's not make a scene now. If you attack me, your little angel will have to be punished."

"What do you want?" asked Sellum, his hands trembling with rage.

"Well, I want the same thing everyone wants. I seek the end of this war," said Sel.

"I don't have the patience for your nonsense right now."

Kaity approached Sellum. "What happened?"

"He has Stabby."

"You never should have brought her here," said Kaity.

"He would have found her no matter where she was. I had my eye on her. I thought she would be safe in Casey's box. The box was just a way of hiding her from my sight."

"It was very kind of Casey to hand her daughter over to me," said Sel with a wicked smile.

"She's just a little girl," said Kaity softly.

"Well, she just so happens to be the perfect bargaining chip. Without Zenero's help, I have to improvise a bit. You should blame him if anything," said Sel.

"What do you want!" yelled Sellum.

"Goodness gracious! There's no need to shout. All I ask is that you fight me alone. Oh, and in a place of my choosing at a time of my choosing." Sel outstretched a spectral hand. "Deal?"

"How can we trust you'll keep your word?" asked Kaity.

"You can't, but you know from experience I'm not squeamish about torturing children. Besides, once Pathos is dead, I have no use for her," said Sel.

"I refuse," said Sellum.

"That's a good...what!?" screamed Sel.

"You heard me."

"You're just going to abandon her after making her your weapon? You really are a monster!" yelled Sel, aghast.

"You're the monster!" yelled Kaity. She turned to Sellum. "We're the only chance she's got."

"Stabby is stronger than you realize, Sel. She would gladly give up her life for the greater good," said Sellum.

"How kind of you to speak on her behalf," said Sel.

"She knows the importance of my mission. You can't sway me. And torturing her will gain you nothing."

"It will certainly help burn off some steam. And I'm feeling quite steamed at the moment."

"Of course! You designed her so she couldn't feel pain, right?" asked Kaity.

"Only at the physical level. There's nothing she can do to guard her soul," said Sel.

"You have my answer. Now leave this place," said Sellum.

"Wait," said Kaity after Sel made a portal. "I don't like this."

"Join the club," said Sel.

Kaity turned to Sellum. "You need my help."

"Indeed I do."

Kaity smiled. "Agree to Bob's terms. Do it or I'm never helping you again."

Sel flew into an embrace with Kaity. He pet her and snuggled her. "And here I thought you were a mere thorn in my side. You're really a good girl, after all."

Kaity's claws pierced Sel and he released her.

"Well, brother. What's your answer now?" asked Sel, circling around him.

"Kaity, why are you helping him?" asked Sellum monotone, his eyes leaking tears.

"I'm helping Stabby. She was forced into this situation, so blame yourself!"

"Ugh. I'm feeling ill. I'm actually dreading that I have to kill the little kitten," said Sel, cradling himself.

"So, if I agree to his terms, you will kill Lum?" asked Sellum, his helmet leaking tears and his hands shaking.

"Asking a sweet girl to kill her own mother. I'm ashamed to call you my brother," said Sel.

"Wait, I won't become Lum. Who is Lum after her?" asked Kaity.

Sellum grabbed her hands. "I need you to promise me."

Kaity nodded.

"I agree to your terms. Now release my daughter."

"She'll be released once our battle ends. I'll see you shortly," said Lord Sel before leaving.

"Don't you still have your Ultimatum? I mean, Bob can't bypass it, can he?" asked Kaity.

"He must believe he has found a way," said Sellum.

"I can't believe you were just going to abandon her," said Kaity.

"There's no way of knowing if he'll keep his word."

"That doesn't matter. If there's even the slightest chance he will, you have to take it. She's your daughter, isn't she? Don't you love her?"

"Of course I do."

"You're so logical that you're forgetting who you're fighting for. They aren't numbers; they're individuals."

Sellum beamed at her. "Thank you."

"When this is over...I don't want to see you ever again."

"I understand."

Etaf appeared directly in front of Kaity. "Kaity, I don't know how she did it but Lum..." said the goddess.

"How did you get here?" asked Kaity

"Huh?"

"I asked how a Lum god found her way to Absence."

"Well Crystal showed up and—"

"Did he have a black hood?" asked Sellum.

"I have to hurry back. I only came here to warn you."

"When Zenero first came to Sellum, you worked with Bob. Care to explain?"

"It's your choice if you want to trust me. I came to tell you Lum has Nina hostage," said Etaf, creating a Lum portal.

"Tell her I got your message," said Kaity with a shaky voice.

"She didn't send me. If you don't come alone, she will kill her," said Etaf before leaving into a portal of light.

"You handled that well," said Sellum, about to pat Kaity's shoulder but stopping.

"Etaf can't be trusted. The fact that she appeared after Bob left makes me even more suspicious. And if she is telling the truth that Lum didn't send her, then that means Sel did."

Sellum beamed at Kaity.

"Stop staring at me," said Kaity, reaching up and covering his eyes.

"My apologies. So, what's the plan?"

"I'll go to Lum and see if it's true. I mean, I know the government has her but...I have to go to be certain," said Kaity softly.

"We should regroup with the others and think this through," said Sellum, creating a portal to Earth.

"If it is true, if she hurt Nina...I am going to make her wish she never birthed me," said Kaity coldly.

"Stay vigilant. And if you're going to strike her down. You're going to need the power of Sel. I'm lending you everything I have," said Sellum, pooling dark energy into Kaity.

"Soon it's going to be over, one way or another. Can you send me to the Observatory?" asked Kaity.

"Against my better judgment?"

"Send me there now."

"The Sel energy I gave you cannot be replenished. Be strong and be vigilant. Lum can be very deceptive."

"You're not my father. You got him killed."

"I'm just...worried for you."

"I can't die. I'll be fine."

"If Lum is coercing you to fight, she may have found a way around that."

"Make the portal."

Sellum created the portal.

Kaity turned to him with a stern look. "Don't get killed, okay? If you do, you're putting me in danger. Don't forget that."

"My prayers are with you," said Sellum, bending down and kissing her forehead.

"Good luck," said Kaity before leaving into the portal.

Kaity arrived in the Observatory. She ran up the clear steps and blasted open the light wall guarding the Quwwat al Nur. At the foot of the steps was her old comrade and friend, Violet Gold. In the Goddess of Love's arms was Napkin.

"If you want to get to Lum, you'll have to kill me," said Evol, her eyes a vacant white.

Kaity ran past Violet and into the mosque of light.

Lum appeared past the model garden of light, safely seated behind a fortified shield of her energy. "Nina has been waiting for you."

"Where is she?" asked Kaity with a glare.

Evol sped in front of Kaity. "Kill me with love and she will be saved."

Lum sat on her aura, which went up like a minaret and crashed against the ceiling. "You had best hurry. Nina doesn't have long before her life ends." A portal appeared and Nina was inside. Her face was twisted with pain and she screamed out in agony. "Never seen her like that, have you?"

"One life in exchange for the balance of Sellum. It's a fair trade," said Evol, creating dual aura blades.

Napkin poured a thin yellow fog into the destined Sellum. He then hopped into a Lum portal, leaving a trail of tears.

Kaity wiped her tears away. "Kill or die. I thought that was how it was. But…I've never really ever put anything on the line. I was immortal as an assassin. I'm not as good as I thought I was, not even half. The third option won't work here. So…I'm sorry Violet, but I'm going to have to kill you."

"I can feel love in every word you say," said Violet, caressing Kaity lovingly.

Kaity hugged her and sobbed.

In the Core, Efil was bound in chains and sobbing.

"Dry your tears," said a voice from the shadows.

Efil beamed at the approaching figure. "Etaf! You've come to rescue me."

Etaf smiled and undid the bindings holding her dear friend.

"I don't know what Sel planned to use me for, but we should hurry and leave. That minion of his is no longer here, but it could return at any moment."

"I know what he's planning," said Etaf.

"You do? How do you know?"

"Well, that's simple really." Etaf flashed her a smile. "I'm a spy."

Efil grabbed her friend's hand. "You were spying on Sel to find out his plans. We must return to the Great Goddess and share what you've learned with her!"

Etaf focused her aura and summoned up the Destiny Sword. "I should have made it clear. I'm Sel's spy."

Efil's eyes shrank. "Huh?"

Kaity's plamsa-claws pierced Evol's chest.

The goddess pulled back and felt the wound.

Kaity sped past her and shot into the light barrier. She clawed at it ferociously.

"You must be patient. I will lower the barrier as soon as she is dead."

"Why do you hate me?" asked Kaity in tears.

Evol appeared behind Kaity and molded the barrier around her, pinning down her arms and legs.

"I gave up everything for you. And in the process, I lost who I was. I became a killer like you. You made me into the monster I am now," said Lum.

Evol slashed at Kaity's back with her astral blades.

"I am a destined Sellum! I won't die so easily!" Kaity's wounds released Sel energy that floated toward her friend.

Evol created a path around the attack and formed an aura spear. She tossed it into Kaity.

The spear was gripped by the encroaching Sel energy and promptly thrust into the light barrier.

The spear was purified almost instantly.

"This shield is so powerful that only the true Sel would be able to penetrate it," said Lum.

Kaity used Sel energy to eat away her hands and feet. She was then pierced by another aura spear. The spear planted itself in the barrier.

Six more aura spears pierced into her back.

Lum looked away. "As a destined Sellum, your soul recreates your body automatically when you die. It does this because Sellum's word is so powerful that your destiny is unavoidable. But what would happen if the soul itself was attacked? Evol's attacks are made from astral energy and can cause harm to the soul. Your life is on the line, my dear. You best fight back before you meet your end."

"Her name is Violet," said Kaity softly. Dark energy erupted from her severed wounds and converged at a single point. The energy pierced through the barrier, creating a small crack in it.

"That's not possible."

"Not alone it wasn't," said Kaity, flashing a smile at Violet. She pierced her own heart with her tail, regenerating her hands and feet as she resurrected. "Napkin took away my fears, and Violet gave me the energy boost I needed. Your allies are leaving you one after another."

Lum smiled. "Your immortality has its limits, my dear. Etaf shall take care of you." The Lum shield shattered, and the Great Goddess teleported Evol away. "Where is Etaf?"

Etaf stood before her dear friend. "I've caused you a great deal of trouble, and for that I apologize," said the goddess with a pained look. "I promise you things will be different once I become Lum. You'll finally be respected the way you deserve to be."

Efil let go of Etaf's hand and backed away.

398

"There's no need to be afraid. I didn't free you so I could kill you. And as long as I don't try to kill you, then you can't kill me either. One of us will die, but not today. Perhaps you'll remove me from the throne when the time comes."

"I don't understand anything you're saying," said Efil in tears.

"Sel needs your power. I can only exert my influence over someone as strong as you when they're emotionally unstable. Just a bit more and I can create a new destiny for you," said Etaf, her sword glowing with energy.

"You're my friend. We both serve Lum devoutly. How can you even say these wretched words?"

Etaf brought her sword down and Efil leaped back. "This isn't easy for me. Seeing my friend look so hurt and betrayed. Let's just get this over with. Don't worry; we won't be using your powers on Lum. She already selected me as an heir. Kaity will kill her. We need you to end Sellum."

"I will not be part of any evil plot."

"There is no good or evil, no right or wrong nor is there truth or fiction. There is only functional and dysfunctional. Some of us are destined to be angels, while others are doomed to live as demons. The threats we've built our society to escape from are unknowingly sewn into the fabric of that society. Angels shine the brightest when compared to detestable demons."

"But you're an angel not a demon. We're both goddesses of Lum."

"I'm sorry, *mataki*. Don't think I decided to walk this path…I had no other choice," said Etaf, grinding her teeth.

"You're being threatened. Whatever threat he made, we can overcome it together."

"Don't be naïve. You're the only one I care about, so Sel can't threaten me. You have no idea just how special you are. Remember the old prophecy deeming you as the key to ending the War of Sellum? Well, maybe this is the moment it was talking about. Your power can render the Omni God mortal."

Fear corrupted Efil's eyes.

"You do understand. Pick up your blade then. That destiny hasn't been written. You still have a chance to stop Sellum from dying."

"Etaf works for Bob. She has been since you first became Lum. You saw her fight your brother back when Zenero betrayed you, so you should know about it," said Kaity, rushing at Lum with her plasma claws.

"You saw what happened? Then you must understand, now more than ever, why Sel must be stopped." Lum created trees to deflect the attacks and mask her location. "There is no one more loyal to me than Etaf. She has no will of her own, which means my will is her will."

"She posed as you while you were posing as Sefiwah. She turned us against you and acted as our friend." Kaity fired Sel energy at the goddess.

"All according to my wishes," said Lum, creating balls of light that deflected the attacks before dispersing.

Kaity coated her claws in darkness and slashed at the light beams. "Why would you have her tarnish your name?"

"I had her act with my authority so that when you learned how treacherous she was, you would come into my arms. Etaf acts upon my will without me even asking. After Exp 8's rebellion, she was the one who captured you on Earth and turned you over to Etah. I needed you to hate Sel so you would stand by my side. And she needed a way to earn Sel's absolute trust. I'll admit I was hurt when I first learned what she had done, but my pain subsided once I knew she was acting for the greater good. Etaf is my spy. Her loyalty to me is absolute. When Sel nearly struck me down inside Samsara, it was she who defended me," said Lum, blinding Kaity with a powerful light.

"If she's so loyal, why isn't she here when you need her most?" Kaity's claws sliced through the darkness and then slashed Lum.

Lum gripped the corrosive wound and healed it. "Etaf is on an important mission to rescue Efil from Sel's clutches. I don't need her to protect me from you. You're the one who must be careful, my kitten. Nina's life is in my hands."

Efil and Etaf were crossing swords.

"I'm surprised you still have enough Lum energy left to create a light sword. Your determination is to be commended, but your form is sloppy. I taught you better," said Etaf, slicing Efil's arm after a successful parry.

Efil increased the speed of her strikes, pushing Etaf into a corner. "Once you are beaten, you shall tell me the truth! I know you love Lum. She shared with me that you rescued her from Sel in Samsara. If you were loyal to him, you never would have done that."

Etaf kicked her dear friend and swung the Destiny Sword. "That's exactly what we wanted her to think. Saving her life put me in the absolute circle of trust. I used that trust to convince her to send you to Absence where Sel's forces lied in wait. I saved her life just to capture you. Killing Lum won't be enough to end Sellum's life; only your power can make him mortal."

"If you truly mean to stand against the Great Goddess, I will cut you down." Efil pooled her aura into a blade and thrust it at Etaf.

The Goddess of Fate parried with her own sword and sliced Efil yet again. "You do realize Lum has already been replaced twice since you became a goddess, don't you? The latest one hasn't even been ruling for a year. Why would you fight for her?"

Efil's time blade pierced through her armor and touched the tip of Etaf's throat. "If you become Lum, I will fight for you too. Until then, I will serve the current Lum. You've lost. Lower your weapon. Whatever is bothering you, it will pass."

Etaf's eyes teared up as she looked at her dearest friend. "History is made tolerable through periodic renewal. As a shaman, I felt that I was a part of bringing in a new era at the end of each year. This new era was supposed to free me of the karmas of my past, but it never did. There are no cycles anymore. It's all linear, and perhaps it always was. Even death just led me into another cursed life. There is eschatological escape from fate. My people, like many humans, were just trying to control that which they had no power over. They're all gone. Every single Shitumbe died because of me. No ceremony could change that. Lord Sel helped me accept my fate. He supported me, and he showed me there was a way around it."

"Let go of your weapon," said Efil, shivering in tears with her blade still pressed to her dear friend's neck.

"The Kali Yuga is the age where there is more darkness than light. It is the age we are living in now. It shall bring about the downfall of mankind, but what if instead of working against it, I nurtured and directed it?"

"But Sel is the home of the humans. If you want to contain the human threat, you must help Lum not Sel."

"That's what I thought at first, but downfall doesn't necessarily mean death. It could simply mean corruption. The rise of the corrupted, of Sel, could be seen as the downfall of humanity."

"So, you're working with Sel because of the age we live in?"

"This isn't just an age. The Iron Age is the final age. I told you before there is no renewal. Time is linear! Thus, bringing about the Kali Yuga will put an end to everything, not just the humans."

"Is that really what you want?"

"It's never been about what I want. I've been cursed since I was born, so my only escape is to join the cursed."

"Regardless, you have lost."

"Not so. The Destiny Sword has a special power that not even you know about."

"Such power is empty without devotion."

"Stigmata!"

The cuts on Efil's arms and legs grew till they severed her limbs entirely.

"Now to carve a new destiny for you!" exclaimed Etaf, slicing up her dear companion with the tip of the blade.

"If my death will stop Sel, then I embrace it!" Efil's Lum energy gripped her severed arm and lifted it. She brought the time blade to her throat but stopped in place. "Why can't I do it? I'm not afraid," she said in tears.

"Our fate has already been written. Unless we are both fighting to the death, neither of us can die. Now that you're full of my essence, let's create a new path together. **Destiny Genesis**!"

The wounds on Efil's body glowed and came together, forming Luminos script above her like a halo.

Etaf collapsed to her knees. "I've done it. I've finally created my own destiny. And this small destiny is just the beginning. Fate will bend to my will before I destroy it entirely!"

Chapter 171: Promises or Lies

In Absence, Riufen approached the realm god.

"So, you're the one Sel sent to kill me," said Absence.

"I only seek an honorable battle."

"And if I die, what will become of my people? What will your honor do for them?"

"I will allow you to choose the location."

"I have no reason to accept your challenge. Tell me, swordsman, why do you serve Sel?"

"I want to surpass his power, but I realize that following this path will cause me to lose my integrity as a warrior. After this battle, I shall sever my ties with him," said Riufen.

"Couldn't you leave before you fight me?" asked Absence.

Riufen shook his head. "Why discard this chance? I want to test your power first hand."

"Why would that matter to me?"

"If I cut you down, I will forbid Sel to harm your realm."

"And if I win?"

"If I give the idea any power, then I have already lost."

"I've been imprisoned for so long that I lost my fighting spirit. I followed my Great Swami's orders and my realm has suffered for it. I failed my realm and him. I accept your challenge. Either I will rise to be the courageous leader this realm needs or Absence will lose what is holding it back."

"Where shall we battle?"

"There is a mountain peak in Lum I've heard about. The tallest in the realm. I believe Olympus will be a fitting venue for our bout. Loyal, send us there."

"Are you certain you want to leave this realm unguarded?" asked the dragon god.

"Sel will not attack again until Lum falls. Occupy, you and Void are in charge until I return."

"We will not fail you," said Occupy.

Absence looked at the bodies of his warriors strewn across the realm. "I pray this conflict ends soon."

Sel appeared before Sellum. "Shall we get started?"

"Started with what?" asked Sellum with a curious look, pouring Lum energy into June.

"Don't play dumb. We had a deal."

"Oh, I just lied about that to get Kaity to do what I wanted."

"No! No! No! No! You can't just back out. That's cheating!"

June smiled. "Nice one, bro. You got him good."

"Liar! Liar! Liar!" yelled Sel.

"I'm not above lying or cheating. There is someone very dear to me who taught me all about it." Sellum patted Sel's head.

"Your little girl is being tortured as we speak!" yelled Sel.

"Not if you're here she isn't."

"Rrrgh! Don't test my patience."

"If you want me to comply with your request, you're going to have to meet my demands first."

"I won't let you control me!"

"Shame, you were so close to achieving your goal."

"Fine! What do you want?"

"What am I saying? There's no way I can trust your word."

"Says the coward who just backed out on our deal!"

"You're going to open the portal to Earth in your realm."

"You're not going to make this easy, are you? How can I trust that you'll follow through once I have?"

"If I don't, you can simply close it. Just keep in mind that each second it is open you lose thousands of souls."

"Do you really want all those dirty souls to return to Earth?"

"You closed the portal to increase the size of your army."

"They don't deserve another chance!"

"Without a sizeable army, you won't be able to mount an offensive on Lum. What do you want more, Lum or Sellum? It's time to choose, brother."

Sel spun around, muttering curses. He then created a portal. "Let's get this over with."

"Wait up." June got up to her feet. "Send me to Earth first. I gotta find July so I can get my powers back."

"As you wish," said Sellum, creating a portal to Earth.

"Enough errands! Let's get this over with!" yelled Sel, pulling Sellum with him into the Sel portal.

They arrived on the molten peak of the highest mountain.

A massive chair of bones and flesh stood atop the peak.

"So, this is where you hid it?"

"Yes. It was. Just so we're clear, if I open up the portal, you will fight me where I choose, and if you flee, your daughter will have her soul taken from her and tormented for all eternity."

"That's the deal," said Sellum, patting his younger brother.

Sel muttered angrily as he lifted up the throne. Veins split apart from the ground, oozing blood down the mountainside.

"Oh wait, there's one more thing. If I follow through, neither you nor any of your pawns are ever allowed to harm my children," said Sellum.

"Not even Abyss? I thought you hated him," said Sel with a disappointed look.

"As the memory fades, so does the resentment. It's unfair, but that's how we learn to forgive. I have faith that he has changed since then, thus I forgive him. You'd never forgive me no matter how much time went by, would you?" asked Sellum.

"My grudges are eternal," said Sel with a smile.

"Is it a deal?" asked Sellum.

"It is an oath," said Lord Sel with a devout bow. The throne was fully removed and thrown aside. The swirling vortex opened up.

Tsul appeared. "What is going on, my lord?"

"We're opening the portal. Moderate who gets through."

"They can only climb this mountain if their soul is not too heavy. Otherwise, they will tumble down back into the inferno. My lord, why are you opening it?"

"Because we've already won. There is no need for an army anymore," said Sel.

"I'll prepare the souls for their next journey," said Tsul with a bow.

"So where do you want to finish this?" asked Sellum.

"We shall go to Lum's throne," said Sel.

"Why there?" asked Sellum.

Sel turned as a smile took over him. "I just want to see them die; that's all."

"Very well then, take us there," said Sellum. A long awkward silence was finally interrupted by Sellum's monotone laughter. "You can't, can you? Oh, this is too funny. You need me to make a portal to the place where you want to kill me."

Sel glared at him.

Sellum composed himself and formed the portal.

Famine arrived in a realm of darkness. "He put her in danger and now he's abandoned her in this hellhole!"

Muffins covered her ears.

"Sorry. I appreciate you bringing me here. Do we know where she is?"

Muffins shook her head.

"I wouldn't trust him to save her, so I guess this works out. He at least knows that I'm more than capable of rescuing her. Sister! Where are you?" he asked, fumbling around in the darkness.

"Bwother!" yelled Stabby.

"Must be nice to have a real sibling," said Yvne.

Famine detached something from his belt.

The device lit up and illuminated the area.

"I'll give you one chance to stand down. I'd rather not have my sister see me transform," said Famine, ready to bite into his arm.

"A transformation? That sounds pretty neat," said Yvne with shimmering eyes.

"Not you too."

"Just as you're loyal to your sister, I'm loyal to my comrades. This little one is what is keeping Sellum in Lord Sel's control. Without her, the Dark One can't kill him."

"My sister isn't some tool for your boss' game. Free her now!"

"Hmmm. Nope," said Yvne.

Famine ran past Yvne and rushed to the prison. He grabbed onto the bars. "I'll get you out of there, just hang on."

Yvne's arm transformed into a drill and plunged into the intruder.

Stabby screamed as her brother was shredded before her eyes, his blood soaking her terrified face.

"Remember, sis…I may not always be around to rescue you. You've got to save yourself sometimes," he said with a weak smile.

Stabby nodded. She lapped up the blood on her face and arms. Knives burst out from her fingertips and her teeth.

"Being a monster doesn't seem so bad now. I don't feel alone anymore," said Famine, touching her metal fingers through the thick bars.

"Bwood!" Stabby's eyes went red, and she sliced open the bars with her super sharp fingers.

Famine hoisted her up into his arms as she cut into his flesh. "Let's go back home."

"As if I'd just let you escape." Yvne turned into a fusion of the two siblings. The new body was short like Stabby but muscular like Famine. Bladed hands and mouths adorned her latest form, though the blades and teeth weren't quite as sharp as the originals.

"Oooh. Stabby…Abyss. Stabbyss!" cheered Stabby.

"That's cute but stay focused," said Abyss, poised for the incoming attack.

Muffins coated her quills in Absence energy and fired at the Sel goddess.

"Not the bunny!" yelled Yvne, failing to shield herself from the needles. Muffins created a portal and they all went in.

Yvne stared blankly. "Did I just fail?" Her eyes widened. She went inside the prison, fixed the bars, and transformed into Stabby. "What Lord Sel doesn't know won't hurt me."

Lum's body emitted vines that coiled around Kaity's arms, keeping her plasma claws out of reach. "You've poisoned me with your miasma, but all that ends today."

"I came here for Nina. Release her now," commanded Kaity.

"It isn't easy for a mother to kill her own daughter. I'm going to use Nina to fully expose the demon within you," said Lum, dispelling the light above.

On the ceiling of the structure was Nina, pierced by blades of light.

"You made this demon!" Kaity's Sel energy seeped into her claws, elongating them.

Lum tossed Kaity aside and fired a spray of light bullets. "Soon I will be free of this pain." Lum gripped her aching chest. "Sel's mere existence is so vile it causes me agony. Your father made you a living weapon, and I infused you with the genetics of the greatest hunter that walks on this planet. We enhanced you together."

"My father was being controlled by Bob. You and he are the ones who turned me into a killing machine!"

"I have cultured you into something that can defeat Sel. You chose to kill. And you chose to make love to me."

"You seduced me with lies!" yelled Kaity, shooting Sel blasts from her fingertips.

Lum teleported behind Kaity and brought her to the ground. Her vines coiled around Kaity's leg. "I wasn't lying. I'm all you'll ever need. I care for you deeply," she said, caressing her kitten.

"Oh yeah? Is that why you slept with Devlin?" Kaity turned around to slash her foe.

"I was testing to see what his intentions were since he was fond of you. I went so far as to try and get pregnant so he would be forced to abandon his quest for your heart," said Lum, stopping the claws with her light-coated fingers.

"And you never even told me! Love is about trust and respect!" Kaity's Sel energy came out from her arms and bit into Lum.

The Great Goddess' wounds released light, dispelling the darkness. "True love is potent and intoxicating. Once you're dead, Kanasta will be next. I shall purge this world of all of its evil," said Lum, washing Kaity away with a torrent of water.

"You're the one holding a hostage," said Kaity, running up the walls.

"Do you love Nina?" asked Lum, sending a homing light arrow at her daughter.

"Absolutely," said Kaity, dodging at the last instant as she closed in on Nina.

"Do you love who she is or what Deceivant made her into?" asked Lum, appearing before her daughter.

"I love both Ninas," said Kaity, firing a Sel beam at the light rope holding up Nina. The future Sellum kicked off the ceiling and cradled Nina in her arms. "It's okay. You're safe now."

Lum appeared once more before Kaity. "I won't allow all my work to be ruined. HEAVEN'S WRATH!" Light erupted from the Great Goddess as a pillar.

Kaity created a shield of Sel energy as the light came crashing down.

The light pierced through and everything went white.

"I'm sorry I couldn't protect you," said Nina, struggling to speak.

Her lips met Kaity's.

The light flare faded.

Nina's body was gone.

Kaity held the empty air where her beloved had been. She turned around, a single thought now coursing through her mind: *Kill Lum!*

Chapter 172: Godhood

Sellum and Sel were at the entrance just outside the main hall of the Observatory.

Sel looked at his brother with weakness in his eyes. "You choose Kaity over your own brother. Is your infatuation with Tranquil really more important than the future of the afterlife?"

"When I first met Kaity, she was only four years old. She was crying about a bee sting. Her mother went to get ointment, but Kaity had run outside to make sure the bee was okay. A gentle soul like that, one who puts those who hurt them before themselves, they are the ones worthy to be Sellum."

"There is far more to being a leader than a kind spirit. I possess all the qualities necessary! You should have chosen me! You owed it to me! I deserved it!"

"You're like a child who didn't get the toy he wanted. Do you honestly think someone like you could keep things in balance?"

"A world where those with merits are not recognized is a world out of balance. But that shall be remedied soon enough." Sel fired a beam.

Sellum erased the beam with an Absence-coated hand. "I'm sure you realize that I am unkillable. Reveal your tricks now. I want to get this over and done with. Either way, your victory is impossible to claim."

"The impossible is merely preposterous. Ah, but you're right. We mustn't waste time." The God of Destruction reached into a portal and pulled out Efil.

"Do what you must, then let Efil go," said Sellum.

"I don't need to do anything," said Sel with a dark grin.

Efil's eyes were coated in Etaf's aura. She raised her hands at Sellum who walked up to her.

"You're not even going to try to dodge her?" asked Sel, floating just above his sworn enemy.

"Why bother?" asked Sellum with a shrug. "ⓇⒺⓋⒺⓇⓈⒺ ⓉⒾⓂⒺ ⓁⒶⓅⓈⒺ, ⓅⓇⓄⓁⓄⒼⓊⒺ!"

Efil's entire aura pooled into Sellum before she collapsed.

Sellum turned to Sel and tapped his chin. "I'm curious. What was that actually supposed to do?"

"How is your shield still standing? She reversed the time around it!" yelled Sel, slamming his spectral arms in a tantrum.

"Sellum's Ultimatum cannot be broken unless all three gods attack. You cannot manipulate time to revert me to the past where I was not Sellum. The God of Gods is eternal. Don't tell me you put all your stakes on this trump card of yours. That would make this entire feud a waste of time."

Sel and Sellum shifted their attention to a massive beam of light coming from the main hall.

"Oh, I've got plenty of backup plans, rest assured!" Sel's energy shot out as black tendrils.

Each tendril was blasted by Lum energy, revealing their spectral core beneath.

The spectral appendages grasped onto Sellum.

"Sellum is linked to all things in this galaxy. Why would the god of the afterlife succumb to soul attacks?"

"You'd be wise not to underestimate me! *Compact!*"

Sellum's armor condensed, making him grunt in pain. "Your ambition will only end when you're dead. So be it!"

Energy orbs came out from the god like pollen. Lum energy connected to the orbs and connected to Sellum's fingertips.

"**ORB ORCHESTRA**!" Sellum waved his hands like a conductor, blasting Sel with the field of orbs.

Sel went into his spectral form and moved through the field. He became physical once more, braving the orb's wrath. "You may be able to resist the power of the artifacts, but you cannot negate them! *Compact!*"

Sellum's armor condensed once more.

Sel knocked the incoming orbs aside. "You may have the power of the gods, but you aren't linked to the artifacts. You're going to be crushed with your own body! Ehahahaha!"

Sellum coated himself in Lum energy but was unable to heal the wounds. "**ZEMBLANITY**!"

The orbs moved in on Sel with a will of their own, following him even as he became incorporeal.

"Don't forget I have the power of all the Sel gods! *Anger Explosion!*" yelled Sel.

The orbs were triggered to burst while Sel was in the spectral realm.

Sel appeared in the aftermath of the blast and fired lasers at Sellum. "*Compact*"

Sellum's arms snapped along with his legs. He pooled Lum energy out to create energy hands and feet from his broken appendages.

"Oh, you look so adorable all broken and wounded. I bet you'll look even cuter after this." Sel's entire body glowed with spectral energy. *Absolute Compact*"

Sellum screamed as his body caved in on itself. The God of Gods was reduced to a small silver sphere.

Riufen looked up at the Observatory from the top of the snowy mountain, gazing at the pillar of light illuminating it. "It appears we aren't the only ones locked in combat."

"Focus on me. I am going to give this fight all that I have." Absence bowed to Riufen who returned the bow.

Riufen sheathed his sword. "Let us start using only our fists."

"As you wish," said Absence before rushing his adversary.

Riufen parried each punch with his own fists. His fingers broke when Absence suddenly increased the force of his punches. He took a few steps back, blocking with his arms. Noticing an opening, the immortal samurai, swiped the god's legs.

Absence caught Riufen's foot under his own and pressed down. He proceeded to assault the samurai with a rapid series of punches. "I will not fail my people!" The god slammed into Riufen who grabbed him by the waist.

The immortal swordsman flung the god over his shoulder only to be pulled down along with him.

Absence grabbed Riufen's arms and brought them behind his back, pinning him to the ground.

"I must improve my hand-to-hand combat. Thank you for this lesson," said Riufen as he was repeatedly slammed into the snow.

Absence coated his fist in energy and brought it down.

Riufen's veins came out from his arms and gripped the god's arm. "You nearly had me."

Absence sliced the veins using his other hand and punched a hole in the samurai's chest.

Lord Sel blasted Absence off with a Sel blast.

The god removed the corrosive energy with a single swipe of his hands.

"Why are you interrupting our battle?" asked Riufen, creating new flesh and bone to heal the wound.

"I've no need for this anymore." Lord Sel flicked the Compact Artifact at his swordsman. Use it to take him down, or don't. As long as you win, I don't care about your method." The God of Destruction flew off back into the Observatory.

"Plan to use my own power against me, do you?" asked Absence, standing firm.

Riufen approached his fellow combatant and pressed the Compact Artifact into his opponent's chest. "Now the real fight can begin."

Lum sent up a ball of light energy that burst and transformed into a rainstorm. "Now no one can see you weep."

Kaity's eyes were shrunken. She slashed at Lum in a crazed state.

"Did you forget that I'm Sefiwah?" asked Lum as she dodged each attack by inches.

Kaity thrust her claws forward.

Lum grabbed them and shoved them into the ground, pinning the wild girl down. "All evil shall be vanquished and light shall prevail. Only a truly just god would sacrifice their child for the sake of peace. You are my Christ," said the Great Goddess with a loving smile.

"Die!" yelled Kaity, tearing her claws out from the ground and pouncing on the murderer.

Lum grabbed Kaity in midair and flung her into a bush of growing vines.

The rainstorm intensified.

"Your words killed Nina. If you didn't love her, she'd be alive right now. Love is something that will only cause you pain."

Kaity wept as she tore herself out of the ever-expanding bramble. Sel energy shot out from her claws, tripling their length.

The weeds were cut, and her next slash was aimed at Lum's throat.

The Great Goddess ducked and pierced Kaity's wrist. She tore out her kitten's veins. Blood soaked the goddess as she wrapped the veins around her arms. "Come to me and die in my embrace."

Lord Sel arrived back at the Observatory and found his adversary floating. "You can still move in that state. Good! I hope you don't bore me!"

A laser shot out of Sel's pupil, hitting Sellum directly. The ray reflected off of Sellum and shot right back at Sel.

"What!?" Caught off guard, Sel was hit by his own laser beam. He passed through it and rushed at his enemy.

Sellum emitted beams of light that transformed into metal and smacked Sel into the ground.

The eyeball bounced right back up, ramming into Sellum.

The two spheres collided, caught in a power struggle. Sel was then sent smashing to the floor once more as Sellum overpowered him. "What? How can I lose to you in your weakest form? I'll devour you!" yelled Sel.

A Jiva appeared behind Sellum and ate him. A Jiva twice the size of the consumer materialized and engulfed the smaller one. Sel then created a spectral mouth and feasted upon his minions.

Sellum burst out of Sel.

Sel summoned a Jiva and thrust the Atma Blade into it. The blade consumed the creature and healed Sel's wound.

Sellum zoomed toward Sel abruptly.

Sel swung his spectral sword as his foe approached.

Sellum swerved out of the way and slammed into Sel, firing a massive beam of Lum energy in the same instant. The God of Gods zoomed behind Sel before slamming into him once more.

As Sel was propelled backward, Sellum slammed him from underneath, shooting him into the air. The ambitious eyeball looked in amazement as the ball then hit him from above. He was slammed into the ground, going into his faze form as he hit it.

"*Fodder Shield!*" yelled Sel. Instantly, his whole body was surrounded by rows of Jiva, making him ten times his size.

The Jiva leaped at Sellum, who either dodged them or busted through them.

Sellum shot through the useless shield, creating a huge gaping hole through Sel.

The Lord of Destruction pulled in all the surrounding Jiva into his Atma Blade.

The vanquished souls invigorated the weapon, coating it in a thick green aura.

"I'm not holding back anymore! *Para Jiva!*" exclaimed Sel as souls soared out from his weapon.

"As expected," said Absence with a smile.

"You knew I would return your artifact to you?"

"I need this artifact if I'm to defend my realm. I came here to retrieve it. You've done Absence a great service. I will remember this," he said, creating a portal to his realm.

Riufen grabbed his arm. "You're going to flee from our battle?"

"To stay would be to needlessly put my people at risk."

"You're abandoning our bout...for honor?" asked Riufen with a contorted face.

"I do so out of loyalty to my people."

"What about your loyalty to the one who returned your property to you?"

"Inconsequential in comparison."

"If I cut you down, I shall protect your realm as the new Absence."

"What?"

"You've stirred my soul with your loyalty. If I become Absence, I shall take up your fighting spirit and keep your people safe."

"I appreciate the offer."

"Whoever is stronger is more able to defend your realm. You have nothing to lose but your life. If you leave now, you are not worthy to defend your realm."

Absence closed the portal. "You're right." He stepped up to Riufen. "We shall fight till one of us no longer draws breath!"

"I shall not disappoint," said Riufen, drawing his spine.

Absence reverted a sword into his hand and blocked the samurai's blade. While stepping back to keep from being overwhelmed, he tossed compacts to the floor with his free hand.

"You're quite skilled," said Riufen, before knocking the sword from his opponent's hand.

"My true skill is accepting my limitations and planning accordingly. **Revert**!"

The balls on the ground unfolded into weapons of all types.

Absence blocked the incoming attack with a shield, picking up a spear in the process. He pierced Riufen's chest, dropped the shield, and fired a full quiver of arrows into the swordsman. After throwing the crossbow aside, he tossed a spear up with his foot. The second spear pierced through the samurai's head.

"It's a good thing I no longer use the Mirror Artifact. I could not stomach another dishonorable conclusion." Riufen broke the spears and pulled out the spearheads with his veins.

"How many times do I have to kill you before you die?" asked Absence, grabbing two crossbows from the ground as he retreated.

Riufen went on his knees and bowed down. "I am deeply sorry. I should have informed you of the only way to vanquish me. This must be a fair fight, after all."

"You're the strangest warrior I've ever met."

"Gladius!"

The crocodile sword had just finished sculpting his visage out of the snow on the mountain peak. "What do you want? Finally going to share the fun?"

Riufen hoisted up Gladius. "You must end the life of both swordsman and sword simultaneously."

Gladius bit Riufen's shoulder. "Fool! Why are you telling him how to kill me! If you want to die, that's fine, but leave me out of it!"

"Come now. Our destinies are intertwined," said Riufen, patting his sword.

"Do the benefits of his skill outweigh the burden of his stupidity?" asked Gladius to himself.

Absence bowed. "I appreciate you being so forthcoming. However, you'll have to figure out how to kill me on your own."

"I wouldn't have it any other way," said Riufen with a smile.

Gladius' tongue shot out and sliced the god's stomach open. "That should do it. He can't heal with Absence energy, after all," said the sword with a smirk.

Red compacts poured out like a waterfall out from Absence's stomach.

"Gladius, eat them," said Riufen.

"What? I don't even know what they are," complained Gladius.

"You betrayed me before. All I ask of you is to take a gamble. It could turn out interesting," said Riufen.

"Fine. I'll do it," said the sword with a grimace, reluctantly eating a pile of the compacts.

"Revert," said Absence, firing arrows at Riufen's chest.

The samurai dodged the arrows and Gladius exploded into bits.

"Ah, they were explosives," said Riufen with a nod.

Gladius reassembled with fury in his eyes. "You eat them next time!"

Riufen tossed Gladius into the air and plunged his spine into his opponent's chest as soon as his enemy reached for a new weapon.

Absence thrust his energy-coated spear at Riufen.

The swordsman grabbed the spear and twisted it, removing it from his foe's hands. He then slammed the weapon into the legs of his combatant.

Absence fell down and rolled toward the samurai. His legs swirled around, kicking the swordsman.

Riufen jumped up, landing on both of his opponent's feet. "It appears your time in prison has given me an unfair advantage over you. You must use your artifact to its full potential!" Riufen helped Absence to his feet.

"Fine then, I won't hold back any longer." Absence sliced open his wrists and gripped two compacts that came out. "ᴿevert!"

The compacts reverted into Gatling guns. Instead of having bullets for ammo, there were rows of compacts connected to one another.

"This is the first time a gun has peaked my interest," said Riufen with a smile.

Kaity's veins were yanked by Lum, bringing her into the goddess' embrace.

"There, there, my dear. Let go of all your worries," said Lum, pooling her energy into her child's head.

The young assassin kicked off. "Don't you touch me!"

"You're speaking again. That will make it harder for me to end you."

The roof of the Observatory opened up and the ground rose, elevating them into the clouds.

"Beautiful, aren't they?" asked Lum, her hand passing through a cloud. "The clouds of Lum show the visitors their desires simply to remind them that they are beyond reach. You see her, don't you? Your beloved Nina. Just like the visitors, you have to let go so you can move on."

"All I see is your mangled body! You can't hide from me," said Kaity with fierce eyes, aiming her sniper.

"DIVINE-DRESS!" Lum aura materialized, coating her body in feathers of light. "White purifies one's soul."

Kaity fired at the goddess.

A feather dispersed itself as wind that deflected the shot.

"Each feather holds the power of creation," said Lum, sending four feathers out that transformed into winged crocodiles.

The assassin's back released black missiles that obliterated Lum's creations.

"You're going to suffer for what you've done," said Kaity, adjusting her aim before firing.

"What do you see in that worthless narcissist!" yelled Lum, sending feathers out and concealing herself in the fog.

"Nina was always true to herself and honest with me! You've always lied to me!" exclaimed Kaity, sending out Sel energy to destroy the feathery projectiles before they could transform.

"Let the light strike the shadows and dispose of the dark stalker," said Lum, sending more feathers at her enemy.

"Your light has created shadows; you've made what you wish to destroy," said Kaity, running on all fours away from the feathers.

"I regret birthing you," said Lum with a sigh.

"And I regret that I ever fell in love with you!" yelled Kaity, sending out Sel beams.

One of the feathers turned into wind, sending the other feathers out of the way of Kaity's assault.

"Cosmic mantras are the wellspring of creation," said Lum, humming joyously.

The feathers turned into chimera of various animals.

"Too slow!" yelled Kaity, binding the mutants with a Sel chain and obliterating them with a quadruple headshot from her sniper.

"You're right. Simple is best." The feathers on Lum's hand disconnected and shot out like speeding bullets at Kaity. They pierced right through her skin, creating plants inside her body.

Kaity's body twisted and her bones snapped as she screamed.

"I can't purify you until I've fully exposed the demon!" exclaimed Lum.

All the feathers left Lum's body and enveloped Kaity as she fired beams at them.

Kaity's body let out a blast of dark energy, destroying the feathers and plants within her all at once. The purple scarf around her neck was also destroyed.

"Nina's final memento is no more," said Lum.

"I don't need an item to remember her," said Kaity with black tears. The dark assassin sliced through the incoming beams with her Sel-coated claws as she rushed up to Lum.

Wave after wave of light slammed into Kaity, the combined force knocking her to the ground.

Kaity leaped into the air and aimed her gun.

Lum's wing grew and disarmed the child.

The assassin stabbed her claws into the wings and rode down them.

Lum fired a beam at Kaity that was deflected by the girl's free hand.

A burst of water erupted from the floor beneath Kaity, sending her into the air.

A single feather attached to the assassin and radiated with light, bringing out the Sel energy hidden inside her.

"HEAVEN—"

A building, fired from the fight on Olympus, suddenly slammed into the goddess.

Kaity took aim and blasted the murderer's head open.

The deity's body fell apart into feathers that dispersed around the area.

Kaity fired Sel beams out until the feathers came together, forming an injured goddess.

"It seems I must provoke the demon one last time," said Lum, blinding Kaity with a beam of light while wiping her eyes.

When the light faded, a familiar face stood before Kaity.

The young assassin was brought to tears.

Chapter 173: Destruction, Creation, Absence

Absence hoisted up his guns after creating some distance between him and the samurai. "Ever hear about the cities that vanished during the Carbon War?"

"I'm not familiar with history of any kind."

"Well, you're about to learn about it firsthand! compact calamity!" exclaimed Absence.

The two Gatling guns launched hundreds of compacts a second. As soon as each compact was disengaged from the gun, it reverted into a building.

"I can shoot over one hundred buildings a second!" exclaimed Absence.

Riufen looked for openings in the ocean of buildings and jumped through them. As soon as he landed, another building was headed straight for him. He ducked, barely dodging it. After looking up, he was smashed by one of the incoming buildings. The immortal samurai was flung into a building behind him. "Now this is exciting!" Riufen leaped off the building, shooting himself above the onslaught.

Absence raised the Gatlin guns to redirect the bullet storm.

"Let's cut through the entire onslaught!" cheered the living sword.

The skillful samurai sliced holes through the buildings big enough for him to run through. With this technique, he made his way to Absence.

Riufen landed in front of the god and ran circles around him, slowly closing in.

"You've lost." Riufen sped by the god and majestically sheathed Gladius. Absence's Gatling guns split in two.

"Your guns weren't quick enough. How about we have a real battle now? My sword versus your true weapon?" proposed Riufen.

"You better be prepared," said Absence.

"I'm more than prepared, I'm anxious," said Riufen with a big smile.

Absence ripped out his eyeball. "revert!"

A staff instantly appeared in the god's hand. The staff was sleek and clear. Inside it were hundreds of compacts.

Absence tossed his staff at Riufen and immediately dashed behind him.

Riufen cracked his neck, dodging the staff.

Absence grabbed the staff and slammed it into Riufen.

"My weapon has many uses. I created it just recently for the sole purpose of defending my realm." The tip of the staff opened up, dropping spheres along the ground. With successive swings, Absence flung the compacts into the samurai.

Each compact became a sword that pierced Riufen's body. The samurai stood firm, smiling as he was barraged.

"You aren't even going to try and dodge?" asked Absence, sending more swords into the samurai.

Riufen ripped out four swords from his chest and spun them around to deflect the oncoming projectiles.

"I can condense anything," said Absence, flipping his staff around before releasing another compact.

The ball reverted into electrical energy. The energy hit the swords and cooked the samurai.

Absence rushed in, slammed his staff into the wounded warrior, and gripped one of the swords pierced into his foe. "As long as you don't die, you can't regenerate." He sliced off the warrior's leg.

"I hope you won't be too disappointed in me," said Riufen, lowering his head.

The severed leg sprang to life and kicked the staff out of Absence's hands and into the air.

The blood from the leg had splashed on the staff and was forcing it to unload all the compacts into the air.

"I wonder, can you dodge rain?" asked Riufen, pressing his sword against the god's.

"I don't need to," said Absence.

The swords came crashing down from above.

Absence's body became coated in his energy, disintegrating the swords on contact.

Riufen held Gladius above him and spun him around, slicing every sword that came into proximity.

As soon as the storm finished, Riufen shoved Gladius into Absence, slicing straight through him.

Red compacts fell to the floor.

"And so, the god dies," said Riufen, pulling out his sword.

Absence's hand moved in a flash, tossing a compact in Riufen's mouth.

The samurai's eyes widened when the compact reverted into a grenade.

Before he could spit it out, the grenade burst.

Gladius was unable to react swiftly enough. The god's Absence-coated spear pierced straight through him.

The swordsman and sword fell, side by side.

"A simultaneous kill was all I needed. Farewell, warrior," said Absence, turning around.

The rainstorm ended as suddenly as it had begun.

Kaity ran to the figure with tearful eyes. "Dad...it's really you."

Lum watched the reunion with tears dripping down her cheeks. "It took me longer than you'd expect to find Konton. After he died, he wasn't sent to Lum."

"He was being controlled! How can he be held accountable for what Bob did to me?" asked Kaity, hugging him.

"I'm so sorry," said Konton, embracing his daughter.

"He was in Sel for all the lives his weapons took. I had to send Etaf there to retrieve him. It wasn't easy."

"It's really you," cried Kaity, burying her face in his chest.

"Isn't this wonderful, Kaity? We're all together again," said Konton, moved to tears.

"Konton, you were just a means to an end. I was originally tasked by Zenero to kill you. After all, you supplied the enemy with armor and weapons," said Lum with a disapproving look.

"What? What are you talking about?"

Lum turned to the man. "I convinced Zenero that I could change you but only because I didn't want to dirty my hands with your blood. That's why I got pregnant. Zenero is cold, but he wouldn't ask me to kill the father of my child."

"You can't trust her! She's just trying to upset you," said Kaity, clenching her father tightly.

"It's the truth. Getting pregnant kept me free from sin and gave me the opportunity to be a mother."

"Wait, your story doesn't add up. You said you made me to stop Bob, but he wasn't an issue until Zenero went to Sellum with his Exps," said Kaity.

"Bob was always dangerous. Pathos was just too blind to notice it. I'm sorry, Konton. Our little girl has changed me. I'm not afraid to kill anymore. Honestly...it excites me," said Lum with a blissful smile.

Kaity stood in front of him. "Don't you dare!"

"I don't understand. What's going on?" asked Konton, in a barely conscious daze.

"I watched him die. I let Kanasta kill him. I was going to come to you and comfort you, but Kanasta beat me to it. Konton, you wouldn't believe it. Our sweet little girl joined the man who killed you. Now she calls him papa. Isn't that funny?" asked Lum, approaching with killer intent.

Kaity broke out into tears. "I'll do anything. Please, don't hurt my daddy."

Lum smiled as her eyes watered up. "We're assassins! What's one more body in the pile?" she asked, rushing in with claws of light.

Kaity countered with Sel-coated claws.

The two clashed as Konton watched in foggy disbelief.

"Assassins kill for money. You kill because it makes you feel self-righteous. You're so obsessed with evil that you now embody it," said Kaity, kicking the goddess.

"You did that to me!" yelled Lum before being blasted off her feet by Sel energy.

Kaity embraced her father. "I'm going to get you out of here," she said, carrying him as she headed toward the exit.

Konton coughed up blood.

Kaity's claws were wrapped in vines. They had been pulled into her father's chest.

Kaity pulled out her Sel-coated claws. Blood splattered on the girl's face. "No. No." The child sobbed and set her anguished father down. "I can do this. I can heal him."

"You can't store both Sel and Lum energy. You only have darkness in you. That darkness is going to eat away at him in mere minutes."

Kaity glared at Lum with hate but shook it away. "Save him!" she pleaded.

"You're the one who killed him," said Lum.

Konton's body was shivering.

"I'll do anything!" cried Kaity.

"If only it were that simple. Oh, I suppose you do have one option. If you were to kill me and take my powers, then—"

Kaity zoomed up and plunged her black claws into Lum. She screamed as she was overtaken by Sel energy.

Sel's Atma Blade poured out souls like a fire hose.

The souls of the fallen Jiva morphed together to create Para Jiva. The massive minion was larger than a building and had tendrils coming out from its sides. It looked at its foe with a vacant stare.

Sellum rammed into Para Jiva, but its skin was too thick to penetrate.

"*Eyeball Ram!*" exclaimed Sel as he slammed into Sellum.

The God of Gods stopped all momentum and shot back at Sel.

Para Jiva bundled up both fists into a battering ram and slammed them down on Sellum as he soared toward Sel.

The two forces battled each other, but Sellum overcame it. The hand was pushed back for an instant before slamming back down.

Sellum was crushed into the ground.

"*Sea of Souls!*" yelled Sel.

Para Jiva covered its mouth as it tried to withhold its regurgitation, but the creature couldn't stop it and regurgitated an ocean of Jivas.

"*Eyeball Laser!*"

A laser shot through all the Jivas, destroying them.

The souls then combined, creating a sword.

"Yin! You have been summoned!" exclaimed Sel.

"Oh really? I thought you only sought my brother Gladius to be your sword," said the weapon as it materialized.

Yin was a paper black katana with a gooey grip.

"I handed Gladius off to my best warrior. But you…you are for me and me alone. Oh, actually, could you be a dear and allow Para Jiva to use you?" asked Sel with a googily eye.

"For my realm I would give up my very soul. Show me your swordsmanship!" commanded Yin in a powerful, guttural voice. The sword changed shape into a Bastard sword and expanded to twenty-five times its original size.

Para Jiva struggled as it lifted Yin to its shoulders. The spectral being lashed Yin at Sellum with great difficulty, missing every time.

"You must use my weight against him. Lift me over your shoulders and slam me on him!" ordered Yin.

Para Jiva lifted Yin high using maximum effort.

Sellum spun around in place, gaining power.

"He's challenging us! Hurry, slam me down on him!" ordered Yin.

Para Jiva thrust Yin downward on Sellum with all his might.

Yin and Sellum clashed, giant sparks shooting from the conflict.

The sparks set the trees in the area aflame.

Sel pooled dark energy into the smoke, turning it into a turret.

Sellum spun around even faster, overcoming Yin's power as he was pelted by the newly formed Sel cloud.

Yin was sent flying into the sky, shattering the ceiling of the observatory.

Sellum shot into the skies, pursuing Yin while Para Jiva moved around, hoping to catch its sword.

Sellum reached the top of Yin as they soared through the sky. The compacted god slammed into the god sword, stopping his propulsion for a second before shooting right back up.

The Sel sword then slammed into Sellum. The spherical deity spun around in place to weaken the momentum. Yin started to fall back down once its momentum was stopped entirely.

Sellum zoomed up and rammed onto the top of Yin, shooting him downward at an increased rate.

Para Jiva held out his hand to catch Yin, but the sword shot right through the spectral warrior, becoming embedded into the ground.

"You should have waited for me to land first! Now I must improvise. **Sinful Samurai**," said Yin.

Veins shot out of Yin's holster, connecting him to Para Jiva's arm. The sword released energy that cloaked the body of the astral warrior.

"You were less than a second off," said Riufen, standing up with Gladius in his grip.

Absence slammed his staff into the ground to jettison himself above the warrior. After his weapon was knocked aside by Gladius, he slammed his head into the swordsman with all his might.

"Still not enough," said Riufen disappointed.

Absence's skull cracked open and he fell to the ground.

Riufen stepped on his head, smashing it beneath his foot.

Absence's fist shot through Riufen, making a gaping hole in his chest. Riufen grabbed his arm and pulled it forward, slamming Absence into his him continuously.

"Each red compact that spilled from my body is another me. My whole body is an assortment of painted compacts! Zenero's army is a single soldier and that soldier is me," said Absence as his compacts came to life around the swordsman.

The Absences ran around Riufen, forming a circle around him.

"**Quarantine Zone Reconstruction**," exclaimed the main Absence.

The compacts in their hands reverted into Gatling guns.

"Now to bury you under the rubble of a thousand cities!" exclaimed the true Absence.

"I asked you to show me your true power, and you continue to deny me. I really didn't want to do this, but I am fed up. **Merror Artifact Activated**!"

"Allow me. **Kusanagi**!" yelled Gladius as his tongue glowed from within.

Riufen spun the blade around, slicing the Absences to bloody bits.

Only one of them remained, covered in the blood of the fallen. "You've run out of copies. I've run out of patience. Go into your Absence form before time is up," said Riufen.

"I haven't lost yet," said Absence, running away in the snow.

Riufen ran up to him, stepping right onto one of Absence's mines. The mine burst and erased him and his sword.

"That should do it." Absence fell to the ground with an exhausted smile.

"It's now or never." Riufen reassembled behind Absence, shoving his spinal cord right through his capsule.

Absence's body was now clear, the spinal cord disappearing as it went through. The god leaped up, swiping his fist at Riufen.

The expert swordsman easily dodged the fist and then jumped behind Absence. "Finally, I get to fight nothingness itself!"

Absence ripped off his finger and tossed it at Riufen.

The finger nicked Riufen's face, making a hole where it hit.

"Projectiles too; this is getting interesting," said Riufen.

Absence bit into his hand, making blood shoot out of it. He coated the blood in his energy before flicking it off.

"This was a lot of fun," said Riufen as he quickly dodged the Absence blood.

"You will die," said Absence, coating his pole in his clear blood and spinning it to spray it on the samurai.

"Not good! Let's end this now." Gladius glowed as his aura coated his body.

Riufen shoved Gladius right through Absence's chest.

"I'm Absence. You can't…." The god's face went pale.

"Enjoy your meal, my sword."

Gladius bit into Absence's capsule.

Riufen ripped out Gladius, Absence's capsule clenched in his teeth. "You lied to me."

"What?" asked Gladius with his mouth full.

"You can't merely cut through anything." Riufen smiled and patted his sword. "You can also slice through nothing."

The capsule was smashed in Gladius's teeth, and Absence fell to the floor with empty eyes.

"Right you are," said Gladius with a sharp grin.

"Every battle must come to an end," said the samurai as the cloud of Absence energy left the fallen god's body.

"Now I am the only family you have," said Lum before being blasted off by pure Sel energy. She wiped the corrosive darkness off with shining fingertips. "May peace rain upon all worlds!"

Lum's light shot into the sky and crashed down on Kaity.

The assassin's aura came out as a jungle cat and swiped away the energy.

"You do realize that this entire structure is made of Lum particles, don't you?"

The ground beneath Kaity glowed and fired a beam of energy into her belly.

The daughter's darkness tried to repel it in vain.

"If you die, I won't have to kill Kanasta. I won't have to dirty my hands for you, ever again." Lum approached.

Kaity was coated in a prison of light energy; her entire body was engulfed by the purity. She stared into Lum's eyes with complete hatred. The hatred manifested itself, causing her to enter her Sel form once more.

"We all come into this world as perfectly clean divine sparks of Allah. You've become so corrupted by the world that your spark is a mere flicker now. Such a pity."

Kaity ran up to Lum, darkness shooting out of her plasma claws. Her claws pierced through Lum, enshrouding her mother's whole body in darkness.

The darkness devoured the feathers that made up the Great Goddess.

A single feather escaped the attack, shining with all of the goddess' glory. The feather recreated Lum perfectly intact before the assassin even noticed it.

"It is time for all of this suffering to end." Lum's whole body radiated. Light shot out of her back, creating six wings of purity. "The struggle of light against darkness shall not go on for eternity! All evil shall soon be blotted out by a pure tranquilizing light!" Lum's wings of light barraged Kaity, making her scream in agony. The wings burrowed into the ground, causing trees of light to sprout out from below.

"It seems you ran out of time." Lum teleported Konton's remains on top of the girl.

Kaity noticed the black hole in his chest and screamed with rage.

Dark energy burst out and consumed all the trees in its path. The darkness was instantly dispelled once it crashed into Lum.

The Sel energy took form as a hand and slammed Lum into the ground repeatedly. It then grew spikes and pierced her.

Lum's energy erupted out of her, consuming the corrosive black goop. "My little girl is gone now. Only the demon remains."

Kaity sprouted wings of concentrated Sel energy.

They fired at the goddess as she took flight.

Feathers created a circle around Lum. Light shot out from the feathers, destroying the dark energy before shooting to the skies.

Kaity ran up the air by stepping on vertical steps of Sel energy. She dragged her plasma claws along the sides of the ascending beam, corrupting it with Sel energy.

The darkness followed Kaity as she zoomed down the beam of light. The corrupted half following closely behind her as it broke through the beam of light.

The corrupted assassin shoved her plasma claws into Lum. The ensuing dark pillar crashed into the goddess.

The darkness and light energy annihilated one another.

They both instantly reverted into their normal forms, the plasma claws now through Lum's capsule.

"All your darkness is gone. Allow a preacher a few words," said Lum with a small smile.

"Shut up," said Kaity, twisting her claws.

"I love you," said Lum, leaning in and giving Kaity a motherly kiss on the forehead.

Kaity's eyes that once burned with hatred now watered with tears. "Then why? Why did you do all of this if that's true?"

"I needed you to stay attached so I could watch over you. I had to seduce you. I had to become your everything," said Lum with a teary smile.

"When Koshi had me at his mercy…you came to rescue me. Even though all he did was touch me, I was so scared. If you hadn't come and saved me…I could have died," said Kaity, gripping her lover's hands.

Lum turned away. "I was the one who sent him after you. Got him all riled up beforehand. I needed you to hate all men. When I explained my reasoning, he hesitantly complied."

"You did that to make me fall for you? That's horrible. You love me, don't you? All those times you told me you loved me, they were real, right?" asked Kaity, backing away.

"You can't fake love. It seduces and binds you. There's no escaping it."

"And yet you tricked me into killing you?" Kaity's hands trembled.

"My days were numbered. Sel has grown too powerful. It had to be you. I…needed you to kill me," said Lum, forcing a smile.

"But why?" asked Kaity trying to hold back her tears.

"It was such a torment, but a joyous torment, to work with you. I was forced to be everything I wasn't, killing savagely and pretending to enjoy it. Each kill we made was a new recruit for Sel's army, but each kill also brought us closer. I bathed in the blood of the dead to get close to you. Even the terrible memories are sweet…for I spent them with you. Being in your presence purified me, yet it simultaneously made me impure. You felt the same, didn't you?"

Kaity nodded with a face full of tears.

Lum smiled. "I crafted Sefiwah to your liking and seduced you to keep you safe. It wasn't easy at first. The guilt of using you nearly drove me to self-destruction. I've contradicted my every preaching with a physical sin. Even so, I persisted in killing and lovemaking to keep you safe."

"Then…you hated being intimate with me?"

"The time we spent together was to keep you away from Sel's clutches. I needed you to love only me in order to keep you safe. Those intimate moments were all necessary. I feel disgusted with what we did…what I did to you. Each time after we made love, I punished myself for my sinful acts," said Lum with a grimace.

"Each time after we made love, I'd snuggle you in my sleep." Kaity grabbed her beloved's hand. "I remember our first kiss. You told me I was no longer a child. You gave me your artifact and then you leaned in and…I could feel electricity dancing on my lips. My whole body lit up with energy. Your eyes softened and you had the cutest blush."

"Kaity, I'm your mother. I only did those shameful things to protect you," said Lum with a deep pink blush.

"See? There it is!" Kaity poked her lover's cheeks.

"How can I love everything I hate when I'm with you? Oh, I can use excuses all I want, but the truth is you make my heart quake," said the Great Goddess with love in her eyes. She grabbed her daughter's hand. "Kaity…you made me a willing sinner. With the wonderful burden of love, I became a demon to share those special moments with you. I learned to enjoy it and…eventually the role took over, and I loved you more than a mother should." Lum caressed Kaity's cheek.

Kaity's cheeks lit up in embarrassment. "Mom…I said it's okay. I don't hate you for being with me…. I hate that you used me. We've both done things we wish we could take back."

"Every kill, every injury…I would do it all over again just to keep you safe. How can something as pure as love transform someone into a monster? I pray that sinners in love turn to saintly practices," said Lum.

Kaity nodded. "You know I love you more than anyone. You've taught me so much. You comforted me after my first kill. My worries just melted away in your loving arms." The girl clenched her soul mate. "I don't regret it. And you don't either, right? What we shared together was magical. You were my first, after all," she said with a deep blush.

"Sefiwah was merely a role, but the love I felt when we were together…it was as real as the sun," said Lum, gazing into her lover's eyes.

"We both loved each other, so there's no shame in what we shared. There was nothing sinful about this," she said, leaning into a kiss with a light blush.

Tranquil pulled away from her daughter's lips. "I took advantage of your loneliness, but know it was all done out of love. Feel my heart racing," said Lum, seizing the girl's hand and pressing it to her chest.

"I feel it. Just like always," said Kaity with a teary-eyed smile.

Lum gave the girl a gentle kiss on the cheek. "I couldn't allow Sel to control you, so I made it so you would trust no one. I had to make you powerful enough so you would be protected from Sel and ultimately be able to kill him. The reason I became an assassin was so I could nurture your strength and keep you safe. I told Kanasta, and he understood my intentions."

"Papa knew you hated killing people?" asked Kaity with wide eyes.

"That's right. My love for you is also the reason I had Ada kill me back on Earth. She was too good-natured; I had to demonize her to keep you at my side. Once you showed up in Lum, I knew I needed you to hate me. I tried to see you as a merciless killer so that you would believe that I despised you. Kaity, no matter how hard I tried to loathe you, I couldn't. I couldn't hate your sweet smile no matter how black I painted it."

"You've been suffering for so long. I'm sorry, momma," said Kaity in tears.

"No more tears, please. You can't show any weakness."

"There's no way I can't cry when my mom is dying in my arms." Kaity held her mother's hand to her chest and sobbed.

"If it hurts to love me…then hate me. Please. I'd rather you abandon all love than suffer anymore."

Kaity looked up and held in her tears. "Was it worth it? Was it really worth it? You killed Nina. You killed Father. You may have been trying to protect me…but you've…you've broken me." The little girl sobbed against her mother's shoulder.

"You're a strong girl. You will move past this. You'll fly out of the ashes, reborn anew. I made you a heartless killer so that I could keep my innocent little kitten safe. How pathetically ironic."

"What am I supposed to do after this? How can you expect me to find the will to fight when everyone I love is dead?"

Lum wiped her eyes and pulled out the claws in her chest. Red leaked from the wound.

"Heal yourself! I won't let you abandon me again," said Kaity in tears, holding onto her lover with all her might.

"I'm sorry, my little kitten. If Sel had kept me captive, he could have made you sacrifice yourself. Now that he is battling Sellum, your time as an immortal may be coming to a close. The Dark One pursues you like a shadow. We both know that no act of cruelty or deception is above him." Lum sobbed and then swept away her tears.

"If you won't do it for me, then do it for Pathos. He's in love with you. Think about what your loss will mean to everyone."

"That's all I've been thinking about since I saw you being experimented on by Sel. Pathos' love is strong but so is his spirit. He won't break from my death. He'll defend you all the more. I have to die to keep you safe from Sel's wrath. I've failed you, but at least you'll survive." Kaity's mother burst into tears.

"Protecting others isn't foolish."

"Don't say that, please. Not after all I've done. You know, the real reason I did not dare show my face to Efil was because I'm the one unworthy to stand next to her. I've become a cruel demon!" Lum sobbed into her hands.

Kaity shook her mother with a face full of tears. "Stop crying. You wanted this, so don't cry."

"You're right. Not another tear. I promise." Lum wiped her eyes.

"Are you just going to abandon your realm? You don't have to die!" yelled Kaity trying to will Lum energy from her hands

"I haven't abandoned this realm. I need you to listen very closely now. My death does not mean the end of Sel's conquest of Lum. After turning Fatima into a Mawali, the goddesses have helped me convince many humans to follow in her steps. The conflict between humans and angels is at an end. I'm going to need you to protect this realm."

"You can protect it better than I ever could."

"I always saw Sellum as an ideal person, like the great prophet Mohammed. But Sellum is both prophet and leader. The Omni God must keep things balanced while pushing them forward. This is your future now. Do you accept it?"

The destined Sellum nodded. "Denying my responsibility will only cause more suffering."

"Kaity, my darling kitten, you're so much more than a destined Sellum," said Lum with a calm smile. "You're the hidden Imam, the mythic prophet who comes to prevent the end times. Lum or not, you are my true successor. I hope you will stand with Evol and the new Lum to lead this empire of faith against Sel's army. I am your sacrifice; my death keeps you alive. Tell them what I've done for your sake. Spread word of my great martyrdom to the people. Forge it into a myth to inspire them to fight for this realm!"

"Who is the new Lum?" asked Kaity.

"One who will never be swayed by Sel. I ask you to keep her safe, but don't endanger yourself in the process," said Lum with a weak smile.

"We can do it together! Violet can help too!"

"She's truly a blessing for me."

"You told her your plan, didn't you? She helped me…kill you," said Kaity, her whole body shivering.

"I never told her anything. She put her faith in the love she felt emanating from me. Pathos is the only one who knew my plan. It wasn't easy convincing him to…Kaity…your color…it's fading away. You look so beautiful all in white," said Lum with shimmering watery eyes.

"Stay with me, please," said Kaity, holding her mother's hands.

Lum looked up at Kaity with a dazed look. "What do you see in the clouds now?"

"It was all black before. All I saw was darkness, but now…I see my mom, holding me in her arms when I was just a baby. Please don't go."

"The last person you love is fading away. No matter who Sel takes hostage, you will live on now. At long last, I look up and see mere clouds, nothing more," said Lum with a weak smile.

"You've taken everything from me. You murdered Nina! You killed my father! Don't take my mother away too!" yelled Kaity, her teary eyes igniting with rage.

"You have every right, but I can't bear to be hated by you in my last moments. Kaity, do not worry about Nina. Sel lent me a demon who shapeshifted into her."

"She's alive?" Kaity's watery eyes lit up. "Is Father alive too?"

Lum shook her head. "I am sorry for everything I have done. My will lives on in you, and you have many friends who will keep you safe. Please live on as incorruptible as tranquility itself. I love you, my little kitten, and I always will," said Lum with her last smile.

Riufen landed in front of the victorious warrior. He tossed Kaity on his shoulders and ran off with her, dodging the clear cloud as long as he could.

Kaity reached out to her dying soul mate. "Mom!" wailed Kaity, crying uncontrollably as she was taken away.

After Lum faded into dust, the white cloud of energy shot into the sky.

Riufen jumped up.

The clear cloud zoomed beneath him. It swerved suddenly and shot into him from below. The samurai shielded with Gladius, but the cloud passed through the sword and entered him.

Riufen was now the God of Absence.

Yin's aura took form around the massive beast as a black armor of swords.

"Gladius can cut anything, and I can be wielded by anyone." Yin sliced up a huge piece of the ground, molding it to become a shield. "Come at me and meet your end."

Sellum's condensed armor fell off, revealing lasers beneath it.

Para Jiva grabbed the shield and slammed it on Sellum, trapping him beneath it.

Explosions were heard from inside the shield.

"Well done. Very well done," said Sel, clapping enthusiastically.

Para Jiva slammed Yin down on the shield with all his might.

The shield suddenly shot up as Sellum rammed into it. The shield knocked into the sword, pushing it backward.

Para Jiva's arm broke as it spun three hundred and sixty degrees.

"That won't stop me!" exclaimed Yin, swiping the sword at the god.

Sellum quickly zoomed into the creature's open mouth, shooting mines all the way down its throat.

The giant beast slammed its chest, trying to throw up Sellum.

Sellum zoomed out of the astral warrior's mouth as all of his mines blew up.

Blood gushed out of Para Jiva as it exploded from within. Its tattered bloody corpse fell to the floor.

Lord Sel shoved the Atma Blade into Para Jiva and absorbed its soul.

The Atma Blade glowed brightly as Sel thrust it through Yin.

"Even though Gladius embodies the essence of a sword, Yin is my preferred weapon because of his versatility," said Lord Sel as the weapon shifted into a twenty-foot long katana. "What do you say we finish him off?"

"For the glory of Sel!" exclaimed Yin.

Sel lifted up Yin with ease and slammed it on Sellum.

The god spun around rapidly as he clashed with Yin.

Yin grew in size to overpower the God of Gods but lost the power struggle regardless. The sword shot up before crashing down on Sellum as a massive thick sword.

Sellum was smashed into the ground, creating a crater around him.

Sel shrank Yin and stabbed it into Sellum with all his might.

The God of Gods spun rapidly, gaining momentum until he was just a blur. Yin shot into the sky, disappearing from sight. Sellum slammed into Sel over and over, pounding him brutally.

"I'll create an opening. *Eyeball Apocalypse!*" Sel spun around rapidly and fired lasers in all directions.

The sphere of Sellum deflected the lasers while closing in on Sel. Once it was right in front of Sel, the ball reverted back to its original form.

Sellum grabbed Sel with eight hands covered in light.

Sel exploded continuously until Sellum let go of him. The God of Destruction fell, not destroyed but unable to move.

"You've lost," said Sellum, creating a clear portal.

"I'm not done," said Sel with crazed charisma.

Giant spectral tentacles shot out of Sel and into the ground. They burst out from below and embedded themselves inside Sellum's energy body.

"For acting impartial while secretly incarnating to raise an army against me, I sentence you to death!" exclaimed Sel.

"If I wasn't so weak…I'd be able to…."

"But you are weak now! Perhaps if you hadn't lent your Sel energy to your fellow gentle soul then you'd be more resilient. No matter. There's no chance of escape for you anymore!" exclaimed Sel.

The white and clear barrier around Sellum shattered into pieces. "A simultaneous kill. Was that your plan?"

"It looks like both Kaity and Riufen have succeeded, and their successes spell your demise! I wouldn't want to let them down after all their hard work!" exclaimed Sel.

The Dark One's weapon released souls, expanding twenty times its original size. It swirled with energy, giving it a special glow.

"Please, brother. There must be another way," said Sellum in tears.

"Yes! Die with that pitiful look on your face!" yelled Sel with a deranged look.

Lord Sel thrust the weapon inside Sellum with all his might.

Sellum shook rapidly as his soul was consumed. Clear energy erupted out of him. He then dissipated into nothingness.

"I have finally succeeded! I am the new Sellum now!" exclaimed Sel.

The clear black and white cloud shot toward Kaity, ruining Sel's fantasy.

"Oh yeah, I have to kill her and Devlin before I become Sellum. Trust me, Pathos, no matter how many obstacles you put in my way, I will destroy them. I am the one who will perfect this corrupt world, and I don't need a prophecy to prove it. You have merely prolonged Kaity's demise, but it will come, and I will become Sellum!" yelled Sel, glowing with infinite charisma.

*To be continued in book 5, **Rise of the Exps: Eternal Rival***

Books from *Sphere of Compassion*
THE MAIN CHARACTER!
Hero's Epic Journey Arc

A Subversive PUNCH to the Face!

Join Main Character and Best Friend, two proud American otakus and ViralTube legends, who are pulled into another world and bribed into joining a growing conflict between victimized villages and deranged dictators. Anime tropes only lead to shattered expectations for our ego-driven hero! He is accompanied by awesome allies, protected by canonical plot armor, and armed with the power of Friendship (a vulgar rocket launcher who uses emotions as ammo). But will these and his encyclopedic knowledge of anime be enough to overcome the threats of a dimension hopping assassin, a guardian angel's sexual advances, a musclebound amazonian, memory erasing mushrooms, a Fearsome Dragon, a charismatic king with a psychotic obsession for our hero and his army of cut throat cat boys?

The Main Character is a 4th wall breaking parody packed with anime references, subversive characters and intense battles!

Be your own Hero!
Before she found the Hero of Destiny, Annie had her own journey!
Join Annie on her adventure through the epic dark fantasy world of The Main
Character series! This young, loving and determined girl will team up with cursed
heroes, adorable angels and mythical creatures to reunite with her cherished
family! Will her bonds with her allies be enough to protect her from mechanized
samurai, shadow hounds, rogue dimensional assassins and an army of CatBoy
soldiers? Or will life's story be closed before she can write her happily ever after?

Immerse yourself in the lives and backstories of Main's companions and
adversaries in the 1st of the Legendary Origin Stories!
This book can be read before OR after any book from **The Main Character** series.

A SUPLEX of Subversion!
Main Character and Best Friend, two legendary otaku heroes, are back in action. They now have a diverse group of otherworldly allies: a guardian angel Stalker, a shy Brawny Babe, a Tomboy Catgirl, a Fruity-scented fortune teller, a foul-mouthed bazooka of Friendship and a freaking Harem of strong female leads! Juggling his harem is the least of his worries though. This time he'll have to go head to head against a psychotic Rival, a mind-manipulating Mascot, a mysterious organization, a blackmailing midget, and horny Harem girls? Even with Point of View manipulation, the ability to Retcon his failures and hair that can punch your lights out, can Main Character overcome his own ego and become a true hero? Or will his backlog of bad choices create a rift between him and his allies?

The Main Character is still a 4th wall breaking parody packed with anime references, subversive characters and intense battles! This time around it also has a Harem of lovely ladies to give it new vigor!

Origins of the Exps

Is clairvoyance a gift or a curse?
Before she became Fate, Ebui fought against her destiny.
Explore the ancient culture and traditions of the Ainu through the lens of a child.
Ebui is a hopeful and brave girl who yearns to become a respected shaman of her
village. Threats loom around every chapter of her life in the form of enemy tribes,
violent ceremonies, sinister plots, and her own cursed prophecies. Will her hope
survive through the supernatural storm of despair, or will her efforts bring about
the end of her people?

Immerse yourself in the lives and backstories of characters from the Of The Exps
series in the first of the Origins of the Exps novels!
*This book can be read before any book from the **Of The Exps** series.*

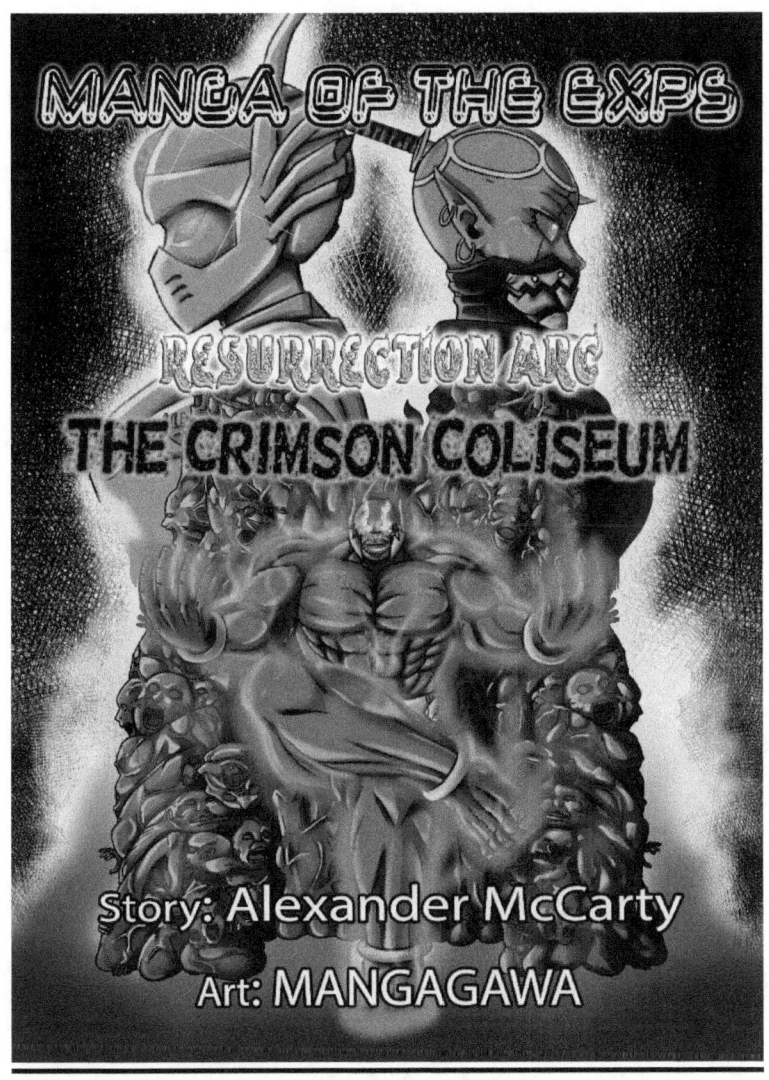

Is freedom worth dying for?
Exp 8 awakens in the Crimson Coliseum, the blood-soaked battle arena where heroes are brought to die. Before he can battle the God of Hate, he must defeat a fellow rebel leader whose body is a gruesome armory. Will Exp 8 be able to conquer the tyrant king of Sel or will he become just another red smear on the Crimson Coliseum?

Get pumped for the first Manga from the ***Of The Exps*** series based on the pivotal battle from the ***Resurrection of the Exps: The Hero of Sel*** novel.
*This manga can be read before any book from the **Of The Exps** series.*
BLACK & WHITE/ FULL COLOR versions sold separately.

FUTURE RELEASES

The Main Character Legendary Origin Stories

In a School of Assassins, Suffering is Growth.

Before Assailant encountered the Hero of Destiny, he crafted his own legend! Discover the dark origins of the fabled Broad-Spectrum assassin. Follow him through deadly exams, covert conspiracies and murderous missions all the while delving deep into the lore of the epic dark fantasy world of The Main Character series! This child of misfortune will work alongside cuddly killers, polymorphous monsters, enslaved heroes, and tragic angels to unravel the secrets hidden by the Assassin's Guild. Armed with mythic knowledge and guided by love, can he wield his truth to conquer skillful students, treacherous assassins, shadowy shapeshifters and secret organizations? Will his legends become a beacon of hope or a seed of despair?

Immerse yourself in the lives and backstories of Main's companions and adversaries in the 2nd of the Legendary Origin Stories!

*This book can be read before OR after any book from **The Main Character** series.*

Rise Arc
Eternal Rival: Rise of the Exps (Summer 2020)

Does competition encourage growth or ensue destruction?
After the aftermath of the realm god death matches, new gods are selected.
Kaity's new responsibilities clash with her desire to save her friends, further
dividing her already splintered forces. Despite already being overwhelmed by
Sel's Pawns and the Exp Hunters, new factions emerge that are hellbent on
claiming the power of Sellum for themselves. The young God of the Afterlife
must forge new alliances to survive. Can she placate her enemies by reaching a
common ground? Or is their thirst for power beyond negotiation?

The 3rd arc of the action-packed series brings the divine conflict to Earth!

Escapades of the Exps
Intimate Interrogation (March 2020)

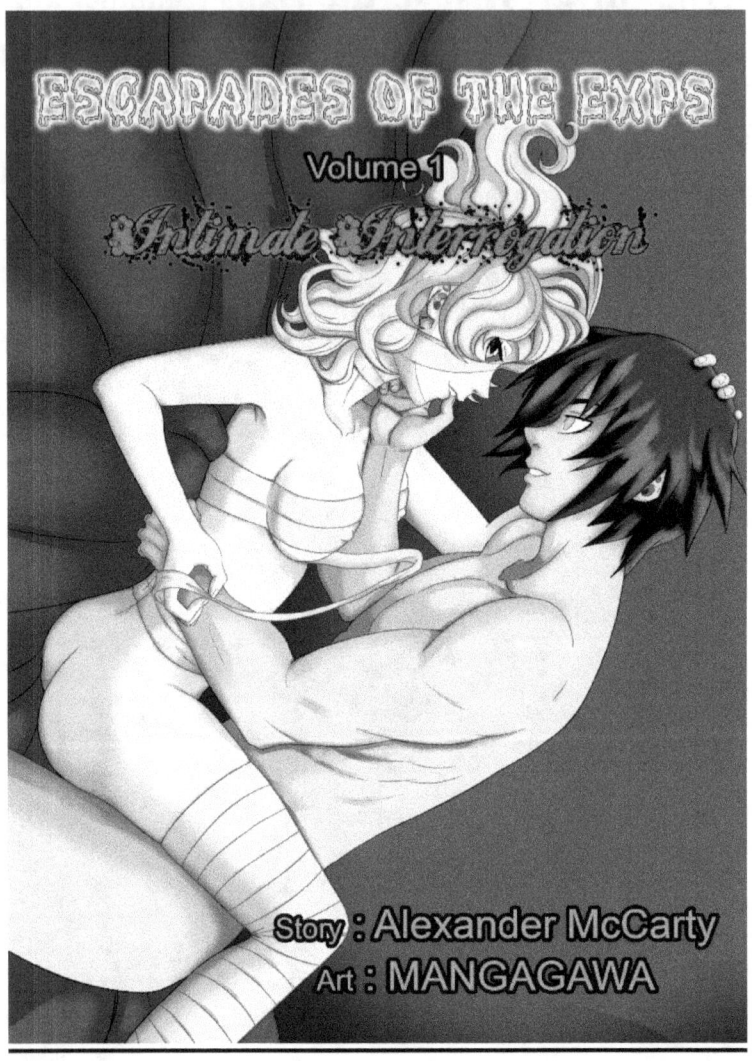

Is sex just another tool for an assassin?
Devlin's new crush already has a girlfriend and she lies beneath the covers of his bed. This seductive assassin has an offer for the hot-blooded scientist and will do whatever she must to seduce him to her cause.

Become entranced by the first Hentai Manga from the *Of The Exps* series based on a scene from the *Rebellion of the Exps: Exp 8* novel.
This manga can be read before any book from the Of The Exps series.
BLACK & WHITE/ FULL COLOR versions sold separately upon release.

About the Author

Alexander McCarty is an animal born on Earth who actively seeks freedom for his fellow animals. At age five, once he realized that the chickens he loved and the chickens he was eating were one in the same, he became an ovolacto-vegetarian along with his nine-year-old brother. In middle-school, he decided to make use of his free time by writing a book. At the age of twenty-one he met vegan activist Gary Yourofsky and vowed to live vegan alongside his brother. They have since dedicated their lives to animal liberation through educational activism. Alexander recently graduated with a bachelor's degree in Religious Studies and holds certificates in Jainism, Asiatic Studies, and Spirituality. He is now a full-time writer and is also the president of Sphere of Compassion Inc. He runs SOC with his brother. SOC is a company whose purpose is to spread innovative media and promote a vegan worldview. When he isn't writing, he is watching anime, reading, or playing videogames. He listens to any and all comments, suggestions, reflections, and criticism.

Please contact me with a link to where you placed a review for any of my books, and I will answer any single question as one of my characters for **FREE**. If you do a review (and point out where) in addition to submitting fan art, I will write a **FREE** short 2–4 page story (with my characters) in a scenario of your choosing. =(:3)*

Bloggers who wish to review my book may request "Review Copies" of *Exp 8: Rebellion of the Exps* at the links below.

authoralexandermccarty@gmail.com
alexanderjmccarty@facebook.com
gabrieloftheexps@instagram.com

We Must Acknowledge Our Condition to Change It

Humans are the cause of the current mass extinction of species on Earth. Our pollutants from animal agriculture have caused soil erosion around the globe and have even made the oceans acidic. There is absolutely no denying the damage we've caused in the last ten thousand years. Despite us living in a mostly ecologically aware age, we still act as though humanity is the pinnacle of creation. If we want to change the future of the planet's life systems, then we cannot ignore the damage we have done.

Humans claim to be the sole proprietors of value and worth. Most often we chalk it up to our advanced intellect, a trait that has nothing to do with morality. If, for example, there were two options—to force either a mathematician or a high school dropout to participate in a lethal medical experiment—which one is the proper choice? The correct answer is neither. Yet we claim that killing animals is alright because of their alleged "lesser" intellect. Ironically it is mankind's claim that we are the sole species of any value that actually makes us the only species without any value.

Let's look at this introspectively. If there was any species that caused as much harm to the other species around it, we would deem it a threat and wipe it out. Humans are the only species on Earth that are invasive no matter where they are located. If we did die out, every species on the planet would benefit, and as long as we live, every species is brought more pain and death.

To move forward we must truly acknowledge our lack of worth and use this new focus to question our current path. Nearly everything we deem as normal is actually an artificial construct. With proper insight, we can determine which constructs are harmful to the planet and which ones are not.

It is not too late to change for the better. Only apathetic cowards choose to do nothing. We must find worth in our identity as animals rather than as humans and must deconstruct harmful constructs, including ideologies and traditions, so that we can coexist with the other animals.

We never were stewards of the Earth and we don't have to be. Humans need to collectively recognize that our extinction would benefit the planet so that we can change our individual selves in order to benefit it. It's not a matter of doing enough, but instead always improving on ways we can reduce the ecological violence we commit.

I ask that you join me in spreading eco-functional misanthropy so that we can coexist with our fellow animals instead of bringing countless species to extinction!

Below are some links to places where we can get informed and get involved with veganism and vegan advocacy!

http://www.adaptt.org/

www.serv-online.org

http://www.abolitionistapproach.com

veganeducationgroup.com

www.ingramcontent.com/pod-product-compliance
Lightning Source LLC
Chambersburg PA
CBHW072253020726
47501CB00002B/255